WITHDRA

D1217543

Officially Noted

9-12-16 Stain bottom corner
here- end nm

FIFTY YEARS OF
UFOs

FIFTY YEARS OF UFOs

FROM DISTANT SIGHTINGS TO CLOSE ENCOUNTERS

JOHN AND ANNE SPENCER

BOXTREE

(Title page) Peter Holding has become an artist and photographer following a UFO experience; one of many personally investigated by the authors. Following a UFO sighting he awoke one night and was drawn to open his curtains, and saw in front of him a huge swirling vortex in which he believed he could 'feel' the presence of entities. In this photograph, as in many of his works, circles and swirls come forward, expressing his feelings from his encounter.

First published in 1997 by Boxtree, an imprint of Macmillan Publishers Ltd, 25 Eccleston Place, London, SW1W 9NF and Basingstoke

Associated companies throughout the world

ISBN 1 85283 924 4

Designed by Mason Linklater

Typeset by SX Composing, Essex

1 3 5 7 9 8 6 4 2

A CIP catalogue record for this book is available from the British Library

Colour Reproduction by Aylesbury Studios Ltd, Bromley, Kent

Printed and bound in Italy by L.E.G.O. Vicenza, Italy

Front jacket photograph:
The Image Bank

Back jacket photographs:
Mary Evans Picture Library *(top right and bottom left)*
Fortean Picture Library *(centre above and centre below)*

Contents

Acknowledgements

Many people from literally every continent of the world have assisted in the research for this book. We are grateful to all of them. We would not wish to understate any individual contributions, but certain people gave up a great deal of time to assist us, and we would like to especially thank Richard Conway, Stan Conway, Tony Eccles, Chris Fowler, Steve Gamble, Leo Rutherford, Mark Pilkington and Matthew Williams.

The opinions expressed by the book overall are our own. None of those who have assisted us are responsible for the views stated, other than where they are clearly expressed as the quoted views of individuals.

Thanks also to Bryan Ellis, who provided many illustrations for the book.

Note: To avoid the repetition of frequently used expressions, common acronyms are used throughout the text. A glossary is provided before the index for the reader's use.

Dedication

To Angus Brooks, whose sighting in Dorset in 1967 was an inspiration to us. We shared a final walk over Moigne Downs with him just months before he died. His enthusiasm for his case, and the subject, never diminished.

Introduction

Fifty years after the birth of the UFO enigma we are able to look back with a special perspective. We now have an opportunity that only time can afford to examine a most important phenomenon, but to do so we must put aside a great deal of nonsense, hype and sensationalism. This book is an exploration not just of the subject itself, but of the political, social and cultural background that has influenced our understanding of Unidentified Flying Objects. The existence of strange lights in the skies is not dependent on such influences, of course, but the way in which they have been studied, believed in, and reacted to owes a great deal to the various 'climates of the times'.

There is much less evidence than is often supposed to support the notion of a physical invasion by aliens from other worlds: the theory that has been promoted more than any other by the media, by 'flying saucer groups' and by the general cultural background of Western society. We shall reveal, however, from a mass of evidence which has emerged from the studies of the last fifty years, something equally significant. That evidence places UFOs within the wider spectrum of the complex world of the paranormal and indicates a great deal about human development in the twentieth century.

Most investigations are a game of question-and-answer. In the study of UFOs there has only been one fundamental question – are they extraterrestrial? But the answers reached have been so complex and diverse that now we are presented with the possibility that perhaps it is the question that is wrong. In more recent decades that single question has been augmented – though never replaced – by more useful questions bordering on the 'What might they be?' variety. Unfortunately, this has

served only to increase the range of non-focused answers. This book provides a much wider perspective on the subject by asking not what, but why? In Michael Crichton's book *Travels*, he explains how, as a medical student, he started asking people why they believed they had had heart attacks, something which, at that time, was thought to be a physical problem and more or less a case of bad luck. He found that, far from being offended or confused, people answered meaningfully from their own intuition: they had failed to get a pay rise; they had had a promotion that brought with it added pressure; they faced stresses with their children, and so on. He had found the impertinent question that, as scientist Jacob Bronowski observed, leads to the pertinent answer. 'Why' is an important question sadly underused in UFO research. Captain Kevin Randle, the prominent American UFO researcher, has commented that 'Sometimes a study of the mood of the public or an understanding of the period can be helpful in understanding a wave of sightings.' This book asks, and answers, the 'why' questions. Why were they seen then, or there? Why did people think that about them? Why did governments act in the way they did? The answers provide a basis for real understanding of the UFO phenomenon.

There are certain obvious influences, not least the significance of the 'seven' years. The first 'flying saucer' sighting identified as such arose in 1947, and the tenth anniversary years – 1957, 1967, 1977, 1987, 1997 – provide scope for natural peaks of interest. Steven Spielberg's film on the subject came out in 1977; Gulf Breeze arose in 1987; Whitley Strieber published *Communion* in 1987, and so on. Moreover, the

Russian Revolution happened in 1917, and Americans have demonstrated a nervousness about the 'seven' years based on their fears of anniversary 'activity' by the Soviets: the first target year for the Apollo moon landing was 1967, because they feared that the Soviets might try a landing to celebrate the fiftieth anniversary of the revolution. And the space programme was a major influence on UFO perceptions.

Having placed the UFO phenomenon within the larger context of paranormal enigmas, we find that in addition to the social influences, the UFO story has an evolution not apparent in other phenomena. It is arguable whether or not it should have. If we compare it to, say, poltergeists, we see this significant difference very clearly. Poltergeists and ghosts have a history, but no evolution: today's stories are largely the same as those recorded 2,000 years ago. This is not the case with UFOs. In 1947 alien abductions were not even hinted at; now they are becoming commonplace.

A good analysis of this evolution was made in 1978 by Isabel Davis and Ted Bloecher in their book *Close Encounter at Kelly and Others of 1955*. Since 1978 events have come to light which change the statistics mentioned in their work, but the point they make still holds good.

For the ten year period from 1946 to 1955 . . . there exist some 250 references to specific CE–III reports (reports which include alien entities) in the case files of the Humanoid Study Group. But in the five year period 1973–1977, the total number of references approaches 450 – nearly double the number for the first decade – and new reports are surfacing all the time. But increased numbers are not the only change over the last 20 years; a significant escalation in the *strangeness* of the reports has taken place. The 1955 incidents at Kelly, Riverside and Mulberry Corners were certainly bizarre at the time, but compared to some later reports, they are almost routine.

For example, we have no abduction reports among the dozen or so CE–III cases discussed in this book, nor indeed, for any date in 1955: if they occurred at all they have not yet come to our attention. But of some 80 CE–III cases in 1976, 20 were abduction reports or on-board experiences – one out of every four reports.

Perhaps the subject is genuinely changing – perhaps aliens are visiting earth and doing something different now from what they were doing fifty years ago – or perhaps the perceived changes are the product of cultural development over time. The question cannot be ignored, and we feel it is central to a subject that will also reveal a great deal about the development of mankind.

It is a real and complex phenomenon, regardless of the ways in which it has been perceived through such influences. J. Allen Hynek, whose name arises many times in this narrative, has said, 'I would not spend one additional moment on the subject of UFOs if I didn't seriously feel that the UFO phenomenon is real and that efforts to investigate and understand it, and eventually to solve it, could have a profound effect – perhaps even be the springboard to a revolution in man's view of himself and his place in the universe.'

John and Anne Spencer, 1997

1947-1957

The Postwar Years

'When your only tool is a hammer, everything looks like a nail.'

UFOLOGY'S FIRST 'MARTYR'

'I've sighted the thing. It looks metallic and it's tremendous in size . . . It's above me and I'm gaining on it.' Captain Thomas F. Mantell, a twenty-five-year-old experienced pilot, radioed back his last words from the skies over Kentucky.

It was 7 January 1948. Several people from Maysville had called the state police barracks to report sightings of something strange flying overhead. The highway patrol had, in turn, contacted nearby Godman Air Force Base to see if they could advise. They could not. Meanwhile, witnesses were phoning in from Owensboro and Irvington some distance away. Whatever it was – generally described by the witnesses as circular and around 250 and 300ft across – it was on the move. Descriptions of a parachute-shaped bright object, perhaps silver or metallic, were fairly consistent. Half an hour after the call from the highway patrol, the assistant tower operator at Godman AFB saw the object himself. Eventually there were several senior personnel watching it, some through binoculars. Apparently none could identify it. There seems to have been some confusion about what response should be initiated, a procrastination that was ended when four National Guard aircraft flew in. The tower operators asked the flight leader, Thomas Mantell, to investigate. One of the planes was low on fuel and so the pilot continued to his landing

at Standiford Field, while the remaining three took up pursuit.

Mantell seems to have thrown himself into the chase with vigour, zooming ahead of his colleagues. He must have been hugely excited at that moment. To the two other pilots, still climbing at 10,000ft, Mantell's plane was just a speck high in the sky. One of the wing radioed: 'What the hell are we looking for?' It was Mantell who answered, and described the object: '. . . metallic . . . tremendous in size . . .' This is an 'approximate' quotation, based on the memories of those in the tower – no recordings were made. Captain Edward Ruppelt, who later investigated the incident, seemed astonished that 'no one can remember exactly what he answered'.

Mantell announced that he was climbing

to 20,000ft in pursuit. The two wingmen recognized that he was, uncharacteristically, approaching the maximum altitude for safety without oxygen. Shortly afterwards, they lost radio contact with him. They descended and continued on to their landing at Standiford. One refuelled and took off again to search in vain for Mantell. Shortly afterwards the news was received that he had died when his plane 'augured in'.

At that time those studying the crash for the Air Force with Project Sign (which is discussed later in this chapter), were not aware of what Mantell had been chasing, and the last thing the Air Force wanted to consider was that it was a 'flying saucer'. Their release explained, almost pathetically, that the sighting 'might have been Venus or it could have been a balloon . . . it probably was Venus except that this is doubtful because Venus was too dim to be seen in the afternoon'. In fact, recently declassified files show that Mantell was chasing a Skyhook balloon carrying a secret naval

The COMING
of the SAUCERS

By Kenneth Arnold & Ray Palmer

project – the saucer-shaped object it was lifting. The theories and speculations continue to this day, though the explanation given is almost certainly correct.

But even the existence of a top-secret project does not on its own explain why Mantell died. Mantell is properly regarded as the first UFO martyr, but it wasn't aliens that killed him: it was his excited reaction to the mood of the time which had arisen from a national media fever. How did that mood arise?

THE START OF A PHENOMENON

Just six months before Mantell's death, America had undergone a wave of sightings of unknown objects in the sky – what Charles Fort, in his curious collections of oddities published earlier in the century, called 'Objects Seen Floating'. In the period of just a few weeks in June and July 1947, an estimated 1,000 or so sightings of such objects were reported. On 14 June, for example, pilot Richard Rankin, flying from Chicago to Los Angeles, had seen ten objects in triangular formation over Bakersfield in California. On 28 June six discs flying in formation were reported by USAF aviator Lieutenant Armstrong over Lake Mead in Nevada.

In 1967, American researcher Ted Bloecher searched through well over 100 references in newspapers, books and the files of the National Investigation Committee on Aerial Phenomena (NICAP) as well as the US Air Force Project Blue Book to piece together the 1947 wave of UFO sightings.[1] He located around 850 sightings, and estimated 1,000 to include the reports he believed he missed. Thirty years further on, we have learned that many sightings find their way into the records even decades after an event, so the real numbers of sightings in that wave

could have been even higher.

But one sighting during that wave took this 'Fortean' phenomenon out of the general bracket of Forteana and gave it an identity all its own.

On 24 June 1947, pilot Kenneth Arnold had been flying through the Cascade Mountains in Washington State in a small light Callair aircraft, modified for mountain search and rescue, searching for a crashed C–46 transport plane which had been missing since January. After taking off at around two o'clock in the afternoon, flying alone from Chehalis to Yakima, he had headed towards Mount Rainier, at around 9,000 to 10,000ft altitude. Alerted by a couple of flashes of bright light, Arnold saw a formation of nine objects in flight. They were flipping up and down in a manner Arnold variously described as 'very similar to a formation of geese', or resembling 'the tail of a Chinese kite that I once saw blowing in the wind' or 'like a saucer would if you skipped it across the water'. He was reported as commenting: 'No orthodox plane would be flying like that.'[2]

This curious movement is not unique and has been described several times, often in much the same terms. For example, Ed J. Sullivan, who, together with Victor Black and Werner Eichler, witnessed a formation of thirty UFOs in May 1951 over Los Angeles, reported: 'They moved with the motion of flat stones skipping across a smooth pond.'[3]

Arnold opened his window to get a clear view and estimated the speed at which the objects were moving to be around 1,700mph. Realizing how unlikely this was, he re-estimated on what he knew to be an overconservative guess, and still produced a figure in excess of 1,300mph. This was several months before Chuck Yeager, flying an experimental aircraft, became the first person to break the sound barrier at half that estimated speed. Arnold

believed the objects to be 23 miles away, and the formation some 5 miles in length. His estimates are questionable: all three – distance, length and speed – are interdependent, so if one is wrong, the others will be too. Since Arnold had nothing he could be certain of his actual observation was of limited value, and the observation had lasted only a short duration.

The sightings of the summer of 1947 were not in themselves an isolated phenomenon: in April of that year a silver ellipsoid object had been seen over Richmond, Virginia by a meteorologist named Minozewski. Byron Savage of Oklahoma City had seen an object in mid-May. In Bloecher's catalogue of sightings, arranged in date order, Arnold's is listed at number 39, and there are nineteen others on the same day. Indeed, it should be remembered that these Fortean aerial phenomena have been recorded down the centuries and include references in Roman writing to 'burning shields' in the sky and descriptions of what seem to be flying machines in ancient religious scripts. So what was significant about the Arnold sighting? And what was the effect that, six months later, resulted in the death of Captain Mantell?

It was the phrase used by Arnold to describe the objects he saw: 'They flew like a saucer would if you skipped it across the water.'

He was, in fact, describing the movements of the objects, the way they flipped up and down, rather than their shape, which he had noted was boomerang-like, similar to a tailless aircraft. But a reporter used his phrase to create an expression: flying saucer. It was the perfect buzz phrase for the moment, totally captivating the public's imagination. It took these aerial sightings out of the gamut of Fortean events and put them into a class of their own.

And there should be no doubt that Arnold's sighting *was* the birth of the modern era of UFOs. As we have seen, it was not the first sighting; it was not even the first time the term 'saucer' had been used. It is the identification of UFOs as a phenomenon in its own right that is important. It is from that date, 24 June 1947 – and as a result of the public attention Arnold attracted merely from the coining of the expression 'flying saucer' – that the government and the military started to show their interest. From that date the exotic possibilities of these objects reached a wider audience than ever before, and the media began their love–hate relationship with UFOs that has persisted to the present day.

'Flying Saucer fever' was fuelled by the media. Bloecher points out: 'The visible record of [the] 1947 emergence of the UFO problem is primarily a journalistic record. Although scientists, the military, and a few governmental spokesmen took minor parts in the dramatic entry of UFOs on to the modern scene, newspapermen wrote and delivered the key lines that made the journalists' role in the drama pre-eminent.'[1] And there was a feverish lust for these reports that summer. During those few weeks, reports were received from all across the North American continent: from forty-eight states, from the district of Columbia and from Canada. It seemed for a time that if your state did not have some reports of aerial visitors, your star was coming off the star-spangled banner.

This hype was almost certainly what killed an experienced pilot with a Skyhook balloon in his distant vision – albeit one with a top-secret saucer-like device hanging below it. The fever, the excitement that had started in the summer of 1947, must surely have played a part in Mantell's apparent recklessness in flying too high, blacking out from lack of oxygen and crashing to his death. And almost certainly it was the novelty of being caught up in the new fad that caused delay and consternation in the control tower that day.

There are aspects of this fad that we have yet to consider when examining why it has been so durable. In time Kenneth Arnold came to believe that the flying saucers were something exceptional, and he went on to dedicate much of the rest of his life to pursuing this enigma. In 1952 he commented to would-be flying saucer photographers, 'If you see the insignia of either the United States or the Soviet Air Force on the objects you have captured with your lens, turn them over to the nearest military intelligence branch . . . *they wouldn't be the*

Kenneth Arnold, whose sighting in 1947 coined the phrase 'Flying Saucer' – against a backdrop of postwar fear of invasion.

flying saucers we're talking about!'[our emphasis][4] Yet at the time of the sighting Arnold reported the objects to the FBI and others precisely because 'I knew that during the war we were flying aircraft over the pole to Russia, and I thought these things could possibly be from Russia.'[5]

THE END OF THE SECOND WORLD WAR

To understand what Arnold meant, and to comprehend the context in which flying saucers came to the fore, we need to go back to the end of the Second World War, and to recognize that, although in one

sense this was the close of a major historical event in another, it was just one moment within a broad canvas of continuous political change. We must therefore look at the world of 1947 from the American perspective.

For the UFO phenomenon was, at birth, exclusively American. Many of those first involved with the subject had lived through two world wars, the second of which had ended less than two years previously. The US entered the First World War on 6 April 1917, and of course, played a prominent part in the 1939–45 war in both the European and the Pacific arenas. Yet despite the many Hollywood images that

Artist's impression of the seminal Kenneth Arnold sighting of June 1947.

have proliferated since then, the Americans were well behind at the denouement in Berlin. It was the Soviet army who took the city, on 2 May 1945 – indeed, it is only in the past couple of years that the Russians have finally told the full story of Hitler's death and their removal of his body. Prior to that the West had only been able to speculate. But Western governments had not wanted to admit that their knowledge was incomplete: it would have shown their dependence on the Soviets in the final days of the war.

In the immediate postwar years the pace of change, both political and social, was astonishing, notably so in the way in which the Russians quickly became the new enemy. It was the Cold War with Russia that became the real backcloth to the paranoia in government and military UFO research.

NAZI TECHNOLOGY

Before we examine the American relationship with its new Russian enemy, we must consider the old enemy, the Nazis, and recognise the advanced technology that they had commanded. Their weaponry had proven itself in the V1 and V2 devices which had devastated London and other cities during the Blitz, and there had been much discussion at the time about other projects they may have been working on. In retrospect, this proved to be no idle speculation: both the Americans and the Russians liberated German scientists whose expertise was shortly put to use on creating the technology for the forthcoming space race. One of the projects the Nazis had been working on was a disc-shaped aircraft which went airborne in experimental flight for the first time in 1945, and which was said to have performed impressively[6].

It seems that later attempts to create similar aircraft by the American and Canadian governments did not meet with much success, however. For example, the Defence Production Department of Canada confirmed, through the Canadian minister for trade, that they had attempted to build a flying saucer but had found it not to be cost-effective. At the time, in the early 1950s, it was believed that had the project been taken to completion, it would have cost $100 million. 'It was dropped a year or so ago after about 18 months work and just a minute fraction of the $100 million estimated total cost was actually spent by the government,'

the minister for trade, Mr C. D. Howe, commented on 3 December 1954. Newspapers of Tuesday 21 April 1953 reported that: 'Field Marshal Montgomery inspected a "flying saucer" during a visit to an aircraft factory at Malton near Toronto yesterday.'[7] What Howe had described was almost certainly the object Montgomery saw. The article goes on to say that the object 'amazed' Montgomery, and that it was said to look like something from the pages of a science-fiction magazine. However, the saucer never actually became airborne.

Many theories, some plausible and others a great deal more implausible, have grown up around the development of flying discs. It is a plausible possibility, for instance, that German scientists continued their work on the disc-shaped aircraft after

the war and that these were some of the UFOs sighted in the early years. If so, and bearing in mind that a great many 'space-age' projects were being developed around the New Mexico desert areas based on the work of German scientists there, this might explain why so many disc-shaped UFOs were seen in that area, and even reportedly crashed there. In the early postwar years there was almost certainly some testing of disc-shaped aircraft – indeed, a document declassified in 1994 shows that from October 1947, Wright-Patterson Air Force Base was undertaking wind-tunnel testing of the flying saucer shape.

A flying disc sketched from Nazi blueprints. German scientists may have continued disc experimentation in New Mexico after the war.

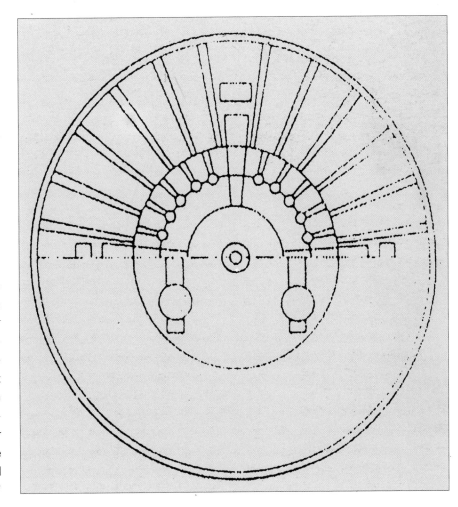

A good deal less plausible is the idea that the Nazis developed their disc-shaped flying saucers in league with aliens, or that they have continued to develop UFOs to this day in hidden bases at either the North or South Pole, or deep inside a hollow Earth. That more extreme belief has it that even modern-day UFOs are in fact Nazi weapons under test, or indeed preparing for their next onslaught on the world.

In spite of the recent emergence of the belief that UFOs are Nazi weapons, in the early postwar period the focus on the Nazis was short-lived. The new fear was that the German scientists 'liberated' from the German Rocket Research Centre at Peenemünde on the Baltic Sea by the Russians might prove more capable than those the Americans had themselves 'liberated'. The Russians had the same reciprocal fears.

THE POSTWAR CLIMATE

When Germany surrendered on 7 May 1945, the loose ends were cleared up swiftly. Germany was partitioned and Churchill memorably described the 'iron curtain' that had descended to divide Europe. The Russians, who had been allies to the West, were now being recast as enemies, and nowhere so fiercely as in the United States. In East Germany the Social Democrats merged with the Communists, and the rise of communism was the main fear and focus of the American people. Symbolic of the tensions was the 1948 Soviet blockade of Berlin, which lasted a year and resulted in the costly and difficult Berlin airlift to bring supplies to the western sector of the city.

In 1947 Communists came to power in Hungary, and Cominform was created by a Communist conference in Warsaw. In 1948, Communists seized Czechoslovakia. In 1949 the German Democratic Republic

was born, and communism spread to China under Chairman Mao Tse-Tung, resulting in the US withdrawing aid to that country. In February 1950, the USSR and China signed a pact in Moscow.

So afraid of communism was the American administration that in the very month of the Arnold sightings – June 1947 – Secretary of State George Marshall announced in a speech at Harvard the Marshall Plan, which would over the subsequent four years commit $13,000 billion to European recovery in order to shore up those economies against possible communist infiltration. (Interestingly, the end of America's financial influence in Europe, in 1973, also came about in precisely the same month as probably the most significant UFO events of that year: the political situation and the UFO cases are fully described in Chapter 3.)

The Cold War began to freeze over. Political crises in the 1950s and 1960s – between Kennedy and Khrushchev in particular – such as the Bay of Pigs and the Cuban Missile Crisis were the result of postwar anti-communist tensions and fears.

So it was during a time when America was watching the march of communism worldwide, and feared internal subversion by communists in influential positions, that the 1947 UFOs were reported. Across the world working people were calling for social change. As Saunders and Harkins comment, 'Thus it was that the year 1947 found many Americans questioning the meaning of their nation and of life itself.'[8]

When Kenneth Arnold saw his flying saucers in June and they seemed to be travelling at speeds no American plane or weapon could achieve, he reported them because he feared they might be Soviet weapons. This also is important because it set a certain standard for the investigation of these objects. From the outset of their

identification as a phenomenon in their own right, they were regarded as *physical*, and the investigations were therefore directed towards objects which were assumed to have physical characteristics. They were described in terms that implied an acceptance of their being physical. When it became apparent, very early on, that these objects were performing manoeuvres that no known technology could match, and no human frame could survive, the leap of logic was not to the possibility that they were not physical, but to the idea that they were physical but, ipso facto, not of this Earth. The theory quickly circulated that the flying saucers had to be extraterrestrial.

Had it not been for the Cold War and fear of enemy attack, then this blinding focus on the physical might not have been so prevalent. The absence of the sonic boom in apparently faster-than-sound sightings might have offered a clue to non-physicality once the phenomenon of the boom became widely known. Alternative possibilities – for example, that the UFOs could be non-physical luminous energies – might have surfaced more strongly and more quickly, and the whole course of UFO research would have been very different, perhaps even to the point where the extraterrestrial hypothesis would have been relegated to a 'fringe' possibility. As it was it was several decades before alternative theories were seriously addressed.

DISINFORMATION BEGINS

It is possible that the US government deliberately put out statements hinting at the possibility of alien invasion precisely because such invasion would unite the American people, whereas fear of Russian invasion might have divided them, considering that they feared communists within their own borders. Such a ploy could explain the otherwise seemingly unnecessary and apparently dramatic statement by the then president, Harry Truman, at a press conference on 4 April 1950: 'I can assure you that flying saucers, given that they exist, are not constructed by any power on earth.'

Where the government did not propagate that view, or drop enough hints to get people thinking it, they must at the very least have smiled quietly when the press speculated on it. In more recent times several comments along these lines by President Reagan have been widely quoted. In 1987 President Gorbachev of the Soviet Union confirmed a 1985 conversation with Reagan: 'At our meeting in Geneva, the US president said that if the Earth faced an invasion by extraterrestrials, the United States and the Soviet Union would join forces to repel such an invasion.' However, Reagan went on to say: 'Well, I don't suppose we can wait for some alien race to come down and threaten us. But I think that between us we can bring about that realization.' If he was hinting that people could be led to believe in the possibility of such an invasion, perhaps government involvement in the subject of UFOs has been in part implementing that policy through controlled disinformation.

Curiously enough, there was another conflicting approach, based on the government's genuine uncertainty as to what flying saucers really were. They also sought to play down possible fears about flying saucers, as we shall see later in this chapter, following the recommendations of the Robertson Panel in 1953. The US government's dichotomy on the matter probably goes a long way to explaining their inconsistencies over the years.

Given that there was a great deal of public focus on the skies and the unknown objects seen there, and given the fears of a postwar, communist-fearing nation whose mainland borders had never been violated by an invader, it is hardly surprising that, whatever the UFOs were thought to be, investigations were started. But UFO researchers have interpreted such investigations as a sign that the American government was taking seriously the flying saucers – and, by implication, the extraterrestrial hypothesis (ETH), the theory that UFOs are alien in origin.

THE US GOVERNMENT UFO PROJECTS

The first such examination of the UFO phenomenon was Project Sign (often publicly known by its nickname of Project Saucer). The trigger for this investigation seems to have been a letter sent on 23 September 1947 by General Twining of USAF Air Material Command to the Army Air Force suggesting that a study project be set up. The 'Saucer Commission' was established on 30 December 1947; the effective starting date was 22 January 1948, just two weeks after the death of Thomas Mantell in Kentucky. So clearly a project had already been intended, but Mantell's death gave them a vigorous push.

They appointed a civilian adviser, J. Allen Hynek, who is arguably the single most significant figure in the early years of UFO study. Hynek, then professor of astronomy at Northwestern University, remained the USAF's scientific adviser for over twenty years. They clearly hoped and intended that he should be their 'scientific debunker'; as it turned out, he became convinced of the importance and reality of the subject and in later years became its leading civilian researcher.

Hynek considered the 237 Project Sign cases interesting enough to be 'worthy of further scientific investigation' but believed they 'did not support "visitors from space"'.[9] However, what he observed and referred to as 'one faction' within Project Sign was responsible for sending an 'Estimate of the Situation' to General Vandenberg, the head of the Air Force, on 8 August 1948, which concluded that UFOs offered evidence of extraterrestrial involvement. Other 'factions' within Sign rejected this; Vandenberg did too.

It would seem that some time between December 1948 and February 1949, the government instigated Project Grudge, a name which said a great deal about the attitude adopted towards a subject that was seen as annoying and trivial. Hynek comments that he filed his 'Sign' report on 11 February 1949 and then found that Sign had 'somewhat mysteriously been transformed into Project Grudge'. Significantly, Grudge relied more on Air Force officers than on civilian experts. Hynek adds: 'The climate toward any serious investigation of flying saucers had become very chilly.' His military equivalent, Captain Edward Ruppelt, later revealed that 'everything was being evaluated on the premise that UFOs couldn't exist'.

Towards the end of 1949, the government indicated that it believed that Grudge had failed and that it would be closed down on 27 December. In fact, as is clear from Ruppelt's writings, it continued, but out of the public eye, as we will see later in this chapter. On 16 September 1951, Captain Ruppelt was invited to head Grudge with a view to ridding the Air Force of this tiresome problem which the government still insisted on pursuing. He requested additional funds and staff, which were granted. In March 1952 Project Grudge was renamed Project Blue Book. Dr Hynek continued as scientific adviser to Blue Book, which would remain the public face of official UFO investigation until it was closed down in 1969. By now the flying saucers had also acquired a new name, designed to be a little less 'pointed'. Ruppelt was the man who coined the expression UFO – Unidentified Flying Object.

Whatever the truth, it is likely that, having accepted there was even a vague possibility of UFOs being extraterrestrial, because of their apparently physicality – and despite rejecting Project Sign's 'Estimate of the Situation' – the American government became concerned that if delicate information fell into civilian hands, panic might ensue. They might have been influenced by a widely held view that this had happened following Orson Welles' famous radio broadcast of *The War of the Worlds* in the Eastern States of the US.* In fact this is a myth, and there was no such widespread panic,[10] but at the time the belief was influential.

THE BIRTH OF THE CIVILIAN PROJECTS

Dissatisfaction with the military and government attitude towards UFOs probably did more than anything to encourage the rise of civilian research groups. This movement began in 1950, when *True* magazine published an article by former Marine Major Donald E. Keyhoe called 'Flying Saucers Are Real', which was based on the disclosures of frustrated and angry former members of Project Sign. Keyhoe, who had been contacted by a 'deep throat' from within, was the first of many to accuse the government of a cover-up. It is important to note that this charge, apart from inevitably angering sections of the military and government, would to some extent have alienated the general public, too: in the 1950s, only 'radicals' challenged the government; loyal citizens supported it. It would take some years and several high-profile fiascos such as the Warren Commission and Watergate for such challenges to become acceptable in a widespread way. The emerging UFO protagonists were therefore perceived as 'radical', which was far from a compliment at that time. Researcher Steuart Campbell relates the story of one group of civilians in these early years complaining to the FBI that the APRO Bulletin was 'communistic' because it 'slurred and criticised the USAF and its officials.'

APRO – the Aerial Phenomena Research Organization – was the first large-scale civilian group, created in Tucson, Arizona by Jim and Carol Lorenzen. Having accelerated, if not caused, the emergence of such organizations the government now determined to keep a watchful eye over their activities. Throughout its early life APRO was under US government scrutiny. Indeed, the CIA's Robertson Panel report, which we shall come to momentarily, cited it as a candidate for surveillance. Presumably there was a fear that civilian groups would discover and expose whatever it was the government was hoping to discover first and perhaps use secretly for its own ends. A more common view in the present day is that the government had already discovered an awful truth, and that they were afraid civilian groups might uncover that truth and create widespread panic.

The Flying Saucer Bureau was another early, and relatively short-lived, civilian group. Its British counterpart, the British Flying Saucer Bureau, still exists today, admirably and indefatigably led by Graham Knewstubbe. It is a member society of the national organization, the British UFO Research Association (BUFORA).

J. Allen Hynek, gamekeeper turned poacher; one of the most influential men in gaining a serious scientific hearing for ufology.

---

*The newspaper reports of the time support the notion of panic. Messages on the Associated Press wire described 'weeping, hysterical women', and people 'gathering in groups and praying'. Later, in *Aliens From Space*, Major Donald Keyhoe wrote: 'Tens of thousands fled their homes, setting off a frantic exodus in several eastern states. Many were hurt in traffic accidents, and others collapsed from heart attacks.' One recent television biography of Welles referred to claims of rape by Martian invaders being made by people at the time.

But the reality is probably somewhat different. The Department of Transportation has no specific data suggesting a panic; the New York City Department of Health has no data available either, and doubt the claims. It is popularly held that the broadcast was presented 'as if live'. That is only partly true: Welles did not disguise the theatrical nature of the performance, and the fact that it was a play was stated at the outset, reiterated during the broadcast and said again at the end. Welles, seeking publicity for his theatre projects, 'warned' the newspapers in advance of the panic that 'might ensue', and the tabloids took the hint – and probably not for Welles' sake: they knew a good story when they were inventing one.

A study by Hadley Cantril confirmed the existence of the panic, and this is the source document for the belief that it occurred which has persisted for the past fifty-nine years. But Cantril's sample was probably a flawed one. It was based on the news-media coverage of the time, and the people questioned in the study are thought to have been a sample of those who reacted most strongly to the broadcast. If only a few individuals reacted adversely, it is likely that Cantril included all of them and extrapolated from there.

Panic specialist Robert Hall suggests: 'The best interpretation appears to be that news media at the time and many persons interpreting the events later greatly exaggerated the amount of wild, panicky behavior that occurred. If there was any panic, it was a panic of the news media, rushing to beat their competitors and to report the attention-grabbing story.'

The most important of the early civilian groups was formed in 1956, based on the work of Donald Keyhoe, with whom it would always be identified. This was NICAP, the National Investigation Committee on Aerial Phenomena. It was created by Navy physicist Thomas Townsend Brown, and later headed by Keyhoe himself. NICAP argued a broadly extraterrestrial line on the subject, reflecting Keyhoe's beliefs, but we now know that government involvement in the group was considerable. NICAP had links with the CIA to a degree perhaps not even fully known today. We do know that Rear Admiral Roscoe Hillenkoetter, first director of the CIA, was a board member of NICAP for many years. Colonel Joseph J. Bryan III was chief of the CIA psychological warfare staff, and also on the board of NICAP. Count Nicolas de Rochefort of the CIA psychological warfare staff was vice-chairman of NICAP. CIA briefing officer Karl Pflock was chairman of NICAP's Washington subcommittee. John Acuff, who took over as head of NICAP when Keyhoe was ousted in 1969, was himself associated with the CIA. He, in turn, was replaced by CIA agent Alan Hall in 1979. Another leading member of NICAP, Bernard Corvalho, was alleged to be an intelligence operative. NICAP was dissolved in 1973.

THE EARLY REPORTS

Whatever the government and the civilians were doing, the UFOs ignored them all and continued unabated. Even by 1950, around 90 per cent of all UFO sightings were still coming out of the United States, although in that year Gerald Heard published *Riddle of the Flying Saucers*, which demonstrated that there was activity elsewhere in the world. As has been shown frequently since, where there are people to report experiences to, and a media which takes an

interest, there are documented cases available anywhere in the world. UFOs, without doubt, are a global phenomenon.

As well as being seen, UFOs were being photographed too. William A. Rhodes of Phoenix, Arizona snapped pictures of a UFO over his home in July 1947; on the same day, near Morristown, New Jersey, John Janssen photographed four brightly lit objects in the sky.

A significant pair of pictures was taken by farmer Paul Trent on 11 May 1950. They appear to show a large, circular object in flight over his farmhouse.

WASHINGTON, 1952

Five years after the first wave of UFO sightings, a focus of reports arose in Washington in July. Researcher Paris Flammonde

The Trent photograph from McMinnville, Oregon. 'One of the few UFO reports in which all factors investigated ... appear to be consistent with the assertion that an extraordinary flying object ... flew within sight of two witnesses.' (Condon Report, 1969)

describes this as 'phase two of the modern era'.[11] Edward Ruppelt, in *The Report On Unidentified Flying Objects*, states that in six months of 1952 US newspapers carried over 16,000 items on UFOs.[12]

These sightings were important first in that the Air Force admitted it scrambled planes to examine and intercept the objects, and secondly because visually observed phenomena were showing up on radar. On 27 July the *New York Times* reported: 'The Air Force said today that jet fighter planes had made an effort to intercept unknown objects in the sky over Washington last night after the objects had been spotted by radar, but that no direct contact had been made. It was the second time within a week that unidentified objects had been observed in the vicinity of the nation's capital, but no planes were sent up on the previous occasion, last Monday.'[13] A press release from the Air Force stated: 'One of the jet pilots reported sighting four lights in front of him, approximately ten miles, and slightly above him, but he reported he had no apparent closing speed. They disappeared before he could overtake them'. Paul R. Hill, an aeronautical research engineer with thirteen years' practical experience behind him, witnessed an apparent rendezvous of UFOs over Chesapeake Bay. Two UFOs, moving at approximately 500mph, were revolving around each other at high speed and were met by a third 'falling in' several hundred feet below the others, creating a V-shaped pattern. A fourth UFO joined the group, which then flew southwards at speed. The Air Force stated that its own aircraft were not in the area at the time. During one spate of encounters, UFOs entered the restricted air corridor near the White House.

Captain S. Pierman of Capital Airlines was one of several pilots who visually confirmed what was being tracked on radar during the wave. For several minutes he observed many bright lights moving horizontally. 'The moment he radioed in his observation of one object it shot away "at terrific speed".'[14] He stated: 'In all my years of flying I have seen a lot of falling or shooting stars – whatever you call them – but these were much faster than anything like that I have ever seen. They couldn't have been aircraft. They were moving too fast for that . . . Please remember, I didn't speak of them as flying saucers – only very fast moving lights.' But Harry Barnes, the senior air-traffic controller that night, commented: 'It was almost as if whatever controlled it had heard us, or had seen Pierman head toward it.' And at the moment it left, the blip also disappeared from the scope. It had therefore been a true radar return.

Major-General Roger S. Ramey, director of operations, gave the Air Force position:

The Air Force, in compliance with its mission of air defense of the United States, must assume responsibility for investigation of any object or phenomena in the air over the United States. Fighter units have been instructed to investigate any object observed or established as existing by radar tracks, and to intercept any air-borne [sic] identified as hostile or showing hostile interest. This should not be interpreted to mean that air-defense pilots have been instructed to fire haphazardly on anything that flies . . .

No orders have been issued to the Air Defense Command or by the Air Defense Command to its fighter units to fire on unidentified aerial phenomena.[14]

Another Air Force spokesman who did not wish to be identified commented in the same interview: 'We don't know what these things are and there's no use pretending we do.'

Captain Ruppelt, a former co-ordinator of UFO investigation for the Air Force and later the author of a book confirming government cover-up, stated: 'The summer of 1952 was just one big swirl of UFO reports, hurried trips, midnight phone calls, reports to the Pentagon, press interviews, and very little sleep.' No one was, however, keeping Ruppelt informed officially, and despite his new position as head of Blue Book, he had to find out about the sightings from the press. When reporters asked what the response would be, Ruppelt's acid reply was: 'I have no idea what the Air Force is doing; in all probability it's doing nothing.'

THE ROBERTSON PANEL

Even so, it is obvious that behind the scenes there was official concern. Just six months later, on 14 January 1953, the Robertson Panel, which we now know was assembled by the CIA, met for the first time. Its task was to define government and military policy on UFOs based on the Cold War-generated fear that UFOs might be physical, and threatening. Five scientists met for a week and concluded that: 'The evidence presented on Unidentified Flying Objects shows no indication that these phenomena constitute a direct physical threat to national security. We firmly believe that there is no residuum of cases which indicates phenomena that are attributable to foreign artefacts capable of hostile acts, and there is no evidence that the phenomena indicate a need for revision of current scientific concepts.'

However, in the wake of the comments of the Robertson Panel, the military put into effect JANAP (Joint-Army-Navy-Airforce-Publication) 146, which imposed severe penalties on anyone in the military who released information about 'unidentifieds', and issued Air Force Regulation 200–2, which related to sightings by Air Force personnel. This was updated in November 1953, and again the following year, on 12 August. Extracts from the 1954 issue indicate: 'Objectives. Air Force interest in unidentified flying objects is two-fold. First as a possible threat to the security of the United States and its forces, and secondly, to determine technical aspects involved.'

The detection of the Washington UFOs on radar implied yet again that they were 'solid' and the sightings of lights seemed to support this. Radar is not totally reliable – it can 'detect' many non-solid anomalies – but, there are many radar/visual sightings that have corroborated a real phenomenon. Radar-detected UFOs were not confined to

the US, either: Project Blue Book records the August 1952 case at Kaneda Air Force Base in Tokyo, for example. In England, perhaps the most famous early radar–visual case took place in 1956, at Bentwaters USAF base.

BENTWATERS 1956

Between 21.30 and 03.30 hours GMT on the night of 13–14 August, there were multiple sightings on radar and by eyewitnesses of apparently high-speed, brilliantly lit objects displaying what researcher Martin Shough has described as 'unconventional manoeuvrability'.[15] Five separate incidents were reported, involving seven different radar units, one airborne. Twenty radar personnel were involved, and nine visual observers. The first incident occurred when Bentwaters ground-controlled approach (GCA) radar detected what appeared to be an object moving at 4,000mph. At around the same time, fifteen slower-moving objects were seen on scope. Several other sightings were noted within a short space of time. Bentwaters asked nearby RAF–USAF Lakenheath for confirmation. The Lakenheath radar was detecting similar anomalies to those reported by Bentwaters, and there was visual confirmation at Lakenheath of something manoeuvring close by. The decision was taken to scramble two RAF interceptors for closer examination. One Venom nightfighter was vectored on to the target and reported both radar and visual sighting. But the hunter became the hunted: ground radar showed the object circling round the plane and then chasing it, staying on its tail for several minutes notwithstanding the pilot's attempts to shake it off. Eventually the UFO was lost, and the plane returned safely home. Shough has described the events of this case as 'probably the most impressive of their kind on record'.[15]

PILOT SIGHTINGS

Although pilots are not encouraged to report UFO encounters – indeed, they are actively discouraged from doing so – many have revealed their experiences of these early years.

On 27 April 1950, Captain Robert Adickes and his co-pilot, Robert Manning, were flying in a DC3 towards Goshen, Indiana at approximately 2,000ft and 175mph, when they encountered a glowing, saucer-shaped object. It easily overtook them, then paced their plane and ultimately dived off at a speed Adickes estimated to be nearly 400mph.

Major Charles Scarborough was a Marine Corps squadron leader who encountered sixteen discs while flying over Texas in 1952. He believed they were responding to his ground-to-air communications, and therefore listening in and acting intelligently.

Also over Texas, one evening in 1952, was the encounter of Captain G.W. Schemel of TWA. He was flying at 18,000ft when the lights of an object appeared less than a mile away from his plane and flashed towards the plane at incredible speed. Schemel dived, and the UFO disappeared overhead in a burst of light. Several passengers not wearing seatbelts hit the ceiling and were injured during the emergency manoeuvre, showing that Schemel took very severe action in the face of the oncoming object. In fact he was so concerned that he requested an emergency landing.

In England, Captain Peter Fletcher and First Officer R.L. Lemon took off from London Airport at 9 o'clock on the morning of 9 October 1953.[16] After passing through a low cloud bank, they found themselves in very clear air with good visibility. Flying towards Paris and over the English Channel, they were passed by an aircraft which they could then see maintaining a position ahead and above them. It was then that they noticed another aircraft, which they later came to identify as being saucer-shaped, maintaining a position more or less relative to themselves. For thirty minutes they watched the object. 'We have no doubt whatsoever that object was solid, having a shape approximately that of an aircraft wing and that it was constructed of a metal similar to that used for aircraft construction, only much more highly polished,' said Captain Fletcher. 'In 18 years of flying I have never seen anything like it.'

In October 1954, Flight Lieutenant James Saladin of the Royal Auxiliary Air Force was flying over Essex, England when he saw three UFOs heading towards him. One, described by Saladin as saucer-shaped with cupolas above and below, came so close that it virtually obscured forward vision. He reported the sighting to the Air Ministry but got no response. Researcher Timothy Good described the incident as 'one of the most important sightings to have been reported by an RAF pilot'.

THE GOOSE BAY SIGHTINGS

The encounter with a UFO experienced by Captain James Howard, who was flying a Boeing Stratocruiser over Goose Bay, Labrador on 29 June 1954, is a well-known case, but the fact that he appears to have reported a 'shape-shifting' UFO is perhaps less well known. In

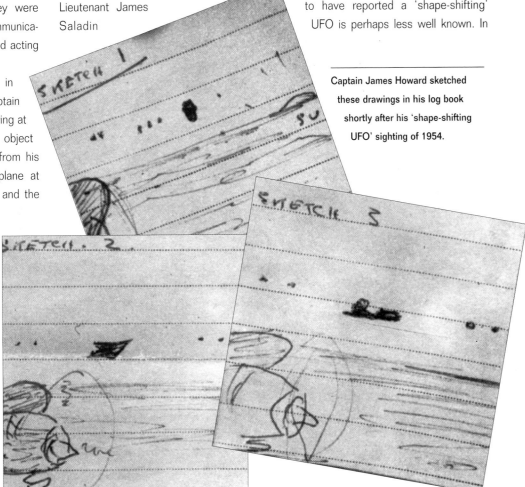

Captain James Howard sketched these drawings in his log book shortly after his 'shape-shifting UFO' sighting of 1954.

Captain Howard's own report, published just months after the incident, he said: 'It seemed to keep changing its shape as it flew beside me, very much like a jellyfish assumes varying patterns as it swims through the water. Or maybe the apparent changes in shape were due to the different angles we viewed it from as it banked and turned about five miles off.'

Howard had taken off from Idlewild Airfield on what BOAC pilots had in those days nicknamed the 'champagne and caviar' run – the North Atlantic crossing from New York to London. Although this was often a non-stop flight, on this occasion the plane was heavily laden and Howard was planning a refuelling stop at Goose Bay in Labrador. At 9.05 Labrador time, looking out at the sky in perfect visibility, Howard first sighted 'the thing'. His first impression was of a 'dark blob . . . with several smaller blobs dancing attendance on it'. The object was also seen by his co-pilot, First Officer Lee Boyd. They were watching a formation. In Howard's words: 'The big one was roughly centre of the group, with the smaller ones extended fore and aft like a destroyer screen convoying a battleship.' During the observation, 'The big central thing began to change shape – or maybe it altered its angle of flight, giving the appearance of changing shape . . . What I do know is that during the entire 18 minutes it flew along with us, it changed shape continually while the smaller attendant things switched position around it.' Howard, knowing that he would be questioned about his sighting, counted the objects and was certain he could see six. However, he was also sure that he had seen more earlier. Lee Boyd speculated that the smaller objects were 'flying in and out of a large central object like aircraft entering and leaving a flight hangar'.

Approach Control at Goose Bay confirmed that there was no other traffic in the area. When Boyd reported the sighting, Approach Control stated: 'We will send a fighter up to take a look-see.' Other crew members joined in the observation: George Allen, navigating officer; Doug Cox, radio officer; Dan Godfrey, engineering officer; Bill Stewart, engineering officer; the steward, and Daphne Webster, the stewardess. Indeed, the steward and stewardess had gone to the cockpit to ask the crew what the objects were as some of the passengers had noticed them and were asking questions. Howard said: 'I was tempted to change course and take a closer look at the things, but I didn't. After all, I didn't know what the blazes they were, and I had fifty-one passengers to consider.'

Shortly afterwards the pilot of the intercepting flight contacted Howard by radio, asking, 'Those things still with you?' Howard confirmed that they were, and almost immediately he realized that, 'The things were no longer there – not all of them. The half dozen attendant things had suddenly vanished.' Navigating Officer Allen commented that he believed they had gone inside the larger object and shortly afterwards they noticed that the larger object was getting smaller, 'as if it was shearing away from us at terrific speed'. In a matter of seconds the object was a pinhead and then it was gone altogether.

In his initial interview Howard does not speculate on the disappearance of the objects but later theories included the possibility that the objects had monitored radio transmission from the interceptor and had decided to leave. Of course, if the objects were a natural phenomenon, then their disappearance at that moment must have been coincidental.

Twenty minutes later Howard landed at Goose Bay, where Lee Boyd, George Allen and himself were interviewed by a USAF intelligence officer. Howard summed up his considerations about the sighting:

It was a solid thing. I am sure of that. Manoeuvrable and controlled intelligently – a sort of base ship linked somehow with those smaller attendant satellites. There is no rational explanation – except on the basis of space ships and flying saucers. On that basis, it must have been some weird form of space ship from another world . . . One day we shall know. That day, I am sure, will be pretty important for the human race. I hope I am here to see it.

Howard's experience was not the only incident to have occurred over Goose Bay. On 29 October 1948, an object had been tracked by radar, and a similar return was received two days later. On the following night, 1 November, an object moving at 600mph was tracked for four minutes. On 19 June 1952, a strange red light was seen over Goose Bay Air Force Base just after midnight, which was also being returned on the radar scope. At approximately 4,000ft, observers saw it suddenly turn bright white – the return on the radar scope 'brightened' at this moment – and then the blip returned to normal size and vanished. The light which had been visible to the eye disappeared at the same moment: a clear correlation between visual and radar sighting.

If these cases had arisen in later years, a connection might have been made between these recurrent phenomena and the geology of the area, as became clear at Hessdalen, which is dealt with in Chapter 4.

EARLY CLASSIFICATIONS

Analysis of the first decade of UFOs concentrated for the most part on the 'things seen in the skies'. For example, Aimé Michel, writing in 1957, more or less divides the phenomenon into three basic types of sighting: saucers, of course; cigar shapes; and lights in the sky (LITS).[17] A few examples of each type serves to illustrate the variety.

SAUCERS

Saucer-shapes, of course, had been prominent even before the eponymous Arnold sighting. Washington housewife Mrs Emma Shingler watched several platter-like objects moving at tremendous speed over Washington State a week prior to Arnold's sighting, during the afternoon of 17 June 1947. What would appear to have been the same objects were also seen by Mr and Mrs Wheeler near the same location. A disc shape was reported by a Mrs H. Atkins and others as being present for fifteen minutes over Green Springs, Alabama the following day. And eight or ten discs, described as 'lighted from within', were reported by R.D. Taylor at Cedar Rapids the day after that. The 'unidentifieds' in Project Blue Book[18] include a dome-shaped disc seen on 22 December 1952 by a technician driving towards an air-force base, who observed the object for fifteen minutes; a similar, perhaps slightly flatter

object seen on 31 July 1948 by an electrician from his home; a ground-hugging disc seen by a farmer and his two sons on 13 August 1947. Disc sightings are too numerous to list comprehensively, even in the early waves, let alone from the last fifty years.

CIGAR SHAPES

Flying cigar shapes have also been frequently reported. The most famous of these is probably the Chiles–Whitted sighting of 23 July 1948. Commanded by Clarence S. Chiles and co-pilot John B. Whitted, a DC3 belonging to Eastern Airlines took off at 8.30 pm from Houston, Texas bound for Boston, Massachusetts. Both pilots were reliable, solid people with good war records and considerable flying hours under their belts. At 2.45am, near Montgomery, Alabama, they saw what looked like a missile coming straight at them. 'It flashed down towards us at terrific

Cigars were commonly reported shapes in the early years of UFOs as depicted in this magazine cover illustration from 'Flying Saucer News' of summer 1955. Many viewed them as the 'motherships' of the smaller flying saucers.

speed,' Chiles later said. 'We veered to the left and it passed us about 700 feet to the right.' The object was cigar-shaped, metallic in appearance, about 30yds long and double the girth of a Dakota. It had no wings. It had two rows of portholes, brilliantly lit as if by a magnesium flash. At the front Chiles saw what looked like a radar aerial; at the rear the tail was blasting out a flame 10 to 15yds long. At the point of closest approach to the plane it 'pulled up', the flame was replaced by 'a weird bundle of rays' and the object shot upwards at right angles and disappeared from view. Only one passenger on the plane, Clarence McKelvie, had been awake, and he also witnessed the event. Investigation suggested that an hour before this sighting the same or a similar object had been seen at the Robbins Aviation Base near Macon, Georgia. No known aircraft was on that flightplan at the time.

Another cigar-shaped object was seen on 20 August 1949 by Professor Clyde W. Tombaugh, the discoverer of the planet Pluto. He saw six to eight brightly lit rectangles which he took to be the windows of an otherwise dark cylindrical shape. He stated: 'In all of my several thousand hours of night-sky watching I have never seen anything so strange as this.'

Cigar shapes were an early category of UFOs reported over Europe, and were known as the 'ghost rockets'. They were first reported over Scandinavia in the 1930s, and in January 1934 up to forty reports a day were being received. Over time the rockets were seen as far south as Greece. In the summer of 1946, almost 1,000 reports were received across Europe, though these included sightings of some disc-like objects.

LITS

The category of sightings that are generally seen as lights in the sky has always been prominent. Whether the lights are themselves UFOs, or merely lights *on* UFOs is not always clear. Even at this level of examination, the UFO phenomenon is not one thing, but several. Gerald Heard prophetically referred to these UFOs as 'thinking lights',[19] decades ahead of the researchers at such places as Hessdalen Valley, which is covered in Chapter 4.

Perhaps the simplest, and most famous, of LITS sightings are the Lubbock Lights. On 25 August 1951, in Lubbock, Texas, an employee of a classified division of the Atomic Energy Commission and his wife saw a huge, fast, apparently structured craft fly over them at no more than 1,000ft in their estimation. It was described as a fuselage-less flying wing resembling the

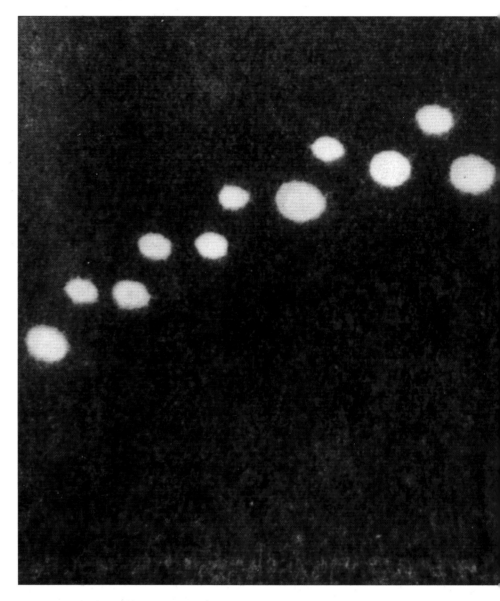

Carl Hart's 1951 photograph of the Lubbock Lights. They were reported by many people, and impressed several scientists. Ruppelt first regarded them as valuable evidence but in his rewritten book dismissed them as reflections from moths.

letter V. It appeared to have dark stripes and a half-dozen or so blue lights on its trailing edge. Then a group of professors (of geology, chemical engineering, physics and the head of the department of petroleum engineering) all saw a formation of between twelve and thirty-six turquoise lights. The following

morning a target was registered on radar by Air Defence Command at 900mph. Captain Ruppelt of Project Blue Book commented that it was 'by far the best combination of UFO reports I had ever read'.

The Lubbock Lights produced witnesses in their hundreds and photographs such as the famous Carl Hart picture of 31 August 1951. According to Ruppelt, the lights were studied by one group of 'rocket experts, nuclear physicists and intelligence experts' and 'convinced them all the more that their ideas of how an (extraterrestrial) spaceship might operate were correct'.

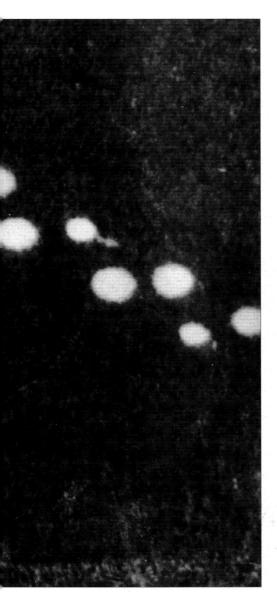

an estimated 3,500ft below him, moving at around 250mph. He had been given clearance to land, and questioned the control tower about the object apparently in his way. 'What do you mean?' he asked. 'You've said I can land, but I can see the tail light of a plane messing about between a thousand and twelve hundred feet above the runway. What am I to do?'

'What are you talking about?' the control tower replied, somewhat curtly. The only other aircraft on their scope was a Piper Cub due to land after Gorman. Gorman watched the light fly over the football ground near the aerodrome, and discovered that it was not visible in silhouette as an object: the light was just a light. He could see the silhouette of the Piper Cub in the football ground lighting. Then L.D. Jensen, the air-traffic controller in the tower, and a friend who was with him, Manuel Johnson, saw the light too. Jensen radioed Gorman, 'Don't come down. I'll see what it is.'

Gorman described the light as 'clear white and completely round, with a sort of fuzz at the edges. It was blinking on and off. As I approached, however, the light suddenly became steady and pulled into a sharp left bank.' Gorman swooped down towards the object, watched by the tower personnel and the occupants of the Piper Cub. As he got near, the light did a tight turn and swiftly ascended. Gorman gave chase, but the tightness of the turn caused him to black out momentarily. The pursuit lasted several minutes, and reached around 13,000ft at one point. Gorman and the light were on several occasions heading directly at one another. On the first such approach, Gorman 'lost his nerve', went into a dive and the object passed over the top of him; then he circled and chased again. This manoeuvre was repeated several times.

Eventually Gorman took a gamble. Reasoning that it could do him no harm if he

hit it, he decided to 'bump' the light. But it continued to outmanoeuvre him, and eventually it headed upwards at tremendous speed, and was quickly lost from sight.

Gorman believed that the object was intelligently controlled, and although it was clearly highly manoeuvrable, he thought it was governed by the normal laws of inertia: 'Although it was able to turn fairly tightly at considerable speed, it still followed a natural curve.'

This was not an isolated sighting. Just six weeks later, a Lieutenant H. Combs, together with a Lieutenant Jackson, encountered a similar light over Andrews Field near Washington. Combs, too, chased the light, and also had to perform several tight turns in the manoeuvring. On straight-line chases he noticed that the light was much faster than he was – he estimated its speed at 600mph, which suggested that sometimes it was having to 'wait for him', and was presumably 'playing with him'. When Combs was on a 'chicken-run' with the light, he turned on his own bright landing lights, and the object darted away at high speed, ending the encounter.

Such lights had been reported as early as the Second World War, when they were known as 'foo fighters'. Each of the opposing forces had believed they were weapons of the other side. For example, the Associated Press of 13 December 1944 reported: 'As the Allied Armies ground out new gains on the western front today, the Germans were disclosed to have thrown a new "device" into the war – mysterious silvery balls which float in the air. Pilots report seeing these objects, both individually and in clusters, during forays over the Reich.'[20]

It has since been suggested that these lights were a form of ball lightning or plasma energy, perhaps forming because of the structural or electrical nature of the aircraft in use at that time. And indeed there

However, in the second edition of his book, Ruppelt suggested that the explanation could have been light reflecting off moths. The circumstances of the rewriting of his book are interesting and are dealt with later in this chapter.

Of more interactive LITS sightings, the aerial 'dogfight' of Lieutenant George F. Gorman is one of the best-witnessed accounts. On 1 October 1948, Gorman, a National Guardsman, was flying back to Fargo, North Dakota in a Mustang F51, having finished his patrol. He was at 4,500ft and, looking down, saw a brilliant white light are fewer such close-approach cases in modern times, though unexplained lights still feature strongly in the UFO reports. The Office of Strategic Services (the forerunner of the CIA), indicated shortly after the Second World War that they believed that foo fighters were an unusual but natural phenomenon.

CAPTAIN EDWARD RUPPELT

The early days of the UFO phenomenon thus established a matter which has never been disproved: that something strange is, and has been, moving about in our atmosphere and that it is worthy of, as J. Allen Hynek put it, 'further scientific investigation'.

And yet after Hynek's military counterpart, USAF Intelligence Officer Captain Edward Ruppelt, took over the US government's study, Project Blue Book, he found that it – and, by implication, he – was not being taken seriously. His thoroughness, which he assumed was the reason for his appointment, was immediately ignored; resources were not made available to him and his status was undermined. For example, he was told to use public transport to investigate cases rather than a staff car. He examined the wave of radar–visual cases in Washington only after reading about them in the press: there was no help from the Air Force. He managed to employ a radar specialist to assist him, but when this specialist's evaluations were overturned, he resigned and joined a private UFO research group. Rather than seeing himself as the investigator he had thought he was, Ruppelt began to feel like the front man in a USAF cover-up. He was probably right: Dr Walter Orr Roberts of the National Oceanic and Atmospheric Administration had turned down the opportunity to chair Blue Book because he took the view that it had predetermined, negative, conclusions.

Perhaps others similarly rejected the chance, and Blue Book was looking for a 'patsy'.

As 1952 gave way to 1953 Ruppelt's powers diminished further still. Blue Book representatives were downgraded at the Robertson hearings, and with further requests for resources being ignored, Ruppelt and Hynek found themselves funding case researches out of their own pockets. Hynek admitted years later that he had played by the USAF rules so he could stay at the centre and would not lose sight of the good cases in what he increasingly viewed as a cover-up. He was disillusioned about the anti-UFO position the scientists on the Robertson Panel were taking, and even withheld his best data from the panel. During a TV interview in 1974 he was asked if he had any outstanding evidence. He replied, 'Well, I thought I might have had, but in the face of that onslaught, I wasn't about to bring it up . . .' Ruppelt, disillusioned with the Air Force – and possibly with Hynek, if he believed the scientific adviser really was a 'company man' – resigned in 1953.

In 1954 he published an article in *True* magazine which detailed unexplained cases from the Blue Book files and word got out that he was planning to write a book on the subject. Embittered as he was, it was obvious that it would not be flattering or helpful to the Air Force.

In 1955 Ruppelt's book was published, making the case for UFOs as something extraordinary, and worthy of further study.[12] It created a storm, but the USAF fought back, and they had a dirty trick up their sleeve. A report had been produced by the Battelle Memorial Institute, which had analysed the Blue Book files. It, too, concluded that UFOs were not all easily explainable, and that 22 per cent of the Blue Book cases had not been solved. But the USAF published a doctored version of

the report, referring to that 22 per cent merely as 'a few remaining unknowns'. The timing of the release was clearly intended to stop Ruppelt in his tracks. The score in terms of public perception was for some time: USAF 1, Ruppelt 0. (The report was eventually issued as Blue Book Special Report Number 14.)

As far as Ruppelt was concerned, the sad end of the story came just five years later, in 1960. Ruppelt issued a new version of his book, and it might as well have been a completely new work. It reversed the conclusions of much of the original, and claimed that all UFOs were cases of misidentification. Quite why he changed his mind so dramatically is unclear: his wife says it was a genuine change of heart; others have speculated that he wanted to curry favour with the Air Force for reasons of patriotism or pride. Still others have suggested that the Air Force put pressure on him. Whatever the truth, tragically, it died with him. In the year the revised book was published, at just thirty-seven years old, he died of a heart attack. Almost certainly his battle with the USAF had taken its toll.

DEBUNK – AND THAT'S OFFICIAL!

One concern was obviously to the forefront of thinking in official circles at that time, and it was manifest in the conclusions of the Robertson Panel. In 1953 they concluded that:

The continued emphasis on the reporting of these phenomena does, in these parlous times, result in a threat to the orderly functioning of the protective organs of the body politic. We cite as examples the clogging of channels of communication by irrelevant reports, the danger of being led by continued false alarms to ignore real indications of

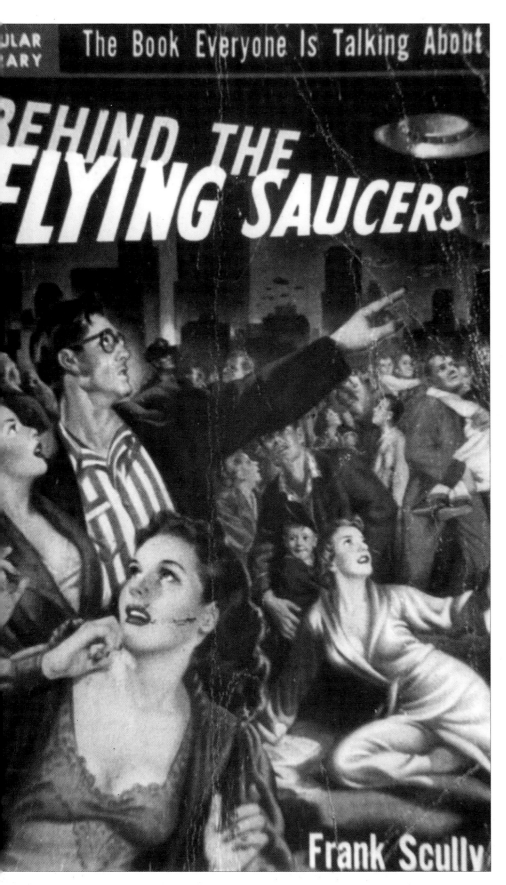

hostile action, and the cultivation of a morbid national psychology in which skilful hostile propaganda could induce hysterical behaviour and harmful distrust of duly constituted authority.

Five scientists with just a week to deliberate do not waste time on areas they have not been asked to examine, so we can be sure that the social effects of belief in UFOs were a serious consideration for the government. The panel recommended that steps be taken to strip UFOs of the status they were acquiring as 'special phenomena' and that, 'The national security agencies institute policies on intelligence, training, and public education designed to prepare the country to recognize most promptly and to react most effectively to true indications of hostile intent or action.' Debunking flying saucers to reduce public concern was now an official recommendation. Moreover, the panel also ordered the monitoring of the emerging civilian flying-saucer research groups such as APRO.

Believing in the 'Orson Welles panic' the panel suggested that Dr Hadley Cantril (who had authored the study of that 'panic') should prepare a programme of public education. They even suggested enlisting Mickey Mouse to put the message over. In more recent years, there have been conspiratorial suggestions at UFO conferences that films such as Steven Spielberg's *Close Encounters of the Third Kind* were made at the government's behest in order to further this policy. The reality is that, given a subject of such special interest, the film-makers were going to step forward anyway. All the government had to do was wait and watch.

Typical of the imagery of UFOs in the 1950s: hysteria and fear based on beliefs generated by science fiction. The impact of science-fiction films of the 1950s was a strong influence on the way UFOs were viewed by researchers and witnesses alike.

THE EARLY INFLUENCE OF SCIENCE FICTION

Given that the UFO phenomenon was born and bred in America, it is important to understand the influence of science fiction in that country at that time. The development of this genre was a major factor in making a belief in aliens acceptable. Some researchers have pointed to the role played by Ray Palmer, the 1930s and 1940s editor of *Amazing Stories* and *Fantastic Adventures*. He was already promoting stories that aliens were visiting earth, and he seized on the Arnold incident and promoted it widely in an extraterrestrial context. The first edition of *Fate* magazine in 1948, strongly emphasized the Arnold story; moreover, Palmer co-authored Arnold's book on the subject.[4] In the 1950s, when Palmer moved on to magazines such as *Mystic Universe* and *Other Worlds Science Stories*, flying saucers were a constant theme. There is no question that Palmer was a major influence, but this would not have been possible without a pre-existing context that appealed to mass readerships not usually given to reading science fiction. This was the context of alien invasion – where 'alien' equalled 'Russian' – during the Cold War.

One popular book of the day that drew from the flying-saucer stories was *Star of Ill-Omen* by Dennis Wheatley, published in 1952.[21] Wheatley, most famous for his occult books and for the themes of witches and Atlantis, was by then a very well-known and bestselling writer. He thoroughly researched the saucer reports and brilliantly mixed fact with fiction to produce a post-war, James Bond-like story of atomic secrets and agents kidnapped by Martian giants and taken to Mars in flying saucers. Most of the theories of the time are worked into the story, whose conclusion was that the saucers had to be of extraterrestrial origin. The fact that the book was well researched gave it added plausibility: moreover, it included references to real characters such as Argentinian leader General Peron (prominent in the public consciousness at the time since 1952 was the year of the death of his internationally known wife Eva), and such tensions as the contemporary Falklands Crisis (which was similar to the crisis of the 1980s, although the earlier event did not escalate into war). The book would have reinforced in some minds a few extreme flying-saucer theories that were being bandied about at the time.

But for mass audiences, it was science fiction on the screen that was most influential, a genre typified by the famous serials of the 1930s such as *Flash Gordon* and *Buck Rogers*. The concept of aliens, albeit fictional ones, was therefore probably more accepted in America than anywhere else in the world at that time.

After Arnold's sighting the subject of flying saucers was put firmly on the cultural map, and films started to depict the imagery, extending it, of course, into the extraterrestrial realm. The consequent effect on the development of the UFO phenomenon has been examined in some detail in John Spencer's books *Perspectives*[22] and *Gifts of the Gods?*[23] Science fiction in films was highly popular in the 1950s: many classics – and a good few ridiculous examples – were produced then, and their imagery has proved lasting. And

The Day the Earth Stood Still: a film made in 1951 which contains much of the imagery later reported in UFO claims. This frame shows the platform bed, medical treatment and concealed lighting which have all been reported frequently since 1961.

such films were not the exclusive province of sci-fi buffs: the habit of going to the cinema to see particular films was not the norm then, since people saw the cinema as a regular night out, regardless of what was showing. Science-fiction films therefore reached a very wide audience.

Of crucial importance is the film *The Day the Earth Stood Still*, released in 1951, which, more than any other, formed a bridge from the idea that UFOs were extraterrestrial to the possibility of contact between aliens and humans. Alien visitors Gort and Klaatu arrive to warn the Earth that it should take better control of its atomic development or suffer the consequences, a message that reflected the fears of the Cold War era and the warnings of the contactee messengers (see below). For example, Klaatu comes from a world of advanced medicine and science, something which was to become a feature of many contactee claims. The ship – circular, of course – has an outer corridor and an inner room for medical work, which contains a platform bed and has no obvious source for its bright lighting. By the end of the film we have seen many images that would in later decades recur in reports of crash retrievals and abductions.

THE CONTACTEE ERA

The UFO phenomenon was about to gain a new dimension: contactees, which can be defined as those humans who claim the privilege of direct meetings with caring, benevolent aliens on a mutual, agreeable basis. In 1953, sixty-two-year-old George Adamski published *Flying Saucers Have Landed*,[24] his story of contact with an extraterrestrial whom he met in a desert in California in 1952. The first alleged contact was at 12.30pm on Thursday 20 November, 1952, ten miles from Desert Centre. The alien was human-looking, about 5ft 6in in

George Adamski – the first 'contactee' – next to a painting of the alien he met at Desert Centre, California, in 1952.

height, and appeared to be about 135lbs weight and around thirty years old. He had beautiful white teeth, grey-green eyes, long blond hair and tanned skin. He wore a one-piece chocolate-brown outfit very similar to the one worn by Klaatu in *The Day the Earth Stood Still*. According to Adamski, the alien conversed with him in a form of sign language and by telepathy. The alien apparently came from Venus. Adamski's adventures included several jaunts with the aliens around the solar system on board flying saucers, meeting the beings of other worlds.

Flying Saucers Have Landed was an incredibly successful book, and if it was a true story, it was the most exciting thing that had ever happened to a human being. Adamski was a real-life Professor Aronnax, travelling as a guest on a trip far more thrilling than one that went merely 20,000 leagues under the sea. Even if it was a fiction, or contained some fiction, it still appealed to a broad audience ready for

something that detracted from the Cold War, supported human fears of the emerging atomic age and offered salvation by 'superior beings' watching over us. It was a mood exemplified by the story of an Argentinian air-force officer who, on 20 August 1957, heard a voice from a disc tell him that 'they' were here to warn the Earth peoples about the consequences of the misuse of atomic energy. There was also a great deal in Adamski's book to appeal to the emerging thinking that marked the beginning of the development of the spiritualist 'New Age'.

Many of the contactees of the 1950s, like Adamski, claimed to have received messages warning the people of Earth to take care with their development of atomic power. The atomic bomb was developed by the Manhattan Project, which was set up in 1942, and first tested on 16 July 1945, at

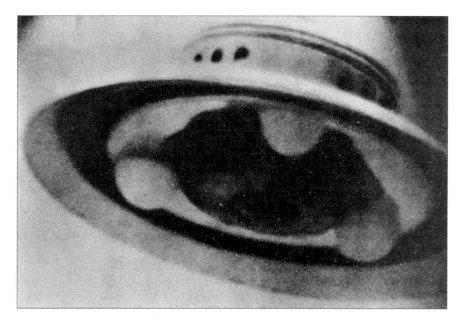

Photographed by George Adamski, this is for many the classic image of the flying saucer. Several cases since then have involved similar saucer-shapes including a Finnish close encounter, a photograph from near Lake Coniston and a close encounter in Belgium.

Alamogordo, New Mexico, a site later associated with one of the most extraordinary claims in UFO literature (see Chapter 4). The aggressive use of atomic weapons had been limited to the two dropped on Japan, at Hiroshima and Nagasaki, in 1945, acts which brought the Second World War to a conclusion, and which had seemed necessary to achieve this end. But when the entire population of Bikini Atoll was resettled to make way for further tests, the public were shocked – not just by the technology, but by the political power of those who wielded it. To that extent, fears about the atomic age were born on Bikini as much as at Alamogordo or Japan. Operation Ivy exploded the first Hydrogen Bomb on 1 November 1952: the first meeting Adamski claimed he had with aliens took place less then three weeks later.

Many claimants followed Adamski straight into the arms of waiting publishers,

and in true Hollywood style, the sequels became more and more dramatic. Few but the most devoted believe the literal truth of Adamski's claims, but if he was making up stories to augment genuine channelled 'feelings' or 'beliefs', or trying to make sense of some sort of imagery with which he believed he was in contact, all of which might be possible, then some of those who came in his wake seemed to have even less claim to the truth. In 1954, Truman Bethurum published his adventures with aliens from the planet Clarion.[25] That same year Daniel Fry met in a desert in New Mexico an extraterrestrial who had landed his flying saucer near the top-security White Sands Proving Ground. The alien's name was Alan and he spoke slang American ('Take it easy, pal, you're among friends,' he said from inside the flying saucer.) Alan warned of the emergence of nuclear power:

The entire population of your planet is now in constant danger of total destruction by an agency which you yourselves have created, with great labor and diligence, and at great expense in time and money. Why should a race be threatened by its own creations? The answer, of course, is simply that the

race has not progressed far enough in the foundation sciences to enable its people to control their own creations, and so their creations control them.

Alan's solution was to ask Fry to write a book to alert the Earth to the threat of impending nuclear war, which he promptly did.[26] Sadly, like so many contacting aliens, Alan completely failed to mention what we didn't already know, for example, the developments which were to lead to the hole in the ozone layer. He was telling the world only what the world had already figured out for itself. Fry asked Alan why he didn't just land on the White House lawn and 'ask for worldwide communication facilities' with the whole world. The alien's reply was bizarre, to say the least: apart from voicing concerns about inspiring worship or panic, he complained that it would not be possible to do so because their craft would be violating classified airspace, and because they could not even communicate by radio – 'Our transmitter has not been licensed by your people.' It seems strange that they should fly millions of miles only to expect to queue up at the post office to get a CB licence!

In 1955 Orfeo Angelucci described how he discovered that he had once been an alien in a previous existence.[27] He also met Jesus, another extraterrestrial. There were many other such claims. In addition, religious cults were forming which mediated between the space beings and the people of Earth through a few chosen special people. In 1954 George King, a London taxi-driver, claimed he had become the voice of Cosmic Parliament, and went on to form the Aetherius Society, a worldwide religion of which he was the centre.

A secret study of one cult during the 1960s[28] revealed some interesting views on the part of its members, not least when the group failed. It was infiltrated by sociologists seeking to understand the dynamics and motivations of such sects. The con-tactee, Mrs Marian Keech, channelled mes-sages via automatic writing from space beings known as 'the Guardians'. 'Without knowing why,' she said, 'I picked up a pencil and a pad that were lying on the table near my bed. My hand began to write in another handwriting.' As well as receiving descriptions of life beyond, she had acquired a personal guardian and communi-cator. The cult which had grown up around her channellings had gradually taken on the air of a pseudo-religion, and forecast a disaster, a massive flood on a biblical scale. Those who truly believed would be rescued by the Guardians in flying saucers.

The early stage of the break-up was interesting. At first the failure of the group's predictions was perceived as a success: when no flood came, the sect took the credit for having averted the disaster. But then, their focus lost, the group turned to infighting. The fact that the flying saucers did not turn up must have been the most important factor in the realization of the members that 'something was wrong'. The reaction of the sect is typified by the comment of one member as he began to acknowledge that his beliefs were not going to be borne out: 'I've had to go a long way. I've given up just about everything. I've cut every tie. I've burned every bridge. I've turned my back on the world. I can't afford to doubt. I have to believe.'

A recent, more humorous example of the failure of contactee belief was reported in late 1996 in Russell, Kansas. A teacher at Russell High School had claimed she was receiving messages from extraterres-trials, and was visited by an alien which also borrowed her physical body. She claimed she had acquired the ability to affect technology telepathically and had acquired healing powers.

As the story spread, several school-children reported seeing UFOs and hearing voices. In the end, twenty to thirty people formed a 'chosen group' which took on slightly sinister overtones. They could iden-tify each other by crosses on their hands and received a series of predictions about the world. It was when it was predicted that Bob Dole was going to become the greatest president in American history that 'people started to have their doubts.'[29]

Whatever the truth of the claims, they were unprovable. But this was the goal of the research organizations of the time: they wanted to know what these UFOs were, how they did what they did and where they came from, This generated a schism within UFO research. Unfortunately, the press attached itself to the most sensational aspects – no surprises there. The image of the UFO phenomenon as crazy people believing crazy stories was set in stone by the contactees, to the great long-term detri-ment of the subject. It is likely, and under-standable, that the more serious scientists, psychologists and physicists who joined the research in later years were put off in these early years by this negative image.

OTHER REPORTS OF ALIENS

The graceful, beautiful aliens of the contactee claims were not the only ones reported, even from the outset. Other claims were, however, virtually suppressed by UFO researchers themselves. Ted Bloecher states: 'At the beginning of the first contemporary wave of unidentified fly-ing objects . . . in this country in 1947, little was said about the possible occupants of these mysterious devices.'[30] John Keel points out that Bloecher's co-author Isabel Davis was one of a few who 'quietly kept track of these "humanoid" reports for years'.[31] Keel offers an explanation of why the lid was kept on these cases: 'NICAP's official policy has been to downgrade, ridicule, and reject nearly all UFO landing cases . . . devoting their main efforts to a twelve-year campaign to prove the reliability of UFO witnesses.' The implication is that reporting flying saucers, even the belief that they were extraterrestrial, was accept-able, but to report landings or alien pilots was not. This was a curious logic perhaps, but one that showed that early UFO researchers were not completely unable to play media relations or political games in order to gain a foothold for their subject by first seeking to establish the credibility of 'acceptable' parts of the phenomenon. Even when Hynek published The Hynek UFO Report[32] in 1977, the famous chapter title 'Close Encounters of the Third Kind' is prefixed 'Approaching the Edge of Reality', though it is true that he was happy enough with the title alone in his earlier work The UFO Experience[9]. In the first book, however, he starts the chapter with the comment: 'We now come to the most. bizarre and seemingly incredible aspect of the entire UFO phenomenon. To be frank, I would gladly omit this part if I could without offence to scientific integrity . . . unfortu-nately one may not omit data simply because they may not be to one's liking.'

But the humanoid reports were there. For example, on 19 June 1947 in Massachusetts, a woman saw a 'moon-sized' object fly past containing a slim figure dressed in what appeared to be a Navy uniform.[33] Gene Gamachi and others at Tacoma in Washington reported several 'little people' in connection with UFOs. Another report from Houston, Texas described a 2ft tall being with a head 'the size of a basketball' who flew off in a silver saucer.

It was not until the early to mid-1950s, however, that reports of 'aliens' became reasonably acceptable, even within the UFO field of study. It seems that their release from obscurity may have been forced by the claims of George Adamski and others. The media was paying attention to these high-profile claims, and they at least offered a suggestion towards explaining what the UFOs were and why they were here. From the media's point of view these claims also provided a sequel to the 'objects and lights' claims which were no longer novel enough for the readership – the media needs to be able to develop its stories to sustain interest. Serious UFO researchers, without any conscious decision being taken by any person or organization, would have felt that it was better to offer their own truth than to let the contactee claims become the 'established truth'. Cynics might remember that Napoleon recognized history 'as a collection of lies agreed upon by the winners', and even a collection of truths has to have its winners and losers.

The claims of communication with, and guidance from, aliens as offered by Adamski were clearing taking the subject down a religious, or at least a pseudo-religious road, and that was anathema to scientific study. The early claims of alien sightings, outside the contactee claims, described what seemed to be astronauts, not 'gods', and seemed to offer an opportunity to bring science into the study.

The year 1954 provided the real breakthrough in terms of the publication of reports which details witness accounts of humanoid aliens. There was a worldwide, but particularly European, wave of sightings, and UFOs were reported flying, and landing, in many countries. Indeed, researcher Milos Krmelj attributes the birth of UFO study in Yugoslavia to this wave.

In October in Libya a farmer witnessed an egg-shaped craft land near him and saw in it six human-like beings wearing gasmasks. One of the 'people' warned the farmer off, possibly to protect him from the effects of work they were undertaking, and later from their take-off. The case included a radio set operated by a 'man' with earphones and instrument panels. In September, Marius Dewilde saw what seemed to be a landed object on railway tracks in Quarouble in France. He was paralysed as he approached the two beings he saw there, and watched helpless as they boarded their craft and took off. The beings were short, and seemed to be wearing diving suits.

The importance of these cases is that they seemed more credible than the contactee claims. The aliens seemed to need devices to breathe; they used technology such as radio sets, earphones and camera-like objects. Their interaction with the witnesses was limited: no religious themes here, just a few terse warnings to keep out of the way of the technology. Explorers, perhaps, taking samples and tending their technological craft. All good scientific 'right stuff', and perceived as an antidote to the contactee claims.

DIVERSITY IN THE EARLY YEARS

—

What perhaps most characterized early alien reports was diversity. It seemed that no two sets of aliens were the same, and there were certain characteristics specific to particular countries. Jacques Vallee points out: 'In the United States, they appear as science-fiction monsters. In South America, they are sanguinary and quick to get into a fight. In France, they behave like rational, Cartesian, peace-loving tourists.[34]

The diversity in appearance is huge, as the following small sample of hundreds of cases shows:

• In July 1947, in Sao Paulo, Brazil: 7ft entities with 'transparent suits covering head and body, and inflated like rubber bags, and with metal boxes on their backs'. The clothing seen through the suits was brightly coloured, and like paper. They had huge round eyes, huge round bald heads and no facial hair. The encounter, experienced by José Higgins following his sighting of a disc landing, is regarded as the first significant entity report of the modern era.

• Near Oran, Algeria in 1954: a small man with glowing eyes.

• In Sainte-Catherine, France in 1954: a man dressed in red clothes that looked as if they were made of iron. He had long hair, and a hairy face.

• In Venezuela in 1954: a small creature with claws and glowing eyes which attacked one of two witnesses.

• At Villares del Saz in Spain in 1953: three little men, 65cm tall, with yellow faces and narrow eyes.

• At Minduri, Brazil in 1958: two giants 6m tall dressed in bright red clothing.

• At Torrent in Argentina in 1965: five beings 2m tall, each with just one eye in the middle of their foreheads.

• At Belo Horizonte in Brazil in 1963: tall, slim beings with bright red skin and one eye and no ears or nose.

• In Peru in 1965: a blackish-coloured creature resembling a shrub, 80cm tall, with one eye.

• At Belo Horizonte, Brazil in May 1969: two humanoids around 1.3m tall, wearing matt silver suits and masks covering their faces. They took a victim on to a flying saucer, where he met a dwarf-like creature covered in long red hair, with a long beard and a face very similar to that of a troll. He had thick eyebrows, pale skin and large greenish eyes.

An artist's impression of the George Adamski encounter of 1952. Adamski became the first 'Contactee' – the first person to claim a mutually beneficial meeting with an alien. In doing so he introduced a whole new aspect to UFOs.

THE VILLAS BOAS ENCOUNTER

It is Latin America which provides us with the last twist of the UFO phenomenon for this chapter: the extraordinary Villas Boas case. This is a very well-known case, so we have summarized it briefly. The experience was reported in response to a magazine article by journalist João Martins. Martins, together with the respected South American UFO investigator Dr Olavo Fontes, questioned the witness, Antonio Villas Boas, five months after the experience, and both were impressed by his testimony.

Following a couple of UFO sightings earlier that month experienced with his brothers, on 15 October 1957 Villas Boas, who was alone this time, saw another light and discerned within it an oval-shaped object. He decided to escape on his tractor, but before he was able to do so, the egg-shaped object landed some 40ft in front of him on three metal legs. The tractor seems to have suffered classic UFO vehicle interference: the lights and engine suddenly died simultaneously. Villas Boas, presumably unaware of the literature dealing with this phenomenon, commented: 'I am unable to explain how this happened, for the starting-key was in and the lights were on.' He leaped down from the tractor and ran, but was quickly captured by five beings from the craft who hauled him aboard. The entities were similar to others reported around the world, and, like those noted in this chapter from reports in Italy, Libya and France, they wore tight-fitting grey suits and helmets. Villas Boas could see tubes running into their clothing.

On board the craft Villas Boas was incarcerated in a small, brightly lit room with polished metal walls. He was joined there by a female alien who was certainly humanoid, and apparently pleasingly so.

Bryan Ellis's impression of the entities who abducted Antonio Villas Boas in 1957 leading to an extraordinary encounter on board a flying saucer. (An 'experiencer' himself, Bryan has drawn from his own encounters to add an emotional interpretation of the cases he is depicting.)

'Her body was much more beautiful than any I have ever seen before,' he said. 'It was slim, and her breasts stood up high and well separated. Her waistline was thin, her belly flat, her hips well developed, and her thighs were large.' The alien was naked, so blonde her hair was almost white, pale-skinned with freckled arms, and had large blue slanted eyes and very small lips, nose and ears. Her high, flat cheekbones gave the impression of a sharply pointed chin. Villas Boas said in his statement to the investigators: 'This feature gave the lower half of her face a quite triangular shape.' Pubic and other body hair was blood-red. She was approximately 4ft 8ins tall.

Villas Boas stated that she was 'look-ing at me all the while as if she wanted something from me'. She made it very clear what it was she wanted from him when she came towards him in silence, and led him to twice copulate with her. In an interview twenty-one years after his experience Villas Boas added a feature he had not earlier revealed: that after the second act of intercourse the woman had used a container to extract sperm from him. He assumes this was kept for later use. Perhaps his earlier refusal to report this detail was a reflection of the macho self-image so prevalent in South America: being used as a stud might have been acceptable, being used as a laboratory rat was not.

Having completed her 'task', the alien backed off coldly, and Villas Boas was allowed to get dressed and was given a tour of the craft. He was caught attempting to purloin an instrument to prove his experience to others and was somewhat aggressively turned off the craft. In the field he watched as the object took off, glowed brilliant red, and disappeared at incredible speed.

The case offers another important bridge in the evolution of UFO encounters, this time between the claims of contactees and those of the abductees who were to follow Villas Boas. The description of the female alien as beautiful, with long blondish hair, and as being very human-like in most respects, reflects the reports of contactees, whereas her other characteristics – the stature, the thin pointed chin, the slanting eyes and the reduced facial features – resemble the descriptions given by abductees. There is a similar 'bridge' in the behaviour shown by aliens. Contactees have reported mutually respectful meetings while the abductees claim to have been treated as subjects for experiments. Clearly, Villas Boas experienced shades of both relationships.

The self-editing that has often governed the release of UFO-related information by researchers was evident here too. Dr Fontes, writing to Gordon Creighton, editor of *Flying Saucer Review*, in 1966, the year after the account was published, commented on the delay from 1958, when they had first received the report, 'We decided not to publish the results of our investigation because the case was too "wild".'

So the first decade of the UFO phenomenon offered a wide range of examples of the different aspects of the subject. We see in the accounts of these early years the first nodal points of change in the UFO phenomenon: 1947 saw the identification of UFOs as a subject in its own right and the fixation of physicality; 1952 brought the first contactee claims, and 1957 the

ground-breaking Villas Boas claims. The next forty years would see twists and turns within these various areas which would have seemed scarcely believable in those first ten years. The assumption that these phenomena – sightings in the skies, radar cases, contacts, abductions and so on – are interrelated was prevalent then, and remains, for many, the probability today. Yet perhaps the connections are more tenuous than they might at first seem, as we shall see in later chapters.

CARL JUNG

One book written during this first decade was prophetic in many ways. In the late 1950s, psychologist Carl Jung penned *Flying Saucers – A Modern Myth of Things Seen in the Sky*.[35] This was a basically psychological study and largely concerned itself with the symbolism and 'inner' meanings or significance of the UFO phenomenon, and was thus a book written well before its time. Given the reputation of the author, sceptics and believers alike clamoured to claim him for their side, and even today many articles hold that Jung believed UFOs were extraterrestrial, a belief which is not at all evident from his book. In summing up, while he reminds his readers, 'It was the purpose of this essay to treat UFOs primarily as a psychological phenomenon,' he does introduce a section on their possible physicality and the link to mental processes. 'There are good reasons why the UFOs cannot be disposed of in this simple manner. So far as I know it remains an established fact, supported by numerous observations, that UFOs have not only been seen visually but have also been picked up on the radar screen and have left traces on photographic plate . . . either psychic projections throw back a radar echo, or else the appearance of real objects affords an

opportunity for mythological projections.' However, an observation he made after disclosing his views to the press is also of significant interest. He said:

I gave an interview . . . in which I expressed myself in a sceptical way, though I spoke with due respect of the serious opinion of a relatively large number of air specialists who believe in the reality of UFOs . . . this interview was suddenly discovered by the world press and the 'news' spread like wildfire . . . but – alas – in distorted form. I was quoted as a saucer-believer. I issued a statement to the United Press and gave a true version of my opinion, but this time the wire went dead: nobody, so far as I know, took any notice of it . . . One must draw the conclusion that news affirming the existence of UFOs is welcome, but that scepticism seems to be undesirable. To believe that UFOs are real suits the general opinion, whereas disbelief is to be discouraged.

Truly ahead of his time!

Certainly the answer to this complex enigma will not come easily. It is with a rueful humour that we recall the words of the United Press radio broadcaster who interviewed Kenneth Arnold the day after his seminal sighting in June 1947. 'I understand the United Press is checking on it out of New York now with the Army, and also with the Navy. We hope to have some concrete answer before nightfall.'

That was an optimistic remark to say the least, for we are now fifty years on and still counting.

So the first decade of UFOs was a complex period, and the phenomenon was interrelated socially and politically with the mood of the time. It ranged from the sober to the outright crazy, but even so, the perspective from later decades might well be that the phenomenon would never again be as sane as it was then.

1957-1967

The 'Sixties'

'The times they are a-changin'.'
Bob Dylan

THE SPACE RACE

On Saturday 5 October 1957, Americans woke up to headlines that missed their intellect almost entirely and struck a visceral fear deep in their psyches. The Soviet Union – home of anything but the free, a stranger to Mom's apple pie and the centre of the hated communist influence – had put mankind's first artificial satellite into orbit above the Earth. Sputnik 1, less than 2ft across and weighing no more than the average man, with a few antennae looking like a cat's whiskers, was now bleeping its way around the earth.

'It gets the American people alarmed that a foreign country – especially an enemy country – can do this. We fear this. We fear that they have something out there that the majority of the people don't know about,' said an alarmed young woman in the street interviewed for her response to the news.

When they had gone to bed the night before the American people had been secure in the knowledge that the heavens were made up entirely of stars, planets, asteroids and meteors created solely by God. Over their breakfast coffee that morning, they discovered that one new item had been added to the list – an item manufactured by their communist enemy. The scientist C.P. (later Lord) Snow remarked that Americans had a 'technological conceit' which he thought was in part based on their

belief that science and totalitarianism were incompatible. Sputnik shocked them out of that belief. And the British historian D.W. Brogan once commented that Americans had grown up with 'the illusion of American omnipotence'. He observed that 'nothing is so shocking for the Americans as to be potentially defeated'. This fear was probably best summed up by one man asked by a reporter if he admired the Russian achievement. 'No, definitely not,' he said bitterly. 'I say we should have been the first ones to have it if there's such a thing.'

Officials in America, for the most part in the military, dismissed Sputnik 1 fairly lightly, and for good reasons. It was in effect, some said, just 'a hunk of iron' or 'a silly bauble'. The launch of the satellite was initially dismissed by the president, Dwight D. Eisenhower, himself a military man, as an event of 'scientific interest', and he famously refused to interrupt a game of golf to discuss the matter. In fact, documents declassified in 1996 showed that Eisenhower knew America had the technology to launch something similar to Sputnik, but that he was afraid to be the first to fly an object over enemy territory. He gambled that after the Soviets had launched Sputnik he would gain, by default, permission to fly spy satellites over their territory. This gamble totally failed in the public's perception, and his presidency lost credibility. Americans believed that their country was behind the Soviets, and blamed

what they saw as a military failure on their leading military figure – the president himself.

Within the Air Force, too, Sputnik 1 was met with a shrug of the shoulders at the most. Plans were well underway to launch a small satellite into orbit, perhaps in 1958 as a contribution to International Geophysical Year. And, as stated above, the Americans could have done this earlier if they had chosen to. A rocket? So what? They had been flying rockets – rocket planes – for over a decade. Chuck Yeager had broken the so-called sound barrier ten years earlier in one. Work was progressing on the X15, and there were plans for an X15B, which would be an aircraft-like rocket capable of flying into space, orbiting the earth and landing again on a runway. Most of the test pilots at Edwards Air Force Base, where this project was under development, had flown rockets many times in their careers.

So the military may have had an intellectual and technological overview of the situation, but where the president miscalculated was in not recognizing that the public had no such knowledge to comfort them.

The concept of 'man in space' seemed to confirm that life could exist in outer space, and brought a new generation of UFO enthusiasts forward based on that scientific belief. Against a background of the emerging 'space race', UFOs entered their second decade.

They didn't know the technology was there; they didn't see the political problems. Americans merely looked upwards into the heavens and saw that the Soviets were over their heads and believed they could rain down terror upon them. Their one intellectual appreciation of Sputnik 1 was that it meant the Soviets had rockets capable of delivering an intercontinental ballistic missile into the heart of America. Almost immediately, Americans recognized Sputnik 1 as the first hammer blow in a new war: the war for control of the realm of the gods. Senate majority leader Lyndon Johnson described space as 'the high ground', and indicated that he believed those who controlled it would win the war, just as in ancient battles those who had fortified the high ground had had the advantage over their attackers.

The first reference to a 'space race' was made in an editorial in the New York Times and it was not, as many have believed since, a reference to a race into space between the Americans and the Soviets based purely on a competition of technology. It was connected to another reference in the editorial, which described the United States as being in a 'race for survival'. After a later Soviet satellite launch, house speaker John McCormack, heading the House Select Committee on Astronautics, commented that America faced 'national extinction'. He said, 'It cannot be overemphasized that the survival of the free world – indeed, all the world – is caught up in the stakes.' The 'space race' was therefore another phrase that first hit viscerally rather than intellectually.

The government and the military were pushed by such public opinion to respond. They attempted to launch an American satellite into orbit on a Vanguard rocket just two months later, possibly rushing the procedures a little. It rose a few inches, collapsed backwards and exploded. 'KAPUT-

NIK!' was the inspired newspaper banner.

In 1997 it is perhaps difficult to appreciate the effect of these events forty years ago. Today the space shuttle has made space travel almost commonplace, but in 1957 it had occurred only in science fiction, and to the vast majority of people, it looked as though that was where it would remain. Science fiction itself was generally viewed as almost laughable escapism, and the few serious examinations of a future in space were widely and easily dismissed. The astronomer royal, Dr Richard van der Riet Woolley, had commented prior to the launch of Sputnik 1 that space travel was 'utter bilge'. Astonishingly enough, Dr Woolley reaffirmed that belief later, even though there had been by then several successful unmanned excursions into Earth orbit.[1] Indeed, the Soviets' Luna 1 had passed within 4,000 miles of the moon, and subsequent Lunas had struck the moon and photographed its far side. Yet Dr Woolley remarked, 'I said it was "utter bilge" when I arrived four and a half years ago and it remains "utter bilge".' By the time Dr Woolley left office in 1971 the manned lunar landing programme was well underway.

It was not one of astronomy's most successful predictions, though Dr Woolley may have been prodded into a somewhat polarized viewpoint by the comments at the time of Professor R. Bracewell of California's Stanford University, who had speculated that other worlds might be sending robot reconnaissance vehicles to study us. In short, a respectable scientist publishing his work in respectable scientific journals was giving credence to the extraterrestrial hypothesis for UFOs. Once Sputnik 1 was in orbit, the possibilities that UFOs were extraterrestrial visitors instantly seemed to become more likely. And in the next few years – particularly by the time cosmonaut Yuri Gagarin and astronaut Alan Shepherd had flown in

space – the concept of space travel obviously became widely accepted. Perhaps a more subtle effect as far as we are concerned is that, for the first time, it could be proven that life could exist in outer space. Agreed, it was only a few dogs, monkeys and a couple of people in specially controlled environments – they were effectively taking a part of the Earth's environment into space with them – but the public began to accept the idea. Many of the realms of science fiction had suddenly become science fact. And like most things that go from being unlikely to likely, for many people the concept of aliens coming from other planets quickly became almost a certainty. Suddenly those UFO things were somebody else's Sputniks, Mercuries and Voskhods, and the people in them were somebody else's Yuri Gagarins and Alan Shepherds. For many, flying-saucer reports suddenly seemed to deserve more serious examination than they had previously been given. UFO interest was reaching beyond its initial devotees.

The space race (the race for survival!) and the continuing Cold War were inexorably linked through 1957 to 1964 and formed a vivid contextual background for UFO claims in those years. If fear of Soviet weaponry had forced the American government and military to view UFOs initially as physical, and triggered among UFO devotees a belief in the 'physical and extraterrestrial', as shown in Chapter 1, then the space race and the Cold War somehow strengthened those images and that connection. For example, consider the leader to a newspaper article headed 'Flying Saucers – Fact or Fiction?' and subtitled 'Are They Watching Us Now?' It starts: 'The triumphant flight into space of U.S. astronaut Scott Carpenter last week – following on earlier successful Russian and U.S. orbits – has again focused attention on other planets, as man reaches for the moon. Perhaps it's not all one-way

The Redstone rocket (right) and space capsule that boosted Alan Shepherd into space in 1961, followed by a flight by John Glenn boosted into orbit by (left) the Atlas rocket. These flights brought the idea of 'outer space' to wide public attention.

traffic. For years strange objects and mysterious lights have been seen . . . is it possible that in this tremendous age of science and spacemen that the objects seen are indeed "flying saucers" – proof of life on other planets?'[2]

Robert Chapman, science correspondent of the *Sunday Express*, commented, 'It was not until the launching of Sputnik 1 in 1957, when people generally had a new reason for looking up at the sky, that UFO reports made a fresh impact on the public press.'[3]

TRINDADE ISLAND

Whatever the cultural background against which they were being measured, UFOs were still very much a global experience. After the 'Kaputnik' disaster of 6 December 1957, the Americans finally got their first satellite, Explorer 1, into orbit on 31 January the following year, a contribution towards International Geophysical Year (IGY). By coincidence, just two weeks previously one of the most famous UFO photographs was taken by a survey ship owned by the Brazilian navy, which was engaged on research for IGY. The *Almirante Saldanha* was anchored off Trindade Island in the South Atlantic, approximately 600 miles east of Rio de Janeiro. At around noon on 16 January, a 'flattened, Saturn-shaped' object was spotted by someone on deck. It flew over the island, 'orbited' Desejado Peak, and then sped away, more or less in the direction from which it had come, pausing briefly to hover once. Its flight pattern was reminiscent of the description Kenneth

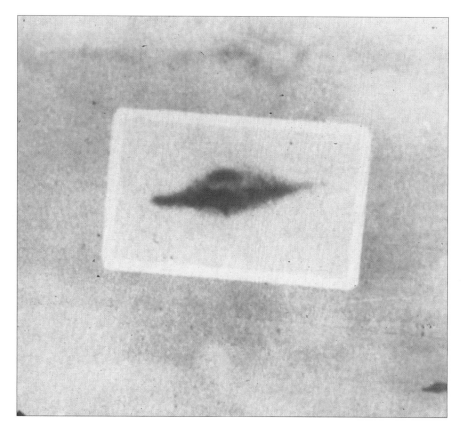

Photographed over Trindade Island in 1958, this UFO was witnessed flying around the mountain peak by large groups of people aboard the vessel 'The Almirante Saldanha'. Four photographs were taken, consistent with the witness descriptions.

Despite the numbers of witnesses and photographic evidence, the Blue Book files classify the case as a hoax. The reporting officer for Blue Book seems to have reached a nadir of mockery in his comments: 'It is the reporting officer's private opinion that a flying saucer sighting would be unlikely at the very barren island of Trindade, as everyone knows Martians are extremely comfort-loving creatures.'

What is perhaps less well known is that the sighting was far from an isolated incident. In November the previous year, when a balloon was launched from the recently opened oceanographic post and meteorological station, witnesses had seen an object, ovoid and silvery-white, in the sky near the balloon. It remained visible for three hours. On Christmas Day 1957 a silver, round object was sighted by a labourer, and on 31 December a silver, circular object was seen by five workers, a sailor, a doctor and Lieutenant Inacio Carlos Moreira of the navy. The following day a bright light flashed over the sea at high speed, witnessed by many people who confirmed that it was the object they had seen before. The day after that there was a brief sighting from Trindade Island, and that same night the naval vessel *Triunfo*, at sea 400 miles from the island, was buzzed for ten minutes by an unknown object. It was circular, glowed orange, flew at high speed, made extraordinary changes of direction and sometimes hovered briefly. On 6 January a radiosonde balloon carrying meteorological instrumentation was seemingly sucked into a cloud. When it emerged, it

Arnold had used of his sighting: an undulating movement 'like the flight of a bat'. It was dark grey in colour, silent in flight, and surrounded by a cloud of greenish phosphorescence.

The object was photographed by one of the witnesses, Almiro Barauna. His pictures were overexposed, but the UFO was visible, if blurred. However, the witnesses maintained that it actually did look like that, presumably as a result of the surrounding 'cloud'. Barauna's photographs were examined by commercial and aerial photographer John T. Hopf on behalf of APRO. He concluded that they were 'without a doubt the finest record of an UAO [unidentified aerial object] to come into my hands'. Whatever the object was, it is worth remembering that the sighting had been corroborated by scores of people.

The Brazilian navy refused to make any immediate comment on the sighting. The

president of Brazil, however, received copies of the photographs and was so impressed by the case that he personally authorized their release. The Navy Ministry, now, it would seem, well and truly miffed, then issued their statement:

With reference to the reports appearing in the press that the Navy is opposed to divulge the facts concerning the appearance of a strange object over Trindade Island, this Cabinet declares that such information has no basis. This Ministry has no motive to impede the release of photographs of the referred to object taken by —— [sic] who was at Trindade Island at the invitation of the Navy, and in the presence of a large number of the crew of the ALMIRANTE SALDANHA from whose deck the photographs were taken. Clearly, this Ministry will not be able to make any pronouncement concerning the object seen because the photographs do not constitute sufficient proof for such purpose.

had lost its package of equipment. Shortly afterwards, another silvery object appeared to leave the cloud and to manoeuvre as it flew away. Although the instruments were designed to be jettisoned, no one could find them. Then, just days before the photographed incident, there was a further sighting of an object strikingly similar to that which Barauna and others would describe.

Whatever it was, it seems very clear that some genuine, unknown object was flying around the newly opened base on an otherwise unremarkable and isolated island. And it made news around the world and in high places because of the surge of interest generated by the space programme.

PAPUA NEW GUINEA

During June of 1959 there was a wave of UFO reports from Papua New Guinea, on the other side of the world. Strange lights in the sky were often seen, and the people high in the mountains reported sightings of large circular objects in flight. There were almost eighty detailed reports from Boianai, Banaira, Giwa, Menapi and the Ruaba Plain.

The most famous and most extraordinary reports came from the Boianai Mission and were documented by the Reverend William Gill. They are mostly sightings, yet the craft came close enough to merit close-encounter classification and, more importantly, a large group of witnesses reported seeing entities which interacted with them.[4]

The Reverend William Booth Gill was an ordained priest in the Church of England and a graduate of Brisbane University. He had been on the staff of the Anglican Mission in Papua for thirteen years when the event took place, and had always believed that UFOs were either a figment of the imagination or an electrical phenomenon. But then in the early evening of 26 June, he left the main mission building to search in the sky for the planet Venus. It was bright and easily visible at that time and in that location, and he quickly found it, but while observing it he saw another light. This was bright, sparkling and situated above Venus, though it seemed to be flying downwards towards him. Gill called two of the mission staff, Stephen Moi and Eric Langford, to join him. Later that evening several others from the mission also arrived to watch the light.

Eventually it became a very large object in the sky. Moi said that if he had stretched out his fist it would have covered only half of it. The description they gave was of a structured craft of some sort, circular, and with a wide base. It had an upper platform deck and legs protruding underneath. Every so often the mission staff saw a blue beam flash up into the sky from the open-topped upper deck, and on that upper deck, most extraordinarily, they could see four human-shaped figures. 'As we watched, men came out . . . on what seemed to be a deck on top of the huge disc. One figure seemed to be looking down at us. I stretched my arm above my head and waved. To our surprise the figure did the same.'

During the sighting several smaller lights were also seen flying around the mission. It has been suggested that the blue light was some sort of communication between the larger – or, at least, closer – object and the other UFOs. After almost three hours of close-proximity observation the object flew away at astonishing speed.

The following night the same object, or one very like it, returned to the mission and the four humanoid figures were seen again. This time they were reported moving about on the open deck and possibly operating some equipment at the centre of the object, beyond the view of the witnesses, who could not see over the rim of the saucer into the centre. Gill waved at the figures, and again, they waved back.

Eventually a large number of the mission staff and all four figures on the object were enthusiastically waving at each other. Gill decided to move the communication up a notch. He took a torch from the mission and flashed a series of light patterns at the UFO. He believed that the UFO responded by swaying from side to side in a swinging motion and coming closer. After a while the figures disappeared, apparently having gone inside the object. Then two of them reappeared and seemed to be working at something, illuminated by the blue beam on the top of the object. At 6.30 Gill went in for his tea, and stayed inside the mission buildings for half an hour. When he came back out again the object had moved

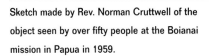

Sketch made by Rev. Norman Cruttwell of the object seen by over fifty people at the Boianai mission in Papua in 1959.

much further away into the distance. In 1977 Gill explained his actions as follows. 'We were a bit fed up that they wouldn't come down after all the waving. This is the difficult thing to get across to people: here was a flying saucer; therefore it must have been a traumatic experience. It was nothing of the kind.'

The following night the object was seen for a third time, but this time it remained much more distant and indistinct, and no figures were reported.

In total, Gill and thirty-seven other people at the mission saw the object or objects. The official report on the case by the Australian Department of Air concluded that: 'Most probably they were reflections on a cloud of a major light source of unknown origin.' That explanation hardly took into account the weight of numbers of witnesses, the duration of the sightings or the related reports from the area at that time.

1961: MAN REACHES SPACE AND ABDUCTIONS BEGIN

On 20 January 1961 a new US president, John F. Kennedy, was inaugurated, promised great things, and then went through three months of hell which culminated in two blows to American pride and to his presidency. On 12 April the world learned that the Soviets had beaten the Americans yet again: Yuri Gagarin, in Vostok 1, had completed one orbit of the Earth. Just five days later, on 17 April, the American-backed assault on Cuba turned into the Bay of Pigs fiasco, leaving Kennedy in despair: 1,500 Cuban exiles, backed by the US, had invaded Cuba; of these 1,173 were taken prisoner. This eventually served only to strengthen the links between Cuba and the USSR. 'What a lousy, fouled-up job this has turned out to be,' Kennedy told Senator Barry

Goldwater. The president badly needed something to revitalize his flagging administration and to put hope and spirit into the hearts of Americans. He immediately got his advisers to examine the realistic likelihood of landing a man on the Moon. Their prognosis was positive, and Kennedy must have been heartened when, on 5 May 1961, Alan Shepherd was lobbed into sub-orbital flight in a Mercury space capsule. On 25 May Kennedy delivered a special message to the joint session of Congress, which he described as a second state-of-the-union address. That alone shows the depths to which the president had sunk, for this was the first time the once-a-year state-of-the-union address had been modified. 'These are extraordinary times,' Kennedy explained, 'and we face an extraordinary challenge.' He went on to make his famous speech committing America to the Man on the Moon project.

BARNEY AND BETTY HILL

On 19 September 1961, an American couple from New Hampshire, Betty and Barney Hill, reported a UFO encounter which was to change the face of the UFO phenomenon for ever. The impact of this case cannot be overstated. It should never be forgotten, however, that it arose during the middle of the space race, the Cold War, and the conversion of science fiction and UFOs into at least potential reality. Equally significant was the fact that the first American in space, Alan Shepherd, who had flown the first Mercury mission just four months before and was then a national hero of almost unbelievable proportions, came from the same New Hampshire locality as the Hills.

A more detailed analysis of this case has been written up in John Spencer's book *Perspectives*,[5] but the account we give here contains some interesting new

information relating to the John G. Fuller book on the story,[6] and which arose as a response to John's earlier publication, *Perspectives*.

The publicity surrounding the Betty and Barney Hill case gave the details of the abduction phenomenon which are now so familiar their first major public exposure.

This was largely due to Fuller's best-selling book. For example, a huge headline in the British *Sunday Mirror*, illustrated by a picture of Betty Hill, declared 'KIDNAPPERS FROM OUTER SPACE – JUDGE THE EVIDENCE FOR YOURSELF.'[7] The article inside ran over three pages and was only the first in the series. It promoted Fuller's book and was written by Fuller himself.

The Hills' story was that during an overnight drive from Canada to their home in New Hampshire, they encountered a bright light which circled around them, causing Barney some concern. He stopped the car and, taking his binoculars, he walked across the road and into a field directly towards the light, which was coming from an object at tree-top height. Betty stayed with the car. Through the binoculars Barney believed he could see at least a dozen people looking back at him from a craft. Convinced that he was about to be captured, he ran screaming back across the field to Betty and the car and they drove off. Betty tried unsuccessfully to catch sight of the object. They could hear a beeping noise which Betty Hill later said 'seemed to be striking the trunk of our car'. The Hills then apparently became drowsy, although it seems they continued driving.

When they saw a sign indicating that they were 17 miles away from Concord, Betty commented to Barney that they now knew where they were, so they must have been feeling lost or disoriented beforehand. When they were discussing the events of that night with a team of investigators some two months later, one of the investigators pointed out that the time it had taken them to cover the distance did not seem to add up. Barney Hill remarked: 'To think I realized *for the first time* [our emphasis] that at the rate of speed I always travel we should have arrived home at least two hours earlier than we did.' We believe that we are seeing here the origins of claims of 'missing time' in abductions, now frequently reported in such cases; and it was brought to the fore not by the witnesses themselves but by investigators.

Betty was inspired by the event. Just two days after the encounter she started gathering data on UFOs. She read a book by Major Donald Keyhoe and wrote to him exactly a week later. A few days after writing to Major Keyhoe, Betty started to have a series of vivid dreams, which went on for five nights. The dreams contained the outline of the abduction that regression hypnosis would later 'reveal'. They included the couple being stopped by the landed UFO, being taken aboard and being given an examination. It is possible that the dreams represented Betty's fears and fascinations rather than reality, but she is adamant that they are recovered memories, as she made clear in a telephone interview with us several years ago (11 December 1988). However, Fuller's book on the subject indicates that the psychiatrist conducting the regression hypnosis, Dr Simon, noted after a meeting with the couple: 'There are definite indications that her dreams had been suggested as a reality by her supervisor (at work).'

It is held that the couple's experience is a corroborated sighting – an encounter they both shared – but what they did not share is important. Betty stayed in the car while Barney ran into the fields to examine the vehicle more closely; Betty's drawing of the craft shows no detail, and, notably, no occupants, whereas Barney's, from his much closer perspective, does. And their descriptions of the humanoids on board the landed craft do not tally in quite significant ways. 'For example Betty recalled their noses as 'larger than the average . . . like Jimmy Durante's', whereas Barney said: 'I didn't notice any proboscis, there just seemed to be two slits that represented the nostrils.' Betty alone had the nightmares, and Betty alone was inspired to follow up the experience by learning about the subject of UFOs, although it is clear that,

Betty and Barney Hill were the first true abductees, reporting capture and medical examination. Their story was first revealed by the use of regression hypnosis. The significance of their claims cannot be overstated in their effect on the evolution of UFO reports.

Betty and Barney Hill's encounter was of the classic 'lonely road at night' type. In so many ways, this case set the standards for those that were to follow.

before the first hypnotic-regression with Dr Simon, she had communicated the substance of her dreams to Barney. In one session with the doctor, Barney says, 'She told me a great many of the details of the dreams.'

Barney had his first regression session on 22 February 1964. During it he says: 'But I have not talked about flying saucers since 1957, when we were talking about Sputnik.' This was just after the Shepherd flight and the resultant acclaim – local officials were even considering renaming his home town Space Town USA.[8] If the launch of Sputnik involved the Hills in a discussion of flying saucers, then surely the launching of local hero Shepherd would have inspired similar conversation.

Betty had her first regression session on 7 March. Of one exchange she says: 'And I laughed and asked him [Dr Simon] if he had watched The Twilight Zone recently on TV.' This gives a few clues to her thinking: she associated the event with science fiction. Researcher Mark Pilkington points out that on 10 February 1964, just weeks

before the Hills' first hypnosis sessions, an episode of The Outer Limits called 'The Bellero Shield' had been broadcast, featuring 'an alien with large eyes that stretch almost to the sides of its head'.[9]

Sorting out the components of the case is difficult after so much time has elapsed. There seems little doubt that the Hills did see a UFO in the air during their drive – indeed, UFO researcher Jacques Vallee comments that report No. 100/1/61 from the files of the 100th Bomb Wing of Strategic Air Command, Pease Air Force Base, New Hampshire also describes an object which was detected on their radar, and which may have been the object the Hills saw.[10] However, the exotic abduction scenario drawn out by regression hypnosis could have been the substance of vivid nightmares, suffered by Betty and related to Barney, rather than recovered memories. Certainly Dr Simon seems to have leaned towards this view: Fuller states: 'The doctor believed this [abduction] to be too improbable, and much material was similar to dream material.'

If this is the case, then it is very significant to the whole abduction phenomenon, for identical cases have been reported from around the world. If the Hills encounter did not happen, then it is unlikely that similar, subsequent events occurred; either – at least, not exactly as reported. So why have so many similar reports been received?

One possibility which must be considered is that there has been faulty research. Witnesses across many countries may not know of each other or swap stories, but the investigators do have knowledge of other cases, and they could be a conduit through which information travels between cases. If they hold in their minds a stereotype of abductions, based on the Hills encounter, then they could be subconsciously influencing other witnesses. This would be relevant where regression hypnosis has been used,

(Opposite) The book that brought abductions to the mass audience. Certainly it became a role model for investigations which many UFO researchers carried in their heads from case to case. But just how accurate an analysis was it?

since that process promotes in the subject a state of suggestibility. None of this should be used to dismiss the abduction or UFO phenomena out of hand, but it might mean that we must look for other explanations. (In Chapters 5 and 6 we shall examine similarities between abduction, the near-death experience and also shamanistic experiences.)

The cause for concern is that there are real problems raised by Fuller's book, and by his research and presentations, of which many researchers do not seem to be aware. The publicity and attention sparked by the Hill case brought a number of prominent researchers of later years into the subject, and provided a framework which, it seems, many could not put aside when examining other reports. Many of the details of subsequent abductions follow a pattern laid down in this encounter, and no single case has influenced subsequent cases, to such an extent, despite the protestations of those ufologists who would like to proclaim otherwise.

Given the vital role it has played in dictating abduction research for over thirty years, these problems are significant.

For example, in his book Fuller states of a meeting with investigators in February 1962 that 'the idea of hypnosis was temporarily tabled'. The implication presented is that it was the investigators who suggested this and that the Hills were reluctant to agree until much later, and in response to the subsequent discovery of missing time. Indeed, the book suggests that Betty was not persuaded until March 1962. This is all good innocent-witness stuff: the witness's testimony seems more credible

THE INTERRUPTED JOURNEY

TWO LOST HOURS
ABOARD A
FLYING SAUCER

JOHN G. FULLER
Author of
THE GHOST OF
FLIGHT 401

because 'the truth' has to be extracted from them using methods independent of their control or knowledge. However, Fuller knew that this was not true and seems to have deliberately omitted something which would prove it. He duplicates a letter from Betty Hill to Keyhoe, apparently in full. But we have a copy of that letter – written,

The next day we did make a report to an Air Force office who seemed to be very interested in the wings and red li[ghts] We did not report my husband's observation of the interi[or] as it seems too fantastic to be true.

At this time we are searching for any clue that might be helpful to my husband, in recalling whatever it was he saw that caused him to panic. His mind has completely blacked out at this point. Every attempt to recall, leaves him ve[ry] frightened. We are considering the possibility of a compe[tent] psychiatrist who uses hypnotism.

This flying object was at least as large as a four motor pl[ane] itselflight was noiseless, and the lighting from the interio[r] did not reflect on the grounds. There doesnot appear to be any damage to our car from the beeping sounds.

We both ha[ve] been quite frightened by this experience, but [we] feel a compelling urge to return to the spot [inte]rested in the hope that we may again come in [contact] [thi]s object. We realize this possibility is [remote?] [w]ould, however, have more recent information [devel]opments in the last six years.

[Your fee]lings would be greatly appreciated. Your book [would] help to us and a reassurance that we are not [ha]ve undergone an interesting and informative

Very truly yours,

(Mrs.) Barney Hill

Portsmouth, N. H.
September 26, 1961

Dear Mr. Keyhoe:

The purpose of this letter is twofold. We wish to inquire if you have written any more books about unidentified flying objects since The Flying Saucer Conspiracy was published. If so, it would certainly be appreciated if you would send us the name of the publisher as we have been unsuccessful in finding any information more upto date than this book. A stamped self-addressed envelope is being included for your convenience.

My husband and I have become immensely interested in this topic, as we recently had quite a frightening experience, which does seem to differ from others of which we are aware. About mid-night on September 20th, we were driving in a National Forest area in the White Mountains, in N. H. This is a desolate, uninhabited area. At first we noticed a bright object in the sky which seemed to be moving rapidly. We stopped our car and got out to observe it more closely with our binoculars. Suddenly it reversed its flight from the north to the southwest and appeared to be flying in a very erratic pattern. As we continued driving and then stopping to watch it, we observed the following flight pattern /\/\/\ :

The object was spinning and appeared to be lighted only on one side which gave it a twinkling effect.

At it approached our car, we stopped again. As it hovered in the air in front of us, it appeared to be pancake in shape, ringed with windows in the front through which we could see bright blue-white lights. Suddenly two red lights appeared on each side. By this time my husband was standing in the road, watching closely. He saw wings protrude on each side and the red lights were on the wing tips.

As it glided closer he was able to see inside this object, but not too closely. He did see many figures scurrying about as though they were making some hurried type of preparation. One figure was observing us from the windows. From the distance, this was seen, the figures appeared to be about the size of a pencil, and seemed to be dressed in some type of shiny black uniform.

At this point, my husband became shocked and got back in the car, in a hysterical condition, laughing and repeating that they were going to capture us. He started driving the car - the motor had been left running. As we started to move, we heard several buzzing or beeping sounds which seemed to be striking the trunk of our car.

We did not observe this object leaving, but we did not see it again, although about thirty miles further south we were again bombarded by these same beeping sounds.

Betty Hill's letter to Major Donald Keyhoe written just one week after the encounter involving her and her husband. In reproducing the letter in his book, Fuller omitted Betty's suggestion of using a hypnotist.

remember, by Betty just one week after the incident – and note that in Fuller's book just one line is omitted: 'We are considering the possibility of a competent psychiatrist who uses hypnotism.'[11] So in fact hypnosis was almost immediately on the Hills' minds, and mentioned in the same paragraph where Betty expresses concern over Barney's inability to recall 'suppressed memories'.

Perhaps of even greater concern is the content of a letter from Fuller in response to articles John Spencer had written about the case challenging his interpretation of the Hills' story. Given that the event happened in 1961, that Fuller's book was published in 1966, and that it should be evident to anyone involved with the subject that the case was a crucial one for research, any responsible researcher surely has a duty to be as honest and open about it as possible. So what are we to make of Fuller's statement in 1989 that he had sat in on taped 'trance sessions' which were never released? In his letter he says: 'These trance sessions have never been published. I am the only one in possession of the tapes, each over two hours long. No one could *possibly* assess the Hill story without the knowledge of what is on these tapes . . .'[12] Thirty years is a long time to keep secret whatever evidence this was supposed to be. Either Fuller was lying about the quality of information revealed, or he was doing ufology a great disservice by withholding it. And it does not bode well for abduction research if he was clumsily tinkering with the most important case in the genre.

The idea that hypnotism could be used to unlock suppressed memories was in Betty Hill's mind just a week after the incident, and Fuller knew that it weakened the dramatic effect of his presentation to admit this when writing up the story. And we discover that Fuller, by his own admission, withheld information about the case from

researchers all around the world.

One aspect of the case that seems to come through clearly is that the Hills were honest and courageous in telling their story, and that theirs was a real experience, whatever interpretation they, Fuller, we, or others put on it. We know from conversation and correspondence with Betty that she believes she was kidnapped by aliens from outer space, and she has always been polite and courteous in discussing her beliefs. We have never had reason to doubt her honesty in the claims she has made. Yet perhaps even now the case has not been fully and properly evaluated without prejudicial predisposition. And, sadly, it might by now, be impossible to analyse it with any more accuracy.

SOCORRO, NEW MEXICO

Between the date of the Hills' encounter and the time it was made public, another case of importance arose.

'Lonnie was white as a corpse, and he ain't exactly no paleface, normally. He was sweatin' like a spent horse. But it was cold sweat.' Thus were the after-effects of a UFO encounter on police officer Lonnie Zamora described by Undersheriff James Luckie.

Socorro, New Mexico stands at the edge of the huge White Sands missile complex, the development and test area where some of the most sophisticated technology of the space race was developed. At around 5.45pm on Friday 24 April 1964, a couple and their three children, driving north on Highway 85 towards Socorro, were astonished when the road ahead of them was crossed by an egg-shaped, smooth, aluminium-like craft flying from north-east to south-west. The couple estimated that the object passed within 3ft of the car's roof, only just missing the tip of the radio aerial. They heard no sound. They

Lonnie Zamora was the highly credible witness to the highly credible report at Socorro.

were able to watch as it hovered for a few seconds and then seemed to gently land just on the other side of a small hill. At the same moment they saw a white Pontiac police car, which had been heading south out of Socorro towards US 85, veer off the road and drive across rough terrain down a small dirt road, apparently following the object. The couple took the object to be some 'new-type aircraft': the husband was angry that a pilot should fly so recklessly low, and assumed that the police car was on its way to castigate him, while the wife thought maybe the aircraft was in trouble and that the police car was responding to some kind of SOS. As they continued their journey into town the pair saw another police car heading south. When they arrived in Socorro they told their story to a service-station manager, Opel Grinder, and his teenaged son, Jimmy. Grinder and his son later signed an affidavit stating that the family had reported the incident to them. This was later to confirm that Lonnie Zamora, the driver of the first police car they had seen, was not the only person to see the object.

Zamora, who had been driving with his car windows open, heard a roaring sound and saw a brilliant blue 'cone of flame' to the south-south-west. Concerned that a

The Socorro close encounter impressed Hynek, the Air Force's investigator. 'Of all the close encounters of the third kind, this is the one that most clearly suggests a "nuts and bolts" physical craft along with accompanying noises and propulsion,' he stated.

nearby dynamite shack might have exploded, he had driven off the road towards the landing craft. He approached the object for approximately twenty seconds, keeping his eye on the flame, which he later described as blue with a little orange around the edges, narrow and streamlined, and flaring out towards the bottom. Once he topped a small hill on the road, he noticed that the flame had gone and the sound had stopped. Looking around for the dynamite shack, Zamora saw a white metal-looking egg-shaped object standing in a ravine. He described it as smooth, oval-shaped and with no windows or doors. He also noticed what appeared to be some kind of insignia on the side of the craft.

There were two figures in white coveralls standing near the object as if inspecting it. Zamora got the impression that they were startled as he and his car appeared on the brow of the hill. Although he was approximately 150yds away, Zamora was able to estimate the height of the figures by comparing them with nearby bushes. He believed that the figures were the size of boys – noticeably short. He reported by radio to the sheriff's office that he was going to investigate a possible accident. He was clinging to the possibility that the craft was a conventional car which had been spun off the road, perhaps by kids. However, he was also wondering whether it might be an experimental vehicle from White Sands proving grounds, which perhaps he was not supposed to have seen, or maybe something even more frighteningly strange.

Zamora wanted a reliable witness to confirm what he was seeing, but, concerned that he might have stumbled upon a secret government experiment, he requested that Police Sergeant Samuel Chavez should come to the location alone. Zamora believed Chavez could be relied upon to keep the matter confidential should it turn out to be necessary.

Zamora, now only 50ft away from the object, was able to clearly see what he thought was landing gear. He heard two very loud noises. Getting out of the car, he started towards the object but he had gone only a few paces when he heard a 'sudden, very loud, ear-splitting roar' and saw a flame. He 'hit the dirt', fearing that the craft might explode. Realizing that the roar was

steeply and rapidly. As it disappeared from sight, Chavez's patrol car appeared, heading towards the position Zamora had given him. Chavez finally spotted Zamora's patrol car, but was too late to see the disappearing object.

While he waited for Chavez to reach him, Zamora went down to the area where the craft had been and examined the terrain. The bushes were smouldering and smoking, presumably having been ignited by the blue flame from beneath the object.

Zamora was undoubtedly shaken by the incident. Chavez exclaimed when he first saw him, 'You look like you've seen the Devil!'

Zamora, sweating, could only reply, 'Maybe I have.'

An inspection of the site located not just the burning bushes but also the imprint of the landing gear, which was marked out and photographed the following morning. Socorro's local newspaper, the *El Defensor Chieftain*, described the landing marks: 'They did not appear to have been made by an object striking the Earth with great force, but by an object of considerable weight settling to Earth at slow speed and not moving after touching the ground.'

Along with the landing-gear impressions there were some footprints close to the area where the craft had come down which were consistent with both Zamora's sighting and the very short time the figures would have been outside the object. Given the duration of the event, it is likely that the craft landed, the figures got out, almost immediately saw Zamora, got back in again and took off – hardly time for very much activity around the object. Furthermore, it appears that sand had vitrified into glass: some 'melted' or 'bubbly' rock was recovered from the site and examined by the Public Health Service in Las Vegas. UFO investigator Ray Stanford also recovered rocks from the landing site which he

steady and that the object was not exploding, he got up and ran back to his car. Looking back over his shoulder, he noticed that the object had risen about 20ft out of the valley and was now approximately level with the height of his parked car. Then the roar stopped, to be replaced by a whining sound, and then no sound at all. Zamora

said of that moment: 'You could'a heard a pin drop.' The object was now moving towards the west-south-west, and very fast.

According to Zamora, the object remained very low, probably no more than approximately 10 to 15ft above ground-level, until it was approximately a mile away, over Highway 60, after which it climbed believes contained metal fragments scraped off the landing gear. However, the evidence to support this was lost when Stanford took the rocks to the Public Health Service for analysis. It appears that all metal fragments were removed from the rocks, despite Stanford's request that they should not be.

The incident was reported to Captain Ord.C Richard Holder, uprange commander at White Sands, by FBI agent J. Arthur Byrnes, who had happened to be at the police station when the report from Zamora had been radioed in. The FBI have a long history of denying being involved in UFO research, which is apparently due to the pique of one man, J. Edgar Hoover, at not being included in the government's studies of the 1950s with the prominence he wished. Therefore Byrnes apparently requested that the FBI not be mentioned in any investigative work, saying that the 'use of local law-enforcement authorities is acceptable'. However, in the 1970s the FBI's file on the Socorro event was declassified, and interestingly Byrnes advised Zamora not to report seeing the figures dressed in white on the basis that 'no one will believe you'. Zamora complied with this request at first. The agent also told Zamora not to describe the symbol he had seen on the side of the vehicle 'to anyone except official investigators'. Captain Holder made the following statement to the press the day after the incident: 'Neither White Sands Missile Range nor Holloman [Air Force Base] has an object that would compare to the object described. And there was no known firing mission in progress at the time of the occurrence that would produce the conditions reported.'

Investigation of the sighting took place almost immediately – J. Allen Hynek and NICAP investigator Ray Stanford were on site within just a couple of days. At the time Hynek attempted to pass himself off as an independent investigator, but in his own

book many years later he admitted that he had been there in an official capacity as the scientific consultant of the Air Force's Project Blue Book. In fact, at the time, Hynek suggested that the Air Force did not try to cover up its UFO investigations.

There was further corroboration of the Socorro incident. An Albuquerque television station had received a call at 5.25pm, a quarter of an hour before the family on Highway 85 had sighted the object. The sighting was entirely consistent with Officer Zamora's: an egg-shaped object travelling at very low altitude at about the same speed as an ordinary prop-driven light aircraft. In fact, travelling at just that sort of speed, approximately 160 to 170mph, an object flying from Albuquerque towards Socorro would take approximately twenty-five minutes. Other witnesses included Larry Kratzer and Paul Kies, who had been driving north on Highway 60 at roughly the same time as Zamora had seen the craft.

The Air Force released a 'fact sheet' on the Socorro sighting which was dutifully,

A clip from *Earth vs. The Flying Saucers.* This film – strongly promoting ETH – was based on the writings of Major Donald Keyhoe. Keyhoe was the first military man to 'break ranks' in a highly public way and accuse the government of a cover up.

and masterfully, ripped to shreds by investigator Ray Stanford in his book *Socorro Saucer.*[13] It shows that either the Air Force was astonishingly incompetent, or – and this is our reading of the inaccuracies – extremely competent at making Zamora's report seem insubstantial or inaccurate. For example, the Air Force fact sheet claims that Zamora was driving north on US 85 when in fact he was driving south and not on, but near the highway. It states that he saw the object from approximately 800ft away when in fact he was about 450ft away, and, later, that he got no closer than 150 to 200ft when he got to within approximately 50ft. The Air Force states that Zamora saw one or two figures in coveralls (providing ' for both vagueness and normality in the type of clothing), whereas Zamora was quite certain he saw two figures, and described their clothes as something 'resembling' coveralls. The fact sheet suggests that he saw the marking on the side of the craft after he had lost his glasses, whereas in fact he had seen it before he lost his glasses, which had fallen off when he stumbled running away from the object. Chavez, according to the fact sheet, must have appeared so quickly that he should have seen the object leaving and yet did not. As it was, the time frame was perfectly consistent with his arriving too late. The fact sheet indicates that the bushes in the area were cold to the touch, whereas they were still smoking; that Zamora had seen smoke as well as flames beneath the craft, whereas Zamora reported only one flame and distinctly no smoke. Indeed, it is especially interesting, given that Hynek was the Air Force's official investigator, that in his book *The Hynek UFO Report* he copies out Zamora's statement, which contains the three-word phrase 'no smoke noted'.[14]

To throw the sighting into further confusion, Jim and Coral Lorenzen of APRO reported that six days after Lonnie Zamora's report a similar object had landed and had been captured at Holloman–White Sands Range. The Lorenzens' informant, whom they described as reliable, indicated that the UFO had been retrieved and was under guard in a hangar at the Holloman base. Stanford was able to use his own high-level contacts to discover that such a craft had indeed been captured. He was also told: 'I think it could be the same one that came to Socorro six days before that, but although the policeman's description was pretty accurate, we don't know for sure it was the same.' Even more extraordinarily, the military officer who spoke to Stanford indicated that they did not yet

know the specific origin of the craft: 'They will probably know, eventually, where it came from, but we already know that the thing was not made by terrestrials.' Stanford speculates in *Socorro Saucer*[13] published in 1976, that the technology for back-engineering a captured UFO and learning what could be learned about it must have gone 'underground' and was 'operating at a super-secret level just as did the Manhattan Project'. This, of course, was to become one of the most popular theories to emerge from crash-retrieval lore in the 1980s and 1990s.

J. Allen Hynek confirms the solidity of the Socorro case and comments: 'Of all the close encounters of the third kind, this is the one that most clearly suggests a "nuts and bolts" physical craft along with accompanying noises and propulsion.'[14] Hynek officially listed the report as 'unidentified' in the Blue Book files, finding Zamora's character 'unimpeachable'. He further comments that even Major Quintanilla, then head of Blue Book, was convinced that 'an actual physical craft had been present'. Hynek remarks that Quintanilla 'attempted . . . to establish that it had been some sort of test vehicle, perhaps a lunar landing module. All of his efforts (and they were indeed considerable) failed to give any indication that a man-made craft had landed at Socorro on the afternoon in question.'

Perhaps the incident inspired the comment of John W. McCormack, speaker of the House of Representatives who, in January 1965, stated: 'I feel that the Air Force has not been giving out all the available information on the unidentified flying objects. You cannot disregard so many unimpeachable sources.'

Crash-retrieval specialists Stanton Friedman and Don Berliner say: 'Half-hearted official efforts to explain the UFO as a rancher's helicopter or a NASA moon-landing test vehicle were quickly dropped, as neither

could possibly account for the main characteristics of the sighting, especially the silent hovering.'[15] They go on to point out that 'this UFO gave every indication of being a solid object . . . something manufactured . . . a machine'.

We are not quite as confident as Friedman and Berliner that the UFO could not have been a government test vehicle, given that the incident happened just at the time when the space programme technologies, including the lunar module and astronaut-training vehicles for the lunar module, were being developed. The length of time for which such innovations are kept secret can be surprising: for example, the triangle-shaped radar-invisible Stealth aircraft, first announced in the late 1980s, had apparently been under development since the mid-1960s, far earlier than is generally supposed.

But at the same time we recognize that this case was an important landmark. A phenomenon which many people were reporting around the world had now, in Socorro, been well observed and documented by a reliable witness in conditions which left almost no grounds for believing that this object was anything less than purely physical. And if we have any doubts about the sighting, they certainly do not approach those of UFO sceptic Philip Klass, who believed that the Socorro report was fabricated to stimulate tourism in the locality. He seems to have based this view on the fact that the landing took place on land owned then by the mayor of Socorro, but in doing so he seems to have ignored the character of Officer Zamora. We might add here – and much to the consternation of some UFO researchers, we are sure – that we believe Klass adds a valuable dimension to UFO research where scepticism is much needed, but on this occasion we think he has overstepped the mark and fallen into a common trap, but in reverse: he seems to show the same desperate need to disbelieve as so many proponents of UFOs seem to do to believe. (Klass's introduction to the subject is described later in this chapter.)

But even if some test vehicle, perhaps relating to the space programme, looked like a fairly likely explanation, just the following year a case was to arise which would increase the possibility that Zamora had indeed encountered something 'other-worldly'. At Valensole in France, a farmer found something in his lavender patch that was remarkably similar to the object at Socorro. But this time the occupants were more clearly seen, were less human in appearance, and apparently used some kind of 'beam' to paralyse the witness. The Valensole incident is covered more fully later in this chapter.

THE END OF THE COLD WAR

The Berlin border had been sealed since 13 August 1961, but the Cold War had been at its iciest for only a few years between 1961 and 1964. Its nadir was probably between 22 October and 2 November 1962, the time of the Cuban Missile Crisis, when Kennedy and Khrushchev were eyeball to eyeball over the deployment of Soviet missiles in Cuba, close to the US mainland. But by the summer of 1963 Kennedy was announcing a nuclear-test-ban agreement with the Soviet Union following the proposal of Soviet foreign minister Andrei Gromyko to ban nuclear weapons in Earth orbit. The possibility that Americans had feared from the outset – that the Soviets could hurl nuclear weapons on to their territory from outer space – was thus effectively removed by the Soviets themselves.

Probably the greatest symbol of US–USSR co-operation was opened up on 30 August 1963, when the 'hotline' telephone between the White House and the Kremlin was instigated in order to allow the

respective heads of state to talk directly and thereby to avoid an incident escalating into the prospect of the much-feared nuclear war. The Cold War was beginning to thaw, and many political analysts believe that 1964 represents the end of 'phase 1' of this postwar era.

With the end of that phase, the political, social and cultural background against which UFOs were being perceived altered abruptly. As we have seen, from 1947 to 1963, it had been one of fear and apprehension: fear that the UFOs might be an alien invasion force was inspired in Americans who had never been threatened at their own mainland borders and supported by the imagery of the science-fiction films of the time; fear that the UFOs might be Soviet weaponry reinforced by the astonishing lead they were able to take in the space race and their hostile adventures near American territory, and particularly in Cuba.

In social terms, a dramatic change was about to sweep the West, and it would be this, rather than politics, that would create the ruling climate against which beliefs about UFOs would now be viewed.

This period of history will forever be known simply as 'the sixties', though it is generally held to have run from around 1963 to the mid-1970s. But even this era is perceived differently in America and in England, though from both viewpoints it is still characterized by a new generation rejecting the values of their parents. In America the revolution had stronger political overtones: it is said that the sixties started with the assassination of Kennedy in 1963 and ended with the USA's withdrawal from Vietnam in 1975. In England, the sixties were more about social change, cultural styles and sexual permissiveness.

It was in this period that the seeds of distrust of governments were sown. If the Cold War had thawed in 1964, then what

almost immediately surfaced in its wake would remain the most burning issue in America for years to come: the Vietnam War. Throughout that year the American government had debated how it could support its allies in the Republic of Vietnam. Circumstances, including an attack on the USS Maddox by the North Vietnamese, dictated that the support would be in the form of military aggression. In 1965, and going into 1966, the first big troop deployments were instigated. On 3 July 1966 there were huge Vietnam War protests at the American Embassy in London. The public were outraged as never before, but the administration remained firm. On 26 October President Lyndon Johnson visited the troops in Vietnam. On 14 February 1967, 100 Labour MPs in Britain condemned Vietnam bombing; on 26 March 10,000 hippies gathered together in New York Central Park, focused on ending the war, and on 15 April 100,000 demonstrators marched from Central Park to the United Nations Building. On 12 September 1967 Ronald Reagan, then governor of California, called for the war in Vietnam to be escalated, a stance which earned him the nickname 'Ronald Ray-Guns'. On 16 October Joan Baez was arrested at an anti-Vietnamese war rally.

Along with such overt protests a more subtle rejection of authority was also laid down. When President Kennedy was assassinated in November 1963, seemingly by a lone gunman, almost immediately a theory was propounded that there had been more than one gunman, and therefore a conspiracy to murder him. On 27 September 1964, the Warren Commission report on the assassination was published, concluding that the assassin, Lee Harvey Oswald, had acted alone, and that there was no conspiracy. Gallup poll statistics indicated that two-thirds of the public found the conclusion unacceptable. Their doubts were to lead to a belief that, far from being wrong or bungled, the Warren Commission had been part of a cover-up, and that the assassination conspiracy might have been perpetrated from within the American administration.

The effect of this distrust on the UFO phenomenon was only marginal then, but the mood created was undoubtedly part of the reason why a strong belief in 'cover-up and conspiracy' permeated the subject in the late 1970s.

THE DAWNING OF A NEW AGE

Probably the most obvious revolution brought by the winds of change in the 1960s was in fashion, music, literature and the arts, plus the opening up of mass communication across the world. London, notably Carnaby Street, and San Francisco, particularly Haight-Ashbury, were pop-culture centres. The miniskirt was created and the Beatles and the Rolling Stones came to symbolize the rejection by the young of parental values. It was during the sixties that the Kray twins and the Great Train Robbers became cultural heroes – proof if any were needed that everything previously held to be right was being stood on its head. Andy Warhol's pop art drew a huge cult following, 'permissive' became a household word and sexual and social taboos were challenged by the introduction of the contraceptive pill and the widespread use of marijuana. In America in 1965, the Beatnik poet Allen Ginsberg first used the phrase 'flower power' to describe the hippy revolution in California. Bob Dylan wrote a song that became an anthem of the times, and one that could as easily have applied to UFOs as to any other aspect of life: 'The Times They are a-'Changin''. As actress Julie Christie put it: 'The sixties was an experiment I was glad to be part of. We were rejecting consumerism

– the power of multinationals – and discovering hedonistic and spiritual values.'[16]

The 1960s marked the birth of the new age. Up to this point UFOs in Britain had been largely a matter of British interest in an American phenomenon. British sightings had occurred, but were viewed only in comparison to the much better publicized American cases. Now, in this new social climate, the UFO was imported into Britain – not against a political tapestry of the Cold War and the space race, but as part of the emerging New Age. In America the places where UFOs were typically reported were seen as military sites, such as the New Mexico desert; in Britain they were seen at what were regarded as mythical sites: Glastonbury, the highly haunted and

Warminster 'happened' at a time when youth was searching for new meanings. Many of the young 'skywatching' on the hills were looking for a 'cosmic saviour', a replacement for conventional religion which many thought had failed them.

legend-ridden Wessex area, and a small town in Wiltshire called Warminster.

Interestingly, however, this is more a perceived difference than a true one, because the legendary sites in the UK were often near military sites, and the military sites in the US were often also the ancient sacred lands of the native Americans. Nevertheless, the way in which UFOs were perceived revealed something of the cultural interpretation of the time.

WARMINSTER

Warminster had been invaded. Bizarre creatures roamed the area, carrying strange devices for all kinds of unknown purposes, survival equipment, apparatus designed to allow them to examine the environment without actually having to touch it. They carried food supplies so that they were not dependent on local availability. They resembled our astronauts on lunar excursions, protected from their surroundings by their clothing and their vehicles. Their ways were alien. They interacted with humanity – indeed, the humans living in the area had come to depend on their visitations – yet they were resented. The invaders were tourists.

They scaled the hills of the Vale of the White Horse and flocked in their hordes to the Marlborough Downs to pay homage to the Avebury Stone Circle and Silbury Hill. They so terrified the custodians of nearby Stonehenge that the authorities later had to rope off the ancient artefact as if it were the site of a police murder investigation.

But if the locals in the small market town in the mid-1960s thought they had suffered at the hands of the Rons and Ethels in their Ford Populars, it was only because they had no idea of what was to follow. Warminster had been invaded so often it should have put up 'Welcome' signs and left the doors open: the Celts had settled there, the Romans had had a go; in modern times the Army had invaded and settled in at Battlesbury Barracks, and now they were annoying the local boys by chatting up the local girls. Once cars had become affordable, the increased mobility they allowed brought the tourists.

The *Warminster Journal* was an important media outlet for journalist Arthur Shuttlewood, and helped to boost the public awareness of what they locally called 'The Thing'. Shuttlewood took a picture first published in the *Journal* to the national *Daily Mirror*.

But now Warminster was going to get an even ruder awakening.

On 23 July 1966 the ufologists invaded Warminster. They had made scouting visits for a year or so before that, but now they arrived en masse. 'Warminster Week' ran from 23 to 30 July, taking in the two Saturdays. Despite the cold, and the rain and clouds that made their skywatching ineffective at best, ant-like lines of dedicated young, and not so young, people plodded up the muddy hills with their cameras, binoculars, Thermos flasks and waterproofs to set up their observation posts. Their mission was to monitor the skies; to observe, photograph and interview witnesses. They set up a post on Cley Hill, another on Cradle Hill and, briefly, a third at Westbury White Horse, which was soon abandoned due to 'communication difficulties'.[17]

There were several 'lights-in-the-sky' sightings during this week-long skywatch but none were particularly conclusive or important. One of the most interesting reports was logged by BUFORA investigator John Cleary-Baker and Arnold West, currently a vice-president of the organization. They saw a bright object in the sky for several minutes, moving at various speeds. Arnold West flashed a powerful signal lamp towards the object and the pair believed that on each occasion it flickered as if in reply. 'No flickering was noted at any other time while it was in view.'[17]

The ufologists didn't come alone, of course. If they had they would have been little problem, for they were a fairly regimented and retiring lot on the whole. But they brought in their wake a barmy army of TV interviewers and camera crews, newspaper journalists and radio reporters. All week smartly dressed media people could be seen cutting their teeth on the Warminster phenomenon. They would stand in the street outside the offices of the *Warminster Journal* and interview anyone

with any opinion on almost anything.

So why Warminster? The town is located in a part of England steeped in mysticism. It lies approximately midway between Stonehenge and Glastonbury, and at least fourteen known leys converge on the site. The region is rich in the paranormal: ghosts, poltergeist activity, and so on. It was not, of course, the only site of UFO activity in the UK, nor the first, but it became the focus.

A starting point for all this is difficult to determine. The history of the area is such that strange phenomena in the skies can be traced back through history – a 'fireball in the sky' during the seventeenth century, for example, is described in John Aubrey's *A Natural History of Wiltshire*. But in the modern era it seems that the Warminster phenomenon started with The Sound.

On 11 April 1964, a local person heard a strange sound which disturbed a flock of pigeons. The witness said that 'several of the birds wheeled over and dropped lifeless to the ground'.[18] On Christmas morning that same year, Roger Rump, the head postmaster of Warminster, was woken at 6.15am by strange sounds above the roof of his house. 'It was a terrific clatter, as though the tiles on the roof were being rattled about and being plucked off by some tremendous force. Then came a scrambling sound, as if they were being hurriedly replaced – loudly slammed back at that.' At around the same time Marjorie Bye heard an odd sound nearby, a droning with vibration, and a young couple simultaneously sent their nine-year-old daughter to see why their dog was barking. She discovered it in a woodshed, clearly agitated. At that point the girl also heard 'a weird crackling high-pitched whine'.[17]

Although the town is near army exercise grounds on Salisbury Plain, there were no military exercises on Christmas morning – indeed, the majority of personnel were

absent on leave from the camp. Those who were there themselves reported the sounds. One sergeant said: 'It was as if a huge chimney stack from the main block was ripped from the rooftop and then scattered in solid chunks of masonry across the whole camp area.'[17] No explanation could be found for the sounds.

Such sounds were reported by many witnesses throughout 1965 and beyond, described variously as being like 'a giant bird's wings flapping overhead', or 'tons of coal being emptied from sacks and sent tumbling all over the place. It all began with an electric crackling.' 'What seemed at first to be a loud crackling of electricity. It came from the roof space above my bedroom. Then it changed from a whining crackle to a more frightening noise.' 'As though buckets of gravel were hurled against the glass, heavy and rasping.' 'The crashing of pebbles on the roof.'[17]

But of course it is the visual sightings of objects in the sky which form the core of the UFO phenomenon, and Warminster had its share of these, too. On 19 May 1965 Hilda Hebdidge saw cigar-shaped objects covered with bright lights. 'They were quite stationary, with no beams or rays and no noise whatsoever.' She saw a similar object on 6 November of the same year. On Thursday 3 June 1965, a 'fiery cigar-shaped object' was seen by many Warminster citizens between 8.30 and 9pm, and on 7 July a large red ball was sighted over the town. Other reports included 'bright spherical objects seen over a lake', 'a ball of flaming crimson light', 'an outsize car headlight in the sky . . . resembled a human eye as it came closer', 'two twinkling stars, specks of light a long way up . . . they came flashing down on us, growing in size enormously before blacking out over our heads', 'in addition to changing from red to silver blue, it also changed at intervals from one to two minutes, from round to pencil-shaped', 'like a harvest moon, which flew quietly and gently overhead towards the north', 'an object silver grey in colour, circular in shape with no wings or tail and it made no noise . . . performed unbelievable aerobatics . . . played leapfrog with a jet aircraft passing by'. On 20 September 1965 something 'amber in colour flew over the grounds of the West Wilts Golf Club . . . changed colour from amber to pink, then to a glowing red'; 'the golden sphere that rolled steadily over the edge of hills to the left of the golf course . . . large, luminous and languid'. And on 30 November 1965, 'a bright silver ball twice the size of the moon, hurtling through the sky', was seen by Police Constable Eric Pinnock.[17]

Warminster was divided between those who thought the UFO sightings were fascinating and those who scoffed at them.

There was very little fear, but a good deal of interest in some quarters. The locals were probably heartily sick of the tourist–UFO-spotter–reporter invasion as well. So the chairman of Warminster Urban District Council, Emlyn Rees, called a public meeting in the town hall on 26 August 1965. A panel – consisting of Mr Rees, the chairman of BUFORA, Dr Geoffrey Doel, BUFORA investigator Dr John Cleary-Baker and Reverend Lawrence Inge, the vicar of Orcheston and then President of the Salisbury Plain Astronomical Society[17] – was assembled to answer questions from the public.

What a night it was! Over 500 people crammed their way into a hall built for 200. One man brought his own stepladder so that he could see over the crowd. One description said that the press gallery appeared to be in danger of collapsing.

Many more gave up and waited for the reports in the local paper instead. The BUFORA contingent clearly wished to pursue a belief in extraterrestrials, and Dr Doel said: 'We defy sceptics to find any explanation that will satisfy people that these things are not from outer space.' However he went on to add: 'You should not feel afraid. You are privileged to be able to investigate them.' Reverend Inge urged that reports should continue to be collected, commented that he believed life was possible elsewhere but did not necessarily see this as the cause of the sightings over Warminster. David Holton, who had earlier suggested that spacecraft might be responsible,

---

The hills around Warminster, particularly Starr Hill, Cley Hill and Cradle Hill were the UFO spotters' Mecca in the 1960s in England. Organized 'skywatches' were set up by UFO enthusiasts, one lasting a week.

and who had discussed the evidence of pigeons flying into 'soundwave barriers', refused to attend the meeting, believing that: 'This is a serious matter and must not be thrashed out in a halfhearted way by local people in front of the press and TV cameras.' A final analysis of the meeting in one national newspaper was that 'most people went away no better informed or the wiser than when they went'.

All this excitement apart, there were two factors which really crystallized Warminster as the UK centre – indeed, for a long time, the world centre – of UFOs. One was a picture by Gordon Faulkner; the second was the influence of Arthur Shuttlewood. In September 1965 Faulkner photographed a UFO nicknamed 'the Thing' in Warminster, and local reporter and UFO enthusiast Shuttlewood had written a report and given it with the photo to the *Daily Mirror*. It made the front pages, and a double-page spread in the centre pages.[19] It was not a particularly impressive photo, and offered little in the way of substantial evidence for UFO researchers, but nonetheless it was important. In 1994 Faulkner described the incident to us: 'I just came out and there it was. The camera was in my hand, I saw it, and I thought, I must get this. It was moving but it wasn't making any noise. It was moving really fast.' Perhaps significantly, the photo came at a key moment – after the public meeting in Warminster Town Hall, when interest was at its highest and the media was craving a 'visual'. The photo became a symbol of Warminster and gave the Thing an identity. In that respect it was of enormous social significance, for it provided a visual image for those who craved one and forged a connection between the town and UFOs.

Response to the photograph reflected the wide range of views on the subject. Readers commented: 'The Thing . . . is a gas-filled balloon', 'it's a mirage', 'space visitors will be more advanced than we are',

'a burnt cottage loaf slung out of a baker's window', 'people from other planets are coming to bring peace and love', 'people are being taken in by experiments by local scientists', and so on.[20]

In 1992, Roger Hooton sought us out to tell us that he had faked the photo with Gordon Faulkner. He presented a good case, though oddly enough, a researcher named Steve Dewey later unearthed a story which held that Faulkner had indeed faked the photograph – but with his brother-in-law, not Hooton, whom Faulkner claimed not to know. Faulkner, of course, maintains that the photograph is genuine. We interviewed both Faulkner and Hooton, and both stand by their claims. One of the two has to be lying. But further analysis is probably impossible: Faulkner told us that he had lost the negative in the intervening years. But whether or not the photo was faked is now secondary to the effect it had. The Warminster phenomenon would not have been what it was without the involvement of one man: Arthur Shuttlewood.

Arthur Shuttlewood's role tells us a great deal about the UFO phenomenon. What was important about Shuttlewood was that not only was he a highly public figure eager to suck up every UFO report on offer, but he had the media connections to broadcast them loudly – and he did. Anyone who had had a sighting anywhere near Warminster knew exactly who to go to. This probably accounts for why Warminster became the focus for UFOs, because such phenomena were not confined to that town: they had in fact been reported all around the country since the 1950s. Such influences often arise in the analysis of UFO 'flaps' (waves). After the first burst of activity in the 1960s, there was a second surge in the early to mid-1970s, and Shuttlewood was prominent and active in both periods.

Shuttlewood was a local man, a diligent

'The Thing' was publicized by Gordon Faulkner's photograph. But was it genuine? Roger Hooton (pictured) claims to have helped fake it.

reporter for the *Warminster Journal*, a member of the local council and a former grenadier guardsman. In 1967 he wrote *The Warminster Mystery*, in which he describes the UFO events in the town.[21]

On 28 September 1965, Shuttlewood saw a bright cigar-shaped object 80yds in length and ran for his movie camera. Nothing of value came out; the film was later found scorched and coiled up inside its casing. And Shuttlewood himself began to suffer: his face twitched and his eye was sore and inflamed and watered for eight weeks. His left hand and wrist and the left side of his face were partially paralysed, he believes, by rays thrown out by 'the machine' to thwart the action of his camera. Shuttlewood also noticed that his wristwatch had stopped and did not keep good time thereafter.

Shuttlewood was also one of many to report the sounds of footsteps of the so-called 'invisible walker' one morning in March 1966. He said: 'It was a heavy footstep. I walked to the building [a barn] – no one was in or around it; yet the sound was repeated several times, as though someone was walking in front of me and away from me. I hurried to catch it up, whereupon it changed direction and I heard the shrill cackle of a laugh that chilled my spine.' Ghostly footsteps were heard by Shuttlewood and two others, Bob Strong and Sybil Champion, in April 1967 along with cough-like sounds.

On 27 August 1967, while lying in bed, Shuttlewood had a vision of a figure with long flowing hair, 'glorious eyes' and a high, broad forehead jutting outward over finely chiselled features. A brilliant light illuminated the room all around him. That day he

became a contactee. Two days later he saw what he believed to be the landing of a cone-shaped UFO on top of Cradle Hill. 'I advised onlookers to stay at a safe distance while I explored the area.' He investigated alone, and saw the landed UFO 'shooting out beams of bright light from a conical and revolving rim'. Somewhat mysteriously, he went on to say, 'It will tax the reader too harshly if I account exactly what happened some 300 yards from the glowing UFO and "whom" I spoke to near a rustic gate separating two large fields. I became terrified soon afterwards, in spite of the reassuring meeting.' His 1968 book, *Warnings From Flying Friends*,[22] is much

more speculative than the first, and charts his contacts with 'Nordic-like' aliens who are here to guide and protect us. And one of his later books was called *UFO – Key to the New Age*.

If not the Californian cult-leader type of contactee, Shuttlewood, who died in 1996, certainly became a local guru. John Spencer spent a few days walking over the hills of Warminster with him as part of a large group while he described his more extreme beliefs. He could see flying saucers while most others saw only stars and planets. But he was meeting a need, in himself and in others. The drive for new religions, new myths – any change arising from the social motivation of the 1960s – was expressing itself in the way many were perceiving the UFO phenomenon.

In the space of just a few years Warminster experienced almost every aspect of the UFO phenomenon, in many cases years ahead of reports from other parts of the world.

VEHICLE INTERFERENCE

Among many reports of vehicle interference were:

• August 1965. Don Parratt, his daughter and three friends saw a cigar-shaped form in the sky and simultaneously their car engine cut out and the electrical circuitry failed. The object remained in the sky for about ten minutes. When the car was taken to a garage it was found that the high-tension lead from the coil had burned out.

• 20 August 1965. Robert Payne, riding a scooter, also suffered a cut-out when out

Maurice Masse's encounter at Valensole in France was all the more thought-provoking because of the Socorro case. But significantly, while the physical appearance of the entities reported by Zamora could have been human, those reported by Masse could not have been.

with his girlfriend, Wendy Gulliford. They saw two large spheres of silver light in the sky. 'They were the spitting image of human eyes lit up.' After the lights had gone the scooter started with no hint of trouble.[17]

• 7 September 1965. Major William Hill, driving near Colloway Clump, suffered engine failure at the same time as a feeling of something 'menacing in the air'.[17] The following day the car was found to be in first-class condition.

HUMANOIDS

• 7 October 1965. Annabelle Randell, driving alone near Heytesbury, saw a bright orange glow. Her car lights dimmed and the engine began to cough and splutter. The bright object spun into the road and the car engine cut out. Then the object flew off into the sky. In front of Annabelle two figures were standing where the light had been. 'They were right in the middle of the road, one more on my side than on the other. I almost bowled them over . . . they wore dark balaclavas on their heads. These clung tight and showed only a small portion of their faces. I could see only their noses, in fact, and the merest suspicion of eyes, wide spaced and deep sunk. Their clothes were of darkish material, either black or deep grey, and skin tight. From the thigh down, the material glistened as though wet, very much like skin-divers or frogmen.' From the time that the orange ball flew off the engine of the car worked perfectly; Annabelle drove past the strange figures and into the night at full speed.[18]

• January 1966. Another witness saw figures he described as 'frogmen'. 'They were very similar to us, but shorter, I would say, with big shoulders, rather large heads and thinner legs.'[18]

• 8 July 1967. A figure was seen dressed in 'dark and close fitting garment, shining as if made of shiny leather'.[18]

• Winter 1967. Near Warminster a pensioner saw a UFO land and two figures drop from it. Believing them to be something to do with the Air Force he watched the visitors walking to the woodland. They were tall and wore dark grey close-fitting clothing with a particular sheen and rounded helmets. At a distance of around 60ft from the witness, one of them raised a hand and instantly they both vanished. The object, when he looked at it, was shrouded in yellow vapour and it took off into the air.[17]

ANIMAL INTERFERENCE

In the summer of 1967 a herd of several dozen cows disappeared from farmland at Chitterne. An extensive search by the farmer and many others could locate neither the cattle nor any tracks showing where they had gone. The following morning all the cows were back in the field. UFO enthusiasts, now camped in the area, suggested that aliens had abducted them for experimentation and study and returned them safely. This has a parallel in the animal-mutilation stories in the United States, and arose at more or less the same time as the first identified case there, of the colt Lady (see Chapter 5). If nothing else, the Warminster report shows the ease with which such stories become enmeshed with the UFO phenomenon.

Warminster survived the military-like invasion of ufologists – clean cut , trainspotter types; boy scouts to a man. They had poked and prodded and photographed the locality and everything that moved in it, but they had done so with respect, or at least with as much discretion as could reasonably be expected from a group of people convinced they were at the Mecca of galactic invasion. But the invasions were not over yet. The first wave of ufologists had dismissed aliens as 'untouchable' – they

were after the Thing in the sky. But over the years the contactee mentality infiltrated UFO research, and, given Arthur Shuttlewood's prominence, it therefore infiltrated Warminster, and a new breed of seeker came to the town.

In their droves the residue of the hippy period made pilgrimages to this new-age Lourdes and the hills around Warminster became the UFO-spotters' altar. And the phenomenon treated each new disciple with kindness, providing for his or her every need, every fantasy. Those who needed to would see great starships which ploughed the trade routes between the galaxies; others would see the scout ships of visiting saviours from higher civilizations. Still others saw lights they believed to be the very spirits of the birth of the age of Aquarius.

The locals might have been somewhat stressed by the barmy-army invasions, but they had seen the advantages of them, too. Ken Rogers, a reporter with the *Daily Express* and an investigator for BUFORA, studied the Warminster phenomenon in great depth, and of the later 'demise' of the attention there he wrote:

Towards the end of the 1970s the frequency of strange happenings in the Warminster triangle appeared to peter out. Sightings became rarer giving rise to the suggestion that the phenomenon had run its course and that the UFOs had decided to leave the town and its inhabitants in peace. In fact, for a while the subject became somewhat 'unfashionable' . . . Certainly the town's traders began to miss the deluge of visitors.[18]

No doubt they cheered up again in the late 1980s when crop-circle mania struck the Wessex area, and Warminster in particular. By then the New Age was well underway – indeed, the phrase itself had become almost a cliché – and there was little to disguise the needs of the pilgrims. This time they were overtly searching for new meanings to life in the patterns and markings in the flattened crops. They meditated and chanted and kept night-time candlelit vigils in the fields, seeking contact. The new seekers didn't just march through the town poking, prodding, photographing and interviewing – though they did all that too, of course. To get the best pictures of the increasingly elaborate crop-circle formations, the new invaders overflew the town and the locality. Now they *were* the UFOs.

At this time belief was moving towards the contactee side of UFOs in England. Twenty-one-year-old Garry Byers of Hackney, for example, claimed he 'heard a voice' telling him to go to the green in Theydon Bois where, as he expected, he saw a silver-black, egg-shaped object overhead. He had already been 'directed' to another spot where he had seen an object 15 months earlier. The voice told him: 'We have brought you here to reassure you. We know that G.A's films are being shown widely, and that people are taking interest.' (G.A. almost certainly refers to George Adamski.) Byers was so taken aback that he did not think to ask questions, something he later regretted. 'It's as if I was just on the fringe of discovering something tremendous,' he said, 'but couldn't grasp it in time.'[23]

ELSEWHERE

From the Warminster experiences, and the contactees and devotees of the new age, it is very easy to assume that the UFOs had turned into something angelic and wondrous. This is not the case. The way in which they were interpreted reflected the cultural beliefs of the time, but ignored claims that were coming in from around the world which suggested, if not demonstrated, more sinister interaction. There are many instances where people seem to have been attacked, or at least adversely physically affected by their encounters.

Most famous is the case which arose early on the morning of 1 July 1965 in Valensole in France. Farmer Maurice Masse, saw an egg-shaped object 15ft across which had landed in his lavender field. Assuming it to be of terrestrial origin, he approached it to tell the pilots what he thought of their chosen landing spot. But as he got closer he changed his mind. The object had a small cockpit on top and was supported by six spindly legs arranged in a way reminiscent of a spider's legs. Two figures, less than 4ft tall and dressed in grey-green one-piece suits, stood in front of it. Masse noticed that they had larger heads than usual and small mouths. They saw him coming and pointed a rod at him, which immobilized him. He was not knocked out, or paralysed in any literal sense; his breathing and other body functions were unaffected. Masse watched the figures for a time. They appeared to be observing him with curiosity rather than animosity; indeed, he felt they gave him a certain sense of peace. Around a minute later the figures boarded the craft, the door closed and Masse saw them in the cockpit. The object took off 'backwards' – that is, the entities were facing him as the craft lifted off the ground. It hovered briefly and then accelerated away. At a distance of some 200ft the craft vanished. Whether it literally disappeared, or moved too fast for him to watch its departure is unclear even to the witness. Around twenty minutes later Masse found that he could move again. Strangely, the farmer found that no lavender plants would grow at the landing site for ten years. A common characteristic of such experiences, which we have had reported to us many times by close-encounter witnesses, is that Masse needed a great deal of sleep, and suffered from drowsiness, for several weeks.

Earlier in the chapter we noted the similarity between this case and the UFO sighting at Socorro in New Mexico. According to Ralph and Judy Blum, French researcher Aimé Michel showed Maurice Masse a photograph of a model of the object seen there by police officer Lonnie Zamora. Michel apparently reported that Masse stared at the picture 'as though he had just looked upon his own death' and exclaimed: 'Monsieur, when did you photograph my machine?'[24]

The Valensole report also has similarities to one from 24 April 1950 in Abbiate Buazzone in Italy, where Bruno Facchini saw figures standing near a dark, hovering UFO. They were wearing helmets and flexible tubes. Facchini offered his help but the entities responded by shooting him with a beam of light which pushed him along the ground for several yards. Shortly afterwards, the object took off.

On 14 March 1965 rancher James Flynn was also knocked out by a beam of light from a UFO. Ground traces in the area were also found. Flynn's doctor found impairment of muscle and tendon reflexes which he believed could not have been faked. And on 14 February 1975 Antoine Severin, on Reunion Island in the Indian Ocean, saw the landing of a small domed object in a field at Petite Ile. Several short entities left the object and fired a white beam at Severin, knocking him out. For several days he suffered from poor vision and impaired speech.

Towards the end of the decade an account of UFO sightings in Exeter, New Hampshire, brought into the field a figure who, to the present day, maintains a love–hate relationship with the subject: Philip Klass.

Around September 1965 a number of UFO reports were received from the area. Probably the most famous was that of Norman Muscarello, who reported five bright red lights moving around over a field near a spot where he was hitch-hiking. The sighting was corroborated by police patrolman Eugene Bertrand, who accompanied Muscarello back to the scene of the incident. They watched together as the lights continued to move around the sky. Another patrolman, David Hunt, was called to the area and also witnessed the phenomenon.

The sightings came to the attention of journalist John G. Fuller, who first wrote about them in an article for the *Saturday Review* and then published a bestselling book on the subject entitled *Incident at Exeter*. Unfortunately, Fuller's role in the development of ufology has not always been a satisfactory one, as a careful study of *The Interrupted Journey*, his book on the Betty and Barney Hill case, has shown. Similar problems arose with this case. To quote Danish researcher Kim Moller Hansen: 'The great number of observations reported by Fuller in "Incident at Exeter" are impressive at first sight, but closer reading reveals their unsatisfactory nature.'[25] Other more sceptical researchers have explained away many of the sightings as planets and mass hysteria. Probably all played their part in such a UFO wave, but equally probably, there had to be some source cases that started the ball rolling.

One man thought he had worked out the answer. Aviation journalist Philip Klass took exception to Fuller's *Incident at Exeter* deciding that the sightings reported in the book were almost certainly natural energy emission caused by power lines. The actual identification of the sightings at Exeter is probably now less important than the effect they had as a result of bringing Klass into the field. Klass's role in ufology by the end of this decade had barely been defined, but in later years he would play a challenging role in the UFO scene in the USA. He describes himself as 'the skunk at the garden party' and since 1966 he has

endeavoured to prove that UFOs are not what their most ardent advocates would have the public believe they are. Klass always makes himself prominent at UFO conferences and apparently enjoys his role as the villain of the piece: 'The louder they bellow, the better a job I guess I am doing,' he says. It was interesting to see the reaction of 'committed UFO believers' at a conference of the US group Mutual UFO Network (MUFON) in Florida in 1990, when John Spencer first met Philip Klass, in the corridor outside the main convention hall. They were chatting about the subject generally and the various approaches to abduction claims in particular when John was politely interrupted because a leading local UFO representative wanted to have a word

---

Angus Brooks saw a cross-shaped UFO in October 1967 and kept an interest in the subject all his life.

with him. John went over to the person, who, no doubt, saw John as an overseas visitor and potentially naive about American ufology, because he whispered conspiratorially, 'Do you realize who you are speaking to?' When John replied that he knew it was Philip Klass – indeed, that he had sought him out – the local man was perplexed and not a little irritated. 'Well, take care,' he advised. 'Don't get a reputation for being too close to Phil.'

MOIGNE DOWNS

At the end of this decade a case arose on the south coast of England which, we think, has probably not been given the prominence it deserves. The investigation, by the Ministry of Defence, seems to have been somewhat dismissive. Since the sighting took place in an area of high-security defence establishments, this may well have

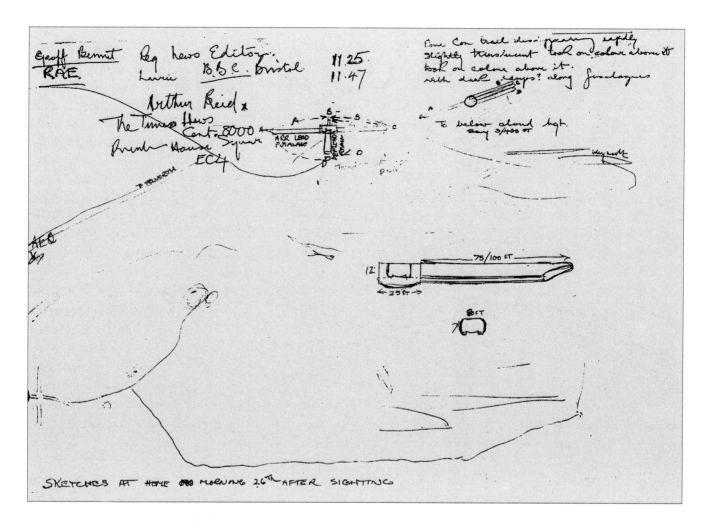

SKETCHES AT HOME MORNING 26TH AFTER SIGHTING

reflected a knowledge that the UFO was 'one of their own'. If so, this must be seen as an early example of cover-up which, if a card somewhat overplayed in ufological circles, is still hard to deny altogether.

The story of Mr J.B.W. (Angus) Brooks was taken up by a UFO magazine called *Flying Saucer Review* in two editions in 1968.[27] *FSR* as it is generally known, was arguably one of the most well-read of such magazines for a time and has been an important influence on the subject. It was first published in spring 1955 and this decade, and possibly the next, were its heyday. It had international connections and collected UFO reports from the widest sources. One name closely associated with the magazine for many years was that of Gordon Creighton, a former intelligence

officer with a devotion to the subject and a working knowledge of many languages, who played a major role.

In the late morning of 26 October 1967, Angus Brooks, a former flight-administration officer then in his fifties, saw a UFO while walking his dog over Moigne Downs in Dorset. 'His' UFO was somewhat unique in structure, though at the time seemed to fit reports being received of 'flying crosses' of lights, seen at night, such as an object which Constables Weycott and Willey had seen and chased for 14 miles between Okehampton and Holsworthy just days before. And on the day before Angus's sighting, a police motorcyclist near Lewes saw a large bright object 'in the shape of a cross'; an object which was also reported by a patrol car just moments later.[28] With

hindsight, perhaps Angus's sighting should also be viewed in the light of Jacques Vallee's contention that many 'shape-shifting' UFOs have been reported over the decades.

During his walk Angus and his dog had sheltered from high winds in a shallow hollow on the hillside. As he lay back he saw an object in the sky approaching him from the Portland direction. As he watched it, it came towards him, decelerated, levelled off and hovered above the ground some 400yds away. He could hear no noise, though the howling wind might have drowned out any usually audible sounds. In flight the object appeared to be of a central saucer-like shape with one 'arm' stretched out ahead and three aerodynamically swept behind, but when it hovered the arms took

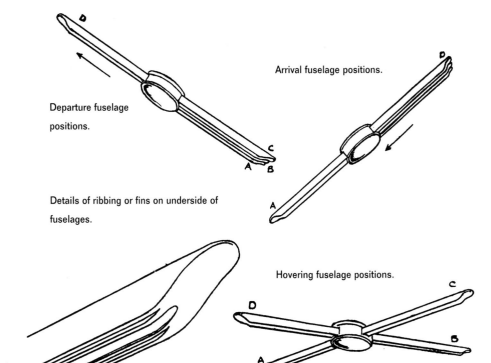

Departure fuselage
positions.

Arrival fuselage positions.

Details of ribbing or fins on underside of
fuselages.

Hovering fuselage positions.

(Opposite) Angus Brooks was meticulous in keeping a record of his sighting. This is his sketch from the file of his own 'case', drawn the morning after the sighting.

(Above) Refined diagrams of the Moigne Downs craft drawn by Angus Brooks. This particularly shows the cross-shape that was so significant; cross-shaped lights having been widely reported by others at that time.

up an equidistant position in relation to each other, forming a cross with the 'saucer' at the centre. He could see no windows or portholes. As Angus watched the object it rotated clockwise but maintained its position, despite the strong winds, above the valley on the downs which runs more or less between the Winfrith Atomic Station and the Portland Underwater Defence Station. The object may have flown across Ringstead Bay which, at the time, according to Angus, was the location of the American Army Aircorp 'Bouncers' Radar Station. Angus later spoke to the base commander, who assured him they had no reports of the object.

The craft seemed to be made of a translucent material. Angus estimated it to be approximately the size of a Comet air-liner, with which he was very familiar. He watched the craft hovering motionless for around twenty minutes before it resumed its original shape and shot away at high speed into the sky beyond Winfrith.

Angus's Alsatian dog, usually quite happy on the downs, was on this occasion distraught and agitated. The following day Angus took his daughter-in-law to the site to show her where he had seen the object and took his Alsatian with him. Again the animal was agitated at the location.

At the time of the sighting Angus was, to quote author Robert Chapman, 'in no doubt that he had seen an alien craft'.[29] He had been concerned enough to consider the possibility of being captured, though he felt at the time his green anorak may have camouflaged him. 'When it first arrived, I was obviously scared. This was something new.'

We met Angus in late 1996 and walked over the downs to the location of his sighting. He is as solid and dependable a witness as you are likely to find. At eighty-three he is fully fit both mentally and physically, and very clear about his sighting. His story, told as we walked, differs not at all from the original report he made nearly thirty years ago. It had not been embroidered over time: a reliable story for sure. He kept a log of his sighting, and a file of the letters he wrote and received about it, with a precision that would be envied by most UFO investigators.[30] By 1996 Angus had formed the opinion that what he had seen may have been a government, terrestrial, device. 'I have come to the conclusion that it wasn't an extraterrestrial craft. There must have been something going on on this planet that could produce this thing. If you had seen Stealth years ago, you would have thought you were crazy [to believe] anything could look like that.' Although the object may well have been military in origin, Angus preferred to talk about it in terms of 'research and development', commenting that it showed no armaments or hostile devices or actions.

Angus reported the incident out of a sense of duty and on the advice of the local vicar. He met three investigators from the Ministry of Defence, Leslie Akhurst, Alec Cassie and Dr John Dickison, to explain his report in detail. They came to the conclusion that what he had probably seen was a 'floater' in his eyeball. Their theory was based on the supposition that Angus had 'dozed off' while lying on the hill and that his dog was agitated only because this was unusual. Angus was quite clear on that point. In a letter to the investigators he wrote: 'The fact that the gale was howling and my Alsatian was painfully clawing me to leave the spot was hardly conducive to "dropping off".'

When we spoke to Angus in 1996 he was very charitable about the ministry's possible intentions, accepting that it was part of their job not to 'frighten old ladies' by seeming to confirm the possibility of something alarming. Nonetheless he remained adamant that what he had seen had been physically in the air and not, to use Chapman's masterful summing up of the account, 'simply in the eye of the beholder'.

In 1965 Lieutenant-Colonel Spaulding of the Department of the Air Force in the US wrote to the Ministry of Defence asking if there was an equivalent to Blue Book in the UK. The reply was: 'Our policy is to play down the subject of UFOs and to avoid attaching undue attention or publicity to it.' It seems as if their analysis of Angus's sighting was part of that 'playing down'.

THE MEN IN BLACK (MIBS)

Fears of government cover-up and conspiracy in these early years probably led to the peaking in the 1960s of 'men-in-black' stories. MIBs almost certainly became associated with the UFO phenomenon after a man named Albert K. Bender wrote to another researcher in 1952 claiming to have worked out a theory to explain UFOs. Bender was subsequently visited by three men, one of them apparently carrying his letter. Their arrival and nature, according to Bender in his book *Flying Saucers and the Three Men* was extraordinary. He was lying down in his bedroom when he became aware of three shadowy figures in the room.

All of them were dressed in black clothes, they looked like clergymen, but wore hats similar to Homburg style. The faces were not discernible, for the hats partly hid and shaded them . . . The eyes of all three

figures suddenly lit up like flashlight bulbs, and all these were focused upon me. They seemed to burn into my very soul as the pains above my eyes became almost unbearable. It was then I sensed that they were conveying a message to me by telepathy.

Bender was threatened: 'If I hear another word from your office, you are in trouble.' Later, he telephoned a friend and mentioned the visit and the discussion. Immediately he hung up the telephone rang. A voice told him that he had made a 'bad slip' and warned him not to make another one.'

In subsequent years many UFO witnesses allegedly received visits from MIBs. This typical story, related by Jim and Coral Lorenzen, founders of APRO, comes from 1967.[31]

Driving one night, Robert Richardson saw a light in the road ahead of him, braked but thought he had hit an object. He found a small lump of metal which he believed had come from whatever it was he had hit. Richardson contacted the Lorenzens and gave APRO the piece of metal. The Lorenzens wrote: 'One of the most interesting aspects of this case was the series of visitors received by Mr Richardson in the days following the incident.' Two unidentified young men visited Richardson's home to talk to him about the incident, and as they left he noticed that they were driving a 1953 Cadillac with, as it turned out, a licence plate number which had not yet been issued. A week later two other men in black suits arrived seeking the fragment he had found. When Richardson told them he had sent the material to APRO and that it could not be recovered, one of the men said: 'If you want your wife to stay as pretty as she is, then you had better get the metal back.' As the Lorenzens point out: 'In view of the fact that the piece of metal was discussed only on the telephone between

Mrs Lorenzen and Mr Richardson, and later in private between Richardson and Paquette [APRO's local investigator], those concerned are wondering how the information got out . . . It would seem that the telephone call from Mrs Lorenzen to Richardson was somehow monitored.' APRO, we now know, had been singled out for surveillance by the CIA's Robertson Panel, as we related in Chapter 1.

Nothing untoward happened, and this is typical of the MIB stories, where much is threatened but action is never taken. It is almost as if the MIBs merely want to draw attention to themselves rather than to actually do anything.

Trying to make some sense of MIB reports forces us to take different pathways. Typically they went around in twos and threes, were well dressed – always in dark suits – and looked like FBI agents. There is a suggestion that they were in fact government agents trying to suppress stories of UFOs, and in a few cases this must be true, given that we now know a good deal more about the CIA's early concerns with those involved in the subject. Another variation is that they were government agents with a different aim: to reinforce belief in aliens.

Some of the MIB phenomenon was almost certainly a projection of fear and paranoia on the part of 'victims'. And we can also be certain that some telephone calls and the occasional personal appearance were simply practical jokes played on people by mischievous or even malevolent locals.

But the most popular theory is that the men in black were themselves alien. Typically they would drive old cars, but ones that were in pristine condition, suggesting somehow that they had been 'created' for a specific purpose. And the men sometimes dressed and acted very strangely, almost highlighting their

non-human qualities. Sometimes they even seemed to exhibit telepathy.

The result of their intervention was often to make the mundane memorable. (Indeed, Bender ended up turning an article into a full-length book with MIBs in the title.) If the MIBs were alien, and if suppression was their goal, then they failed miserably. On the other hand, if they were government agents spreading rumours that UFOs were alien, then they did a very good job indeed. We shall see again later, that governments might well have reasons for wanting their enemies to think they were in possession of alien technology.

THE SCHIRMER ENCOUNTER

Just as the decade was coming to an end a case arose which seemed to indicate that not only was understanding UFOs confusing, but that the intelligence behind UFOs deliberately sought to make it so. The sighting came during a UFO flap in Nebraska at around 2.30 on the morning of 3 December 1967. Police patrolman Herbert Schirmer had been cruising around the town of Ashland with some apprehension, noting agitated dogs and a bull in a corral that was 'really upset'. Since midnight he had the feeling that 'something was wrong'. Driving to the outskirts, he saw a lighted object on Highway 63 which he took to be a broken-down truck. As he approached the vehicle it suddenly took off fast into the sky.

Schirmer drove back to his base to write a report – 'Saw a flying saucer at the junction of Highway 6 and 63. Believe it or not!' – noting the time of the commencement of the event as around 2.30am. He commented: 'I always glanced at my watch before starting on something. Police reports have to be accurate on time.' Representatives of the Condon Committee charged with investigating UFOs (see Chapter 3) visited Schirmer at Ashland. They apparently noted a time discrepancy. It had been three o'clock when Schirmer filed his report, and given the distance from the sighting location to the station, it was estimated that some twenty minutes had been lost to him. 'I was really shook when they found the missing half-hour in my log,' Schirmer said.

A hypnotic-regression session with Dr Leo Sprinkle revealed that during the missing time Schirmer had had contact with beings on board the flying saucer. It appears that Schirmer was 'prevented' from drawing a gun or using his police radio to alert others, and that the aliens approached the police car. During that session some rudimentary detail emerged about where the beings were operating from, that they did not intend harming people, that they took electricity from power lines and their craft operated by working 'against gravity'. The session started as something of a fiasco, which gave Schirmer reason to question the validity of the Condon Committee staff. Schirmer had wanted to meet Professor Condon, having been

assured of his interest in the case and its potential for scientific study. Since Condon was not around when Schirmer arrived, the staff apparently introduced someone else to him as Condon, but Schirmer realized that he was being fooled.

On the basis of their investigation the Condon Committee dropped the case, concluding: 'Evaluation of psychological assessment tests, the lack of any evidence, and interviews with the patrolmen, left project staff members with no confidence that the trooper's reported UFO experience was physically real.'[26] After the research had been completed, Schirmer returned to duty and shortly afterwards was appointed as head of the Police Department, becoming the youngest police chief in the mid-west. But he resigned after only two months – not as a result of any adverse pressure or ridicule, but simply because, as he says, 'I simply was not paying attention to my job. I kept wondering what had really happened that night. My headaches were getting pretty fierce; I was gobbling down aspirin like it was popcorn.

You can't be a good policeman if you have personal problems. So I quit.'

Schirmer was troubled by the possibility that there was still information in his mind which had not yet come out. He contacted UFO investigator and writer Warren Smith, who, at that time, had written magazine articles on UFOs under the pen name Eric Norman. Smith, together with another researcher, Brad Steiger, and hypnotist Loring G. Williams, used regression hypnosis to take Schirmer back to the time of the encounter. During this session much more detail emerged. He was captured and taken aboard the object, and as he was being abducted, one alien grabbed him on the side of his neck below his ear, hurting him. As he was taken out of the police cruiser he was asked, 'Are you the watchman over this place?' The aliens asked him if there was a local power plant, water reservoir and so on.

During a later hypnosis it was revealed that the alien ship 'operated through reversible electromagnetism', and the beings took him on board, where he could

see 'a couple of funny chairs and machines that looked like computers'. They gave him information in considerable detail, for example that this was 'an observation ship with a four-man crew'; that they were preparing us for a showing of themselves; that they were from another galaxy and had bases on Venus and several in and around the United States, including within the Bermuda Triangle. Then they made it clear to Schirmer that he should not remember the things they had told him, and that they would have to impose a cover story on his mind. 'You are to say that the craft landed in the highway and you approached it and it shot up into the air . . . You will tell this and nothing more. You will not speak wisely of this night . . .' Schirmer was then taken back to his car and the crew reboarded the spacecraft, which took off, shooting straight up into the sky.

The aliens themselves were described as being approximately 4½ to 5ft tall and muscular, with larger chests than might be expected of people of their size. Their skin was grey-white and they had large, slanted cat-like eyes. They had very little in the way of lips, but a long, flat, prominent nose. Over the left ear they appeared to have a small radio-like device with a 2in high antenna sticking up from it. While on board the saucer, it seems Schirmer was shown a monitor picture of the outside of the craft, on which he could see guardsmen apparently guarding the entrance to the ship. 'They paced back and forth like regular soldiers on guard duty,' he said.

The aliens indicated that they kidnapped people as part of a 'breeding-analysis' programme. 'I think some people have been picked up and their brains have been changed in some way,' Schirmer explained.

The Schirmer case has been likened to that of Betty and Barney Hill, which had just become well known across the world following the release of John G. Fuller's book.[6] The two abductions bear some comparison: the capture of the 'victim' from a car; the desire by the aliens to suppress the witness's memory (which in both cases failed), and so on. Interestingly, we might note other comparisons, too. Both incidents started as sightings of brightly lit objects; neither witness had conscious recall of an abduction. Both abductions were indicated by missing time – two hours in the case of Betty and Barney Hill and twenty minutes in the case of Schirmer – and both periods of missing time were 'discovered' not by the witnesses, but by the UFO investigators, and in both cases suggested by the investigators to the witnesses.

But if we have no doubts about the reality of the UFO sighting, and some doubts about the reality of the missing time and therefore the more extraordinary components of the cases, we certainly cannot have any about the absurdity of the UFO phenomenon as presented by the Schirmer case in particular. First, the logic of the encounter itself. We would have to assume that for some reason we cannot fathom selected people must be given snippets of information and that these snippets must remain buried, otherwise there is no obvious reason why aliens should take someone aboard a flying saucer and then impress on them that they have to forget what they saw. Secondly, the 'cover story' suggested to Schirmer by the aliens is absurd in itself. Why propose anything to do with a flying saucer, which would immediately begin to put the person on their track?· Better to have suggested to Schirmer that he met some driver in a broken-down car, spent half an hour chatting to him and fixing his

car and sent him on his way. The probability of Schirmer ever discovering that this was not true would be much more remote, since the assumption in his memory would be that because it was a logical scenario it was therefore probably correct, whereas to leave the memory of a UFO encounter invariably leaves question-marks and interest.

But even if we grant that for some unknown reason these are necessary parts of the experience, what about the actual details? The question: 'Are you the watchman over this place?' is a line straight from the cheapest of Hollywood B-movies. Indeed the whole manner of the aliens – stiff, robot-like walking, their strange telepathic communications, their guards marching up and down like robots outside the UFO – are reminiscent of the extraterrestrials from several 1950s sci-fi movies, perhaps most obviously the 'human form' of the two replicated electricians in the film *It Came From Outer Space*. If the aliens had actively wanted to appear plainly absurd they could hardly have done better than to have the little radio over the ear with a 2in antenna sticking up: this is exactly what the robo-men wore in the 1966 children's film *Dr Who and the Daleks*. (And they tended to strut up and down, robot-like, on guard outside their flying saucer as well.) And of course, 1967 had seen the recent release of the first series of *Star Trek*, which contained – guess what – a cold, emotionless alien, Spock, who comes up behind you and knocks you out by pinching you on the neck just below the ear. And he's got strangely upward-slanting eyebrows as well.

So from the Schirmer case onward – and therefore, by implication, also backwards in time – we have a huge question-mark over the UFO phenomenon, and particularly the abduction element. One explanation is that these experiences are

not physically real but self-generated, pulling out the fears and apprehensions of people confronted by mysteries such as strange light-sightings. Perhaps we are drawing from our image bank of science fiction to colour in the details.

On the other hand, perhaps the abductions are physically real, and actually happening, in which case it is far more credible that the information being gleaned by the witnesses themselves and by researchers is the information that the intelligence behind the abduction wishes us to believe, but is not the truth. The implication therefore is that regression hypnosis brings to the surface memories which have been implanted specifically for that purpose. Given the astonishing range of talents attributed to the intelligence behind the UFOs by proponents of the reality of abductions, it would be one arrogance too far to assume that we were getting through their best defences and finding out what they did not want us to discover. Furthermore, the aliens are acting in a way that will make recollection of them not credible, not least by copying our science fiction to make the stories told sound unbelievable.

So we are left with an extremely uncertain view of the abduction phenomenon, whether we believe in it or not. Either it is a mythology and we are falsely trying to read into it an objective reality or it *does* represent an objective reality, but one which the aliens are manipulating through the false perceptions, or selective memories, of the abductees in order to imply an obvious mythology, which in turn diverts attention away from their real purpose.

Clearly the next decade and onwards was going to be a trying time.

1967-1977

The Decade of Endings and Changes

'Necessity is the mother of invention.'

The first two decades of the modern UFO era were decades of beginnings: of postwar reconstruction; of new states, such as Israel, and of new divisions, such as the division of Germany; of the Cold War; of the rise of communism; of the start of the atomic era. They saw the beginning of the space race, of the sixties, and the new age.

This third decade, by contrast, is characterized by endings, and it is in this context that the UFO phenomenon was studied at this time. It saw the end of the space programme, and of the dream it had promised; the end of the excitement of the sixties and of the possibilities of universal love the era had seemed to foretell; the end of trust in governments.

The UFOs in this decade served to dispel the disillusionment surrounding, and causing, these endings. In the heyday of the space programme, the general mood had been one of admiration for science: they could put a man in space. Within just a few years the mood changed: they could put a man in space – so what? The permissive society didn't create happier or more fulfilled people – if anything, it shot away stability and left everyone drifting out of control on an uncharted sea, knocked about by ebb and flow. And when Nixon did for the White House what the Boston Strangler had done for door-to-door salesmen, the effect was not just to make distrust of

government the right and duty of every solid citizen, it was to generate paranoia. For a while Nixon had become known as the only president to lie in state while still alive, but in the aftermath of Watergate uncertainty soon arose. The new view was: 'Surely Nixon was just the one who got caught.'

Before we examine the direct effects of the events of this decade on the UFO phenomenon we must examine one important development within ufology itself which had started at the end of the previous decade, but whose effect became significant at the beginning of this period: the University of Colorado Study of UFOs, and the resultant Condon Report.

THE COLORADO STUDY (CONDON REPORT)
—

It was what was to become known as the 'swamp-gas débâcle' that was the trigger – or the final straw, at least – which forced the US government to take some public, official action in the matter of UFOs. Several 'anomalous lights' had been sighted in Washtenaw County, Michigan in March 1966, and the Air Force's civilian adviser on UFOs, J. Allen Hynek, had investigated the claims and concluded that they were the product of glowing methane deposits: swamp gas. Whether or not he was right, this certainly was not what the public wanted to hear. Many people

believed his statement was not only a cover-up of the truth, but one that failed even to respect their intelligence. Western governments have never been trusted by all their peoples, but as we have discussed, open distrust had hitherto been regarded as the purview of 'radicals' and 'commies'. Following the publication of the Warren Commission report on the assassination of

The Saturn Five/Apollo on display at Kennedy Space Centre (below) was never launched because of a lack of funding. Public interest diminished when the images from the moon landings became repetitive. But for a time the space race represented wondrous science; the Vertical Assembly Building (opposite) was the largest enclosed space on Earth – so vast that clouds formed inside it.

President Kennedy, it became more common, and less radical, to be seen to be criticizing your government, although at that time it was still more a case of 'my government is incompetent' than 'my government keeps big secrets from me', and the swamp gas débâcle became a symbol of that perceived incompetence. The result of the public dissatisfaction was that on 28 March 1966, Congressman (later President) Gerald Ford wrote to L. Mendel Rivers, chairman of the Armed Services Committee: 'In the firm belief that the American public deserves a better explanation than that thus far given by the Air Force, I strongly recommend that there be a committee investigation of the UFO phenomena. I think we owe it to the people to establish credibility regarding UFOs and to produce the greatest possible enlightenment on this subject.' Ford's call was echoed by that of democrat Congressman Weston E. Vivian. As Colorado Study member David Saunders and co-author R. Robert Harkins comment in their book UFOs? Yes!, 'Nothing gets results like the demands of an important congressman's constituency, and when Democrats and Republicans join forces, the Congressional machinery shifts into high gear.'[1]

Hynek himself had only months before suggested the idea of a special investigation panel to the Air Force: 'So far I have come across no convincing evidence that any of these mysterious objects come from outer space or from other worlds. I have recommended to the Air Force that a panel, including sociologists and psychologists, should examine the growth of rumour, possibly the study of some of the people who report the sighting of U.F.O.s would be more rewarding than the investigation of what they saw.'[2]

As it happened there had also already been secret discussions in an ad-hoc committee of the prestigious Scientific Advisory Body, involving optical physicist Brian O'Brien and astronomer Carl Sagan. They

had concluded that top universities might like to offer expert teams to study UFO claims. They also recommended that the Blue Book files be declassified and made available for such research. Ford took that up, and announced his support for the recommendations on 21 April, but the result was not quite what they had intended.

The aim had been that one university would be given a grant to take on a study project, but it seemed for a while that no one wanted to touch UFOs with an intergalactic barge pole. For many universities the subject was 'unclean': the Massachusetts Institute of Technology, for example, flatly turned it down. When the 'opportunity' was put to the University of Colorado, their administrator, Robert Low, accepted the idea but then found himself involved in an uphill struggle to convince the university heads to go with it.

The way in which he convinced them was an alarming portent of the study that was to follow. On 9 August 1966 he described the project in an internal memorandum: 'The trick would be, I think, to describe the project so that to the public, it would appear a totally objective study but, to the scientific community, it would present the image of a group of non-believers trying their best to be objective, but having an almost zero expectation of finding a saucer.' Perhaps they were also encouraged by the $313,000 contract price on offer for the work, for universities the world over have almost permanent funding problems. The final cost was in fact $525,000. This 'price' on UFOs was later put into chilling perspective by the project head, Dr Edward Uhler Condon, when he said: 'It's less than we spend to kill one Viet Cong, and we go in for that by the thousands.'

The contract for the study was signed with the University of Colorado on 6 October 1966. Low would be the project administrator, and the project head would be Dr Condon, a leading nuclear physicist, who

said of himself: 'I raise a little hell when I run things.'

Thus UFOs suddenly became respectable – or at least, relatively so. The highly prestigious journal Science, the organ of the American Association for the Advancement of Science, now published a letter from J. Allen Hynek which it had previously rejected. In it he wrote: 'There is a tendency in 20th-century science to forget that there will be a 21st-century science, and indeed, a 30th-century science, from which vantage points our knowledge of the universe may appear quite different.'

Not that this respectability extended to the views of the 'believers' in the subject. There was a widespread view within scientific circles that the advantage of the Colorado study would be that it would do to death 'this nonsense of UFOs once and for all'. The most accurate forewarning, however, came from an editorial in the Statesman in Salem, Oregon, which, ironically, likened the study to the Warren Commission, which had undoubtedly brought about in part the public's willingness to shout loudly in the first place. 'The investigation begins with the best possible credentials. As with the Warren report, however, even the best of credentials do not assure acceptance of conclusions.'

Science and UFOs have never made easy bedfellows, and in the context of the climate of 1966 their relationship was particularly uneasy. The space programme was well underway, and in the latter half of the year the final long-duration flights of the Gemini programme were in progress. Astronaut Jim Lovell and his co-author Jeffrey Kluger comment in their book Lost Moon (later republished as Apollo 13) of the high-tech, computerized mission-control room: 'During the sixties there was no greater place for a scientist to work, no facility that more completely represented the heart, the soul, the very forebrain of the

Jacques Vallee (centre – pictured with researchers Bob Digby and Hilary Evans) has been one of the leading researchers to propose alternatives to ETH. He was the model for the character of Lancome in *Close Encounters of the Third Kind.*

scientific world than this big, foreboding, thrilling room.'[3] In other words, science in those days was hardware; science was technology. Science did not like having to deal with sociological concepts (as many of the Condon Committee believed UFOs either to be, or at least to encompass) or having to prove or disprove the 'hardware' attributes of objects many believed were misperceptions or atmospheric phenomena. So the exploration of UFOs by the scientific establishment at this time was a major breakthrough.

To begin with, the committee interviewed a few key players in the UFO business. They took statements from J. Allen Hynek, Jacques Vallee (they had wanted Vallee to join them, but his public interest in the subject, and published views on UFOs, effectively excluded him); from Major Hector Quintanilla, the head of Blue Book; from Donald Keyhoe and Richard Hall of NICAP, and later from Jim and Coral Lorenzen of APRO and physicist Dr James E. McDonald.

The committee got down to its basic work: reviewing the reports available. They set up a network they called the Early-Warning Network: people around the country who would flag up local UFO reports in the media and alert the study team, thereby ensuring that investigators got to incidents quickly. It is a system that is still used by most civilian UFO research organizations. Their approach, however, was still somewhat haphazard. They reviewed only a limited number of cases, and their selection was dubious at best. But the credibility of the whole study was severely, and permanently, dented within months when a report was published on an address Condon gave in New York on 25 January 1967. Speaking to a packed audience from two local science societies, the American Chemical Society and the Glass Works Chapter, Condon stated: 'It is my inclination right now to recommend that the government get out of this business. My attitude right now is that there's nothing to it. But I'm not supposed to reach a conclusion for another year.'

There is little doubt that Condon's negative attitude affected the direction of the Colorado Study Project. Project member David Saunders comments: 'I could not have objected if Condon and Low merely held private views that would have made them unusually difficult to convince – among any balanced group of scientists, such views

ought to be represented. But I did object to the idea that such views were determining policy for the Project in such a way that they reduced the ability of the Project to do its job.' Then Saunders and colleague Norman Levine discovered the 'trick' memorandum written by Low in the files, and morale hit an all-time low. Why a scientist of Condon's reputation should have been so willing to act as a government patsy is uncertain, but it is known that he was investigated during the communist witch-hunts of the 1940s and 1950s, and researcher Raymond Fowler alleges that, 'Dr Condon helped the government put the kiss of death on civilian interest in UFOs in exchange for his past record being cleared from national security problems he had incurred with the House un-American Activities Committee during the McCarthy and Nixon witchhunts that had begun in 1947.'

On 9 February 1968 Saunders and Levine were fired from the project, allegedly for incompetence. Saunders took his revenge in the media. He pre-empted the publication of the Condon report with a book of his own: *UFOs? Yes! Where The Condon Committee went wrong.*[1] Saunders and Levine also gave the 'trick' memorandum to journalist and prominent UFO writer John Fuller, who published it in a scathing article which gained it nationwide publicity. Morale finally crashed, team members left, and the work effectively came to an end.

The resignation comments of Mary Louise Armstrong, Condon's administrative assistant, bear consideration. 'Bob's [Low] attitude from the beginning has been one of negativism . . . Very little time has been spent on reviewing the data on which he might base his conclusions . . . I think there is a fairly good consensus among the team members that there is enough data in the UFO question to warrant further study . . . it seems as if he is trying hard to say as little as possible in the final report, but to say it in the most negative way possible.'

Condon prepared his final report, which was approved by the Air Force for publication on 31 October 1968 and by the National Academy of Sciences on 15 November. The report was actually published on 9 January 1969. The National Academy of Science reviewed the report 'immediately after the review became available'.[4] Their panel included representatives from Yale University, the University of Michigan, Rockefeller University, Stanford University and the University of California. They accepted the findings of the study. The review concluded: 'In our opinion the scope of the study was adequate to its purpose: a scientific study of UFO phenomena,' and observed: 'The methodology and approach were well-chosen, in accordance with accepted standards of scientific investigation'. The panel agreed that there was no evidence that the subject was shrouded in 'official secrecy'; that no UFOs had offered evidence of being a defence or national-security hazard; that there was no need for a special investigative agency to be set up; that nothing from the study had contributed to science. They conceded that there might be some value in a study of atmospheric optics, and that UFO reports and beliefs might be of interest to 'the social scientist and the communications specialist'. The review ended by stating: 'On the basis of present knowledge the least likely explanation of UFOs is the hypothesis of extraterrestrial visitations by intelligent beings.'

The Air Force summarized their position based on the report. 'The report concluded that little if anything had come from the study of UFOs in the past 21 years that had added to scientific knowledge.' They were clearly getting ready to shut down Project Blue Book. Indeed, we received, from the British Ministry of Defence, a copy of a preliminary report of Blue Book which makes clear its views to that point, which were very much in line with its eventual final conclusions.[5] It was dated 1 February 1966. Project Blue Book was cancelled on 17 December 1969.

So the US government and the Air Force were, ostensibly, out of the UFO business. Donald Keyhoe of NICAP commented on the release of the Condon report: 'We are publicly challenging the attempt to dismiss UFOs. Dr Condon started off as a non-believer and made his findings fit his beliefs.' That is evident when one reads the report in full. The conclusions are presented first, but the data that should support the conclusion does anything but, and leaves many, perhaps a third, of the interesting cases dangling tantalizingly.

If anyone believed at the start that the Colorado Study would put an end to interest in UFOs, they were hopelessly wrong. It damaged public interest in UFOs for a number of years, it is true, but in the end it served only to encourage the interested groups to consolidate and re-examine their own procedures and data. And it fixed interest within those groups on the possibility that incompetence alone did not explain the government and the Air Force's apparent lack of interest in the subject. Conspiracy theory was therefore given a longer-term shot in the arm by the report. By the time Watergate was exposed, it was distrust – even fear – of government that had become the driving motivation for UFO researchers to question officialdom.

For the moment, however, interest in UFOs certainly waned. As Stanton Friedman and Don Berliner indicate: 'The major private organisation – NICAP – rapidly lost its mass appeal, its funding which came almost entirely from membership fees, and its ability to pressure the government . . . For several years so little was heard about UFOs that it was as if they had never existed in the first place.'[6] Their observation is totally correct, but sometimes even a manipulative government is helped by synchronicity. It can hardly be a coincidence that this lull in interest also coincided with the period of moonwalking from 1969 to 1972. Throughout that time the focus on 'outer space' which UFOs had seemed to provide was being presented in physical reality by the Apollo programme, and all media attention was concentrated on that.

But by 1972, even previous advocates of the Apollo programme were becoming bored by the repetitive images coming back from the Moon. When man last left the Moon that year, the search for a new dream resurfaced, and 1973 became a hot time for UFOs, particularly in America. If officialdom had sought to rid itself of the UFO problem, it was about to find out that it had failed miserably. On 28 November 1973, a Gallup survey indicated that 51 per cent of Americans believed UFOs were real, a 5 per cent rise over the Gallup poll of the mid-1960s. And in that later poll, 15 million Americans were held to have seen a UFO.

USSR

As we have seen, the UFO as a modern, media-influenced phenomenon, was born in America and flourished in the West. It touched the military, technological USA and the mystical, historic UK. But we have also shown that it is a global phenomenon, that reports have been received from all around the world. That those reports have been examined through 'Western eyes' has meant that the interpretation we have put on them has reflected our own cultural values, social viewpoints and political situations. However, if we look at a land mass the size of the former Soviet Union, we realise that if UFOs are a real phenomenon then they should be widely reported there too, and so they are. It was in this decade that the Soviet Union entered the fray.

The value of studying the birth of the modern UFO in the context of the rich variations of cultures within the Soviet Union has unfortunately been lost for ever because UFOs, as a modern, identified, separate phenomenon, came to the fore in exactly the same conditions in the USSR as they did in the USA – that is, in the aftermath of the Second World War, during the specific conditions of the Cold War, against a backdrop of space exploration and through military and political channels. In short it was, sadly, America all over again. And indeed, comparisons between cases in the USA and the USSR show them to be remarkably similar, more so even than, say, those in the USA and the UK.

The Soviet Union has a history of 'things seen in the sky' which dates back into earlier centuries – for example, a sighting of three lights in formation which tracked their way through a ravine and suddenly disappeared, reported from St Petersburg in July 1880. But, as we were later to discover, it was in 1946 – more or less the same time as the birth of the modern era in the USA that a great deal of official, military and governmental attention was paid to these 'things in the sky'. There seems to have been no Soviet Kenneth Arnold to give the phenomenon a name for public consumption, but that hardly mattered since the Soviet Union's officials had no intention of making the studies public and the media in Stalin's Russia had no way of 'outing' the subject. What is important is that the birth coincided with the same postwar and Cold War paranoia as it did in the USA. Timothy Good demonstrates that in 1952 the GRU (Glavnoye Razvedyvatelnoye Upravleniye)

the Russian equivalent of the CIA, requested an examination of UFOs to discover if they were:

a) Secret vehicles of foreign powers which are penetrating Soviet airspace
b) Misinformative activity by imperialistic secret services
c) Manned or unmanned extraterrestrial probes engaged in the investigation of Earth, or
d) An unknown natural phenomenon.[7]

Ion Hobana and Julien Weverbergh comment:

The fact that Russia kept quiet about UFOs until the 1960s has its reasons. First of all the Russian authorities just after the Second World War (the Cold War period) felt that UFO reports whether from abroad or originating at home had to be linked with psychological warfare tactics since these 'mysterious' and excited accounts were looked upon as likely to have the sole purpose of creating unrest and fear amongst the people. The second cause – an extension of the first – is that the Russian authorities, just like their colleagues in the West, did not know what to do apart from debunking all such accounts or hushing them up. [After the Cold War] . . . the Soviet authorities found that the UFO was as big a problem (in the West) as it was to them.[8]

The thawing of the Cold War brought about many exchanges of ideas between West and East. Computer scientist Jacques Vallee addressed a world congress of mathematicians in Moscow in 1966 on the subject of UFOs, encouraging a professor of higher mathematics and astronomy at the Moscow Aeronautical Institute to make details of UFOs in Russia more accessible and public. That professor was Dr Felix Yurevich Zigel, without doubt the most influential figure in the development of UFO analysis in Russia and one of the most

important figures in releasing that information to the wider world.

The Russians are a people who do not like to risk looking foolish, and even in the midst of their highly successful space programme which, at the time, was whipping the Americans at every turn, they rarely announced anything until it had already been achieved. However, three things conspired to encourage them to 'come out' on the question of UFOs.

The first was a high level of UFO activity across Russia and several Eastern Bloc countries in late 1966, though this alone would not have encouraged them to go public – after all, it had happened before. The second factor was that, on 8 April 1960 at the National Radio Astronomy Observatory at Green Bank, West Virginia, Frank Drake fired the opening shots of Project Ozma, the first attempt to search for extraterrestrial intelligence by scanning the heavens for intelligent radio transmissions. It was assumed that either advanced cultures might be broadcasting a 'hello' signal, or at least that transmissions 'leaking' from a technological culture would be recognizable as such. After 150 hours of searching Ozma found nothing conclusive, although two bursts of pulses were a source of controversy. But the project had a high public profile, coming as it did in the midst of the space race and the daring exploits of astronauts and cosmonauts alike, when the mood of the moment was definitely towards the skies. Not to be outdone, the Soviets quietly undertook their own searches. The Americans later called their radio examination of the stars SETI – the Search for Extraterrestrial Intelligence. The Russians, more optimistically, named theirs CETI – Communication with Extraterrestrial Intelligence.

On 12 April 1965, Tass, the official Soviet news agency, announced that CETI had had a success, and indeed it seemed that they had hooked a big one. Astronomer Gennady Sholomitsky at Sternberg Astronomical Institute had discovered what was believed to be an intelligent source of radio transmission from a distant point in the Andromeda galaxy. CTA–102, as it was designated, was believed to be a 'super-civilization', according to the usually taciturn Tass. 'We are not alone . . .' the news agency announced. It appeared, therefore, to Western eyes, that the Russians had whipped the Americans yet again: their cosmonauts could beat the pants off American astronauts, and now their radio telescopes had been blessed with the first radio contact with another race.

The slightly negative after-effects of this announcement may, ironically, themselves have played a part in the 'outing' of UFOs in Russia. For the announcement turned out to have been a little reckless: the next morning several astronomers, including Sholomitsky, admitted that this extreme conclusion was 'premature'. Within the year the rhythms they had believed to be the product of intelligence were identified as the natural 'beat' of a quasar. So they were embarrassed, but so what? The world laughed for a day and then forgot about it. Some new crisis, the love-life of an actress or a new political scandal, would soon come along and take the limelight. Perhaps the Russians learned that looking foolish once in a while didn't hurt that much.

The third influence was the recognition of the serious stance being taken by the USA on UFOs through the seemingly impressive Condon Study (little did the Russians know!). Here was another opportunity to beat the pants off the Americans, and, again, in an arena that looked as if it might have something to do with outer space.

These three factors combined to create a climate in which, to some scientists, the examination of the UFO phenomenon seemed to be a respectable use of time. It

culminated in a red-letter day for Russian ufology: 18 October 1967. On that day 400 people attended a meeting of the Cosmonaut Committee. The president of the committee was Major-General Porfiri Stoljarov, and the vice-president Dr Zigel. On 10 November the two officials each took a deep breath and opened up on Russian TV – and to the world – showing drawings and photographs of UFOs. They explained that the role of the Stoljarov Committee was to expose pseudoscientific interpretations of a genuine and unexplained phenomenon. 'Unidentified flying objects are a very serious subject which we must study fully. We appeal to all viewers to send us details of any observations of strange flying craft seen over the territories of the Soviet Union. This is a serious challenge to science, and we need the help of all Soviet citizens. Please write to us at the following address in Moscow . . .' Within days they had over 200 reports of sightings.

An announcement was made on the world news that the Russians had formed an organization, like the Condon Committee, to study UFOs.

It was a huge breakthrough. Bear in mind that there were no civilian groups like NICAP or APRO in the Soviet Union. As Hobana and Weverbergh put it: 'Although ufology is not entirely taboo in that country, people have to proceed very carefully if they wish to pursue it. The influence of important "anti-UFO" scholars is considerably greater than it is in the U.S.A. today, and the attacks made there by the scientific establishment on those who study UFOs are fiercer and more spiteful.'[8]

The New York Times bannered: 'A SOVIET ASTRONOMER SUGGESTS WORLD STUDY OF FLYING SAUCERS', and sub-titled their report, in a reference to the Condon Study, 'Soviet U.F.O. Plan Has Familiar Ring'.[9] Most critically for the fallout that was to follow, the newspaper claimed that the study was

'off-icial'. The more conservative scientists in the Soviet Union were horrified. The New York Times! The Soviet Academy for Sciences took fright. If certain scientists had felt that the CETI fiasco showed that looking foolish wasn't the end of the world, the more conservative elements were of the completely opposite view. And the conservatives had the floor in the Soviet Union, even more so than in the West. Soviet science had dipped its toe in the water, but it looked as if this time it was not being nibbled by the minnow of the CETI announcement but grabbed by the great white shark.

The academy retreated. The Stoljarov Committee, it protested, was not at all official – it was just a group of scientists working in their spare time. The only government approval was that which had, in that country, to be given to any association for any purpose. This is blatantly absurd, of course, as anyone with a knowledge of the former Soviet Union would see immediately: top scientists do not get whole programmes on television like the one Stoljarov and Zigel had aired without official blessing. But denying the facts after the event was a common feature of the Soviet Union in those days, and this matter was no exception. One Dr L.A. Artsimovitch went on the rampage. At a meeting of the Bureau of General Physics and Astrophysics section of the Academy for Sciences, he accused the scientists of making Russians look foolish to the world. It is said he waved a copy – that copy – of the New York Times in their faces. Shortly afterwards the secretary of the National Committee of Soviet Physicists, Vladimir Lechkoutsov, stated in interview with The West that there was no Russian UFO organization.

The Stoljarov Committee was dead in the water. On 27 February 1968, Pravda published the official line: not one single object had ever been seen over Russia which could not be identified. People who reported such things were mistaken, or lying. They wheeled out American sceptic Donald Menzel to confirm his belief that even if there were other civilizations in the universe, UFOs were not a manifestation of them. By the time the Americans announced the negative outcome of the Condon Study and closed down Project Blue Book, Russian officials were also ready to bury ufology deep in its grave.

But what was learned during this brief glimpse behind the Iron Curtain was interesting in a worldwide context. As we have said, the characteristics of the Russian phenomenon largely matched those of the West, a fact that was highly suggestive of a genuine, global, phenomenon, whatever its true origin. And these comparisons were across the UFO spectrum. Dr Zigel, vice-president of the Stoljarov Committee, had explained in the magazine *Smena* in April 1967 that UFOs seen by Russian pilots were comparable to those seen by their Western counterparts. At an earlier conference it had been revealed that Soviet cosmonauts had reported seeing UFOs while in space. In the USA, the Condon report's clearest chapter is the one which describes the sightings by American astronauts during their own missions. Mention was made of the study of fragments of UFOs, in a context suggestive of small pieces of metal akin to the Ubatuba recovery (small fragments of magnesium recovered following the airborne explosion of an object over a lake in Ubatuba, Brazil). Russian landing and entity reports were few, but they did exist. The official response to such cases in Kazakhstan and Uzbekistan was to wheel out Dr L.A. Artsimovitch to explain that the reports had been stirred up by the American press for the purpose of propaganda and, by implication, destabilization.

Zigel was forbidden to continue his associations with the West. He kept his own records and maintained his own interest, but

it would be many years before he was able to officially communicate with his Western colleagues again. He died in December 1988. During the years of isolation he allegedly amassed 50,000 reports, including sufficient detail on which to base his belief on entities associated with UFOs. He seems to have managed to steer a delicate course through totalitarian Russia's censorship: many of his comments indicate a belief in the extraterrestrial hypothesis, not least his classification of entities, but when pushed to a statement he always kept all options open. His statement that 'not one of the existing hypotheses can boast of authoritatively clearing up the UFO problem' was typical. He even made a few comments that the ETH was fantasy and speculation and still managed to keep the debate going. Many of his most private views were circulated in small reprints of articles (ten at most, usually) distributed only to trusted colleagues, some of which have since found a place in Western archives.

The Apollo programme that placed men on the moon took UFOs off the public interest map for the three years of the landings. But combined with other factors, they brought 'ancient astronaut' beliefs to the fore.

It would be 1979 before the Russians would feel safe enough to dip their toes back into these murky waters again, at least publicly.

With tongue in cheek we note one positive outcome in Soviet ufology: UFOs were the subject of the only joke ever known to have been uttered by Soviet foreign minister Andrei Gromyko. 'Some people say these objects are due to the excessive consumption in the United States of Scotch whisky,' he quipped. 'I say that is not so. They are due to the activities of a Soviet athlete, a discus-thrower, in eastern Siberia, practising for the Olympic Games and quite unconscious of his strength.'[10]

THREE POWERFUL INFLUENCES COME TOGETHER

The almost constant interest in UFOs since their identification as an individual phenomenon in 1947 has ensured that when actual UFO reports dry up or public interest is diminished, other forms of research and lateral examination of UFOs and related phenomena tend to take over. In 1968–69 a triple coincidence occurred which gave

UFO enthusiasts in the West an incredible shot in the arm during a time of lack of interest in 'conventional' ufology.

The most prominent event of those years, and on its own one which might well have diminished interest in UFOs, was the Apollo Moon-landing programme. At 3.30pm eastern daylight time on 23 December 1968, the astronauts of Apollo 8 – Frank Borman, James Lovell and William Anders – were the first to cross a great divide. At that moment they passed the 'equigravisphere', the point at which the Earth's gravitational force gives way to the Moon's gravitational force, on their journey to orbit the Moon. They thus became the first people to truly leave Earth. Their successful mission paved the way for the first Moon landing and had many memorable moments, probably the most lasting being the view of the Earth rising over the lunar horizon. The Apollo programme moved on apace. In March 1969, Apollo 9 was launched into Earth orbit to test the lunar module; in May Apollo 10 performed a dress rehearsal for the lunar landing with the lunar

---

Erich von Däniken, whose books sold in their millions, promoted the idea that Earth had been visited in ancient times by extraterrestrials.

module separating from the command module in orbit around the Moon, and flying to within 47,000ft of the Moon's surface. Finally, in July 1969, Neil Armstrong and Edwin 'Buzz' Aldrin first set foot upon the Moon. It has been estimated that one-sixth of the world's population watched the Apollo 11 mission live on television.[11,12]

Although a trip from the Earth to the Moon is barely a flea hop in astronomical terms, the perception from Earth was that man had now ventured out into the cosmos and travelled among the stars. This was the stepping stone to a real life *Star Trek*. And, significantly, as we shall see, the focus was the Moon.

The second of the three events started life in 1966, when the manager of the Hotel Rosenhügel in Davos, Switzerland, was staying up most nights until 4am writing a book called *Erinnerungen an die Zukunft* (Memories of the Future). In March 1968, 6,000 copies of the book were published, Swiss newspaper serializations began and the work gathered a considerable following across Switzerland and Germany. By December it was the number one bestselling book in West Germany. It was first published in England in 1969, and in

America in 1970 under its now familiar title *Chariots of the Gods?*[13] and Erich von Däniken became a household name across the world. His book struck a chord with the mood of the time. Von Däniken was to become a prolific author promoting his central question: was God an astronaut?

In England and America the revolution that would historically be viewed as the sixties had transformed youth culture, and there was a driving search for some new meaning to life – indeed, Von Däniken's early writing may well have been inspired by the 1966 'God is Dead' movement. Ironically, it might also have been inspired by the book *Intelligent Life in the Universe* by astronomers Carl Sagan and I.S. Shklovskii, which considered the possibility that ancient extraterrestrial visitation may have affected the development of the human race. However, this was a 'mind game' and not an attempt at archaeological examination, as Von Däniken's book was. Although Von Däniken is widely credited with these theories, they had in fact previously been examined by several authors and quite widely published.* The difference was the timing: Von Däniken published his ideas at the precise moment when the world was looking for some new theory.

Briefly, what Von Däniken was suggesting was that in ancient times extraterrestrials had visited the Earth and had intervened in the development of mankind genetically, spiritually and socially. In various books he gives differing reasons: deliberate intervention, astronauts stranded on Earth by accident and so on. He proposes that the actions of these technological giants were construed by our primitive ancestors as being 'godlike', and that many of our beliefs about ancient history come from misinterpretation of technology. So, for example, an Old Testament story such as the destruction of Sodom and Gomorrah by God becomes a destructive atomic blast by astronauts who

were perceived as gods. Von Däniken uses as his physical evidence archaeology, arguing, for example, that the pyramids could not have been created by the technologies available to people of the time. Indeed, he goes all around the world interpreting archaeological structures, cave paintings, statues and the stories of various religions' holy books and scriptures, seeing in them proof of ancient astronaut visitations.

Von Däniken's theories therefore provided a new mythology in the sixties for those seeking new 'gods'. This way, we could have our gods back again and still believe them to be physically real because they were technological.

For UFO enthusiasts, here was a whole new branch of research and inquiry, for Von Däniken's theories suggested that UFOs did not start in 1947, or even a few years earlier, but had in fact been visiting the Earth throughout history and prehistory. Many UFO enthusiasts, lacking current UFO reports and bemused by the lack of governmental and press interest, took up the threads of the ancient astronaut ideas.

Although the subject is perhaps slightly tangential to the purpose of this book it is worth recording that subsequent analysis of Von Däniken's work has shown it to be considerably unreliable. Ronald Story referred to ancient-astronaut theorizing as 'shabby pseudoscience' and pinpointed fallacies in Von Däniken's research.[14] In particular his book re-examines the claims of the Piri Re'is map, the Nazca Plains,

Ancient astronaut theories were given a boost when the film *2001 – A Space Odyssey* seemed to bridge the images from the Apollo programme and the books of Erich Von Daniken. Extraterrestrial visitation in Earth's ancient past became a popular theme.

Easter Island, the carvings at Pelenque, and the pyramids. Colin Wilson comments:

In a later book, Gold of the Gods,[15] he [Von Däniken] indulges in actual deceit. He describes in detail how he descended into a vast underground cave system in Ecuador and examined an ancient library of strange metal leaves engraved with unknown characters. Later exploration of the caves revealed no such library, and when his companion

---

*They had been promoted by, among others, Louis Pauwels and Jacques Bergier in *The Morning of the Magicians* (1960), Robert Sharroux in *100,000 Years of Man's Unknown History* (early 1960s), Yusuke J. Matsumura in Volume 2 Numbers 1–4 of *Brothers* – the *Worldwide Unique Magazine for Flying Saucer and Space People* (1964) and *Northern Neighbours*, a Canadian magazine, in an

article called 'Did the Gods and Prophets come to Earth from Space?' (April 1962). Other writers on the theme that predated Von Däniken have included Posnasky and Kiess; Epstein; Alexander Kazantsev, a Russian astronomer, in *Australian Flying Saucer Review*, Volume 1 Number 3, in an article entitled 'Did ancients meet spacemen?'; Professor Agrest, a Russian, in *Australian Flying*

Saucer Review, Volume 4 Number 1 (February 1961, interviewed by Galkin and Chernin); British author Brinsley Le Poer Trench; Brad Steiger, in *Strangers from the Skies* (1966); W. Raymond Drake; Paul Misraki; Dr Viatcheslaw Zaitsev; George Hunt Williamson in *Secret Places of the Lion* in 1958.

revealed that he had not even ventured underground, he himself admitted that this was true, but explained that the writers of books like Gold of the Gods 'are permitted to embroider their facts' . . . The result of all this is that he [Von Däniken] has now been totally discredited, and that the 'ancient astronaut' theory associated with his name has few serious supporters.[16]

It may be that rejecting Von Däniken completely because of his errors in his writings is throwing out the baby with the bathwater, and that some aspects of the theory, the possibility of ancient extraterrestrial visitation, may have some validity. Nonetheless it seems highly unlikely that Von Däniken's theories and the lunar landing programme would have been associated with each other in any broad public perception on their own merits had it not been for the third event, which bridged the apparent gulf between ancient astronauts and modern astronauts. This boost for ufology was offered by none other than the science-fiction writer Arthur C. Clarke, who, ironically, is no advocate of UFOs. The year 1968 saw first the publication of the book[17] and then the release of the film *2001 – A Space Odyssey*, to huge public attention and acclaim. Both works, of course, unashamedly latched on to the mood of the Apollo space programme and featured astronauts living and working on the Moon as the starting point of its odyssey of exploration.

But the theme of *2001* was of ancient astronaut visitation. Not the visitation of humanoids as depicted by Von Däniken, agreed, but nonetheless the visitation to Earth 3 million years ago of extraterrestrials, embodied by the monolith, which promoted the creation of the human race from primitive animals then living on the planet (an idea very much akin to the Von Däniken theory). In the film, the discovery of this history was made by the archaeological excavation of an extraterrestrial device

buried on the Moon. So here, too, we have the link between extraterrestrial visitation and archaeology. And what's more, archaeology on the Moon, the very place where American astronauts were venturing when Von Däniken's book was published in England and America.

There is little doubt that it is the three strands coming together which promoted the ancient astronaut theory so strongly, and which gave UFOs a temporary lease of life during a time when interest in conventional UFO research was on the wane.

THE ASTRONAUTS' SIGHTINGS

The importance of sightings by astronauts, to UFO researchers has been significant, perhaps especially so in recent years. Just as in Chapter 1 we noted that UFO proponents wanted to 'claim' Carl Jung for themselves, so, similarly in this decade – and indeed up to the present day – there is a desire to claim the astronauts to support UFO theories, in particular the extraterrestrial hypothesis. So much has been written on this matter that a review of the prevalent beliefs about just what astronauts did, or did not, see during their space missions is in order. Despite the claims and the hype, the truth is that there seems to be very little to suggest that our astronauts have any great or secret knowledge or experience of UFOs.

However, NASA's public figures have been thought-provoking at times. 'I've been convinced for a long time that the flying saucers are real and interplanetary. In other words we are being watched by beings from outer space.' So stated Albert M. Chop, deputy public relations director for NASA and a former USAF spokesman for Blue Book. And Maurice Chatelain, former chief of NASA communications, has written: 'All Apollo and Gemini flights were followed, both at a distance and sometimes

also quite closely, by space vehicles of extraterrestrial origin . . .'[18]

And astronauts have had UFO sightings of course; in the strictest and proper sense of the term, they were unidentified. For example, Tim Good mentions objects seen during the test flights of the X–15 'rocket plane' by Joseph Walker and Robert White,[7] for which a possible explanation suggested by one analysis was ice flaking off the aircraft. Good also refers to radar technicians at Cape Kennedy tracking a UFO 'in pursuit' of an unmanned Gemini spacecraft, which remained unidentified. The late 'Deke' Slayton, one of the original astronauts chosen for the Mercury programme (but who eventually flew much later), pursued a disc-shaped object in 1951 while flying over St Paul, Minnesota, but lost it. However, he confided in a letter to J. Allen Hynek that he attached 'no great importance to it'.

Scott Carpenter was rumoured to have photographed a UFO during his 1962 Mercury flight, but the object he pictured is widely considered to have been a tracking balloon jettisoned from his own capsule. Tim Good, a friend of Carpenter's, pursued the point, but, as he relates, he was soundly rebuked by Carpenter, who complained of 'your continuing implication that I am lying and/or withholding truths'.[7]

During the flight of Gemini 4 in 1965, James McDivitt reported a UFO with 'arms sticking out of it', and captured it on film. A photograph reproduced in Frank Edwards' book[19] shows an oval shape with a trail behind it, but no arms. McDivitt states that the picture is not of the object he filmed. From his description the object sounds like a satellite, and indeed, he seems to believe that this is what it was – a secret satellite, perhaps one with defence implications. He denies having seen an 'alien spacecraft'.

During the flight of Gemini 5, Houston asked the astronauts to look out for something they were tracking near the spacecraft, but nothing of an exotic nature features in the transcripts of their communications. Other Gemini flights are associated with 'bogeys' and 'targets', but nothing of a defined or even precisely described nature.

Pete Conrad of Apollo 12 said that if an alien turned up, 'it wouldn't surprise me', but he gave no indication he was speaking about anything of which he had special knowledge.[20]

Maurice Chatelain suggests that the code name for flying saucers used by astronauts was 'Santa Claus'[18] He seems to be justifying, or reading too much into a remark made by Jim Lovell aboard Apollo 8: 'Please be informed that there is a Santa Claus.' Chatelain comments: 'Even though this happened on Christmas Day 1968, many people sensed a hidden meaning in those words.' But Lovell himself says that the 'Santa Claus' phrase was used because they had just tested the rocket burn that would either bring them back safely to Earth, or leave them, in Lovell's words 'permanent satellites of Earth's lunar satellite, expiring from suffocation in about a week . . .'[4] Apollo 8 went behind the Moon, and out of radio contact with Earth, where it would – or would not – success-fully fire its engine. It was when the spaceship re-emerged into radio contact, its engine firing successfully and their lives safe, that Lovell spoke those words. Arthur C. Clarke in his 'author's note' to 2010 – Odyssey Two, reveals: 'The Apollo astronauts had already seen the film (2001) when they left for the Moon. The crew of Apollo 8 . . . told me they had been tempted to radio back the discovery of a large black monolith . . .'[21] Heaven only knows what Chatelain would have made of that if they had!

Inevitably, the first lunar landing flight has attracted massive attention and not just a few rumours. The most popular is that two UFOs hovered nearby as Armstrong stepped down the ladder of the lunar module for the first moon walk. That unidentified lights might have been visible is possible, but whether or not the astronauts were able to identify alien spaceships is only open to speculation. A documentary, SAGA UFO Special, suggested that unnamed radio hams had picked up the following conversation:

Mission Control: What's there? Mission control calling Apollo 11.
Apollo 11: These babies are huge, sir ... enormous . . . Oh, God, you wouldn't believe it! I'm telling you there are other spacecraft out there . . . lined up on the far side of the crater edge . . . they're on the Moon watching us.

Timothy Good relates this story in Above Top Secret,[7] and goes on to say that an unnamed source claimed to have had a conversation with Neil Armstrong in which the astronaut had confirmed this. However, when Good wrote to Armstrong directly, he replied: 'Your "reliable sources" are unreliable. There were no objects reported, found, or seen on Apollo 11 or any other Apollo flight other than of natural origin.' Aldrin makes no reference to any such event in his book Return to Earth,[22] but he does, interestingly, include a cautious note on UFO buffs. Of an unclear L shape the astronauts saw he states: 'It could possibly have been one of the panels of the Saturn third stage which flew off to expose the LM [lunar mo-dule] and cannot be traced from Earth . . . We debated whether or not to tell the ground we had spotted something, and decided against it. Our reason was simple: The UFO people would descend on the message in hordes, setting off another rash of UFO spottings back on earth. We concluded it was most likely one of the panels.' Command-module pilot Michael Collins does not even mention the incident in his own book.[23]

Their wariness of misinterpretation seems reasonable. For some 'UFO people' nothing can happen by accident. When, on the Apollo 12 mission astronauts broke their camera by pointing it straight into the sun and burning it out, UFO enthusiasts believed the crew had been 'censored' because there were 'things' on the moon with them. When Apollo 13 blew up mid-flight, the rumour spread among the UFO community that they had been 'got at' by aliens because they were carrying a nuclear device which the extraterrestrials had wanted to prevent being used on them, or near their bases on the Moon.

One astronaut who has been very vocal about his beliefs is Gordon Cooper, who flew the final Mercury mission. He has denied rumours about a sighting during that mission, and given that elsewhere he has expressed very clear beliefs about UFOs, as we shall see, we should view that denial as reliable. Cooper has been open about an incident in 1951 over Germany, when he saw a group of 'double lenticular-shaped' objects, classic flying saucers, flying in formation. They were, he believed, flying higher and faster than any plane of the day could fly. Several hundred of these were apparently seen by him and other pilots around that time. In an interview for CNI News with Michael Lindemann, Cooper said that he and the other witnesses 'were uniformly convinced they were seeing a technology that wasn't human'. The explanation given to him from 'higher authorities' was that the objects were 'high-flying seed pods'. Cooper didn't believe that, but swallowed his argument. 'I was in the Air Force. I wanted to fly,' he explained.

In an article in UFO magazine by Robert T. Leach,[24] Cooper acknowledged that in 1957 he was at Mojave dry-lake bed in California (now the area used for space-shuttle landings) when several USAF photographers brought in a film of a UFO.

The object, they said, had taken off when they had approached it. Cooper did not witness the event himself, but confirmed that he saw on the film a 'lenticular saucer' shape, metallic-looking, with landing gear, and that he watched it land and take off. Cooper never got to the bottom of the mystery, but he also admitted that he was never ordered not to discuss it. 'Nobody paid much attention to it,' he said.

When the United Nations opened a debate on the subject, Cooper wrote to them stating his view:

I do believe UFOs exist and that the truly unexplained ones are from some other technically advanced civilisation . . . I believe that these extraterrestrial vehicles and their crews are visiting this planet from other planets, which are obviously a little more advanced than we are here on earth . . . I feel that we need to have a top-level, co-ordinated program to scientifically collect and analyse data from all over the earth concerning any type of encounter, and to determine how best to interface with these visitors in a friendly fashion.

Timothy Green Beckley quotes Cooper: 'UFOs are, I believe, very likely travellers from some other planet; visitors from some other world that is hundreds of thousands of years more advanced than we are, and they certainly have a far more efficient system of propulsion than we have.'[25] In the interview with Lindemann, Cooper commented that he believed that these travellers would make themselves known when they were ready, and that he would like to meet them.

Cooper also expressed his belief that a UFO might have landed at Holloman Air Force Base, and that scientists might well have worked on retrieved alien spacecraft, as has been more recently speculated. But in *UFO* magazine, he states clearly that he has no certain or inside knowledge of any such 'back engineering'.

So Cooper believes that UFOs are extraterrestrial, and he is as entitled to his view as anyone else, but what about proof? Lindemann asked him if he had ever seen anything 'other-worldly' in space. 'Nothing,' Cooper replied. He also admitted that he did not believe that other astronauts had either, in space or on the Moon. In the *UFO* magazine article Cooper reaffirms this. This is crucial, because in this obviously truthful and honest presentation we can separate fact from belief, a distinction it is all too often very difficult to make in the statements of UFO witnesses. Cooper knows the limits of his facts and presents them; and he has beliefs, too, which he presumably holds dear, but accepts that they are a separate issue. And he recognizes that distortions are rife. For example, he denies the rumours that he saw a UFO landing in Florida. 'That's something somebody made up.'[24] In the Lindemann interview he speculated about Roswell – 'I'm pretty sure something was picked up at Roswell' – and even that alien bodies, and living aliens, might have been recovered. But he admits that these are only suppositions.

Cooper said he had been given the opportunity to meet aliens, but that 'it fell through'. The phrase suggests that he was dealing with a contactee group. Lindemann reports: 'The day before the scheduled event, there was a preliminary meeting where something went wrong. Gordon said he wasn't there and doesn't know exactly what happened; but it resulted in cancelling the next day's events. He had assumed he would see one or more craft and alien occupants up close, in daylight. He says he never saw any such thing.' We have had similar offers which have had similar results: we have been promised meetings with extraterrestrials, but something usually goes wrong and the aliens don't show up. On one occasion John Spencer was told the aliens could not deal with the

metal-framed glasses he was wearing. Occasionally we have been shown photographs of such 'meetings'; but on examination the glittering spaceships described are reduced to vague lights in the distance. Cooper, frankly, probably didn't miss as much as he might have hoped for.

So what can we make of all this? It appears that we have no astronauts claiming proof that UFOs are extraterrestrial vehicles, although the opposite is still widely believed by some 'UFO buffs'. We have one astronaut who is a firm advocate of ETH, but who has no proof from his own experiences or those of his colleagues.

Could NASA have staged a massive cover-up during the years of the space programme? Cooper is very open about that. 'The space programme was totally under the public's eyes continuously. There was certainly . . . no capability of withholding anything or hiding anything.[24] This is important, because some writers claim that when astronauts are broadcasting to Earth there are 'technical' and 'medical' channels available on which UFO sightings could be reported.

The next obstacle probably brings down most UFO conspiracy theories. NASA is a huge civilian organization, albeit one with military connections. A cover-up of alien intervention during the Apollo programme would have involved thousands of people. For the astronauts we always think of as the public face of the programme are of course only a tiny fraction of the personnel. The idea that a civilian group could have kept everyone 'bottled up' for so long simply flies in the face of credibility. And the claims of NASA's ETH adherents, such as Albert M. Chop and Maurice Chatelain, however thought-provoking, are just claims all the same. Consider the cash and kudos with which anyone who could present proof positive of alien involvement in the space programme would be rewarded. The temptation would have been too great.

Of course, NASA may well be involved in 'clandestine' projects, but Cooper is right to remind us that the Apollo programme was not one of them: it was very public. And if they are involved in such work, then they are keeping their secrets. But in any analysis we must consider the magnitude of any proof that aliens are visiting Earth: it is in quite a different class of secret from a spy satellite or defence system, and it has public appeal that would bring greed and ego to the fore, which any other clandestine operations NASA might be carrying out probably do not have.

What about the credibility of the astronauts in this regard? They are trained observers, after all. Indeed the Condon report stated: 'The training and perspicacity of the astronauts put their reports of sightings in the highest category of credibility.' But those trained observers are the very people who say they saw nothing of an extraterrestrial nature. As for their opinions, there is nothing to suggest they have greater insight or wisdom than anyone else, and in the absence of proof, their opinions carry no more weight than any others.

Lastly, perhaps we should always remember that the astronauts – not to mention anyone else involved in the space programme – are not homogeneous. They are a group of very different individuals. We spoke recently to Apollo 16's Charles Duke when we shared guest spots on a radio pro-

The Space Shuttle has changed the image of 'Man in Space': no longer a place of derring-do by the early pioneers but now a place of work for scientists and engineers.

gramme. He confirmed that each astronaut handled his experiences differently. Some found religion, some sought solitude; others turned to drink, or to mysticism. And they have on several occasions proved themselves capable of speaking their own minds, particularly when freed of job or career constraints. The only logical reason why they should speak with one voice to deny any knowledge of actual alien contact or proof of the existence of extraterrestrials, is almost certainly because they are telling the truth.

THE INVISIBLE COLLEGE

Another important factor which paved the way for the serious continuation of UFO research was the status of J. Allen Hynek. At the symposium of the American Association for the Advancement of Science on 26 December 1969, he presented a paper which firmly set out his belief that the subject was worthy of further examination. Since Blue Book had been closed down just weeks earlier he was now free to continue that privately. During his years with the USAF, Hynek had, loosely and secretly, gathered a 'society' around him. Now it could come out into the open and offer the subject better treatment than the debunking he had been employed to do. This 'society', made up of scientists ready to do quality scientific work in the field, has become known as the 'invisible college'. Hynek formed them into the Center for UFO Studies (now the J. Allen Hynek Center for UFO Studies), which became the first group set up by and for scientists to study UFOs. It provided the quality that Blue Book had lacked, despite Hynek's best, but constrained, efforts.

It was much needed, if the speculations about the death of Professor James E. McDonald are correct. McDonald was professor of meteorology and a senior physicist at the Institute of Atmospheric Physics at the University of Arizona. He was one of the first scientists to openly support the idea of UFO investigation, and to treat the subject as worthy of study. In 'UFOs: Greatest Scientific Problem of our Times?', a talk prepared for the American Society of Newspaper Editors in 1967, he put the case for 'getting the whole problem out of the mainstream of our military-intelligence channels and into some primarily scientific channels where the problem could have been more adequately examined'. The peer pressure against him was frightful. In 1971

he committed suicide, and many believe that the ridicule he suffered for his open-mindedness led to his despair. Researcher Steuart Campbell is less charitable. 'His suicide indicates an instability that may have been the cause and not the effect of his interest in UFOs.'[26] Whatever the truth of that, support for UFOs in the first few decades of the subject was a tricky balancing act, and Hynek's move to make the 'invisible college' visible was a turning point in the study of UFOs.

THE AMERICAN FLAP OF 1973

Hynek's work in keeping the flame burning meant the UFO researchers were ready when the flap of 1973 occurred. On 1 March, 40 brightly lit circular objects were witnessed manoeuvring around each other above the small resort town of Saylor's Lake by some twelve people over a two-hour period. The witnesses were concerned enough to telephone the local police, who joined them watching the objects for some thirty minutes. State Trooper Jeffrey Hontz said: 'They looked like flying Christmas trees.'[27]

The events over that tiny community some 60 miles inland from New York were the first salvo of a most extraordinary year of UFOs – arguably one of the most extraordinary in the history of the subject. By late summer and early autumn, some of the most legendary cases ever recorded had arisen. Eight of the incidents occurred in a period of just nineteen days.

Moreover, 1973 could arguably be regarded as the most significant year not only for UFOs but, socially and politically, in American history. For the three previous years the USA had flown Apollo space missions, landing a succession of astronauts on the Moon. When Neil Armstrong first set foot on the Moon in late 1969, the

world watched in awe; by the time Apollo 17 blasted off for the same destination on 7 December 1972, few Americans, let alone the rest of the world, were impressed by the first launch at night or the long duration of the lunar excursion itself. In a world of fast communications and rapid technological change, Apollo 17 was just more of the same. The world in general, and America in particular, was disappointed by the failure of the promise of the 'Star Trek' exploits into outer space, and many were looking elsewhere for their astonishment and excitement. Even the launch of an orbiting space station, Skylab, in May 1973, failed to provide that.

Perhaps the most significant assault on America's sense of self-esteem and security was the effect of the Middle East crisis which signalled the end of the special American involvement in Europe which had been ongoing since June 1947. After the Second World War, the Americans had put into action the Marshall Plan (a.k.a. the European Recovery Programme), which had provided huge amounts of financial aid to devastated Europe: $13,000 billion was poured into the continent between 1948 and 1952. This was no act of altruism: it was a two-pronged plan to support American interests. First, it was designed to shore up the European economies against communist infiltration – a poor country blighted with homelessness and unemployment is vulnerable to predators. The Americans preferred Europeans to take their money rather than that of communists. The second aim was to provide markets for US exports to ensure a postwar economic boom. American factories could be converted from war work to consumer-oriented production safe in the knowledge that the whole European continental market was ready to buy. As a result there was an influx in Europe of the luxury goods which so typify the American lifestyle. Between 1948 and 1952 many Europeans, and the British in particular, became what amounted to pseudo-Americans. This influence lasted decades – indeed, the effect on British culture is still clearly evident today – and the claim that Britain was another state of the USA was not so far removed from the truth. Interestingly, when Winston Churchill first described his vision of a united Europe (prior to the formation of the EU), it did not include Britain, which he believed would remain closely allied to the USA through its 'special relationship' with that country.

But in 1973 the boom finally went bust. The Middle East crisis exploded on 6 October when Egypt and Syria chose a Jewish holiday, Yom Kippur, to join forces and attack Israel. Just eleven days later oil prices around the world rose by 70 per cent, decimating the economies – and certainly the luxury-goods markets – of Europe. America's hold on Europe was loosened immeasurably, and there was immediate fear of communist insurgence. And it was this very month that was arguably the most significant ever for UFOs.

But most importantly, 1972–73 saw the American people learning to distrust their government. As we discussed in Chapter 2, for many years there had been student unrest and demonstrations relating to, in particular, the Vietnam War, but up to now the man in the street still believed that if his government said it was right, then it was right. Then, on 17 June 1972, a team of burglars attempted to bug the headquarters of the Democrats' offices in the Watergate complex in Washington.

America was holding its head very high. Its president, Richard Nixon, had in early 1972 become the first US president to visit China for what was described as 'serious and frank' talks with Chairman Mao Tse-Tung, the Chinese leader. Just months later, Nixon was in the USSR on a state

visit which was to lead to Soviet leader Brezhnev reciprocating by coming to Washington the following year. As 1972 became 1973, the Vietnam War reached its conclusion and Nixon took the credit for a peace treaty signed in Paris in January 1973. At the end of March, the last US troops left Vietnam.

But while the Americans were applauding themselves and their leader for demonstrating that they were the only great superpower, and one that was travelling the world embracing it with peace, Nixon was, virtually daily, defending attacks in the American media about his involvement in the Watergate burglary. In May 1973 the US Senate hearings on Watergate began. By November the burglars had been jailed and before 1974 was out Nixon was forced to resign in disgrace. Towards the end of 1973 Gerald Ford had been sworn in as US vice-president following the resignation of Spiro Agnew over allegations of tax evasion. *The CIA and the Cult of Intelligence* by Victor Marchetti, in which the CIA was exposed as having been involved in highly dubious, and often illegal, activities, was published the same year. So over these two years the American people had learned that their government lied, cheated and betrayed them.

It was J. Allen Hynek, speaking in London in 1973, who made the connection. 'If our government has been covering up Watergate, then their handling of UFOs is a cosmic Watergate.'

The USA in 1973 was therefore a shocked country being forced to face the reality of corruption at the highest level, disappointed by the failure of the Apollo space programme to live up to President Kennedy's Camelot dream, and searching for something. It was searching for a purpose, even an enemy, that could unite its people in war, but without the inconvenience or horror of real war and bloodshed.

It was searching for a force from somewhere that was greater than the corrupt and base instincts of man. It was searching for new beliefs that might prove more solid than the old, frayed ones.

That search was a manifestation of what many in authority knew already: that people need a unifying purpose if they are not to turn in on themselves. Harvard professor Henry A. Kissinger, later secretary of state, commented in his book *Nuclear Weapons and Foreign Policy*[28] that survival for America 'depends not only on our strength, but also on our ability to recognize (and fight) aggression in all its forms'. And in 1959, political columnist Walter Lippmann commented: 'The critical weakness of our society is that for the time being our people do not have a great purpose in which they are united and wanting to achieve.' In this and later decades we shall see many times that the American government seems to have used the UFO subject, and the espionage technique of disinformation, to direct and control public thinking. There are occasions when, directly or indirectly, they have implied – or led UFO researchers to believe – that UFOs are indeed the manifestation of alien invasion. Are they hinting at the truth? Or are they playing a game of 'unite the people against a common enemy'? Remember Hynek's own comments to the Robertson Panel about the value of a study of UFOs with regard to rumour: 'Possibly the study of some of the people who report the sighting of U.F.O.s would be more rewarding than the investigation of what they saw.'

OFFERING A BOUNTY

If further pressure were needed to create a climate in which UFOs would come to the fore, the American tabloid publication the *National Enquirer* offered an annual $5,000 prize for the story which supplied 'the most scientifically valuable evidence' of the year. On 27 May 1973 they reviewed the Delphos case and announced that it was 'the most baffling case the panel encountered in a full year of investigation'. After reviewing over 1,000 cases, the judging panel awarded the $5,000 prize to Durel Johnson. One of the cases in the 1973 flap, the Coyne helicopter case, was another winner of the *Enquirer's* annual $5,000 prize.

These awards were no doubt good for circulation, but such an 'incentive' can only have been bad for UFO reporting. There must have been a temptation to 'dress up' real stories with a few 'extras' that might secure the prize. Whether they won the prize or not, some fictionalized stories will inevitably have formed part of the UFO literature.

As well as these annual prizes, the *National Enquirer* was dangling an even larger carrot: a $50,000 prize for the case that proved an extraterrestrial origin for UFOs. So there was still further incentive for those entering the field not just as witnesses, but as investigators, to look for evidence of UFOs as extraterrestrial. We suspect that these negative effects on ufology, now firmly established as an American institution, are the reason why the *Enquirer* has constantly refused to answer our questions about the prizes.

The Delphos case began on 2 November 1971, when, at seven o'clock in the evening, young Ronnie Johnson saw a mushroom-shaped UFO hovering over a patch of land near the family's farmhouse. He later claimed he was blinded and paralysed for about five minutes during the observation. For around fifteen minutes he could not focus his vision, then he ran in to tell his parents, Durel and Erma what he had seen. They rushed outside just in time to see something moving away. Erma compared it with 'a giant washtub'. A glowing circle of white powder was found on the ground above which the UFO had hovered.

Mr Johnson took photographs and reported the event to a local newspaper.

There have been many suspicions surrounding the case, not least of the fact that the medical effects on the family, who felt a paralysis when touching the powder, were not reported to a doctor. The Johnsons also refused to report the event to the police, or to take a lie-detector test, yet they clearly enjoyed the fame the case brought, to say nothing of the $5,000 prize. When the spotlight moved on to the Pascagoula abduction and the Coyne helicopter case, which are covered later, the Johnsons then reported the return of the object over their farm, followed by a host of paranormal activity. Suspicion was rife, and all in all, they have received much criticism. Analysis of the ground traces did not produce any astonishing results, and many believe that it was a 'fairy ring', a natural ring of fungus, and that the Johnsons made up the story on the strength of the ring. More generously, it has been suggested that they perhaps erroneously linked a distant sighting of a UFO with a ground trace.

UFOs had been reported in the local and national press throughout the month of March 1973 and interest, particularly in Pennsylvania and New Jersey, was high. Sightings and reports continued through the summer and into the autumn. Then, in a crescent-like swathe of states extending through Pennsylvania, Ohio, Indiana and down to Mississippi and Alabama, eight major UFO incidents occurred within a nineteen-day period.

On 7 October, Forest County constable Charles W. Delk was called out from his home at 8.15 in the evening by reports of a UFO. He had read about that year's UFO sightings in the press and was singularly unimpressed by them, believing them to be a figment of people's imaginations. In fact he ignored the first request to investigate and only acted when he received a second

call from his office to say that the witness was frightened. When he arrived at the witness's home at 8.30 the UFO was gone. He was annoyed, but not surprised. Getting back into his car, he drove back towards his house. Along the road he realized that just above the treetops was an egg-shaped object topped by a globe apparently held on an antenna. Delk compared it to a child's spinning top: glowing yellow and with many small yellow lights blinking on and off around the edge. Convinced that the object was going to land, Delk tried to follow it, keeping in radio contact with his base. For 4 or 5 miles out of the town of Petal in Mississippi, he followed the object towards Leeville, driving at around 25mph. On reaching a nearby electrical power station, the object paused over it, apparently braking by means of hissing blue flame jets. It moved off again and Delk continued to follow. As happens in many UFO cases, there was a point when Delk was virtually underneath the object and his car lights and engine cut out. The object moved away, leaving Delk trying to restart the car and, for the first time, feeling somewhat afraid, realizing that he was isolated and incapacitated. Some fifteen minutes later the car lights spontaneously came back on. He started the engine, and shortly afterwards the radio began working as well. Delk resumed his pursuits, catching up with the object a few miles on. Just after he relocated it, the object vanished. Delk is sure that it did not fly away: it appeared to have instantaneously dematerialized.

On the evening of 11 October, Larry Booth of Pascagoula was shutting up his house for the night at around 9pm. Through the glass of his front door he could see a bright light above the streetlights outside. An object hung in the air, many red lights moving around the inside rim. The object appears to have had a small dome on top lit from the inside. Booth could not hear any

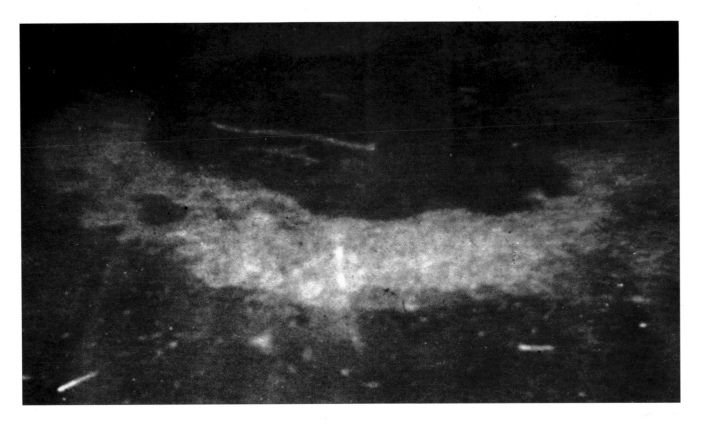

The Delphos Ring is probably the most famous ground trace case in UFO literature, yet it is a case that has generated much controversy. When publicity waned, the witnesses subsequently produced extraordinary and sensational claims, which many people doubted.

sound from the object, even when it began to move off slowly. From his doorway he watched it until it was out of sight. Booth was untroubled: he thought the object probably came from the nearby naval station and only connected it with the subject of UFOs when he read of another encounter that same night. (This was the abduction of Charles Hick and Calvin Parker by a landed UFO in Pascagoula, which we will explore in detail shortly.) Booth learned that during the flight of his object, and therefore presumably during the other encounter, televisions in the area were 'acting up', a problem which suggested a similar electrical interference to that which had affected Officer Delk's car.

In the neighbouring state of Alabama, on 17 October, police chief Jeff Greenhaw received a report that a UFO with flashing lights was apparently landing near the town of Falkville. He investigated, taking a camera with him. As he was driving along just outside the town, he suddenly saw in the middle of the road a 6ft figure dressed in a silver suit. Greenhaw took four photographs of the humanoid before getting back into his police car and turning on the blue flashing lights on the roof. At this the creature ran off down the road. Greenhaw apparently chased the 'person', reporting that he was apparently able to run at some 40mph, since Greenhaw was unable to catch him in the police car. In fact Greenhaw ditched the car off the road in the excitement of the chase. His photographs of the entity are pretty unconvincing, and if he was not party to a hoax, which seems unlikely given what was to follow, then it seems quite possible that he was the victim of one.

The following month he resigned his post as chief of police, apparently having been asked to do so by the mayor. The story that came out was one of tragedy following his UFO–entity encounter. Even at the time, it seems, Greenhaw's wife laughed off the incident – 'She wouldn't be laughing if she saw what I saw,' he said – but the following month she left him and later filed for divorce. His car blew up apparently spontaneously; his home burned down while he was at a high-school football game. Eventually he felt that he would have to leave Falkville. Whether his beliefs had made him the victim of local antagonism is unclear; whatever the truth, he must have regretted the day he responded to that UFO report.

The day following Greenhaw's encounter, on 18 October, Captain Laurence Coyne, First Lieutenant Arrigo Jezzy, Sergeant John Healey and Sergeant Robert Yanacsek were flying a helicopter from Columbus, Ohio to Cleveland Hopkins Air Force Base. It was a clear night, and they were flying at around

165kph at approximately 800m altitude. They had started out at 10.30 in the evening for a 150km journey. Around 70km out, Jezzy saw a bright red light to the left which he thought was might brighter than the navigation lights of an aircraft. Just a few minutes later, Yanacsek spotted a red light to the right which seemed to be following them. Soon they thought it might be closing in on them. Coyne contacted Mansfield flight control for identification of the object, but they were unable to assist. As the light got bigger and closer, it appeared to be on a collision course with their helicopter. Coyne brought the helicopter down to some 500 to 600m as collision with the light seemed imminent. However, the light stopped abruptly, hovering in front of the helicopter. Coyne, Healey and Yanacsek saw a grey cigar-shaped metallic object in front of the helicopter which filled its entire front window. From its base a green cone of light swept over their aircraft, as if scanning it. The object hovered briefly and then moved off at speed, manoeuvring as it flew.

It seems that during the encounter the helicopter crew had either lost control or had subconsciously manoeuvred, for they were now at 1,150m altitude and climbing at 330m per minute. Coyne brought the helicopter down to its designated altitude of around 800m and continued the flight. (Almost exactly five years later, pilot Frederick Valentich was not so lucky. He encountered over Australia an object emitting a green light which appeared to scan his aircraft. Although he was in radio contact with the ground at the time and reported the incident, he was reported missing, believed killed.)

What gave Coyne's subsequent report credibility was that five other people on the ground witnessed the sequence of events, and their descriptions largely corroborate the claims of Coyne and his crew.

The *Pensacola News Journal* of 18 October 1973 reports the sighting by a local businessman of a flying saucer which swooped over his truck on Interstate 10 and drew it up into the craft. Clarence Ray Patterson claimed that he was abducted and examined by creatures for half an hour before being released. The description of the creatures was said to be 'similar to other reports, such as the Mississippi incident where the two fishermen were pulled inside a spacecraft' (again, a reference to the Hickson–Parker abduction which we shall come to).

On 22 October, at Blackford County, Indiana, DeWayne Donathan and Gary Flatter had separate bizarre encounters with entities. Donathan and his wife, driving home early in the evening, saw what seemed to be a parked tractor by the roadside next to which silver-suited figures were dancing, as if to music. Donathan looked at them as he drove past and somehow formed the opinion that the entities could not move from their position in the road. Overcome by curiosity, a little further on the Donathans turned round and retracked their route. The figures were gone, although the Donathans associated them with two bright lights which were flickering in the sky. Some three hours later an almost identical report was made by Gary Flatter, who witnessed a similar scene just a mile away from the Donathans' sighting. He reported watching a pair of dancing figures for some five minutes until they drifted into the air.

On 25 October Stephen Polaski and fifteen other witnesses saw a bright red UFO over a field at Greensburg, Pennsylvania. Stephen took two ten-year-old boys with him towards the field to investigate. As they approached they could hear the object making a sound 'like a lawn-mower'. Polaski and the witnesses saw two bear-like humanoids in the field, which they believed came from the UFO. These crea-

tures seemed to have been something more like sasquatch: over 7ft tall, covered in hair, and with green-yellow eyes. They smelled of burning rubber. Polaski fired a gun over the heads of the entities and eventually directly into them. One of the boys ran back to the house they had started from, very scared. The creatures seemed unaffected by the shots and walked back into the woods near where the UFO had been seen. Investigation of the site showed that the ground glowed for some time afterwards and that animals avoided the location. Around three quarters of an hour later, a state trooper and Polaski examined the site of the glowing ring and heard what was obviously something large crashing its way through the trees and foliage. The state trooper apparently wanted to pursue it, but Polaski backed off. Returning to the car, the two noticed a large creature coming towards them which they fired at. Then they got safely into the car and fled.

Polaski appears to have suffered some sort of immediate breakdown as a result of the incident. He began growling like an animal, attacked his own father and a local UFO investigator, and chased his dog. He finally collapsed, growling, before apparently reverting to 'normal'. Later he was sure he saw a personification of Death, 'a man in a black hat and cloak carrying a sickle', in the field, and claimed that he was receiving messages warning of catastrophe on Earth.

PASCAGOULA
—

The most dramatic of all the 1973 encounters, and arguably one of the most important cases in UFO–abduction history, was the encounter of Charles Hickson and Calvin Parker at Pascagoula.[29]

Charles Hickson is a rational, calm, uncomplicated person, as we found after meeting him in Florida in 1990. At the time of the incident he was a shipyard worker with a passion for fishing and a liking for the tranquillity of quiet, isolated places. On 11 October, Hickson and a young fellow shipyard worker, Calvin Parker, were enjoying a night's fishing at the abandoned Schaupeter Shipyard when Hickson heard what he described as a 'zipping' sound and saw, some 20m away, an egg-shaped object fast approaching the ground. Parker, turning round immediately, also saw the object, and looked to the older man for support and explanation. They could see a revolving, pulsing blue light emanating from the object, which hovered a few feet off the ground. It was, they thought, approximately 30ft in length, around 10ft high and had a small dome-like structure on the top. It would appear that it was not dissimilar to the object Larry Booth had seen earlier that night.

The two men were alarmed, not least because the object had cut off any possible means of retreat – they were sitting at the end of a pier, and the UFO was blocking the dirt track back to the main road. Their car was parked on a separate track, but they would still have had to have passed the UFO to get to it. While Hickson was hoping it would leave so that they could make their escape, he was also curious, and wondered whether there was anyone inside.

He didn't have long to wait to find out. An opening appeared in the hull of the object and three entities glided out, floating in the air. They were bizarre-looking creatures. 'My flesh crawls now when I think about [them],' Hickson said. They were vaguely humanoid in shape, but where the nose and ears would have been they had pointed projections. Whether there were any eyes has been frequently debated: if so, they were hidden by a covering, which may have been skin or some kind of cloth. The beings had long arms with mitten- or claw-like 'hands' at the end. They may have had two legs, although throughout the

encounter they never separated, giving their owners an almost monopodial appearance. The legs ended in what looked like elephant's feet.

Two of the entities grabbed Hickson and the other took Parker. Their ability to defy gravity seemed to extend to the humans, who were 'floated' back to the craft. Hickson remembers feeling a pain in his arm, after which sensation left him. Whether he was tranquillized or not he isn't sure, but the following day he noticed bleeding from a wound in his arm.

Charles Hickson and Calvin Parker's encounter at Pascagoula in 1973 came during a wave of the most famous cases in the history of UFOs, and at a time of great political, cultural and social significance to the American people.

Parker becomes tangential to the story from this point on, for he appears to have been unconscious for most of the experience. Even so, he was badly traumatized by the event. He suffered a nervous breakdown just three weeks later and a second shortly afterwards. He has since become very solitary and withdrawn, and refuses to discuss the encounter. Hickson, by contrast, dealt with it by discussing it and sharing it; indeed, his subsequent experiences have led him to believe that 'openness' is part of his duty as a contactee.

Hickson, meanwhile, found himself inside the craft. He was afraid that he would be taken away for ever or killed, and that his

family would not know his fate. As it turned out, he was, he believes, 'scanned' by what he described as a moving 'eye', and then removed from the craft along with Parker. Hickson's main concern was Parker's condition. 'My God, what have they done to him?' he said, seeing on Parker's face an expression more terrified than any he had ever seen before. On the dock Hickson saw the craft leave at remarkable speed, directly upwards. Then the night was dark and quiet once more and Hickson and Parker stood alone.

The agitated and confused state of the pair during the next forty-eight hours gives more weight to the credibility of this encounter, at least as it was experienced by the witnesses, than to that of probably any other UFO case. They appear to have driven around, unsure what to do, who to tell, or indeed whether to tell anyone. Eventually they called the sheriff and told him their story. While they were in the sheriff's office they were, both separately and together, asked to record their accounts. By and large their reports are consistent and corroborative, and were delivered in a way which convinced the sheriff that they were sincere people telling the truth.

What was more significant was that at one point the sheriff appears to have deliberately left Parker and Hickson alone together in a room in which he had left a hidden tape-recorder running. More than any other piece of evidence, the conversation recorded supported the witnesses' claims and verified their sincerity to the sheriff, to UFO researchers and to virtually anyone who examined the case. Their exchanges reveal obvious agitation, fear and concern for their own credibility, and clear signs of disorientation and panic. At no time is there any suggestion that their state of mind or the claims they were making were in any way 'put on' or false.

Investigation of the case was almost immediate, and leading UFO researchers

and other investigators, many medically qualified, had access to the two men within days of the encounter. There is very little suggestion of any collaboration between the two, yet their stories are corroborative, and there was little time for Hickson or Parker to have become immersed in the literature of UFOs, and therefore to contaminate their recall of the experience.

Whatever happened to Hickson and Parker, there can be almost no doubt that a genuine, traumatizing experience affected both of them, and one which was not, as was confirmed by medical analysis, likely to be a shared hallucination. Both witnesses were examined by Dr Bernard A. Best, who, like the sheriff, concluded that they were basically honest people honestly relating something which had happened to them. Obviously, no doctor could comment on the validity of the claims themselves, but Dr Best confirmed that nothing in the examination of either witness suggested fantasy or delusion. That said, there are strange aspects to this case. The aliens are of a kind rarely reported: the

Charles Hickson with John Spencer. Hickson has never wavered in his claims of an exceptional abduction in 1973, with entities virtually unique in the literature. Since that time he has become a 'repeater' witness, with many claims of telepathic contact.

only other similar account is a Peruvian case from 1949 from the files of APRO. And the abduction does not appear to have included the medical examination experienced by so many other abductees.

For Charles Hickson the encounters were not yet over. Even at the time the craft was leaving, he felt he received a 'calming' message directly in his mind: 'We are peaceful, we meant you no harm.' Over the subsequent months and years, he has had several further mental contacts with the aliens he believes are guiding him, and possibly others. In some cases these are only impressions, with no corresponding visual image, though he once saw what appeared to be the object from his first encounter. He was alone at the time, and so has no corroboration of this. On another occasion a somewhat different object was seen by several members of his family, causing them considerable concern, and at that time too he felt he received mental impressions.

When we spoke to Hickson in 1990, he confirmed that more contacts were made after 1973, and even in his most recent letters to us, he signs off by commenting, 'The contacts continue.'

Repeater witnesses – that is, those who have frequently seen or experienced UFO phenomena – have been viewed with caution during UFO history. The belief that some people are psychic is long-standing, although it is only recently that this theory has been connected with the UFO phenomenon. At first claims of repeat contacts were regarded as the ramblings of deluded people, but studies carried out since the mid-1980s have indicated that there are certain people who seem to be 'paranormal prone'. It might therefore be expected, rather than surprising, that such people would have multiple experiences. Whether one event creates a mindset which encourages the witness to delusion, or whether the contacts are genuine, is of course debatable. In Hickson's case, his belief that he is being monitored by the aliens so that they can keep in contact with him has led to speculation that the wound on his arm was caused by the implant of a tracking device – a claim now often made of many 'repeater' abductees.

So how much of the 1973 wave of UFOs was the result of social conditioning and political upheaval in the USA? To what degree were the close encounters the product of fantasy or wishful thinking on the part of people 'hyped up' by distant UFO sightings around the United States? Was the UFO flap genuine, or the product of media enhancement?

Part of the answer is almost certainly

that the media and social environment created a situation in which UFO reporting became both acceptable and commonplace. The newspapers of the time make pretty depressing reading, with Watergate and the Middle East crisis to the fore, so there was an incentive for the media to find some novel, entertaining stories. They chose UFOs because of the rash of light-in-the-sky reports from Saylor's Lake, thereby creating a climate in which others could come forward: people are always more ready to tell their stories if they know they are not alone. As a consequence there was a resurgence of UFOs in the media, and the whole spectrum of UFOs came to the fore. All this added to the *Enquirer*'s 'prizes', and the host of other political factors we have discussed, with the result that, when UFOs returned to prominence in 1973, they did so with a vengeance.

THE FREEDOM OF INFORMATION ACT

Another turning point in UFO research occurred in the last years of the decade when the American Freedom of Information Act extended to government files which included those on UFOs. To date it is estimated that this has resulted in 30,000 UFO-related documents being placed in the public domain. The accusation that the 'good stuff' is still withheld may well be true, but the released papers relating to such organizations as the National Security Agency, FBI, CIA and USAF proved one thing: that these institutions were actively concerned about the UFO phenomenon at times when they were publicly stating otherwise. And to forestall any 'over-the-pond' criticisms of the Americans, it is sobering to reflect on the degree of secrecy in such matters of the UK, which has declined to even consider a Freedom of Information Act.*

The efforts of such individuals and organizations as William Spaulding of Ground Saucer Watch of Arizona and Citizens Against UFO Secrecy (CAUS) have brought to the fore many important documents, and revealed many embarrassing skeletons in the official cupboard, yet the act has its limitations. As Friedman and Berliner state in *Crash at Corona*,[6] it 'does not provide entree to highly classified information whose very existence is easy to deny and all but impossible to prove'. A researcher often has to know the precise details of a document he or she wants to be able to ask for it: 'trawling' is very difficult. Moreover, it can take years for requests to be dealt with, and when documents are released they may be substantially edited on grounds of national security. When CAUS petitioned for some National Security Agency documents, the NSA resisted the action in court and swore an affidavit to a judge who was not even cleared to see the files he was pronouncing on. CAUS demanded sight of the affidavit. After three weeks it was released, heavily edited: 412 out of 582 lines had been obliterated, and eleven pages were omitted. And this was not even a 'UFO document' in its own right, only a protective affidavit. This immediately begged the question: just what are the NSA hiding?

Some editing on the grounds of national security may be logical enough, for example information on UFOs which might have been detected, but not identified, through highly secret intelligence-gathering equipment whose details would be of use to aggressor nations, or on UFOs which might be the government's own developments. However, such editing inevitably leads to suspicions about what is being withheld and reinforces the belief that governments are covering up knowledge of an extraterrestrial origin of UFOs.

Nick Pope, of the British Ministry of

Defence, speculates that the Freedom of Information Act also had a downside. 'The release of genuine UFO documents has helped hoaxers by providing them with blueprints for official documents, the names of genuine departments and personnel to use and signatures to copy.'[30]

MEANWHILE, IN EUROPE...

In 1974 French national radio ran a series about UFOs (published in book form as *The Crack in the Universe*), which generated much interest. The French minister of defence, Robert Galley, admitted that the government was investigating UFO reports and had been doing so since the wave of sightings of 1954. In 1977, a team of scientists was put together by the French government to form Groupe d'Etudes Phenomenes Aerospatiaux Non-Identifies (GEPAN), based at Toulouse. Unlike most governmental bodies, they joined in the subject fully, and the group's leaders, doctors Claude Poher and Pierre Guerrin, reported their findings in UFO magazines such as *Flying Saucer Review*. GEPAN's investigations indicated that the subject was worthy of study – a conclusion which was the exact opposite of the declaration of the Condon Report, but which reflected what J. Allen Hynek was saying. However, Jacques Vallee has pointed out that GEPAN had no less difficulty bringing cases to the attention of 'mainstream' science than their American counterparts. Of one case in which the witness was one of their own colleagues, leading French scientists 'would not even take the time to meet with him to review the data because they felt UFOs had no place in a rational world'. Nevertheless, GEPAN's work did seem to create an air of openness for a time, although conspiracy theorists argue that this was a double bluff.

Leading Spanish researcher Vicente-Juan Ballester Olmos is now working on the UFO files declassified by the Spanish Air Force. Many believe these releases to represent an 'openness'; others fear more important files are still being withheld.

In Spain the air force opened some of its files, and in 1976 the Air Ministry handed over a batch of UFO cases to a reporter, Juan Benitez. The file included photographic support for several incidents. In an article in *Flying Saucer Review*, Benitez states: 'When you read these files . . . it becomes definitely and categorically clear that the UFOs exist and, quite evidently, are a matter of the deepest concern to the governments of the whole planet.'

More recently, on 14 April 1992, the joint chiefs of staff of the Spanish army, navy and air force decided to declassify their UFO files – forty-nine of them, involving seventy-one sightings. The reports contain 16 radar detections, military aircraft scrambled to intercept on 14 occasions, 22 sightings from civilian airliners, 10 photographed cases, 9 close-encounter cases and 5 humanoid-entity cases. In his study of the declassification, researcher Vicente-Juan Ballester Olmos finds 'no trace of smoke-screens or any deliberate deceptions'. He expects around 120 cases to be eventually declassified.

AVELEY

The third decade of UFOs was characterized by some extraordinary stories of encounters. In England, for example, there was what is claimed by many to be the first investigated and documented case of a British abduction, the Aveley case. The incident took place in 1974, although it was not made public until August 1977. On Sunday 27 October, a family consisting of a couple around the age of thirty and their three pre-teenage children left Harold Hill in Essex, where they had been visiting relatives, at 9.50pm. During the drive home, as two of the children slept in the back of the car, the third, Kevin (we shall use the pseudonyms chosen by the original investigators of the case[31]), saw a light which appeared to be

travelling in a similar direction to the car. It was lost from sight as they passed a small wooded area. As they continued along the country roads near Aveley they had 'a terrible feeling that something was wrong'. As the car rounded a bend Kevin and his parents, John and Elaine, saw a thick green fog or mist rising around 8 or 9ft high across the road. At this point the radio started crackling and smoking. John pulled out the wires. Then their lights went dead and the car swept into the fog. Inside it was both light and cold. After what seemed just like a second or so there was 'a jolt like a car going over a humpback bridge' and the mist was gone. Both adults seem to have experienced a period of discontinuity. When John 'became aware' again, the car was half a mile further down the road. He later recalled that at first he believed he was on his own in the front of the car. Elaine's first memory starts about half a mile further on. Both reported that the coldness had gone and the car was functioning normally, apart from the disconnected radio. Elaine remembers that the interior light in the car was on, and recalls asking, 'Is everybody here?'

When the family arrived home it was over two and a half hours later than they had expected. John overslept the following day and failed to get to work, and both he and his wife felt tired. There were several other after-effects of the encounter. The 'Personal Changes' section of the Aveley abduction report relates that 'John now felt much more confident in himself'. He was 'working for himself creating things' and had 'written many poems about life'. Elaine, too, became 'more self-confident'. Kevin, 'who was backward in his reading at school suddenly started getting better'. About the time of the encounter, 'John, Elaine, Kevin and Karen all gave up eating meat and now cannot even stand the smell of it'. John and Elaine 'both feel very

strongly about conservation of our environment and our heritage'. Whereas both John and Elaine 'liked "a good drink" before the incident they hardly touch alcohol now'. And John, who had previously smoked between sixty and seventy cigarettes a day, 'suddenly gave up smoking completely'.

Like many close-encounter witnesses, the family have experienced other paranormal phenomena, including typical poltergeists' activity. 'Several items have disappeared from various rooms without trace, or have turned up a few days later somewhere else', and there have been more aggressive phenomena, such as 'the back door flew open wildly crashing against the wall', and ghostly smells, lavender and sweet, sickly smells. Investigator Andy Collins spent the night in the family's house and experienced some of the phenomena, for which, he reports, 'I too can personally vouch.'

It was during regression-hypnosis sessions that the story of the abduction emerged. It appeared that after the car was engulfed in the fog, a white light within the fog surrounded the car and, according to the case report, 'John felt a sensation of ascent' before blacking out. He then found himself on a balcony looking down at a blue car (theirs was white), where he could see a man and woman, slumped and unconscious. There were children in the back seat. Despite the colour of the car, John had the strong impression that he was looking at himself and his own family. He seemed to be viewing all of this within a large 'hangar' area. He then blacked out again and when he came round he was lying on a table where, he feels, he was scanned by equipment and observed by three tall entities and two small, ugly ones. He called the small beings 'examiners', and described them as approximately 4ft in height, covered in hair and having large, slanted, triangular-shaped eyes, a slit for a mouth and pointed ears. They made guttural 'chirping' noises. The tall entities were approximately 6½ft tall in height, moved gracefully and wore seamless one-piece suits.

In conversation with these creatures John was given a complicated description of how they used visors to see, adjusting the light to suit their own optic nerves. There was a good deal of other interaction, some of which made no sense to John. He was taken on a tour of the ship, which included what appeared to be a chemistry laboratory and rest rooms. John was also shown a star map (a feature reminiscent of the report given by Betty and Barney Hill in 1961, which is discussed in Chapter 2) and an image of the aliens' own planet, ruined by pollution and natural problems. They also explained that they had lost their two suns and one of their moons through 'misuse'. Then, suddenly, John found himself inside his moving car.

Elaine, too, recalls the white light engulfing the car and the feeling of ascent, and remembers being on the balcony next to John, looking down at a blue car in the hangar area and seeing in the car John, herself and Kevin, although she also recalls having her arm around Kevin up on the balcony. There are three alternative implications of this corroborated account. They could have been viewing the scene through a time slip – that is, before they were extracted from the car; they may have been abducted out-of-body rather than physically, or the abduction might have been the product of imagination. The degree of 'contamination' – the details possibly transferred between John and Elaine – is uncertain.

Elaine also remembers the examiners, and being laid on a flat table. Much of her description, including that of the examination itself, is similar to John's. She was also taken for a tour of the craft, and at one point she saw John passing the opposite way, though they ignored each other. During one regression-hypnosis session Elaine remembered seeing, from space, the Earth, gradually closing in on the area around Aveley. The investigators' report comments: 'She has no idea as to whether this was a projected image, a good telescope or [whether] they went down to Aveley from outer space.' Later, in the hangar area, Elaine looked at the car again and saw the children inside and John just getting in. 'Next thing, the car starts "fizzling" away or dematerialising out through the wall . . . When the car had completely disappeared, Elaine immediately started worrying . . . Elaine next remembers being able to see the car going along the "lanes" by the woods. Then she remembers getting into the car as it was going along and shutting the door, noticing that the interior light was on.' This corresponds with John's memory of first finding himself alone in the car, and later Elaine being there too.

Perhaps the most interesting response was from Stuart, aged seven at the time, when he was asked what he was going to be when he grew up. The report relates: 'He is going to build a large spacecraft that will take away thousands of people from Earth. In fact he has already started building scale models in Lego bricks!'

VALLENTUNA, SWEDEN

At around midnight on 23 March 1974, a clear, bright, starry night, 'Anders' was walking down a dark country road near Hagalund, south-west of Malmhagen. He had been at a celebration but was not drunk. He lived a few kilometres away, at Lindholmen, and had walked this route before. For reasons set out later, the investigators of the case believe that he might have been 'under the control' of UFO entities – the abduction he was about to walk into occurred at a significant time and place. Suddenly Anders detected a light, a circle all around him. His next clear memory was of being at his house, frantically ringing his doorbell. His wife opened the door and noticed a wound on his forehead. Anders contacted Hardy Brostrom of the local 'home guard', a local group which assisted the police force. During a local flap of UFO sightings, they had played an active role, even attending skywatches alongside local UFO researchers.

Anders underwent two regression-hypnosis sessions in April and May 1974. They indicated that during the 'time out' he had been abducted, 'hoovered up' into a flying saucer within the light that had engulfed him. He met entities which were semitransparent, tall, and apparently wearing hoods. During contact with these entities, Anders was 'pierced' in the forehead by an instrument.

This incident occurred amid a mass of sightings.[32] At exactly the same time as Anders was being abducted, a woman cycling on a nearby road saw a cone of light in a position which completely corroborates Anders' sighting of the light, though not, of course, the abduction (she did not see Anders, nor would she have done from where she was – he would have been obscured by trees). Nevertheless, this is the first substantial case of a third party witnessing facets of a reported abduction experience. The following year, the Travis Walton case would provide a whole group of such witnesses.

The next morning two witnesses independently reported a landed metallic object in the area near where Anders had been abducted. Also, at around 3.15pm the same day 'M.B.' and a friend together saw a white, glowing object flying in the vicinity. At 5pm, another witness saw lights in a nearby forest

and believed them to be coming from a water tower, but later discovered that there was no such tower, or any other construction, for that matter, in the forest. Just over two hours later, 'H.B.' and his mother, who were driving in the area, saw four beams of light high over Lake Uddbysjön, and watched beams from the ground shining up towards the airborne lights. At around 7.20pm, M.B. had a second sighting of the object he had seen earlier which was corroborated by another witness, Mrs H. Andersson. Mrs Andersson saw an unusually bright light descending into the small valley near Söderby, near the site of Anders' encounter. Later, at her parents' home, she, among many others in the locality, reported television and telephone interference. Throughout that night Mrs Andersson and members of

her family watched several curious light phenomena. There was an aftermath, too: the children suffered headaches and stomach aches, and Mrs Andersson had a pain in her kidneys during the subsequent days. She said of the experience, 'It was so horrible I wish it had never happened. I got the impression that we were checked out by someone.' Mrs Andersson went on to become the facilitator of a local support group for UFO-experiencers.

At around the same time, a retired blacksmith who lived just south of Malmhagen was taking his dog for a walk when he saw a very bright glow above his house. He watched it move towards Malmhagen to the exact point where Mrs Andersson and others observed it. He later experienced a feeling of nausea. At around 7.30 to 8pm another

A wave of sightings and encounters in Sweden, at Vallentuna, in 1974 were examined by local researchers – including Arne Groth, pictured – using 'New Age' techniques that would come to the fore again in 1989 in Russia.

witness saw an orange object over Malmen and saw it travel between Skrattbacken and Malmhagen.

These reports, which are just a sample of over 100 cases which occurred in the area within a two-year period seem to indicate that something was in the locality over those two nights. Between 31 May and 2 June 1974, a skywatch was organized, led by home-guard chief Hardy Brostrom, which included prominent UFO researchers. Three observation posts and one central point were manned by fifty home-guard personnel and fifteen ufologists. There were many sightings, mostly of the LITS variety.

Perhaps the interest of a quasi-military unit is not surprising. During the time of East–West tensions, Swedes, although neutral, were quite aware that if Russia attacked Europe it might well be through Scandinavia. In the early days of UFOs in America, one concern was that UFO sightings made through the early-warning defence system could have been mistaken for military aggression. John Keel points out: 'Any phenomenon which could possibly trigger off World War III accidentally has to be taken seriously'.[33] So the Swedish authorities had a good reason for wanting to understand and be aware of the characteristics of UFOs. And using an 'unofficial arm' might have been a sensible measure to maintain official distance from the subject.

In Sweden, the Anders abduction was not studied using the 'American' model of research or on the basis of a predetermined belief in 'medically interfering' aliens. The approach used was an early recognition of the wider paranormal within UFOs, something that would not fully be appreciated for many years. John Spencer spent some time in Sweden investigating this and other cases, and interviewing many of the researchers and witnesses in an attempt to understand how what might clumsily be referred to as 'New-Age' approaches such as dowsing were applied to UFO studies. 'We are using the human mind and body system as a measuring instrument,' researcher Bertil Kuhlemann stated. When entities were reported in Russia in 1989, researchers there would describe much the same approach (see Chapter 5). In the Anders case, it was concluded that the abduction took place at the precise crossing point of many leys.

Like the family in the Aveley case, Anders himself gained through his experience a sense of unity with the Earth. Such life transformations have become more and more evident in the last few decades when empathetic examination of cases has been offered. The wider world of the paranormal was beginning to emerge, although its involvement in the subject of UFOs would become an area of continuing controversy.

One 'New-Age' investigator, Arne Groth, used dowsing-like techniques with crystals to examine the wound in Anders' forehead. He believes that something was implanted, though not necessarily a physical object. He contends that natural-energy lines, akin to leys, can identify individuals with an almost fingerprint-like uniqueness and that perhaps aliens use these to keep tabs on their abductees. This view is basically similar to that of some American abduction researchers such as Budd Hopkins, who believe that abductees are sought out several times through their lives. Groth claims they are tracked 'naturally', Hopkins by technology; perhaps both theories reflect their respective cultural backgrounds.

Groth also believes that the abduction of Anders took place at a critical point in his biorhythms which, coupled with the fact that the incident took place next to ancient runic stones, leads him to conclude that the abduction process is a meaningful rather than a random event for the abductee. This suggests to Groth that Anders was 'under control' when he left the celebration and may even have been 'directed' to take the route he did.

Budd Hopkins echoes this view with his example of a Seattle man who 'felt a need' to take his nephew on a car trip during which the boy was then abducted. Hopkins states: 'There are times when the aliens control people.'[34]

TRAVIS WALTON

On the night of 5 November 1975, a seven-man woodcutting team travelling together in one truck encountered a UFO after clearing trees in the Apache–Sitgreaves National Park in Arizona. They described the object as a golden light, seemingly solid, and of a classic flying saucer-shape some 20ft across. One of the men, Travis Walton, leaped out of the truck and ran towards the object. His colleagues, shouting for him to be cautious, watched as he was hit by a blue beam coming from the object and fell to the ground. Had they stayed around to see what happened next, either we would have had a multiple-witnessed abduction or perhaps Travis Walton would not have undergone the experience he did. As it was, the remaining six woodcutters fled in panic to the nearest town. Three of the gang refused to go back into the woods at night; the rest returned to the site with the police, but no trace of Travis Walton could be found. According to Sheriff Ellison, who headed the search, 'One of the men was weeping. If they were lying, then they were damn good actors.'

Walton was missing for five days, during which time there were allegations that one or more members of the team, which included his brother Duane, had murdered him. Then, unkempt and unshaven, he turned up just outside the nearby town of Snowflake.

Walton remembers only a fraction of those five days. He recalls that he was abducted into the UFO, where he found himself being examined by 'grays'. Walking about in the saucer, he saw a human-like person, and the scenery he could see through the windows suggested that either he was flying in space or watching the holographic projection of space flight. 'When I was returned on 10th November I was in a serious emotional state,' he recounts. 'At that time and for weeks afterwards I did not want to tell anyone about my experiences except those close to me. I avoided the public and the media for several days.'[35]

Walton took several lie-detector tests which became the subject of some controversy between competing UFO groups in America. Of one test he conducted, Dr Jean Rosenbaum of Durango, Colorado, stated: 'This young man is not lying . . . He really believed these things.' Critics of the case have pointed to Walton's previous criminal record, though supporters have argued that this dated back to his youth, and that at the time of the incident he was not in any trouble, nor was he regarded with suspicion by local people. One suggestion was that the whole story was

a fabrication to get the gang out of a financial penalty for delivering late on the tree-cutting contract. And the fact that the case won the $5,000 *National Enquirer*'s prize prompted the suspicion in some that it could have been fraudulently claimed for that purpose.

On the other hand, none of the members of the team have ever come forward and admitted taking part in a hoax in the twenty years since the event, even though there have been times when to do so would have been financially lucrative.

Recently a film, *Fire in the Sky* was made based on the case. Travis Walton admits that it is largely fictionalized: virtually the only part faithful to the original experience is the encounter with the UFO itself. The bizarre

and frightening scenes in the film of the experiences on board the flying saucer owe nothing to Walton's recollections.

There seems to have been something about the late 1970s, in the wake of the genuine flap of UFOs in the United States in 1973, that brought out the best and the worst in the subject. Almost certainly cases which might have gone unreported and remained unknown got attention because of the resurgence of interest, but if ever there was time when 'dubious' cases started to surface, this was it. There would have been hoaxes before, of course, but now it seemed that the stage was more gaudily lit, the greasepaint just a little more thickly applied. The *National Enquirer*'s prize can only have helped to encourage 'try-on' claims, and that would have spawned strange and bizarre stories around the world, even if they were not eligible for the American prize. Inevitably, the contactee claims and cults that drove serious UFO research to distraction were to resurface. Probably the most famous of such claims, which is given little credibility outside the 'believers' camp, is that of Eduard 'Billy' Meier, a Swiss farmer. In 1975 Meier met Semjase, a beautiful female humanoid, and like George Adamski, the first recorded contactee, before him, he often went for trips in flying saucers which he also frequently photographed. The photographs have been challenged continually, partly because they are often taken 'into' the sun, an angle which would obscure any hanging threads, and partly because it was claimed that models of craft just like the ones in the photographs were found at Meier's home. Moreover, it appears that a picture of Semjase was actually a shot of a model from *Vogue* magazine.

The decade had been a rollercoaster ride for UFOs, and it was going out in style.

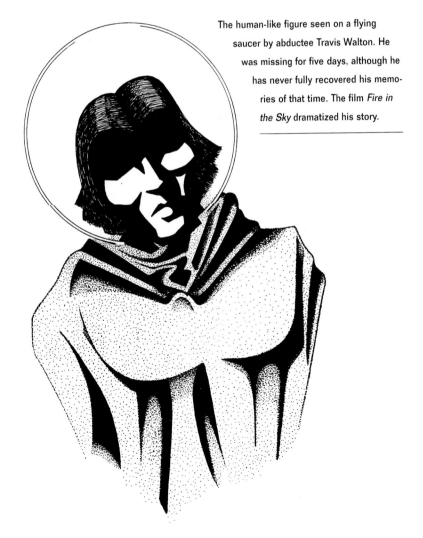

The human-like figure seen on a flying saucer by abductee Travis Walton. He was missing for five days, although he has never fully recovered his memories of that time. The film *Fire in the Sky* dramatized his story.

1977-1987

The Decade of Conspiracy

**'A lie which is all a lie may be met and fought with outright,
but a lie which is part a truth is a harder matter to fight.'**

Alfred Lord Tennyson

CLOSE ENCOUNTERS OF THE THIRD KIND

The fourth decade of UFOs started with a bang. In fact, to be more precise, with the build-up of 'angelic' music, a burst of light and a simultaneous bang: the opening frames of the film *Close Encounters of the Third Kind* (*CEIIIK*), written and directed by Steven Spielberg. The film was the culmination of Spielberg's interest in UFOs, which hold a strong attraction for him: he reminds people they were both born in the same year, 1947. Released through America in 460 cinemas on 14 December 1977, and in the UK in March 1978, it was based entirely on the UFO phenomenon, drawing on its most vibrant imagery. It even included a cameo appearance by Dr J. Allen Hynek, who had acted as a consultant on the film.

A theory has persisted for many years that the US government has used the mass media, and films in particular, to condition the public for an eventual acceptance of extraterrestrials. Certainly there was some indication, for example, in the comments of the Robertson Panel in 1953 (see Chapter 1), that if need be they would use such techniques. Inevitably, *CEIIIK* has been considered by some a major part of that conditioning process, and there have been suggestions that Spielberg was backed by the government. Indeed, Mark Pilkington points out that this rumour was 'even being spread

amongst cast and crew during production'.[1] The film promotes comfortable-looking, friendly, playful-yet-wise aliens who live in a cathedral in the sky and make peace with the people of Earth (represen-ted by the Americans, of course).

(Interestingly, *Independence Day* released in 1996, adopts a contrasting approach and should therefore have thwarted the theory of government propaganda. In that film reptilian aliens without a semblance of pleasantries hang like death over all the major cities of the world before blasting the lot to computer-generated pieces. But no, the Rumour must live! So instead it then mutated to: 'Now the government is preparing us for the worst,' or, 'They are giving us a terrible image to make the reality more easy to take.')

Back in the late 1970s, one effect of *CEIIIK* was that BUFORA experienced their biggest-ever boost in membership during the publicity campaign before its release and during the first few months it was shown. There was also a very large increase in the number of UFO sightings reported. The reason for this might be, as early contactee George Adamski once said, 'Few people have ever learned to look up.' Now many more learned to do exactly that. Films have the effect of increasing the number of misidentifications of mundane objects: people start using their imaginations when their imaginations have been inspired.

Certainly *CEIIIK*, combined with thirtieth anniversary conferences and other public-ity, brought UFOs firmly to the public's attention once again. Furthermore, it gave the media, and particularly the tabloids, a legitimate reason to do UFO spreads and, inevitably, to hype up stories beyond all semblance of the facts. American through and through, the film promoted only one explanation of UFOs: the extraterrestrial hypothesis. It took UFO claims from decades and compressed the 'juicy bits' into two awe-striking hours. It distorted some aspects: the poltergeist-like events suffered by some witnesses were attributed directly to attack by aliens, rather than shown as more tangential effects, which is how they are most often reported. And the creative artistic impulses and passions which can follow close encounters were depicted as being a hidden message from the aliens. But generally it was a good representation of the ETH. Yet the effect it had was to temporarily clear all other theories from the table, and for a time – a time just four years after an extraordinary wave of US sightings and experiences – UFOs just had to be alien.

The film *Close Encounters of the Third Kind*, the name based on a classification system developed by Hynek, was one of the most influential films on the subject. It stimulated a turning point in UFO belief, specifically that of government cover-up.

We are not alone

CLOSE ENCOUNTERS
OF THE THIRD KIND A

A COLUMBIA/EMI Presentation
CLOSE ENCOUNTERS OF THE THIRD KIND A PHILLIPS Production A STEVEN SPIELBERG Film
Starring RICHARD DREYFUSS also starring TERI GARR and MELINDA DILLON with FRANCOIS TRUFFAUT as Lacombe
Music by JOHN WILLIAMS Visual Effects by DOUGLAS TRUMBULL Director of Photography VILMOS ZSIGMOND. A.S.C.
Produced by JULIA PHILLIPS and MICHAEL PHILLIPS Written and Directed by STEVEN SPIELBERG

ORIGINAL SOUNDTRACK ALBUM AVAILABLE ON ARISTA RECORDS. Read the Sphere Book

Sound recorded with the DOLBY SYSTEM ® Panavision ®

But *CEIIIK* was also the trigger for something much more sinister. As we said at the start of this chapter, there was a prevailing suspicion in some camps that the government was using films to prepare the public to acknowledge the existence of aliens, and for those who craved it, this was a suggestion, in full, glorious Technicolor, that the government might know more about aliens than they were disclosing. That they had contact with extraterrestrials, as shown in the final scenes at the Devil's Tower. That they lied and cheated to keep the public in the dark, illustrated in particular by the gas-leak cover story used to quarantine the area for the meeting with the aliens. If this film was government propaganda, then presumably these scenes were designed to prepare the ground for an admission that they had been involved with aliens for some years. Yet the film's message could just as easily be interpreted as one of anti-government propaganda. Mark Pilkington records that Spielberg's original draft was 'centred on a US Air Force officer frustrated at having to cover up UFO reports for the government'.[1]

Perhaps there was a more subliminal message in the character of Roy Neary: that the individual, the common man, could break through it all and get to the Truth. Generations of UFO researchers attracted to the subject with half an eye on David Vincent of *The Invaders* now had a new role model.

And there was perhaps another role model born in those days. In 1976 the Watergate conspiracy of only a few years earlier, which had made confrontation with government acceptable, was made into a film, *All the President's Men*, based on the book of the same name by the journalists who exposed the conspiracy, Bob Woodward and Carl Bernstein. *All the President's Men* introduced 'Deep Throat', the undercover 'inside' man who spilled the beans on the government's lies and corrup-

tion and who helped guide Woodward and Bernstein to their information. From then on, people would sidle up to you at UFO conferences and lectures and whisper that they had some dark secret they wanted you to act on. But we cannot discuss it here: they would want to be met elsewhere, alone, 'where "they" can't overhear us.' In fairness, we can't remember being asked to meet anyone in an unlit underground car park as Woodward and Bernstein were, but nonetheless it was clear some people were living out their conspiratorial fantasies. Crash-retrieval researcher Leonard Stringfield, for example, was contacted by a source known only as 'Mack', who turned out to be offering very dubious photographs of a 'dead alien'.[2] According to Stringfield, he claimed

he was 'in trouble with the FBI on grounds of seditious UFO activities'. Shades of Mulder and Scully of the *X-Files*, who were to become role models in the next decade.

THE START OF CRASH RETRIEVALS

Within a year, lurid stories of crash retrievals and government conspiracy were rife. The basis of these was that the US government had recovered crashed flying saucers and was concealing research on them from the public. Government cover-up had always, with justification, been a mainstay of the subject – indeed, the Freedom of Information Act revealed proof of it in some areas. But to all but the most paranoid, the belief was that the government

Many believe that the US government has retrieved, and is studying, one or many captured flying saucers in facilities similar to that shown in this artist's reconstruction. The most famous such claim relates to the 'Roswell Incident' from 1947.

was covering up its investigations, and its doubts, not its knowledge.

Crash-retrieval stories represent the most speculative beliefs about government conspiracy. *CEIIIK* now became the focus for a theory that it was *knowledge* of – indeed, *involvement* with – aliens that the government had been lying about. Although the film does not explore 'crash retrievals', it created a climate in which 'government lies' could be discussed more freely. It cannot be a coincidence that researcher

Stanton Friedman dates his introduction to Roswell and crash retrievals (his current speciality) from 20 February 1978, just weeks after *CEIIIK*'s American release. Friedman was in Baton Rouge giving a talk when he was told, 'The person you really ought to talk to is Jesse Marcel. He handled pieces of one of those things.'[3]

Of course rumours had been around for decades, but after the release of the film more extreme suggestions were floated, comparing theories with those of *CEIIIK*, at conferences that year. Friedman and Berliner acknowledge these earlier rumours in the opening paragraphs of the same chapter from *Crash at Corona* quoted from above. 'This [the Marcel story] wasn't the first crashed saucer tale Friedman had heard . . . but none had turned out to lead to

any valuable evidence.' But this moment in 1978 was the point when the subject gained 'acceptability'. Leonard Stringfield's book *Situation Red – the UFO Siege*[4] had just been published, and he was invited to talk at the MUFON conference in July. Stringfield called his paper 'Retrievals of the Third Kind'. He commented: 'New sources emerged to tell me, firsthand, about their experiences of involvement in secret military retrieval operations or of having seen the alien craft or cadavers, some on a need-to-know basis. The floodgates had opened . . . Some were new sources with tales to tell, but most were the kind whose uncle, or cousin, or friend, years ago while in the military, had seen the hardware or the critters. Only a few were traceable.'

This has always been the problem with crash retrievals. The solid, confirmable report has always been elusive; crash retrievals have been built on what amounts to well-presented bar rumours which lack substance. Researcher Andy Roberts has compared crash-retrieval lore with folklore, and cites one motif of the 'accidental discovery' variety. He quotes the tale of a Presbyterian minister related by Leonard Stringfield. 'As a child he was taken on a tour of a museum in Chicago by his father, they got lost and by mistake wandered into a room in which small humanoid bodies were seen in a glass case. They were instantly seized by officials, and only released when the boy's father had signed some papers.' Roberts goes on to compare this with a story related in *Folklore Frontiers* by Peter Rogerson. 'A friend . . . when visiting his son in hospital, found himself by accident in a strange ward full of babies with massive and impossible deformities. He was ushered out by a nurse who told him he should not have been there and the room should have been locked.'[5]

Not everybody was happy that crash retrievals were being so prominently promoted, presumably because many people instinctively felt that they were nothing but rumour based on old hoax stories. Leonard Stringfield comments of his presentation to the 1978 MUFON conference: 'One of my contemporaries in research since 1954, a close friend, went into a rage when he learned of my subject, saying it was nonsense and would hurt research and me.'

ROSWELL

The most significant and famous crash-retrieval story is the Roswell incident of 1947, which is the incident that came to the fore in 1978. In fact mention of it had been made in UFO literature several times, but it had usually been dismissed lightly by cautious researchers.

In the first edition of *Flying Saucer Review*[6] there is an article describing a news item heard in 1947 by Hughie Green (later famous in Britain as a television presenter) while he was driving from Hollywood to Philadelphia. 'A commentator interrupted a programme to announce that a Flying Saucer had crashed in New Mexico and that the Army were moving in to investigate . . . quite a few details were given . . .' Later, arriving in Philadelphia and looking for the item in the newspapers, Green found nothing. By then a blackout on the news was presumably in force. The magazine asked: 'Do the Americans have a Flying Saucer in their possession?'

In *The Flying Saucer Story*, published in 1966, Brinsley le Poer Trench speculates briefly on the Americans having captured a flying saucer that year, and refers to Hughie Green's report.[7] This is in any case in keeping with a statement issued by the RAAF (Roswell Army Air Field), and then retracted, to which we shall come later. Roswell is not seriously pursued in Le Poer Trench's book, which shows the lack of significance it was held to have had at the time. Instead the book concentrates on the spurious

claims of Frank Scully explored here later and on a saucer retrieval in Norway, widely thought to be a Soviet experiment, a story which originated in a German magazine. The same year Brad Steiger speculates that the USAF may have captured a flying saucer from near Pittsburgh. Interestingly, he makes no mention of Roswell at all.[8]

Again in 1966, reference was made to the Roswell incident by Frank Edwards. He states: 'There are such difficult cases as the rancher near Roswell, New Mexico, who phoned the Sheriff that a blazing disc-shaped object had passed over his house at low altitude and had crashed and burned on a hillside within view of the house.'[9] He goes on to describe the military security surrounding the retrieval and the explanation – which Edwards clearly did not believe – that the object was a box kite with a disc hanging below it.

We might also consider the writings of Harold T. Wilkins who, in 1956, made several references to crashed saucers reminiscent of the Roswell incident.[10] And Kenneth Arnold and Ray Palmer refer to the 'capture of a "flying disk"' in mid-July 1947, which 'excited residents of Jackson, Ohio. Later, however, the "saucer" was identified as a U.S. Army Signal Corps Radiosonde Transmitter used for gathering weather data.'[11]

The fact that these stories had featured in UFO literature, but had been largely ignored for decades, suddenly coming to prominence at such a specific time, speaks volumes for the degree to which *CEIIIK* influenced thinking and the acceptability of the topic.

Roswell itself is so well documented, and the subject of so many books, speculations, good research and downright nonsense, that we shall provide only the briefest of descriptions here to set the context.

On Thursday 3 July 1947 rancher William 'Mac' Brazel and his neighbour's young son

Dee Proctor, were checking the farm for damage following a thunderstorm the previous evening when they came across a mass of small fragments of shiny material strewn across a field. They took some of them back to the house. Friends suggested that Brazel should report the find, so on Sunday 6 July, he went to see Chaves County sheriff George Wilcox and took him a few samples of the material. The sheriff notified intelligence officer Major Jesse Marcel at Roswell Army Air Field. Marcel and Sheridan Cavitt of the counter-intelligence corps returned to the ranch with Brazel and collected up the rest of the material.

The next event is extraordinary, whatever one believes about Roswell. Frank Joyce at Radio Station KGFL received a press release from Lieutenant Walter Haut, who had hand-delivered it to the station and then left. This effectively stated that the Army had retrieved a crashed flying saucer. Joyce, suspicious, cautious – perhaps even trusting but patriotic – telephoned Haut at the Roswell Army Air Base and expressed his unease about publicizing the release. But Haut confirmed: 'No, it's OK. I have the OK from the C.O.' This would have been Colonel Blanchard. So Joyce sent the release to United Press, and the publicity machine cranked up. The *Roswell Daily Record* of Tuesday 8 July was headlined: 'RAAF CAPTURES FLYING SAUCER ON RANCH IN ROSWELL REGION'.[12] The report made clear the source of the story: 'The intelligence office of the 509th Bombardment group at Roswell Army Air Field announced at noon today that the field has come into possession of a flying saucer.'

The same day ABC News announced the same story in the headline edition of their radio broadcast:

The Army Air Force has announced that a flying disc has been found and is now in the possession of the Army. Army officers say the

Major Jesse Marcel displaying the debris recovered by the Army Air Force from the Brazel ranch near Roswell, New Mexico. He claimed the debris was switched, and that the real debris was of a much more mysterious origin.

give details of what the flying disc looks like. In Forth Worth, Texas, where the object was first sent, Brigadier General Roger Ramey says that it is being shipped by air to the AAF research centre Wright Field, Ohio. A few moments ago I talked to officials at Wright Field who declared that they expect a so-called flying saucer to be delivered there but that it hasn't arrived as yet. In the meantime General Ramey describes the object as being of flimsy construction almost like a box kite. He says it was so battered that he was unable to determine whether it had a disc [form]. He does not indicate its size. Ramey said that so far as can be determined no one saw the object in the air and he describes it as being made as [sic] some sort of tinfoil. Other Army officials say that this* information indicates that the object had a diameter of about 20, 25 feet and that nothing in the apparent construction indicated a capacity for speed and that there was no evidence of a power plant. The disc also appeared too flimsy to carry a man.[13]

missile found some time last week has been inspected at Roswell, New Mexico and sent to Wright Field, Ohio for further inspection.

Late this afternoon a bulletin from New Mexico suggested that the widely publicized mystery of the flying saucers may soon be solved. Army Air Force officers reported that one of the strange discs has been found and inspected some time last week. Our correspondents in Los Angeles and Chicago have been in contact with Army officials endeavouring to attain all possible late information. Joe Wilson reports to us now from Chicago.

Joe Wilson reported:

The Army may be getting to the bottom of all this talk about so-called flying saucers: as a matter of fact, the 509th Atomic Bomb Group headquarters at Roswell, New Mexico reports that it has received one of the discs which landed on a ranch outside Roswell. The disc landed on a ranch at Corona, New Mexico where a rancher turned it over to the Air Force. Rancher W.W. Brazel was the man who discovered the saucer. Colonel William Blanchard of the Roswell Air Base refuses to

But within a short period of time the story was retracted. The very next day the *Roswell Daily Record* was headlined: 'GEN. RAMEY EMPTIES ROSWELL SAUCER' and subtitled: 'Ramey Says Excitement Is Not Justified'.[14] As Hughie Green had discovered, the genie had been quickly stuffed back in the bottle. The story that what had crashed over the ranch was the remains of a weather-balloon was promoted and Major Marcel was paraded out with weather-balloon debris to verify it. The material actually recovered seems to have been something of a mystery to the man who found it.

*'This' implies other information; the information here does not lead to this conclusion.

Light yet strong, it could not be burned or penetrated, and it was covered in hieroglyphics.

This whole story might have died then and there, and as it was it remained dormant until 1978. To understand some of the more speculative rumours about Roswell we have to examine rumours of the early years of flying saucers, starting with a local newspaper, a film-maker called Mike Conrad, two characters called Silas Newton and Leo GeBauer, and the author Frank Scully.

Around 1948, a spoof story was published by the *Aztec Independent Review* about a flying saucer from Venus which had crashed near Aztec, New Mexico. The tale was frequently recycled in the years that followed. Around the same time, Mike Conrad, who wanted to make a film about UFOs, devised a sensational publicity trick to promote himself. He engaged a promoter to pose as an FBI man and 'admit' that the bureau had in their possession some top-secret footage which was going to be used in Conrad's movie. Conrad probably based at least some of this promotion on the rumours started by the *Review* story; some, perhaps, even on the Air Force's 1947 announcements concerning the Roswell 'retrieval'.

Again, around this time two individuals called Silas Newton and Leo GeBauer were spreading the word that they had been involved in a crash retrieval. They were convicted confidence tricksters, and they were advertising and trying to sell a device which, they claimed, was based on retrieved saucer technology, and was capable of locating valuable minerals. They convinced an author, Frank Scully, who wrote up the whole story in his book.[15]

The common thread running through these fabrications was that a flying saucer had crashed and had been recovered, largely intact, along with the corpses of alien humanoids. Yet how closely these strands were intertwined is unclear. Conrad was engaged on film promotion, of course; Scully might or might not have known that Newton and GeBauer's tale was a hoax, but he published it as true. Newton and GeBauer probably did not realize that the same story was being used in Conrad's publicity campaign, but whatever they believed, they had only one motive: money.

Scully's book and the whole fiasco was pretty well exposed back in the 1950s, which helped keep it out of public attention for many years. But when in 1978, the distrust of government and the images of the film *CEIIIK* brought the topic to the fore, the reliable reports of small fragments of material retrieved at Roswell quickly intermingled with the 'Aztec' stories, leading to exaggerated and bizarre claims of whole saucers, dead aliens, even living aliens, being recovered.

In 1994 the Air Force admitted that their 1947 explanation of the Roswell Incident as a crashed weather-balloon was untrue. They now said that 'the crashed vehicle was a then-classified device to detect evidence of possible Soviet nuclear testing'. This spy operation was known as Project Mogul. So Roswell was, according to this explanation, the crash of a disc suspended under a balloon; even perhaps a sister device to the one Thomas Mantell lost his life chasing in 1948. US Congressman Steve Schiff commented: 'At least this effort caused the Air Force to acknowledge that the crashed vehicle was no weather-balloon. That explanation never fit the fact of high military security used at the time.'[16]

Such has been the intensity of investigation since 1978 that on 28 July 1995 Schiff and the General Accounting Office released a report detailing the results of a records audit of the 'Roswell incident from the examination of paperwork relating to it in official files. Given the following extract, controversy is set to continue: 'important documents, which may have shed more light on what happened at Roswell, are missing . . . The GAO report states that the outgoing messages from Roswell Army Air Field (RAAF) for this period of time were destroyed without proper authority.'[16]

Schiff pointed out that these messages would have shown how military officials in Roswell were explaining to their superiors exactly what had happened. 'It is my understanding that these outgoing messages were permanent records, which should never have been destroyed,' he said. 'The GAO could not identify who destroyed the messages, or why.' But he estimated that 'the messages were destroyed over 40 years ago, making further inquiry about their destruction impractical'.[16]

Shortly thereafter, in 1996, an Air Force report by Captain James McAndrew supported the Mogul Project explanation. We spoke to researcher Don Berliner, who examined the huge report in detail, and his scathing opinion was that 'it is Blue Book all over again'. In other words, a cosmetic government cover-up.

In the years since 1978 over 100 claimants have come forward to add their stories to the Roswell dossier, and their various and not always consistent claims have been collected or rejected by various Roswell researchers in support of their own particular beliefs. The leading story, based on hearsay, is that of civil engineer Grady Barnett who, investigating what he thought might be a crashed aircraft, discovered 'some sort of metallic, disc-shaped object and the scattered bodies of small dome-headed humanoids'. Barnett, the story continues, then told of a group of archaeology students, who joined him to look at the object, and that very shortly afterwards the United States Army cordoned off the area. The civilians were removed and told that it was their patriotic duty to remain silent about their observations.

This crash was supposed to have taken place on the Plains of San Agustin, some 180 miles from Roswell, so to tie it in with William Brazel's report, the object would have had to have been damaged over Brazel's ranch, littering the land with small amounts of debris, and then continued on to its final crash site, where Barnett supposedly discovered it. The Barnett story, promoted mainly by Stanton Friedman, contradicts the theory put forward by researchers Kevin Randle and Don Schmitt, who believe that the saucer crashed near the Brazel ranch. The discrepancy would seem to stem from an entry in Barnett's wife's diary which states that he was near to the plains of San Agustin at the time. Friedman and Berliner believe Barnett's diary, and therefore that the saucer crashed at San Agustin. To fit their theory, Randle and Schmitt need to believe Barnett's diary is wrong. Since they do not think he is lying, which would in any case remove his credibility, they believe he falsified his diary entry as part of a patriotic cover-up.

But in fact Barnett himself, a key individual in the claims, is not even a player in this debate, for he died in 1969, before interest in the subject of crashed saucers arose. 'His' story was related by friends of his, Vern and Jean Maltais, years after his death.

Another witness was Gerald Anderson, aged five at the time, who recalled seeing the crash site and the arrival of the military. Glenn Dennis, a mortician, said that the military had requested child-sized sealed coffins. He was later told that alien bodies had been recovered.

There was a certain amount of professional antagonism between Randle and Schmitt and Friedman and his co-author, Don Berliner, over their respective views of

what happened at Roswell. Randle and Schmitt dismissed the Barnett story as hearsay and Gerald Anderson's testimony as unreliable. They were successful in showing that Anderson's recall of New Mexico anthropologist Dr Winfred Buskirk's presence at the site might have been inspired by the fact that he taught Anderson at school in the 1950s. At first Anderson denied this detail, although class photographs located later showed it to be correct. The archaeological-team connection was not to be given up so lightly, however. Randle and Schmitt located one team led by a Dr Holden, but Holden's diaries do not concur with the claim.

The trawl through the writings relating to Roswell, which include magazine articles and an incredible number of entries on the Internet, must lead any seasoned UFO researcher to the conclusion that the truth is never going to be discovered. Or, if it is discovered, that it will never be accepted by committed UFO buffs.

Most importantly, the witnesses who are known to have given fairly reliable recollections, in particular Brazel himself, Jesse Marcel and Sheridan Cavitt made no claims of having seen alien bodies. Furthermore, most of the reliable reports relating to recovery of material describe a bare disc and not a complex aeronautical machine. Indeed, in 1994 Cavitt claimed that the object he saw was 'too flimsy to carry people or anything of that sort. It never crossed my mind it could be anything but a radiosonde.' He went on to say: 'It looked to me somebody lost a weather-balloon. I couldn't care less . . . tough luck.' He was dismissive of committed UFO crash-retrieval researchers: 'They don't believe you when you tell the truth.'

The interesting character is Major Jesse Marcel. Although he does not claim to have seen alien bodies, he seems to have become interested very early on in the

possibility that the object was extraterrestrial, and even at the time he made a great deal of fuss about the hieroglyphic markings on the material. Some researchers have speculated that Marcel had become swept up by the flying-saucer craze that followed Kenneth Arnold's sighting just weeks before. In essence, like so many who were to follow him, he saw in the material what he wanted to see rather than what the evidence presented. By 1978 the story he told Stanton Friedman was almost certainly what he truly believed in his heart. But given that he had had thirty years to think about it, his belief in the extraterrestrial possibilities at Roswell had probably strengthened, despite the lack of hard evidence to support it. He claimed that the material in General Ramey's office, with which he was photographed, was switched for publicity purposes, but even that appears to be in doubt.

Marcel said that he would have known whether the Roswell material was a weather-balloon as he was 'acquainted with virtually every type of weather observation or radar tracking device being used by either the civilians or the military'. In support of that contention, he set out for UFO investigators a CV featuring his successful roles as gunner, bombardier and pilot during the Second World War, and his considerable qualifications. But in December 1995 Robert Todd discovered that Marcel's official record, which had never been questioned by previous examiners of his claims, was exaggerated, to say the least. He had flown in combat, but only as an observer, and his qualifications were much more modest than he had claimed, and would not have necessitated any particular knowledge of radar tracking devices or weather-balloons. Todd's comment was: 'Clearly Marcel had a problem with the truth.'

It is noteworthy that in the first RAAF release reported in the *Roswell Daily*

Record, which seemed to suggest that a flying saucer had been captured, Marcel's name was prominent. It is possible that he had a hand in drafting that release, and if he was committed to the extraterrestrial hypothesis at this early stage, it might account for what appeared to be a reckless release. If so, it would hardly be surprising that more rational minds took over almost immediately to calm the hysteria and retract the release.

So what can we make of Roswell? The best evidence for something having crashed on William Brazel's farm is the material which was found, which is consistent with that used in lifting balloons and a listening dish, even from the witness's own descriptions. And it is important to recognize that not only do none of the rumours of bodies being recovered and of working aeronautical flying machines have any reliable basis in witness testimony, but they can all be tracked back to known hoaxes, and in particular the Scully story.

The probability is that a government test device crashed at Roswell. It should be remembered that the crash site is in an area where some of the most highly secret projects of the time were developed – the atomic bomb, the technology of the space race, and more. As Nick Pope comments: 'White Sands missile range near Roswell has fired an estimated 30,000 pieces of military hardware into the sky in the half century since 1945 . . . White Sands admits that 7 per cent of its tests are aborted, allowing for quite a high incidence of crashes.'[17]

Given that the witnesses were not questioned by UFO researchers until thirty years later, it is probable that their own memories of what they saw had to some degree been embellished. And the memories of those committed to extraordinary beliefs may well have been embellished more than the others. Given the climate in

which these stories began to circulate, it is equally probable that a lot of people jumped to erroneous conclusions drawn from other work going on in the area. For example,

there is evidence that monkeys were being used in experiments there, and if anyone had had to recover their bodies from a crash, then thirty years would be sufficient

Artist's impression of a crash retrieval. Roswell-incident researchers have suggested that the debris found on the Brazel ranch was only a fragment of the full disc which crashed and was recovered largely intact from the Plains of San Agustin.

Add to that groups of totally committed, biased researchers out to prove that Roswell was the cosmic Watergate, and that the government actually knows that UFOs are extraterrestrial, and the ingredients for the greatest UFO story are all in place. The fact that many of these researchers select the facts that suit them is evident from the way in which contrary evidence is twisted to support stories rather than to discredit them. One minor example is the claim of the mortician that child-sized coffins were requested for humanoid bodies. If the government was involved in a highly secret and potentially controversial crash retrieval and wanted to play it down as much as possible, why not order ordinary coffins for 'dead airmen'? Little bodies can easily be put into big boxes and far less attention would have been drawn. That of course assumes that the claim is true in the first place and not itself an embellishment. But either way, why do modern-day researchers not challenge this, and a host of other facts surrounding Roswell, more rigorously, rather than accepting what they want to hear?

The sad truth is that for many researchers, Roswell is all they have. If they ever had to concede that what crashed on the farm was a balloon and a listening device, almost every statement they had ever made would become irrelevant; almost every belief they hold would be overturned and most of what makes life interesting for them would be taken away from them. That is why the Roswell incident will continue to grow in complexity, intrigue and significance, and why in the end no truth will ever be acceptable.

time to remember them 'differently', perhaps to displace them in time and space so that they became a part of the Roswell incident. If a serviceman was sent on a retrieval of some military device in 1947, he might well have begun to wonder after 1978 whether he had been involved in 'that Roswell thing'.

CONSPIRACY

The cornerstone of belief that something important happened at Roswell is not in fact the extraterrestrial hypothesis – although most of the committed ufologists involved would love proof of that to be the outcome – but confirmation of government conspiracy. This 'reason' to hit back at distrusted governments is what fascinates many people about the incident.

This belief is as fiercely defended by those same UFO researchers as the belief in aliens, yet it is patently absurd. That governments can keep secrets is obviously true; that they can keep certain secrets for considerable periods of time is equally true. But that a cover-up such as Roswell could be maintained successfully for fifty years is impossible. A half-dozen or so people involved in, say, a political assassination might well keep their secret for many years, but a half-dozen people cannot hide a crashed flying saucer and do anything meaningful with it. To successfully conceal the retrieval of a crashed flying saucer and alien beings from another planet for fifty years – accepting that during that time some scientific analysis would be expected – would involve too many people having too much knowledge. Very large numbers of soldiers would have been needed to guard the materials and bodies over that extended period of time. And what about the large number of civilians – scientists, cleaners, cooks, administrators and so on – who would acquire some knowledge and who would be in a position to provide more substantial evidence than what is being passed to UFO

Richard Haines, a research scientist for NASA with specialization in aeronautics and astronautics, believes in ETH, yet has doubts about claims of the back-engineering of captured flying saucers. Such sensational claims are the cornerstone of many modern beliefs in UFO research.

researchers? Nor would highly restricted access be sufficient to keep the lid on it all for five decades. Investigative journalists have broken into and filmed many secret locations, and defied threats more frightening than those a government can impose. In recent years we have seen the clandestine filming of the activities of drug barons in Colombia, the exposure of top Mafia dons in Italy, and other similar exposés around the world. And we need be in no doubt that the intelligence networks of such underworld fig-

ures can be highly effective and their punishments brutal – and fatal – given that they can disregard basic laws and have no electorate to whom they are accountable.

And no security is absolute. For example, in 1996 the IRA were able to drive a huge car bomb through the security gates of a British Army barracks in Northern Ireland, and explode it, during a time of maximum-security alert. They merely observed the base and identified the natural lapses of security to which human beings, bored with routine, fall

prey, and this incredible breach of security was engineered with simplicity.

To set aside bureaucracy and officialdom for a moment, let us consider human beings as human beings. Apart from those motivated by greed and ego, there would be a large number concerned, possibly to the extent of risking their own lives, about the moral and ethical questions involved. Many would reveal the truth of an extraterrestrial capture at Roswell on principle, sincerely believing that the US government, or any other government for that matter, should not keep so much valuable science to themselves. Consider the ease with which American atomic secrets, the most highly classified in the world, were smuggled to the Russians in the 1950s by committed ideologists Julius and Ethel Rosenberg. Yet while there are many who already claim to be doing the same for UFO secrets, their revelations inevitably turn out to be third-hand, second-rate and valueless. Real 'insider' revelations simply do not happen.

Richard Haines, a research scientist for NASA who specializes in aeronautics and astronautics, while concluding that the evidence of the UFO data is strongly supportive of the idea that 'Earth is being visited by highly advanced aerospace vehicles under "intelligent" control', nevertheless has doubts about the claims for the Roswell incident.[18] Of speculation that scientists have been back-engineering captured saucers, Haines indicates that the evidence suggests we have not learned anything we might have been expected to learn from studying a retrieved object. 'The progression from fabric wing biplanes to titanium–silicon–asbestos composite wings on supersonic aerospace planes has been progressive, one advancement building upon another. The same thing is true for the fuselage, nacelles, engines, tail structure, and the hundreds of internal systems of

modern airplanes . . . there is almost no evidence for truly revolutionary breakthroughs in the science and technology of flight.'[18] However, when we spoke to Dr Haines in 1996, he emphasized the word 'almost' in that statement: recent sightings of fast-manoeuvring lights around the Nevada area which have not yet been fully investigated had impressed him, and left him with many question-marks.)

For what it is worth, the present US president, Bill Clinton, volunteered his own contribution during a trip to Belfast on Thursday 30 November 1995. Speaking to the public he commented: 'I got a letter from thirteen-year-old Ryan from Belfast. Now, Ryan if you're out in the crowd tonight, here's the answer to your question: no. As far as I know an alien spacecraft did not crash in Roswell, New Mexico in 1947. And Ryan, if the United States Air Force did recover alien bodies, they didn't tell me about it either. And I want to know.'

CAUS (CITIZENS AGAINST UFO SECRECY)

Given the climate of the times, it was inevitable that pressure groups relating to the subject of government secrecy would form in the United States. One in particular, CAUS – Citizens Against UFO Secrecy – has been successful in bringing into the public domain many government documents relating to UFOs which, if they have not confirmed the reality of an extraterrestrial visitation, have certainly confirmed that the government has long been hiding its genuine interest in the subject. True ufo-logy is entitled to examine that government interest, which almost certainly involves studying people, dealing with rumours, and researching communication, the effect of disinformation (which could, of course, be instigated by an enemy power) and the potential of the UFO phenomenon to cause

fear or panic, not because of what it is, but because of what people believe it might be. Moreover, if there is a spontaneous phenomenon in the atmosphere which manifests itself in ways which can trigger radar and other early-warning defence systems, then the potential for accidental triggering of conflict between superpowers must be understood and controlled. It is perfectly acceptable that governments should conduct such investigations in the pursuit of national security, but governments or factions within governments using their powers for improper purposes is precisely what a pressure group is there to determine and protect against. CAUS has proven its integrity in the evenhandedness of its work, regardless of the beliefs of its protagonists.

Also in the US and, more recently, in Britain, 'Operation Right to Know' and its leader, John Holman, has taken a similar, committed, stance.

PARANOIA

As an illustration of the extent to which belief in an extraterrestrial reality inspired by Roswell and the many fraudulent accounts that were circulated have become enmeshed, consider the comments of UFO researcher William Cooper: 'Between January 1947 and December 1952 at least 16 crashed or downed alien craft, 65 alien bodies, and 1 live alien were recovered.'[19] Why would so many crash in so short a space of time and, according to Cooper, eleven of them in New Mexico alone?

Cooper then alleges: 'In 1953 at least 10 more crashed discs were recovered along with 26 dead and 4 live aliens.' With aliens this clumsy, the greatest danger from alien invasion in the USA would appear to be being struck on the head by one of their random-falling spacecraft. Area 51 researcher Glen Campbell has commented, 'If this civilization is so advanced why can't they keep their craft in the air? It would be just our luck that the aliens visiting earth are the drunk drivers of the universe.'[20]

The degree to which paranoia has infiltrated this aspect of UFOlogy knows almost no bounds. When Anglia Television made *Alternative 3*, a spoof documentary for broadcast in the UK on All Fools' Day, 1 April, in 1977, which claimed that man had landed on Mars on 22 May 1962 and that a brain-drain of scientists had been secretly taken there and were working in special facilities on the planet, the producers can hardly have believed that this 'theory' would come to form part of many UFO enthusiasts' beliefs. The programme scarcely set out to be credible: government cover-up and conspiracy theories were mixed with claims by fictitious astronauts; an upside-down shot of the lunar module was presented as a satellite, and the same clip of two people walking through cloistered corridors was used twice in completely different contexts; moreover the producers used known actors. The book of the programme[21] also prominently promoted the 'aliens on the moon' claim for Apollo 11 we referred in Chapter 3.

It is a testimony to beliefs about UFOs that such an obvious joke can have been taken on board as a reality.

DISINFORMATION

We can be fairly certain that official disinformation has played a large part in the later decades of UFO research. The purpose of disinformation is basically to discredit a potentially threatening situation and deflect attention from it to a harmless one. It might also be deemed useful for governments to study the behaviour of a group dealing with rumour, and the way rumour can mutate and circulate, in order to be aware of the power of disinformation in the hands of

the enemy in times of conflict. In wartime governments are very concerned about 'careless talk' ('Careless Talk Costs Lives', and all those posters put up in factories during the Second World War about 'not knowing who might be listening'). Here we must remember the comment of the Academy of Sciences when reviewing the Condon Report: 'UFO reports and beliefs are also of interest to the social scientist and the communications specialist . . . we concur with these evaluations and recommendations.' The crash-retrieval paranoia of the 1970s and 1980s probably provided a good opportunity for the government to use UFO enthusiasts to test certain disinformation techniques, or to extend a game it had been playing for years. Is this the involvement of communications specialists to which the academy was referring?

Howard Blum comments that one group involved in disinformation was 'a diligent band of Air Force Office of Special Investigations agents working out of Kirtland Air Force Base. These airmen and intelligence agents were, by all accounts, imaginative. They had fabricated convincing looking classified AFOSI reports that "revealed" sightings and bizarre UFO research projects; they had spread fantastic stories about cattle surgically massacred by alien invaders.'[22] (These are areas to which we shall come later.)

Mark Pilkington remarks: 'The conspiratorial alliance of government and greys is easily tracked back to several papers received by ufologists in the early 1980s that were soon shown to be misinformation albeit from military sources, hoping to prevent an accidental uncovering of real secrets. The results were successful; the stories were elaborated upon by subsequent writers and ufologists still spend more time arguing among themselves over the authenticity of such stories than they do actually investigating UFOs.'[1]

There have been many examples of disinformation in UFO literature, and the following is just a small sample.

When a supposed government document known as the Aquarius document was given to UFO researcher and self-confessed government spy Bill Moore by some part of the government or military, he assumed it was handed to him 'with the intention that I would pass it to Bennewitz' (UFO researcher Paul Bennewitz – see the end of this chapter). Bennewitz did not publicize the document, however. In an interesting twist to the story, Moore says that a briefcase containing a copy of the Aquarius document was stolen from his car while he was meeting an associate of ufologist Peter Gersten of New York. Gersten apparently later had the document himself. Moore comments: 'To this day, I have never received a satisfactory explanation of how he obtained [it] . . . Whether the San Francisco break-in [of the car] . . . was engineered as a result of that frustration [Bennewitz's failure to make public use of the document] and the document passed to Gersten with the expectation that he would circulate it, remains unknown.'[23] Had Gersten circulated it he would have been held up to ridicule. Certainly the government had its motives in wanting to discredit Gersten, since at the time he was causing them considerable headaches with his continuing efforts to take them to court on matters relating to the Freedom of Information Act (he was the lawyer acting for CAUS) and his plans to make a federal case out of the Cash–Landrum incident (described later).

Perhaps disinformation was also behind a curious incident that followed a television programme in 1992 about computer hackers. An unidentified hacker was shown 'breaking into' secret government files and on his screen the following words were seen: 'Wright-Patterson AFB/Catalogued UFO parts list . . .' and 'Kirtland AFB/Office of Special Investigations, Sandia/NSA Intercept equipment division/key words/names/Sandia Labs, Project Beta (1979–83–?), Paul Bennewitz'. The programme's producer, Susan Adams, was inundated with phone calls about the segment. She confirmed that the information was genuine and had arisen during the hacking. 'We chose to use the UFO data screens because we thought it was interesting material.'[24] If the file was genuine and from a government source, but the information was false, then presumably the hacker broke into files used for disinformation.

In 1983 there was an incident involving TV journalist and 'cattle mutilation' proponent Linda Moulton Howe. On 9 April she was taken to Kirtland Air Force base by Air Force Office of Special Investigations agent Richard C. Doty. A meeting had been set up by Peter Gersten, who, presumably, was already a thorn in the government's side. The first thing Doty did was to confirm to Howe that her documentary *Strange Harvest*, which linked animal mutilation with UFOs (see Chapter 5) was accurate and had the government worried; that it had 'upset some people in Washington. They don't want animal mutilations and UFOs connected together in the public's mind'. Then she was shown the Majestic 12 papers (see end of chapter) or something similar, but told not to make notes. The papers confirmed the existence of a living extraterrestrial, and that the government was in contact with aliens. Project Aquarius was specifically mentioned and the papers seemed to suggest that life on Earth had been originally seeded by aliens. Themes we have seen developing in the UFO story throughout this book were being confirmed, apparently, by government papers.

Howe asked why she was being showed the papers, and why they were not being

Artist's impression of the Valentich encounter of 1978. Valentich was in radio contact with the ground when he reported a light or object 'orbiting' around him. The radio went dead; he has never been seen again.

shown to leading TV networks, or to the *Washington Post*. She was told that these other media were 'on a list the government didn't like'. Howe knew that to accept that answer would be naive. She felt that *Strange Harvest* had upset the government, and that perhaps they wanted to discredit her by giving her information that would not be believed. If she was right, then perhaps it would have discredited Gersten too. Howe kept quiet about the incident for two years. Then, at the MUFON conference in 1987, Bill Moore revealed news of the same supposedly secret government 'MJ12 documents'. Perhaps those involved believe the MJ12 documents are genuine, but it is equally possible that Moore – a self-confessed government spy – was simply trying for a second time (knowingly or unknowingly) to get a false rumour started.

THE VALENTICH ENCOUNTER

As we have seen, in the aftermath of the release of *CEIIIK* and the current climate in general, many UFO reports probably made it in to the media which would not otherwise have done so. However, there are cases which must be reported, and in any climate the following incident, perhaps one of the most important in the subject, would have come to attention. It did not necessarily involve aliens, though many believe it did, but it offers a powerful reason why examination of the UFO mystery is deserving, whatever its meaning.

It is the case of a young pilot, flying alone across the Bass Strait in Australia, who became one of the most famous martyrs in UFO history. His case is a cornerstone in research, as it leaves little doubt that whatever UFOs are, they create effects which should be taken seriously.

The Frederick Valentich encounter occurred in 1978, during one of the most concentrated flaps of UFO sightings in Australian history. Many of them were made in the south-eastern corner of the continent, where the Valentich incident took place. And in this case there were witnesses to aspects of the sighting.

Flying was something of a passion for Valentich: at the age of eighteen he had applied for military pilot training in the Royal Australian Air Force, but he had been turned down because his educational grades had let him down. He was now going for a commercial pilot's licence and had just two courses to complete. He attended a class on the day of his last flight.

In the early evening he filed a flight plan for a 'full-reporting' flight, which called for him to keep in contact at certain points along his route. He had a Class 4 instrument rating, so he was allowed to fly at night on instruments. Ken Llewellyn, senior PR officer for the Royal Australian Air Force, commented: 'It was a fairly normal exercise. He had an appropriate instrument rating for the trip. It was a very straightforward flight. I could see no reason why it shouldn't have been concluded successfully. What happened three quarters of an hour into that flight I think could be one of the great mysteries of Australian aviation.'

Valentich took off nearly forty-five minutes later than the 5.35pm departure his flight plan dictated, but the reasons for this are unknown. Some researchers have considered it significant, but light-aircraft flights are not as precisely scheduled as commercial flights, and are often subject to delays. Preflight checks can take longer than expected, and if the tanks need topping up this can hold things up if there are few pumps available at the field – and Valentich did have to refuel, in fact. Airfields have to accommodate all kinds of last-minute occurrences – student pilots coming back to the field unexpectedly, and so on. (On one occasion we had to remind 'the tower' that we were at the end of the runway, waiting to take off and had been for fifteen minutes; they had simply forgotten about us!) Moreover, Moorabbin Airport is considered to be the busiest domestic airport in Australia: it caters for many charter companies, several regular business and pleasure flights and six flying schools.

Valentich also failed to arrange for the runway lights at his destination, King Island, to be turned on, which would have made his landing dangerous. This has fuelled speculation that he did not plan to arrive – even that he faked his own disappearance – but he could, of course, simply have forgotten. Sinister reasons why he might have delayed his flight, or not expected to land at King Island, or a host of other dark theories, are probably irrelevant and spring mostly from a lack of understanding of light-aircraft flying.

It was 6.19pm when Valentich flew his single-seater Cessna from Melbourne across the Victoria coast towards King Island. He was in radio contact with the ground, and the start of the flight was uneventful. Flight Service wished him well

Frederick Valentich, who went missing during a UFO encounter over the Bass Strait in 1978. He was an experienced flier, going for a commercial pilot's licence. His last words over the radio: 'it is hovering and it's not an aircraft...'

and noted 'We'll expect a call when you reach the Cape.' Valentich responded using his designated call sign: 'Delta Sierra Juliet, Melbourne, roger.'

At 7.06.14, Valentich radioed an inquiry which marked the start of his extraordinary encounter. 'DSJ Melbourne, this is Delta Sierra Juliet. Is there any known traffic below five thousand?'[25]

He was told there was no such traffic; he replied that he could see what looked like a large aircraft. When asked he could not identify it, reporting only what looked to him like four bright landing lights.

A couple of minutes later he commented of the object, 'It seems to me that he's playing some sort of game.' Asked to describe the object, Valentich said it was a long shape and that it had 'a green light and sort of metallic like. It's all shiny on the outside.'

Shortly afterwards Valentich described the closer approach of the object and said: 'The engine [of the Cessna] is rough-idling. I've got it set at twenty-three twenty-four and the thing is coughing.' He returned to his description of the object: 'It is hovering and it's not an aircraft.'

Moments later sounds described as 'metallic' could be heard over the microphone and Melbourne lost contact with Valentich. An intensive search-and-rescue operation was mounted, but the pilot has never been heard of again.

Thereafter everything about the case is speculation. Did Valentich get 'sucked up' by a UFO? Did he fake his own disappearance, and if so, why? Did he encounter some military test which killed him? Did he come up against a rare meteorological phenomenon which alarmed him, confused him even, stalled his plane and caused him to crash into the near-icy waters of the Bass Strait?

We don't know. But we can be clear about one thing: Valentich certainly encountered a UFO. And whatever it was, he died because of the encounter. That fact alone is reason enough to take the subject of UFO research seriously, at least until we know more about the natural energies of the world, or can persuade governments not to endanger lives with secret testing, or can demonstrate intervention by aliens, or all of these.

The Valentich disappearance seems to have been the culmination of a series of sightings in the area. *UFO 1979*, published by the Tasmanian UFO Investigation Centre, reports that there were many sightings in late August and September of what appeared to be 'flares' but which could not be attributed to ships in distress.[26] One anonymous writer to *King Island News* reported being followed by a slow-moving light as he or she drove into Currie. The same correspondent recalled a sighting on 12 September near Camp Creek of a bright white light, oval in shape. A similar report was made by George Newman and his two sons just a few days later in the same area.

The programme *Unsolved Mysteries* related the eyewitness account of a man who, with his family, had been watching the skies above the area when Valentich disappeared. 'I looked up and saw this lime-green light about 1,000 or 2,000ft above the aircraft. So we sat there and watched it for a few seconds. Then the green light got closer to the plane. I said, "That plane is coming down pretty steep, on a 45-degree angle . . . I think it's going to crash."'

There were many accounts from people looking over the water from both King Island and the mainland. Paul Norman of VUFORS commented: 'There were more daytime sightings reported on that same day than in any period of activity I've ever investigated.' Norman visited King Island and found a report of a sighting of a UFO just five to six hours prior to Valentich's disappearance, at around 1pm. A Mrs K.M. saw an object like a huge golf ball, white or silver in colour, moving out towards the sea and then back in the direction in which it had come. She watched it for approximately ten minutes before she had to leave. She did not see the object again. Norman's write-up notes that following the Valentich report, the sightings stopped. This is unusual – as we have seen, high-profile reports usually inspire more reports. In this case, whatever it was Valentich encountered seems to have been the end of a short 'wave'. Yet this small, localized wave might itself have been the end of a much longer event. *UFO 1981*, published by TUFOIC, reported: 'The 4 years from 1974 to 1977 saw the Centre all but overwhelmed with at times a non stop flow of UFO cases of almost every type . . . 1977 saw the end of a prolonged flap.'[27]

OFFICIAL DEBATE

The film *CEIIIK* inspired some people in other quarters. Sir Eric Gairy, the prime minister of Grenada, had tried throughout 1977 and into 1978 to get the subject of UFOs on to the United Nations' agenda. In 1978 he succeeded. *CEIIIK* was shown to the delegates to get them 'in the mood', and J. Allen Hynek and Jacques Vallee, among others, made presentations setting out a basis for a worldwide study of the subject. The General Assembly invited 'interested member states' to co-ordinate research 'on a national level', and to inform the secretary-general of their findings. Sadly, it never materialized as envisaged.

The following year there were a few landmarks in the subject, not least of them being the recognition of the subject by the House of Lords in Britain. On 18 January 1979, Lord Clancarty, better known in UFO circles as the writer Brinsley le Poer Trench, instigated a debate on the subject in the House and promoted it in order to press the government to open its UFO files and prepare the public for alien intervention.[28] In all, fifteen lords spoke on the subject. The subsequent edition of Hansard, the official text of the debate, was a sell-out. Clancarty had ignited public interest and if he had not converted their lordships to the subject, he had at least introduced the House – a place of tradition and mysterious majesty in pretelevised days – to some members of the public who had probably never thought much about it before.

The debate concerned itself with the reality versus the mythology; the confusion between UFOlogy and religion, specifically Christianity (the House of Lords includes two archbishops and twenty-four senior English bishops known as the Lords Spiritual), with the possibilities of life in outer space generally; with misperception and optical illusion, and a host of other concerns. For three hours their lordships debated UFOs displaying more or less the same range of beliefs, theories and knowledge as ufologists and the general public. If anyone in the house had 'above top-secret' knowledge of the subject, he kept it to himself.

What did come out of the debate was the formation of the House of Lords All-Party UFO Study Group. Their first meeting was held on 19 June 1979, and guest speakers were invited to give presentations to the group. However, the group fell into disuse over time and is no longer active.

BACK IN THE USSR

In 1979 the Russians dipped their toes back into UFO waters. Then they took the precaution of avoiding the expression 'UFO' altogether (a ploy that would also be used by a group in Scandinavia studying lights in valleys around Hessdalen in

Norway, as we shall see later in this chapter). The Academy of Sciences Institute for the Study of Terrestrial Magnetism and Radioactivity created a study group to examine what they referred to as an 'anomalous atmospheric phenomenon', and under the auspices of a version of CETI, further studies of UFOs were set up. It appears that semicivilian and fully official investigations were underway even at an overt level. However, at the same time, documents were being secretly copied and passed around among enthusiasts. *Samizdat* is the Russian word for such a document, a common word in the repressive Soviet Union of the time. There is also a suggestion that some of the rivalry which has bedevilled Western UFOlogy existed. There is one report of an incident in which the influential professor Dr Felix Zigel is alleged to have broken up a rival group's meeting. Whether or not he was acting under orders or on his own initiative is unclear. It is also true that private interest in the subject, firmly underground, was strong, as was revealed many years later.

Perhaps there was a little more openness afoot. For example, in 1980 the director of the USSR National Public Library for Science and Technology in Moscow approached BUFORA requesting that they exchange publications. He offered a list of Soviet publications, and asked for a copy of the BUFORA in-house magazine.[29]

By 1983 political changes were afoot in the Soviet Union, and the government found it acceptable to admit that UFO research was still a valid subject. In

February 1984, the Commission for the investigation of Anomalous Atmospheric Phenomena was set up in Moscow, headed by cosmonaut Pavel Popovitch. This commission went further than any group since the 1960s towards admitting that it was studying UFOs as we define the term – it referred to a sighting over Gorky Airport of

Forester Robert Taylor was seriously affected by a UFO encounter in a clearing just off the M8 motorway in Scotland, in 1979. Mine-like objects rolled towards him and apparently fixed themselves to his clothing before he passed out.

an erratically moving, metallic cylinder tracked on radar, for example. An address in Moscow was advertised for reports to be sent to.

Yet it would not be until the fifth decade of ufology that the Russians would feel able to fully 'come out' again – and by then their country would be a very different one.

AND IN SCOTLAND . . .

Back in Britain the UFO mystery rematerialized in a clearing at Livingston, just off the M8 motorway between Edinburgh and Glasgow. On 9 November 1979, forester Robert David Taylor walked into the clearing and was confronted by the sight of a strange

object. Large, globular and hovering, it seemed to almost fade into obscurity. Taylor thought it might be trying to camouflage itself. The object was approximately 20ft wide and 12ft high and bisected by a brim-like protrusion around its centre. Suddenly, two small spiked mine-shaped objects rushed out towards the forester. They attached them-

selves to his trousers and pulled him towards the UFO. He passed out, aware of an overwhelming acrid, choking smell. When he came round the UFO had gone and he was unable to walk or talk properly.

When Taylor got back to his truck he immediately drove it off the road on to soft ground, where it got bogged down, and he had to walk home. He had a headache, and a thirst that lasted for two days. Investigation of the site showed what appeared to be 'track marks' which might have been made by the two 'mines' which had rolled out towards Taylor. He believed that he had indeed been approached by something extraterrestrial, and although he had never previously been interested in the subject thereafter he always carried a camera in the hope, a vain one as it turned out, that he would see, and this time be able to photograph, something like it again.

Investigators, including the police, took his report seriously: Taylor was known to be an honest and responsible person. A work colleague and neighbour said of him: 'Bob is a serious, sober man in his fifties. He is not a fanciful person and there is no question of him drinking.'[30] While no one doubted that his report was honestly given, the debate about what happened continues to this day. One investigator, Steuart Campbell, believes that Taylor had an epileptic attack inspired by a mirage of Venus.[31] Others have speculated about epilepsy without necessarily seeking a trigger for it. And of course, still others believed Taylor's assumption that he encountered an alien spacecraft.

Whatever its origin, the case seemed to have made its mark in autumn 1991, when Livingston Development Corporation put a plaque (which was later stolen) on the site to commemorate not the event, but the fact that it had featured on Arthur C. Clarke's *Mysterious World* programme. Clarke was mentioned, and Taylor wasn't!

BRITAIN'S OWN 'CRASH RETRIEVAL'

Clearly the time was ripe for a crash-retrieval case in the UK, and sure enough, the moment came in 1980, in the early hours of the morning of Friday 26 December. An object was recorded by RAF radar at Watton in Norfolk, heading over the North Sea towards the Suffolk coast. The radar lost the object around Rendlesham Forest, on the edge of which stood a joint American–British Air Base USAF–RAF Woodbridge. At more or less the same time security patrols at the back gate of the base saw something which appeared to be coming down into the forest and went to investigate. According to a memorandum sent by Deputy Base Commander Charles Halt of the United States Air Force, 'Thinking an aircraft might have crashed or been forced down, they called for permission to go outside the gate to investigate. The on-duty flight chief responded and allowed three patrolmen to proceed on foot.' The patrolmen reported finding in the forest an 'object . . . described as being metallic in appearance and triangular in shape, approximately 2–3 meters across the base and approximately 2 meters high. It illuminated the entire forest with a white light. The object itself had a pulsing red light on top and a bank of blue lights underneath. The object was hovering or on legs.' The Halt memorandum records that the object moved away from the patrolmen as they approached it, causing animals in a nearby farm to go into a frenzy. An hour or so later the same object was seen again near the gate.

According to the Halt memorandum, 'The next day, three depressions 1½ inches deep and 7 inches in diameter were found where the object had been sighted on the ground.'

The memorandum continues: 'Later in the night a red sun-like light was seen through the trees. It moved about and pulsed. At one point it appeared to throw off glowing particles and then broke into five separate white objects and then disappeared. Immediately thereafter, three star-like objects were noticed in the sky, two objects to the north and one to the south, all of which were about 10 degrees off the horizon.'

What the Halt memorandum does not include is the report that the following night the UFO was seen again, and Halt was called out. Along with Lieutenant Bruce Englund, Sergeant Bobby Ball and Sergeant Neviles, he went into the woods to investigate. There is a tape-recording of comments he allegedly made during the investigation as he watched several objects and light phenomena in the sky. One object was shining a beam like a searchlight down to the ground. The object then disappeared rapidly. Steuart Campbell comments of the Halt tape: 'It also shows very clearly how people who are convinced that they are at the site of a mysterious event will find what they consider to be evidence for that event.'

As the story deepens so the credibility lessens. The next claim is that USAF intelligence officers arrived at RAF Watton, took away the radar tapes and 'mentioned' that a UFO and aliens had crashed into Rendlesham Forest. Probably the least reliable aspect is a third report, of rescue teams needing to go out to recover confused investigating personnel; of low-level gases all over the forest clearing, and of a UFO landing amid all the activity. These most extreme claims come from Larry Warren (who originally used the pseudonym Art Wallace), at the time a security patrolman at the nearby Bentwaters RAF base. He says that he was ordered to take lights into the forest and that while there he watched military personnel filming and observing something like a huge transparent aspirin tablet hovering above the ground. Suddenly he found himself lying on his bed in his barracks, a suggestion of possible missing time. However, even in BUFORA's summary of the case in February 1984, his claims were regarded as 'distinctly suspect and [containing] a number of inconsistencies'.[32]

One revelation to come out of the investigation was the fact that the British authorities had lied about their involvement in the case. The Halt memorandum was requested of the Ministry of Defence, who denied knowledge of it. A similar request was made in America under the Freedom of Information Act, and it was produced. Ironically, the Americans had destroyed their copy, and the one presented by them came from the British Ministry of Defence.

The release of the Halt memorandum triggered a media response. The *News of the World* of 2 October 1983 carried the headline: 'UFO LANDS IN SUFFOLK – AND THAT'S OFFICIAL'. The article is incredibly sensationalist: 'Cattle and forest animals ran berserk . . .' 'A sloping silver cylinder about 20ft across its base, silently glided to land . . .' 'About 200 military and civilian personnel, British and American, witnessed the astonishing event.' 'The airmen said the visitors appeared to be expected,' and so on.[33]

Of most concern for UFOlogy is the persistent rumour that money was paid by the *News of the World* to British ufologists, although one saving grace is that the newspaper records its story as a '*News of the World* investigation' by their own writer, Keith Beabey. No doubt he had his own sources which offered the detail.

The parallels between this case and the Roswell incident in America are close. The reasonably substantiated evidence boils down to something 'not particularly exciting' happening at the back doors of a USAF–RAF base. Ian Ridpath, a science

writer, discovered that in the early hours of the morning of 26 December a large fireball meteor had been seen which would have been visible from Rendlesham Forest. This fireball may have played a part, and the principle 'hardware' involved may have been some British or American technology under test. In considering this possibility it is worth remembering that this particular part of the Suffolk coast is not short of security establishments, including NATO air bases and the Sizewell nuclear reactors. There are also a good many electronic monitoring locations and highly sensitive military establishments within a few miles (as there are in the area around Roswell, New Mexico). The suggestions of a much more 'exciting something', which have included claims of 'gray' aliens floating in beams coming down from a spacecraft and telepathic communications between aliens and base personnel, are merely bar-rumour stories which came out fairly quickly after the event but have 'improved' with age.

Investigation becomes increasingly impossible with time; the base itself was demobilized as an American base in 1993.

Another comparison with Roswell is that it seems the incident is being promoted partly as a result of rigid belief systems and partly because some ufologists, for whom Rendlesham has become a cause célèbre, refuse to accept a mundane explanation and are determined to promote the ETH, overtly or implicitly, for their own personal ends. That the case is being kept alive artificially is not impossible – there are even rumours of a TV ministeries or blockbuster film being made. All the worst aspects of UFOlogy seen with Roswell seem to be repeating themselves in Rendlesham.

So what can we speculate about Rendlesham? One front-running possibility is that Rendlesham was the most significant disinformation campaign on British

soil. Researcher Andy Roberts points out:

When it became apparent to the USAAF that UFO researchers were not going to give up easily on the case, the USAAF themselves put out (mis)information suggesting that a UFO had landed and even that aliens had been conferred with. This effectively debunked the case from the eyes of the British public and the media . . . In reality it was almost certain to have been a military (possibly space re-entry or 'stealth') test, perhaps not even 'one of ours'.[34]

Perhaps the disinformation was premeditated. As we have noted, it is very evident from the interest of various American institutions that understanding the flow of rumour and information is of interest to US military strategists, and there are indications that on many occasions during American UFO cases, and with Roswell in particular, disinformation has been used, specifically targeted at UFO researchers. It seems that some division of the American government has decided that UFOs provide a good testing ground for this research. After all, if UFOs are not extraterrestrial, then there is no possibility of any actual extraterrestrials turning up to spoil the test.

So studying how UFO rumours can be spread throughout a committed group might well be one of their aims. Rendlesham could have provided, or even been contrived to provide, an 'overseas' test for this American research. It would also be valuable information since America at war would depend on Britain a great deal for military support. They might have wanted to test what they had learned in America on British soil, assessing how sensitive a third-party ally was to rumour-spreading by an enemy. This could at least explain why Colonel Halt has not only stood by the publication of his memorandum but has added to the general background

and pine forest towards Dayton near Houston and encountered an object like a diamond of fire, with flames bursting from beneath it periodically, hovering at treetop height. Several times it dropped down towards the highway, blasted flames and then rose again. The description conjures an image of a lit hot-air balloon, although it is impossible to imagine that such a device could have caused the reaction it did in the witnesses. The heat was so intense that it was difficult to touch the metalwork in the

Betty Cash (third from left), Vickie Landrum (far left) and Colby Landrum (not in picture) suffered radiation-like sickness following an encounter. The two men in the picture helped Betty to fight a financial battle with the US government for compensation.

rumour through various direct involvements with UFO groups and researchers. Probably the most obvious starting point in viewing this incident as a UFO disinformation-testing exercise is when USAF intelligence officers collected tapes from RAF Watton and just happened to mention in passing that an alien spacecraft with aliens inside it had crashed into the forest. If true, this is hardly the sort of thing that should be casually mentioned, but it makes perfect sense as part of a disinformation campaign.

There is also a curious coincidence of UFO cases that might just be linked. Across the Atlantic in Texas, something happened near Huffman Air Force Base on the night of 29 December 1980, just a couple of nights after the Rendlesham Forest encounter. There are certain similarities to some of the reports from Rendlesham Forest (the angu-

lar shape of the UFO, for example), but that said, we admit that this is speculation at best, and a theory not greatly supported by other UFO researchers. However, it is worth noting that the original dates attributed to Rendlesham would have made it difficult 'if not impossible, for these two events on either side of the Atlantic to be connected. At one point it seemed that both incidents happened at more or less the same time. It is only now that Rendlesham is acknowledged to have occurred a day or two earlier than was at first supposed that the timing begins to fall into place. It is possible that the American reports on Rendlesham were deliberately misdated to avoid the connection being made. The Halt memorandum gets the dates at least one day out.

What happened near Huffman Air Force Base in Texas was as follows. At around 9pm on 29 December, a car containing three people – Betty Cash, Vickie Landrum and her grandson, Colby Landrum – was driving on Highway FM1485 through oak

The diamond shape seen by the witnesses in the Cash Landrum case in Texas, in 1980.

car with their hands. The object was surrounded by a large number of black helicopters, and was possibly itself suspended from some sort of heavy lifting vehicle.

The three witnesses got out of their car and walked towards the object. Their subsequent medical difficulties suggest that each of them was affected by radiation sickness in more or less direct proportion to the varying lengths of time they each spent outside the car. Betty Cash suffered the most. She developed cancer leading to

double mastectomy, hair loss, nausea, sickness and diarrhoea. Vickie Landrum reported hair loss and swelling and Colby had burn marks and difficulties with his eyes.

Vickie Landrum became convinced that the object was a secret military machine under test, and she and Betty Cash sued the government for $20 million. In 1986 the case was dismissed because 'no such object was owned, operated or in the inventory of the US military forces or NASA'.

The possibility that this was the object

which crashed into Rendlesham Forest being taken back to America for study should be considered. There are of course many factors which mitigate against this theory, not least the rather clumsy method of transporting the object, though it is possible that there could have been little choice, depending on its size and/or its physical condition.

HESSDALEN: BACK TO CORE BUSINESS

Serious UFO research had not been entirely abandoned in the dash for the exotic in the forest. An astonishing light phenomenon was being reported in Norway, and it became the centre of one of UFO research's few long-term study projects.

In November 1981, people living near the Hessdalen valley in Norway saw various strange lights. They were not astronomical in origin, often being seen with the valley walls behind them as they swept rapidly in and out of the mountains and, in an echo of so many early UFOs deemed to be alien craft, made rapid ascents, turns in direction and fast accelerations. And they were seen by hundreds of witnesses.

An early survey of the lights seen, conducted among 130 local people, indicated various forms: yellow spherical lights, cigar-shaped objects, and egg-shaped objects, in addition to others. There had also been reports of electronic interference with televisions and so on. A typical account is that of Ruth Mary Moe, Age Moe and John Aspass, who all saw a bright egg-shaped shining object hovering over a hilltop near Aspass's farm. They headed towards the mountain pasture over which it had been hovering, but when they got there there was no sign of the object, no traces in the snow and no sound.

Norwegian defence, in the form of two officers, Captain Nyland and Lieutenant

Reymert, visited the Hessdalen valleys to examine the reports. Their comment was:

We didn't see any UFOs. On the other hand, we saw thirty shooting stars and satellites and six or seven planes. And not least, we saw a lot of UFO hunters . . . The people of Hessdalen have been seeing luminous objects since 1944 but many years passed before they dared to talk about the sightings. But the accounts are credible, and we in the Defence must take them seriously. There are more things between Heaven and Earth than can be explained at first sight.[35]

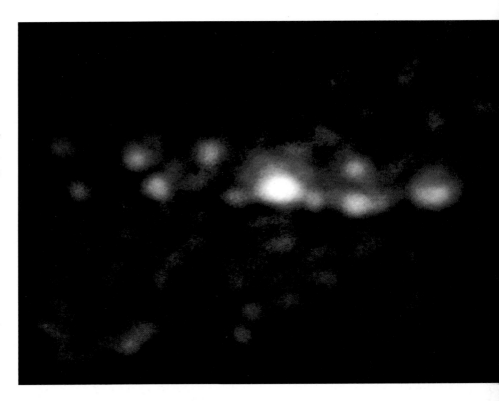

A rational suggestion was put forward by Major-General Schibbye, head of Air Command in southern Norway. 'We have received credible reports about objects which people have not been able to explain. This is something we have to take seriously. There are natural explanations for what people see in the sky at night, but sometimes it can be difficult to indicate the correct cause. The phenomena in Hessdalen may be atmospheric reflections, ball lightning or other meteorological phenomena.'

Project Hessdalen was formed on 3 June 1983 by UFO research organizations from Norway, Sweden and Finland. Also included was the Society for Psychobiophysics. Project leaders were Leif Havik, Håkan Ekstrand, Jan Fjellander, Erling Strand and Odd-Gunnar Røed, who has been prominent in bringing the subject to Britain and the rest of the world. They were funded in part by Scandinavian governments, but only on condition that they did not use the word UFO in their project title, and that they described the project as a study of anomalous lights rather than as anything to do with extraterrestrials. The researchers were equipped with considerable detection devices, including radar, a seismograph, a magnetometer, spectral analysers, infra-red viewers, Geiger

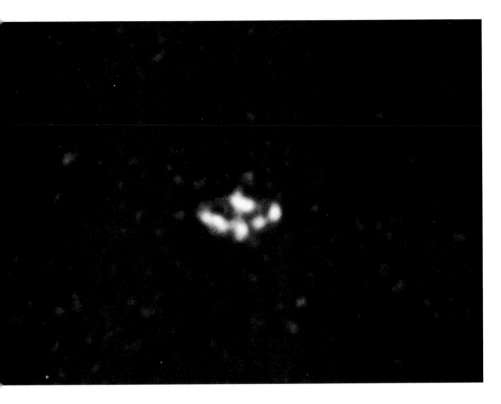

(Opposite top, and above) The lights in and around the Hessdalen Valley in Norway led to research into an important 'core' aspect of the subject. Significant scientific study was possible due to the long period of sightings and the equipment made available to the Project team.

(Opposite, below) Odd-Gunar Røed (centre) one of the original Project Hessdalen team, photographed with John and Anne Spencer.

counters and cameras. In the first winter months of 1984 a recording station was set up.

During the first period of the project, which continued until the end of February 1984, 188 light reports were recorded. Most famous and most strange was the red light reported by Leif Havik from 20 February 1984, which flew around his feet and then disappeared into the air. Age Moe also witnessed the phenomenon. Neither of them could explain it. On another occasion, lasers and lights fired towards the objects seemed to trigger a 'response', or at least a brightening or flashing of the lights suggesting a

reaction. For example, when a laser beam was fired at a flashing light, the flashing accelerated to twice its normal speed and then resumed its former pattern when the laser was switched off. When the laser was turned on again, the flashing sped up again. This occurred eight times out of nine.

The tentative report on Hessdalen was that the phenomenon was real, that it was registering on the instrumentation, but that it was not yet explainable in scientific terms. During the spring of 1984 the Norwegian Institute of Scientific Research and Enlightenment examined the area for plasma phenomena and investigated the possibility that the lights were forming in an inversion layer caused by cold air forced into the valley meeting uprising warmer air. Jan Krogh believed: 'We now have clear indications that plasma phenomena may have been seen, and are currently seen, in Hessdalen.' Some incidence of inversion phenomena was also accepted, but there were still unexplained lights. Krogh explained: 'Most of these are relatively large lights, and often moving in

waves. In the daytime they often look like metallic balls or discs surrounded by a glow or halo. When such lights are seen they often look as though a metallic object has been placed in the light. Such a description is quite fitting with light from plasma. It is the glowing ionised gas which looks like a metallic fuselage.'

In January 1985 the site was visited by J. Allen Hynek, who commented: 'It seems we have something important in Hessdalen – nowhere else in the world has the UFO phenomenon been known to stay put for so long a time.'

Suggestions that the phenomena have been caused by local power lines or 'constant' conditions within the valleys have been rejected to some degree by the Project Hessdalen observers for the very reason that the phenomena have peaked and diminished over time. If the explanation depended on stable conditions, then the phenomena should be continuous and constant.

Odd-Gunnar Røed has kept us up to date with progress at Hessdalen. He is sure the lights are 'a physical phenomenon'. In 1993 the Centre for Research into Unidentified Light Phenomena was set up at Hessdalen by Erling Strand and his colleagues. Scientific research of the best kind will continue, and may yet throw some 'light' on the UFO phenomenon.

One or two of the photographs from Hessdalen show 'clumps' of lights. These may be similar to those reported as foo fighters (see Chapter 1). Lieutenant Donald Meiers described a common type of foo fighter as 'a group of about fifteen lights which appear off in the distance, like a Christmas tree in the air.' State Trooper Jeffrey Hontz at Saylor's Lake had used much the same description: 'Some had white lights, some had blue, and some both. They looked like flying Christmas trees.'[36] But if the lights could not all be explained by the above examinations, a radical suggestion was, at that time, coming to the fore which might also help to explain the localized nature of the lights in terms of both time and place.

EARTHLIGHTS

In 1982 Paul Devereux and Paul McCartney published *Earthlights*, a book which applied the researches of Canadians Michael Persinger and Gyslaine Lafreniere to the subject of UFOs, proposing a radical alternative viewpoint to many reports.[37] It made the link between tectonic, geophysical activity and anomalous sightings of lights. Charting reports of UFOs, it could be seen that many sightings had been made over geological fault lines. The implication was that some UFOs – some LITS – were the product of natural energy released prior to earthquakes while the stresses were building up. Experiments suggested that under pressure certain rocks produce patterns of light emission, perhaps an electrical plasma discharge. Such energies might also be responsible for the vehicle interference sometimes reported in connection with UFOs.

Earthlights would seem to be a plausible explanation for the lights examined by Project Hessdalen. The Norwegian fjords are highly faulted, and indeed the whole of Scandinavia is undergoing isostatic readjustment – the rising up of the land after the melting of the huge weight of ice during the last ice age. The various strains produced might create the necessary conditions for earthlights.

The presentation of a theory that UFOs might be non-physical – energy sources only – was long overdue. It was one of few radical thoughts in UFOs for many years, a coherent and fresh alternative to ETH. The saddest possibility for UFO research is that such a theory could, and probably would, have come to the fore right at the beginning in the 1940s had the subject not arisen during the period of Cold War paranoia and the

resultant fear that the things being seen were physical. It says a lot about the development of the subject that it took thirty-five years for such an idea to gain a hearing.

Devereux has extended his theory to the interaction of energies with witnesses. He has speculated that the plasma itself might respond to the predisposition of a witness, taking on a form agreeable or in some way needed by the witness. Persinger, responding to the UFO context, has taken a different view: that these energies could affect the electrical activity in the brain, creating hallucinations which may even explain contactee and abductions imagery.

ABDUCTIONS

'I was immobilized. I couldn't move and I didn't think to speak. I just watched,' Mrs J. Berte claimed of her 10 December 1979 experience. She had been asleep on a porch at a friend's house when she was awakened, paralysed and taken aboard a flying saucer. There she saw her friend, who had presumably also been abducted. She had a tube-like probe extending from

(Above) Budd Hopkins (left) is probably the single most significant figure in putting abductions on the UFO agenda. He is photographed here with Walt Andrus, the head of MUFON, the largest UFO research network in the world.

(Opposite) Artist's impression of abduction as claimed by many abductees: vulnerable people in lonely houses at night.

her stomach. Her response was one of anger at her circumstances: 'It makes you very angry. They don't ask your permission. They just take you away.'

The subject of UFOs was becoming, if not quite fragmented, then certainly compartmentalized. All the facets of the UFO phenomenon remained, each supported by its own advocates almost independently of others. So, for example, crash retrievals were being investigated by people with a particular interest in crash retrievals, who spent very little if any time on lights-in-the-sky cases, while many studying the LITS phenomenon were not attracted to crash retrievals.

During this decade a subject which had

not so far been particularly popular began to get into high gear: alien abduction. The first of the alien abductions – in what was to become a regular pattern – was the well-publicized case of Betty and Barney Hill in 1965 (see Chapter 2). Although there had been a trickle of cases since that time, such as the famous Pascagoula encounter of Hickson and Parker in 1973, the matter had been regarded as marginal. Now a whole group of UFO researchers came to the fore; they were interested in abductions only and demonstrated only tangential knowledge of LITS, crash retrievals, contactees and so on.

Interestingly, the abduction phenomenon was not triggered by *CEIIIK*, which had been so prominent in kick-starting this fourth decade in other respects. The film does not touch on the details of abduction experiences – short-term aggressive kidnappings, medical examinations and so on.

The current perception of the abduction phenomenon is largely due to the efforts and enthusiasm of one man: Budd Hopkins. In 1980 he wrote *Missing Time*, published in 1981, which was based on several years of examining the subject. He notes in the introduction: 'Since 1976 I have been involved to varying degrees with the investigation of 19 similar abduction cases involving 37 people.'[38] He comments of *CEIIIK*: 'The film, in its junk jewellery vision of the UFOs themselves, its noisy, chaotic *exorcist* type episodes and smiling baby-like humanoids provides a kind of control on witness accounts. Almost nothing within these pages resembles in any way the "Hollywood version" of the UFO phenomenon.'

Hopkins immediately set out his stall. He pointed out that for each known abduction 'there may be dozens still totally unknown, and that's only in the few Western countries – the US, England, France, and Canada – where something of a widespread investigatory network exists. Fragmentary reports from everywhere else, from South Africa to Indonesia, suggest that the phenomenon is worldwide.' Hopkins goes on to add, on the basis of the sample of reports he was working with, 'We can logically theorize that there may be tens of thousands of Americans whose encounters have never been revealed – bearing in mind we are talking about abductions which came to light through the investigation of a routine UFO sighting in which a time lapse and other suspicious details were uncovered. The discovery which impelled me to write this book is one I believe to be of extraordinary importance.'

Within a short space of time Hopkins was extending the phenomenon beyond UFOs and proposing that some abductees 'had *absolutely no conscious memory* of a UFO sighting; for example, of one abductee all that he had to go on was the "feeling" that "something may have happened" to him one night . . . An inescapable conclusion to be drawn from all these cases is that *anyone* could have been abducted, with no memory of it, no conscious recall even of a preliminary event like the sighting of a UFO.' And even in this first book Hopkins speculates that the abduction phenomenon is far from random; that abductees are continually monitored at different times through their life. It was a theme to which he was to return in his second book, *Intruders*.

The matter of alien abductions is very anthropomorphic. Extraterrestrials seem to do precisely what we would do if we were the visiting aliens. Although Hopkins comments that we should not be surprised to find that alien astronauts do not land on Earth to erect little flags and pose for pictures, he does quote astronaut Edgar Mitchell, who effectively confirms that the 'Hill-type' abduction makes anthropomorphically logical sense. 'If we had expected to encounter any kind of living beings, which, of course, we didn't, we would naturally have asked NASA to put us down in some very unpopulated region where we could examine the local fauna in safety and at our discretion. We would have wanted to pick up some living specimens, examine them, and put them back with a minimum of fuss, hoping to get back to Earth safely with as much information as possible.'

Hopkins' book immediately crystallized certain images which have remained largely unchanged in UFO alien-abduction research. One is the concept of missing time: that the abductees are 'taken' for a period during which they are examined and/or manipulated before being returned to their own environment with that period erased from their memory. When noticed, this missing time then becomes the trigger for analysis. Another is the grays, the abducting race of aliens which are basically short, somewhat featureless humanoids, with spindly bodies, large, bald domed heads, huge wraparound black eyes, diminished nose, mouth and ears. The image was reinforced in *Missing Time* by both the illustrations and the recollections recorded. We will return to the grays shortly as they represent a stage in UFO evolution which is itself extremely interesting and which was largely cemented by Hopkins' work until the claims of Whitley Strieber emerged in 1987 (see Chapter 5).

Once Hopkins had opened the floodgates the subject burst forth as if a huge pressure had built up which had hitherto had no means of release. Countless books were written, particularly in England and America, largely promoting the same kind of research and results Hopkins had publicized. Some were questioning and critical of the work; others totally confirmed the concept. Throughout the remainder of the decade

Hopkins' scenario, which echoed the claims of Betty and Barney Hill for the most part, dominated the subject. What he added to it was potentially alarming: that the abduction phenomenon was not random; that not only did most abductees undergo a sequence of events in their own lives, the blood line was followed. He was warning abductees that

Debbie Jordan – 'Kathie Davis' in Budd Hopkins' book *Intruders* – has had a life-long series of experiences.

they were probably abductees because their mother or father or another family member had been, and that their own children or descendants probably would be too.

DEBBIE JORDAN ('KATHIE DAVIS')

At the end of the decade Hopkins' second book, *Intruders*, was published.[39] It was based largely on the abduction of 'Kathie Davis', who later went public under her real

name, Debbie Jordan, and wrote her own book with her sister, Kathy Mitchell.[40] *Intruders* described in detail the repeated abductions of Debbie Jordan, and reinforced again the image of the grays. Debbie's case became the cornerstone of abduction imagery as the UFO phenomenon moved into its fifth decade.

It was something that happened on 30 June 1983 which led Debbie to contact Hopkins. She had tried to read *Missing Time* a month earlier but had found it scary. When a light was seen in the garden of her parents' home, apparently leaving physical traces in the form of a line of hardened soil, she was drawn back to the book and subsequently wrote to the author. He began a long-term search, using regression hypnosis, which revealed a series of lifelong experiences.

At the age of six Debbie had apparently wandered away from her home and encountered a 'gray' who performed a medical examination on her, making a sharp cut on her leg. The indication of 'screen memory' (protective-substitute image) is hinted at here: Debbie remembers the event taking place in 'a strange house' and the alien being a 'little boy'. Then there are several strange encounters during her teenage years. In March 1978 she was abducted and underwent another medical examination. Hopkins has an alarming interpretation of this event: in an earlier 'examination' Debbie had been artificially inseminated, and in this 1978 'examination' an unborn foetus was surgically removed from her. Around a year later, Debbie was abducted from her apartment, taken aboard a flying saucer and an implant was placed deep inside her nasal cavity. Hopkins believes that these implants are tracking devices to enable aliens to keep tabs on abductees.

Three months after the June 1983 'light-in-the-garden' sighting, Debbie experienced what Hopkins describes as a 'two-step abduction . . . unique in the UFO literature.'

Debbie was taken aboard a UFO which, with 'screen memory' she saw as a local supplies store. Later the same night she was abducted again from her home and given a further medical examination. During this experience she was shown a small child which she believed was her own, and conceived with the aliens. Hopkins believes her natural son was also abducted that night.

In February 1986 Debbie saw an alien in her home, heading towards her youngest son's bedroom. It may have been a clue that he is to undergo a lifetime series of experiences. Later experiences suggest that her older son may also be a target. That April Debbie had a dream, of the kind she believes reveals memories, in which she was shown two babies but told there were nine. They are 'hers', and she was allowed to touch and bond with them.

In his foreword to Debbie Jordan and Kathy Mitchell's book *Abducted!* Budd Hopkins comments: 'What Debbie's account revealed is no more or less than the central reason for alien interaction with humans. Despite deep alien curiosity about human sexuality, about our basic maternal and paternal instinct, and about the way human beings form relationships with one

An artist's impression of a lunar landing vehicle from 1947, designed for the British Interplanetary Society. It is remarkably similar to the devices reported by both Debbie Jordan in America and Meagan Quezet in Africa during their close encounter experiences.

B.I.S. LUNAR SPACESHIP, 1947 CONCEPT. KEY:

1   MAIN ROCKET MOTOR
2   VERNIER LANDING ROCKETS
3   ROLL-CONTROL JETS
4   PORTHOLES
5   EARLTH-LANDING PARACHUTE
6   COELOSTAT MIRROR
7   PRESSURE CABIN
8   AIR-LOCK HATCH
9   TAKE-OFF ROCKET MOTORS
10   EXTENSIBLE LANDING-LEGS
11   HATCH TO AIR-LOCK
12   COELOSTAT SUPPORT STRUCTURE
13   ONE OF THE THREE CREW COUCHES.

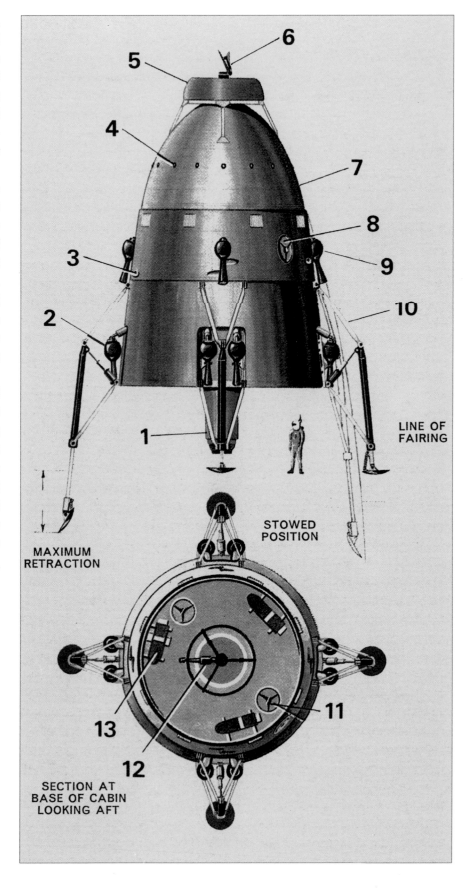

MAXIMUM RETRACTION

STOWED POSITION

LINE OF FAIRING

SECTION AT BASE OF CABIN LOOKING AFT

another, it is our genetic make up that appears to be the focus of alien attention.'

In the book Kathy Mitchell asks an intriguing question. 'If there are extraterrestrial beings who have the power to pull my car off the road at their will, take control of my mind and body, why did they allow me an unobstructed view of their craft for a few fleeting moments, for a memory I would retain forever? Do they want their "victims" to partially remember, to quest for answers, to educate the population at their own mental expense?' Abductees seem to go through a learning process. Whether or not this is the direct result of alien intervention or something inherent in the people undergoing the experiences is something that has been much debated recently. We will discuss it in Chapter 5.

John Spencer met Debbie Jordan at the MUFON conference in America in 1990. She confirmed the accuracy of Hopkins' book, and added:

A lot of what goes on with my family, in the neighbourhood and everything, and all the people involved is not in the book. Because there was so much material it was almost impossible to get it all down without being confusing. It's almost like you've got to be there and you've got to see them . . . to even believe it. And if there wasn't so many damn people to talk to about this . . . if it was just me I would be down to the Seven Steeples right now – that's the local madhouse.

Debbie mentioned her experiences with 'witness support', a growing trend among abductees across the world and particularly in America, Britain and Scandinavia. She had nothing but praise for Hopkins and the way he handled her traumas.

When I started working with Budd . . . I started getting into this network of being with people like me [who] had the same memories and stuff. I can't say I got better. I guess you

never get better . . . but I changed. I grew. I could cope even better and the anxiety is gone. I must be on the right track because something certainly made a big turn-around in me. If you knew me six or seven years ago and you knew me now . . . ask anybody I know. I am not even the same person.

I love Budd. I mean, he's like almost second family after all this time. He's been very good to me. I know how hard he works and how emotional he gets about everything. I don't always agree with his opinion of something. I feel like he has helped me to get control of my life for maybe the first time. He has opened doors for me, you know, and he has helped me learn things and his whole family has treated me and my family so good and I have a tremendous amount of respect for him.

Under hypnosis, the light Debbie had seen in her parents' garden in 1983 was 'revealed' to be a landed craft. On 3 January 1979, in Mindalore, Johannesburg, South Africa a mother and son encountered a strikingly similar object. Both cases include the description of an upright bullet-shaped object with a hatch for entrance and exit, standing on legs spaced equidistantly around the base – similar, in fact, to early depictions of the lunar-landing module, though nothing like the craft eventually used. It resembles, for example, the British Interplanetary Society 1947 concept of a lunar spaceship.[41]

When Meagan and André Quezet went out of their house to get their dog at around midnight, they were surprised to see what looked like streetlighting glowing ahead of them on the road. They knew there were no lights there. As they investigated they could see a landed object standing some 12ft high. They assumed it was some sort of experimental craft. As they got closer they were approached by five or six people coming out of a hatch who spoke to them in a high-pitched Chinese-like language.

They appeared to be human, and were of normal height. They were dressed in coveralls, and one of the men had thick hair and a beard. Upset, Meagan asked her son to 'go and get Daddy'. Their recollections become blurred at this point. Meagan's next clear memory is of the people jumping back into the object. She heard a buzzing and the craft rose up and flew off into the sky. André had not made it to fetch his father and returned to his mother as the object took off. They went back to their house together.

Meagan's husband, Paul, had been on a late shift so they decided not to wake him. They told him about their experience the next day and he suggested telephoning the newspapers. Meagan was originally reluctant to become involved in hypnosis sessions, believing that her memories might be distorted by poor questioning, but when she was persuaded by one of the newspapers to participate it emerged that the aliens had attempted to lure her into the object, and that at one point both she and André had gone aboard. She described seeing chairs and funny lights. Then they leaped out of the craft and it was then that Meagan shouted to André to go and get his father.

The doctor conducting the examination commented: 'The impression I have is that this is a hysterical fantasy . . .' André was not keen to try hypnosis, and would not involve himself further in the investigation. As he died young in a motoring accident, further avenues of investigation as far as he is concerned are closed off.

HYPNOSIS: THERAPY OR RESEARCH?

Great controversy surrounds the use of regression hypnosis. Certainly it is of benefit to release trauma, and to help witnesses to work through their fears, regardless of whether these are generated by actual memories or fantasy. However, there are many doubts about its reliability in terms of producing hard data. The American approach has been to believe that the information which emerges reflects an underlying reality, but there is a great deal of evidence that the technique can create false memory, distort memory and solidify fears into beliefs. Experimental work carried out in the UK by ourselves and teams of researchers indicates that recall under hypnosis is not reliable, even if therapeutic. These experiments are outlined in more detail in *Gifts of the Gods?*.[42] As a result of these and other doubts BUFORA imposed a five-year moratorium on the use of regression hypnosis in its own cases which has been extended periodically and is at the time of writing still in force.

It must of course be remembered that not all accounts are related through regression hypnosis. The Villas Boas account of 1957 is only one example of an experience recalled consciously.

THE ABDUCTION DEBATE

The debate on abductions has remained, since the beginning, a question of whether or not such experiences are physically real. It is a widespread phenomenon which arises all around the Westernized world, and with very similar motifs and imagery, particularly in the increasingly similar descriptions of grays. The experiences of abductees often conform to a pattern which includes capture, examination, some form of communication, perhaps a tour of the craft and in many cases the near-

The modern face of alien visitation. This artist's reconstruction represents the 'gray', a type of humanoid alien frequently reported in modern close-encounter and abduction claims. But over time even this image has evolved, becoming increasingly more alien.

acquisition of tangible proof which is then retracted. Antonio Villas Boas tried to steal a clock-like object but was caught; Betty Hill was offered a book which was then taken back from her. This consistency around the world in tales told by people who clearly have not been in contact with each other or had access to material strongly suggests a reality.

The alternative is that the abduction phenomenon is a developing piece of folklore. Thomas 'Eddie' Bullard, who has a doctorate in folklore from Indiana University, has compiled a statistical survey of over 200 abduction cases. He believes that the evidence points to a reality behind the phenomenon.

If abductions are stories then unreliable reports should compare with reliable reports as one and the same, but they [largely] do not. If abductions are stories then the account should branch off into a different national version for each geographic area, but they do not. If abductions are stories the investigator should be able to impose an individual style on them . . . [which] . . . does not occur. If abductions are stories they should change according to an expected pattern over time, but their history is steady instead, even to the point of opposing external influences.[43]

Although Bullard's arguments are persuasive, there does seem to be more scope to the possibility of the abduction experience as folklore than he credits. Who, for example, decides which reports are reliable and which are not? The reality of UFO research is that there are no commonly accepted standards. Moreover, the abduction experience, as a modern phenomenon, may be the first kind of folklore to develop in a world of hi-tech, instant communication which unquestionably affects the degree to which it can mutate as it travels around the world. Bullard argues that if the reports are fiction, i.e., folklore, they should gradually come

through as a stereotype around the world; that abductions in early years should be less homogenous than those of later years. In fact there is evidence that this has happened in the years since his work. Certainly there has been a standardization of aliens over time, from the wide variety we considered in Chapter 1 to a large number of claims of one type: the 'grays'. And the massive influence of an abduction account by Whitley Strieber, which is described in the next chapter, has certainly served to create a stereotype which is becoming increasingly homogenous around the world.

We might also consider that later cases, if they were only stories, should draw from the imagery of earlier cases. Some abduction researchers have argued this does not happen, but it clearly does, notably in that so many cases follow almost precisely the detail of the Betty and Barney Hill account. However, it would have to be conceded that there have been 'non-leading' cases: for example the Hickson and Parker abduction at Pascagoula in 1973 was unique at the time and has never really been a strong image in subsequent reports. Indeed, similar aliens have only been reported on one other occasion.[44]

IMAGINARY ABDUCTEES

One radical piece of work undertaken in the mid-to-late 1970s was that of Professor Alvin Lawson. He speculated that the similarity of reports might reflect something common to all people. He conducted 'imaginary abductee' experiments, taking a group of test subjects in whom 'imaginary UFO "abductions" were induced hypnotically'. The result was that 'an averaged comparison of the imaginary sessions with "real" abduction regressions from the literature showed no substantive differences'. Lawson further concluded that the ability to fabricate was present, and that '"real" witnesses might

similarly confuse fact with fancy'. He examined the way some of the details raised by the test subjects related to their true medical histories and stated: 'There is an irresistible invitation to see a basis in memory and/or imagination for at least some details of "physical examinations" . . . It tells us that the interplay of imagination and memory may make determination of the unvarnished truth very difficult indeed.' Lawson's results were presented to the MUFON symposium in 1977 and written up in the *MUFON UFO Journal* of November that year.[45]

To explain the commonality of so many reported abductions, Lawson turned to the 'birth trauma hypothesis' – the theory that abductees were reliving their birth. He considered the close similarities between descriptions of 'grays' and the characteristics of the human foetus. 'These striking similarities suggest that the unborn child – particularly in the period of the first eight weeks from conception – may be a model for the humanoids reported in many close encounter cases.' Lawson argued that 'bad womb' experiences might create the 'bad' feelings 'on board flying saucers' and that 'good womb' experiences could engender feelings of 'cosmic unity, transcendence . . . visions . . . and other parallels with mystical or ecstatic experiences.' He noted that many abductees reported tunnel imagery when boarding a UFO, but that seven subjects who had been born by Caesarean section had no such recollections. An eighth subject delivered by Caesarean did describe such imagery, but it turned out that she had spent two hours in the birth canal before the operation.[46]

Controversy rages on. In future years it might be impossible to unscramble the possibilities Lawson identified, for today the abduction experience has 'come of age', as we shall see in the next chapter, and has its own existence as a cultural belief from which people can draw images.

What has to date been underplayed in our view is that UFO research per se has largely been undertaken by a homogenous group of mostly white middle-class males from technological cultures. They therefore inevitably interpret the stories they hear through their own world view. The Betty and Barney Hill case became a stereotype with which every abduction researcher is familiar, and which is carried around by them in every investigation they undertake.[47] It is possible, then, that the recall of witnesses is being subconsciously modified to fit that model. Certainly we have seen examples of the questioning of witnesses where it is evident that their statements are being measured against expectations. For example, a witness referring to 'an object' may have a question put back to him or her which refers to 'the saucer'.

THE MJ12 DOCUMENTS

The decade had been a fraught one, to say the least: the subject had gone from obscurity to madness. Inspired by fiction, it virtually became fiction in all its public faces, even if a real phenomenon was calmly biding its time beneath the surface and being sensibly researched in places such as Hessdalen. In addition, whatever their origin, the importance of the 'abduction experiences' was beginning to be examined. But the decade which had to all intents and purposes begun with Roswell would end with a new Roswell twist, and one which remains the subject of debate to this day.

In 1979 William Moore co-wrote *The Philadelphia Experiment* with Charles Berlitz and later became interested in UFOs as a result of reading Frank Scully's book *Behind Flying Saucers*.[15] Although he later came to recognize that this book contained hoaxes, his appetite for crashed saucers had been whetted. He later co-authored, again with Charles Berlitz, *The*

Roswell Incident, published in 1980.[48] Unsatisfied with aspects of that book, he broke with Berlitz and teamed up with Stanton Friedman, a well-known advocate of the Roswell story. But it was *The Roswell Incident*, the first book on the subject, which, he says, encouraged the US government to recruit him as a 'spy' within the UFO field, something which he admitted in later years. By now a director of APRO, he was approached by a man known as Falcon who was, according to Moore, 'a well-placed individual within the intelligence community who claimed to be directly connected to a high-level government project dealing with UFOs'.

Moore's job was to monitor Paul Bennewitz and his Project Beta. It appears that Bennewitz had filmed top-secret government projects at Kirtland Air Force Base. Moore was unimpressed by Bennewitz's eventual revelations, commenting that his theories had 'blossomed into a tale that rivalled the wildest science-fiction scenario anyone could possibly imagine'. Bennewitz believed that two alien forces who were themselves in opposition to each other had invaded the United States. Something like the 'Adamski aliens', the blond, beautiful Nordics, were promoting a sort of '*Star Trek* federation' brotherhood opposed by the grays, who were into human and animal manipulation. Bennewitz was of the opinion that the government was aware of both forces, had entered into treaties with the aliens, and was working with the grays in underground bases.

Moore learned that the government had been feeding Bennewitz this bizarre information, presumably to discredit him in order to deflect attention away from the real things he had filmed and spoken about. Some of his work might have given away clues to the development of government projects. Moore's job was to determine whether the disinformation campaign was

succeeding. The specific reason why he was asked to target Bennewitz was never made very clear, although it is highly likely that he succeeded in deflecting Bennewitz from filming what were probably government aircraft in development.

Moore presumably undertook this work because he believed it would take him closer to a genuine governmental truth about UFOs. Quite why he believed he would be given credible information when he himself was instrumental in feeding another ufologist garbage is unclear, but Moore continued in hope.

As a researcher, he decided he needed some back-up and teamed up with Jaime Shandera, a TV producer. Shandera was not particularly devoted to UFOs, but had had discussions with Moore about making a fictional film inspired by the Roswell incident. Journalist Howard Blum's description of Shandera is of a man neither successful nor unsuccessful but 'looking for the next deal, scurrying after the rights to the next hot property'.[22]

The team was now established. Stanton Friedman, Bill Moore and Jaime Shandera: the ardent UFO researcher committed to a belief in extraterrestrials and in a genuine crash near Roswell; a convert with a potential door into the US government intelligence services, and an uncommitted but reasonably experienced documentary producer who would have the instinct, they hoped, to separate the wheat from the chaff.

How fortunate then, that it was to this team that the MJ12 documents should have been delivered. Shandera indicates that he believes they came to him from

---

The MJ12 documents are believed by many to be proof of the US government's involvment in UFO crash retrievals. But they came to light under suspicious circumstances. Are they the proof that researchers have sought, government disinformation, or a hoax?

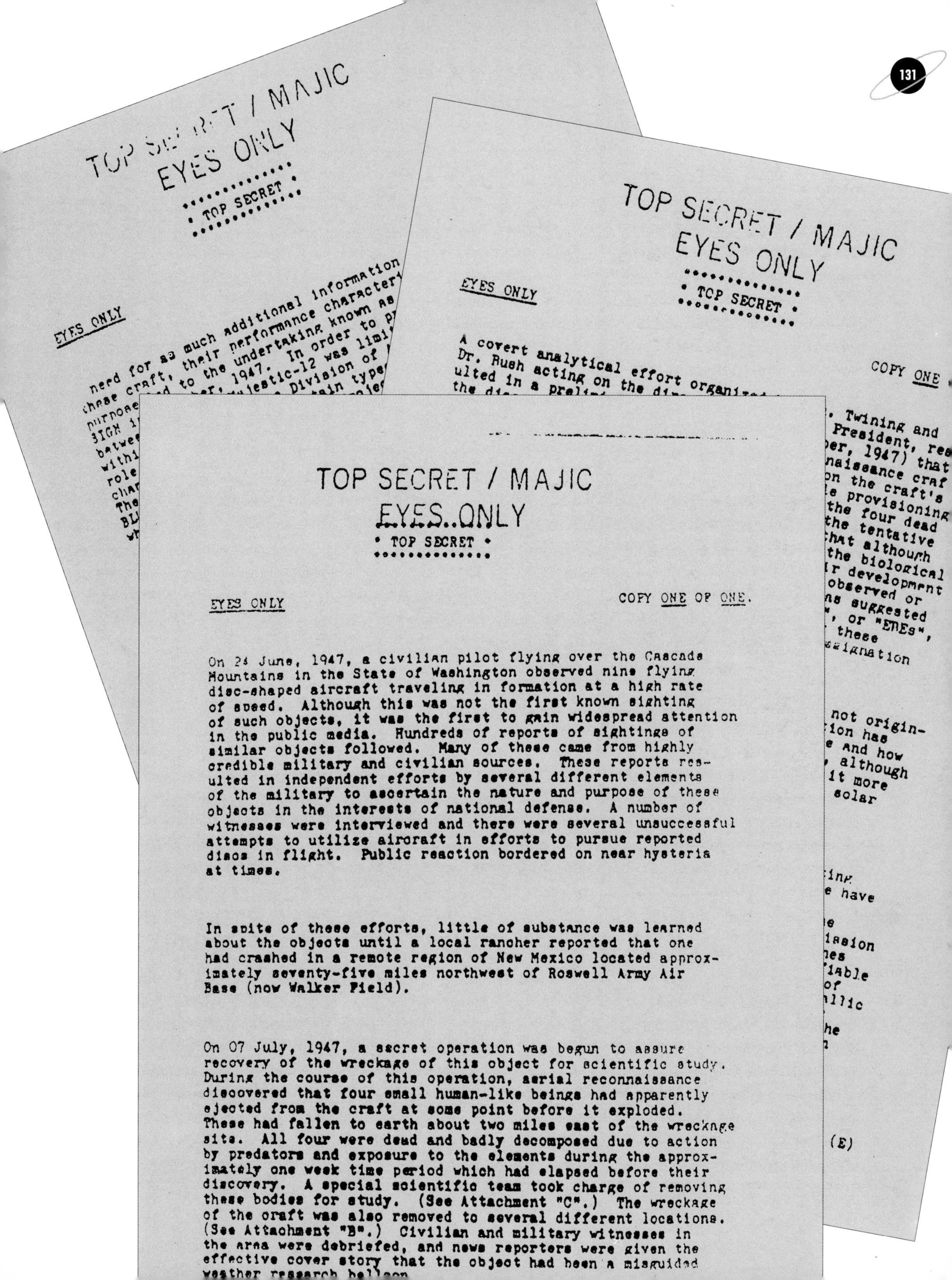

Top (back-left page, partial):

EYES ONLY

need for as much additional information
these craft, their performance character
purpose . . . to the undertaking known as
1947. In order to p
3IGM in . . . er, Majestic-12 was limi
betwee . . . a Division of . . .
withi . . . . . . rtain type
role . . .
The . . .
BL . . .
wh . . .

Right page (partial):

EYES ONLY   COPY ONE

A covert analytical effort organized . . .
Dr. Bush acting on the dir . . .
ulted in a prelim . . .
the dis . . .

. Twining and
. President, re . . .
. . . er, 1947) that
. . . naissance craf
. . . on the craft's
. . . le provisioning
. . . the four dead
. . . the tentative
. . . hat although
. . . the biological
. . . r development
. . . observed or
. . . ns suggested
. . ., or "EBEs",
. . . these
. . . signation

. not origin-
. . . ion has
. . . e and how
. . ., although
. . . it more
. . . solar

. . . ting
. . . e have
. . . e
. . . ission
. . . es
. . . iable
. . . of
. . . lic
. . . he

(E)

Front (center) page:

EYES ONLY   COPY ONE OF ONE.

On 24 June, 1947, a civilian pilot flying over the Cascade
Mountains in the State of Washington observed nine flying
disc-shaped aircraft traveling in formation at a high rate
of speed. Although this was not the first known sighting
of such objects, it was the first to gain widespread attention
in the public media. Hundreds of reports of sightings of
similar objects followed. Many of these came from highly
credible military and civilian sources. These reports resulted in independent efforts by several different elements
of the military to ascertain the nature and purpose of these
objects in the interests of national defense. A number of
witnesses were interviewed and there were several unsuccessful
attempts to utilize aircraft in efforts to pursue reported
discs in flight. Public reaction bordered on near hysteria
at times.

In spite of these efforts, little of substance was learned
about the objects until a local rancher reported that one
had crashed in a remote region of New Mexico located approximately seventy-five miles northwest of Roswell Army Air
Base (now Walker Field).

On 07 July, 1947, a secret operation was begun to assure
recovery of the wreckage of this object for scientific study.
During the course of this operation, aerial reconnaissance
discovered that four small human-like beings had apparently
ejected from the craft at some point before it exploded.
These had fallen to earth about two miles east of the wreckage
site. All four were dead and badly decomposed due to action
by predators and exposure to the elements during the approximately one week time period which had elapsed before their
discovery. A special scientific team took charge of removing
these bodies for study. (See Attachment "C".) The wreckage
of the craft was also removed to several different locations.
(See Attachment "B".) Civilian and military witnesses in
the area were debriefed, and news reporters were given the
effective cover story that the object had been a misguided
weather research balloon.

contacts in the US government. If the documents were genuine, and the US government wanted them to be released in a credible way, even acknowledging that they might have been using the 'deep throat' principle it was a curious decision to pick a team of committed UFO researchers. Release to a large number of highly placed research institutions, universities and investigative journalists, who by definition would have been more objective, along with leads for following up the information, would seem more appropriate. If true, the very fact that the MJ12 documents were given to this team, and in secret, suggests that they were fakes being used for disinformation purposes.

On the other hand, it would be foolish not to acknowledge the possibility that one or more of the team faked the documents themselves. If they were looking for something to inject life into their own personal theories and the subject of the proposed film, they could hardly have chosen anything better.

Howard Blum describes Moore's feelings as 'a rush of victory, a sudden understanding that the four years he had put in with the Falcon had not been in vain'.[22]

The MJ12 documents were photographed on a roll of undeveloped film which was apparently anonymously dropped through Shandera's letterbox on 11 December 1984. Shandera took the film to a meeting with Bill Moore later that day, and they developed the film at Moore's house.

The original documents consist of two items: first, an Eisenhower briefing document dated 18 November 1952, and secondly an executive memorandum from Harry Truman dated 24 September 1947.

They set out details of Operation Majestic 12, which is defined as 'a top secret research and development/intelligence operation . . . established by special classified executive order of President

Truman on 24th September 1947', and describe the retrieval of human-like entities from a flying-saucer crash in 1947 and comment on the likelihood of this being extraterrestrial.

Moore, Shandera and Friedman kept the MJ12 documents secret for two years while they tried to establish their authenticity. Since they were revealed, there have been many debates about this, based on minute details, most of which would seem to be unnecessarily speculative. For example, the memorandum written by Harry Truman was thought to be 'un-Truman-like' in style. Truman's signature was subjected to all sorts of tests which merely proved to one faction that it was genuine and to another that it was a fake. The way the date was written seemed inconsistent with other documents, and whether or not a particular comma should have been inserted was disputed. Again, both sides found evidence to support their viewpoint.

In the end, this focus on detail proved very little, and neither was it likely to do so. Even the best researchers are prone to 'the ratchet effect', where every turn in one direction tightens the screw but a turn in the other does nothing except leave it where it is. So it is with ufological clues. Facts that support your belief are accepted, and those which do not are ignored, in whatever part of the spectrum your belief happens to reside. In short, if the documents were faked and mistakes had been made, the supporters of the documents would hold that perversely, those mistakes were, like scars in fine leather, proof of their authenticity. So when Harry Truman's signature was found to be exactly the same as an example on another document, one faction claimed this as proof of its authenticity and the other pointed out that no one signs his signature in an identical way every time. And so it went on.

The problem with UFOlogy, as we have

seen, is that it often consists of the opposition of polarized viewpoints rather than scientific analysis, particularly where dramatic or exciting possibilities are concerned. Stanton Friedman could hardly have resisted approaching the MJ12 documents with the hope that they were real and Philip Klass, who was shortly to get in on the act, would have set out to determine that they were fakes. It was Philip Klass who wrote to William Baker, assistant director officer of congressional and public affairs at the FBI, on 4 June 1987, asking for clarification regarding the MJ12 documents. Not surprisingly, the FBI offered no clarification.

If the documents are fakes, then the fakers had done their homework in early UFO literature; if they are genuine, then there are supporting clues to be found in some of the lesser-known books of the early years. Brinsley le Poer Trench comments: 'I do not think the US Air Force is the organisation responsible for withholding information about the UFOs. I consider that the policy on UFOs comes from a higher level and that various government agencies, including the Central Intelligence Agency (CIA) are instruments used to keep the truth withheld.' He refers to an article recounting a conversation between Wilbert Smith and C.W. Fitch. 'Mr Smith told him that it was not the US Air Force but "a small group very high up in the government."'

And he mentions a book published in America in 1964 called *The Invisible Government* which hints at the same possibilities. The group, it is said, was 'instigated during the Truman administration . . . it is called the 54/12 group.' Is this MJ12?[7]

The Moore–Shandera–Friedman team were blessed – some would say suspiciously blessed – with good luck. Next they were sent a postcard which set them off on a treasure hunt culminating in the discovery of a third document, the Cutler–Twining memo. This is the last of the papers known as the MJ12 documents. It was located in the National Archives in July 1985. The Cutler–Twining memo complemented the other two MJ12 documents perfectly. Signed by Robert Cutler, the special assistant to the president, and dated 14 July 1954, it referred to the MJ12 briefing and asked General Twining to rearrange his plans for a White House meeting. Bearing in mind that this was discovered in the National Archives and not on a roll delivered to Moore or Shandera, this document seemed to confirm the existence of MJ12 and therefore to strengthen the reliability of its counterparts. But the possibility that the Cutler–Twining document had been deliberately planted in the archives for Moore and Shandera to find, as part of the disinformation, must be considered. Indeed, there were arguments about its authenticity, for example, whether the paper was of a type in use by the government at that time.

Philip Klass was highly suspicious of the way the document was found, pointing out that it was a very small needle within the National Archives' huge haystack. However, fake or not, planted or not, they did find it. If the document was unlikely to be discovered but discovery was needed – and it did confirm Moore and Shandera's beliefs – then there could also be some suspicion that it was put there by Moore or Shandera. This would mean they would have had to have taken it into the archives with them. Howard Blum indicates that he feels this is unlikely as the archives are so highly secure.[22] That remains a matter for speculation. If the stakes were high enough, presumably the document could have been concealed. Whether this scenario is feasible for the National Archives Maryland branch in 1985 is unclear, but no security is impregnable, as we have discussed.

In response to inquiries, the National Archives examined the document and issued a statement on 22 July 1987 which expressed concerns over its authenticity. Many doubts were listed: incorrect references, security markings and an apparently incongruous filing location. It was indicated that Eisenhower's appointments as officially recorded did not agree with the memo, and that apparently no support could be found for the document in other inquiries to official records.[49]

The Fund for UFO Research raised $16,000 to support investigation of the Majestic 12 documents, but in the end the analysis proved exactly what might have been expected – nothing. In his book *Out There* Howard Blum quotes 'an exasperated FBI agent' as having said: 'It wouldn't surprise me if we never know if the papers are genuine or not.'[22] He might have been speaking for ufologists the world over.

DONALD MENZEL

One character in the story of UFOs who merits a mention is the American archsceptic Donald Menzel, professor of astrophysics at Harvard University and one-time chairman of the department of astronomy. He was active in the first decade of UFOs, but it is in this later one that an astonishing twist in his story arises.

Menzel believed UFOs to be the product of misidentification and bad science. He wrote a book rubbishing the subject in 1953. Hilary Evans comments: 'The impression we get is that Menzel was willing to entertain any conjecture, no matter how implausible, rather than admit that the [witnesses] may have actually seen what they claimed to see.'[50] Evans cites the example of Menzel's appreciation of the case outlined in Chapter 1 in which Lieutenant Gorman engaged in an aerial 'dogfight' with

a UFO. Menzel believes several witnesses were seeing a lighted balloon for a time and a mirage of Jupiter for the rest. As Evans says, almost in an echo of Oscar Wilde, 'To mistake one natural object for a UFO could happen to anyone; but to mistake two, on a single occasion, strains credibility more than the possibility that Gorman was really confronted by an unknown object'.

Asked what should be done about UFO reports that 'can't be explained' Menzel's written reply was, 'Throw them in the wastebasket!' In fact his beliefs, though possibly genuinely and passionately held, might have been the result of his now well-known associations with both the CIA and the NSA. However, when the MJ12 documents turned up Menzel was included in the list of twelve government specialists charged with crash-retrieval examinations. The implication is too good to be true: that Menzel, while rubbishing the subject, was actually studying captured flying saucers!

Stanton Friedman examined this unlikely claim and believes it has merit. He uncovered what he believes was Menzel's 'dual life' in working on 'black' projects hitherto unknown to UFO researchers. However, if the MJ12 documents are fakes, then the presence of Menzel's name on the list greatly increases the probability that they were created by ufologists: his inclusion in the documents would be an act of almost exquisite mischief.

If crash retrieval and conspiracy had been the principle themes of this decade then the abduction phenomenon had run them a close second. Budd Hopkins' work had encouraged many others to enter the field, and analysis of 'alien abductions' was now a worldwide aspect of the subject. But in 1987 *Communion*, a book by an American horror writer, was published and dramatically changed even this embryonic area.[51]

1987-1997

The Decade of Autonomy

'May you live in interesting times.'
Ancient Chinese Curse

What most characterizes the UFO advances in this most recent decade is that there was no particular political or social pressure for them to be achieved. The phenomenon had taken on a momentum of its own and was only now justified as being a 'force' in its own right. Yet at the start of this period it was still very much a minority-interest subject. That was to change with the release of just one book.

COMMUNION

Whitley Strieber's *Communion*, published in 1987, was an account of his own abduction experiences.[1] The story is similar to the claims of many, but it is both well explored and well written, for he was already a successful novelist. *Communion* and its successors recount a possibly life-long interaction with 'the visitors' – perhaps extraterrestrial beings, or else something more intertwined with the human race over centuries. His experiences have included abduction aboard strange craft-like objects, medical and other examinations, and 'visitor' interaction with his family. His first recollection is of an entity encounter in December 1985, which happened during the night and involved a figure in his bedroom. 'I saw two dark holes for eyes,' he recalls, 'and a black down-turning line of a mouth that later became an O.'

American horror writer Whitley Strieber made the best-seller lists with his account of his own abduction in the book *Communion*.

Strieber confirmed to us his earliest feelings about his experiences when we spoke to him in April 1996.

I thought that my encounter in December '85 had been physically real, but that it had been a rape. That the house had been invaded by crazies, and that I was remembering these big eyes and stuff because of the fear. Maybe they were wearing dark glasses. And eventually when [the doctor] placed me under hypnosis I had expected – and I think he had expected too – that we would see human faces. And his objective – as a forensic hypnotist he had worked with the police for many

years – was to obtain access to evidence of the crime. That was what he thought he was doing. Among the things that happened during this hypnosis session that really threw him, and eventually for that reason also threw me, was that I spontaneously flashed back . . . to an experience of the same kind that had happened when I was a child.

Strieber accepted that hypnosis is not always accurate; indeed, 'I don't think it is accurate very often,' he said. But he added:

In my case it's a little different because first of all the hypnotist was highly sceptical. And second, there was quite some extensive background of normal conscious memory at the time of hypnosis. And the hypnosis – except for that regression back to the earlier experience – didn't really bring out any new narratives. It was all the same but just more vivid, which is exactly what forensic hypnosis is meant to do. That's how it works . . . [the doctor] was viewing it as a case of traumatic amnesia. It was very familiar to him; he had extracted forensic information from hundreds of witnesses in his career.

(Opposite) One of the most photographed cases in UFO history is the Gulf Breeze case triggered by the claims of Ed Walters in 1987. One feature was the 'blue beam' which 'attacked' both Walters and his wife (see pages 153 – 156).

One of the most significant effects of the release of the book, and subsequent film, was the introduction of the subject to a much wider audience. There can be no doubt that *Communion* influenced millions of people who might never have done more than glance at reports in their tabloid newspapers and dismiss them. And it was almost certainly one of the earliest triggers for such current astonishing successes as *The X-Files*.

Another important effect was the hardening of the motifs of the abduction experience. In particular Strieber's accounts include missing time and screen memory, reinforcing a 'model' for experiencers and researchers alike. This had happened once with Betty and Barney Hill; now it was happening on an even wider scale. In some cases this is helpful: those experiencing similar life events can more easily deal with them if they are given a pre-existing 'template'. But in spite of the fact that Strieber himself made it clear he was struggling to understand the template, many experiencers and researchers alike have viewed it almost as if cast in stone and ignored his cautions.

IMPLANTS

A strong belief has grown up that abductees are 'implanted' with technological devices. Typically, they are inserted in the nasal cavities, in the ear or behind the eye. Such positions imply to some that they are designed in some way to affect the brain. That said, there are claims of implants elsewhere in the body, in the toes and penis, for example.

If the implants are genuine, and technological, then what are they for? It has been suggested that they may be tracking devices which enable the aliens to locate their abductees, or psychotronic ones designed to impel abductees to particular actions or beliefs. A third theory is that they enhance certain brain activity, perhaps psychic abilities.

UFO researcher Doctor David Jacobs discovered during his work: 'Towards the end of the examination, the aliens either implant a small, round seemingly metallic object in the abductee's ear, nose, or sinus cavity, or remove such an object. The object is . . . small, it usually is smooth, or has small spikes sticking out of it, or has holes in it.'[2] John Mack, professor of psychiatry at Harvard Medical School, comments: 'I have myself studied a $\frac{1}{2}$ to $\frac{3}{4}$-inch thin, wiry object that was given to me by one of my clients.'[3]

In *Witnessed*, Budd Hopkins tells us that an X-ray on abductee 'Linda Cortile' showed 'the presence of a complex, radiopaque, metallic object in Linda's nasal cavity . . . it provided solid evidence of an alien implant, a radiologic smoking gun.'[4] But before the device could be removed for examination, Linda was apparently abducted again and the implant removed. Hopkins claims this was evident when she woke up one morning with an extensive nosebleed. He believes that aliens know when their devices have been located and that: 'It is unlikely that they would ever let us capture such a prize if they could possibly prevent it.' In this instance the device shown in the X-ray seems more clearly 'technological' than those that are allegedly recovered, but since it could not be retrieved many doubts about its origin must remain.

The search for implants has been ambiguous. Several such 'devices' have been found, but nothing has yet proven them to be of manufactured design. Some researchers maintain that manufactured devices have been retrieved, but the counter-argument runs that what has been extracted from abductees are normal tissue secretions of the body.

Another possibility is that this motif of implants reflects beliefs. Certainly more is believed about them than has been proven

by examining them. Given that the abduction experience may be a 'Western' interpretation of an unknown experience, then the suggestion of implants might be a manifestation of a fear of modern technology. The idea of being 'turned into a machine, or robot' is a very deep-seated fear in the West, and perhaps, like so many facets in the history of UFO beliefs, this fear is materializing.

THE GENETIC STUDY THEORY

Researchers have been at pains to discover not only whether UFOs are extraterrestrial, but, if they are, what they are doing. Budd Hopkins said of UFO research many years ago: 'It was as if we were trying to record the license plate number on the getaway car without having understood what the crime was.'[5] The most commonly held theory at present, particularly among American researchers, is that aliens are engaged on a study programme of genetic examination and manipulation. Current elaborate theories have been presented suggesting that either the human race is a biological experimental programme which the aliens are monitoring and updating, or they require something from humans which is absent in their own genetic make-up. These theories are rejected by Whitley Strieber, who states in *Breakthrough*, his third book on his experiences: 'They didn't want slaves or genes or souls . . . you don't get wooed by someone who is attacking you.'[6] Strieber believes that the 'visitor' contacts are beneficial and not a form of aggressive invasion. Strieber is interesting in that he has, for many, crystallized the abduction experience as real, while at the same time rejecting much that is theorized about it.

In the first abduction case, that of Betty and Barney Hill, each claimed to have been examined by the aliens separately. This has been a feature of many reports since then, although there have been occasions when two or three people have been examined in the same room. Dr David Jacobs describes accounts of possibly hundreds of subjects in one huge room being examined all together.[2]

Most of the medical examinations centre on the reproductive and sexual systems and involve samples of sperm and ova being removed. Several female abductees claim, like 'Kathie Davis' (Debbie Jordan) in Chapter 4, that they have been impregnated and that the hybrid alien–human offspring has been removed during a later experience on a flying saucer. The women are sometimes later 'bonded' with their 'children' during subsequent abductions. British abductee Maria Ward suffered a 'bedroom visitation' abduction following which she remembered 'having something done to me in my womb – I could feel something moving around inside me.'

John E. Mack comments: 'The purely physical or biological aspect of the abduction phenomenon seems to have to do with some sort of genetic or quasi-genetic engineering for the purpose of creating human/alien hybrid offspring. We have no evidence of alien-induced genetic alteration in the strictly biological sense, although it is possible that this has occurred.'[3] Mack mentions one abductee, Ed, who was sexually stimulated by his abductors, who admitted that they needed his sperm 'to create special babies' and 'for work we are doing to help the people on your planet'. Budd Hopkins is very clear that this is a central theme:

We know a great deal now about what's going on. Whoever, or whatever, the UFO occupants are they seem extremely interested in studying us on the physical level: human reproduction, our DNA, the way on the emotional level we treat one another in sexual or loving relationships. But most especially how we treat our children. And it seems to be, even though this sounds totally crazy, that they are interested in producing some kind of hybrid mix of themselves and ourselves.

This emerging theory of hybridization is offered as an explanation for many claims, and it is one we cannot ignore in a study which seeks to examine the cultural and social background against which the UFO phenomenon has been reported, examined and measured. We have already seen the clear correlation between certain early science-fiction images and some key UFO reports, and this particular image also exists within science fiction – almost exclusively American science fiction.

American science fiction seems to be almost obsessed with duality of identity, and with exploring the inner conflict that arises in individuals of mixed background. Perhaps the most obvious example is the character of Spock in *Star Trek*, who is half Vulcan and half human. Many episodes of the series involved the inner struggle between the fierce logic of one half of his personality and the fierce passions of the other. In the first film of the series, *Star Trek – The Motion Picture*, this theme is expanded, setting Spock's own dilemma against a subplot involving the inner struggle of a hybrid machine formed from a reconstituted Voyager probe and an alien probe searching for its 'creator', and determined to meet it's 'father' face to face.

Data, the android in *Star Trek – the Next Generation* struggles to become human despite himself, and many of the episodes of that series examine that theme, exploring Data's emerging consciousness, his dreams and something akin to a near-death experience. In the episode 'Unification' Spock and Data work together, and discuss Spock's attempts to suppress his humanity and Data's attempts to develop his. 'You have abandoned,' Data tells Spock, 'what I have sought all my life.'

Other characters include Worf, a Klingon virtually cast out by his own race, who works within the disciplines of the human-dominated Federation. Counsellor

Troi is half-human, half-Betazoid. And in a story running through several programmes the fully-human Tasha Yar is killed, returned to the series in a time warp, and killed again – but not before, as it later turns out, becoming concubine to a Romulan and producing a half-human, half-Romulan daughter who hates the Federation that created her.

If the only examples we could find were in *Star Trek* then we might dismiss the whole theme as the obsession of Gene Roddenberry, its creator. But it goes much deeper, and starts much earlier, than that. America is the country that invented the superheroes, perhaps most famously Superman and Batman, who have become global characters. One advertising survey indicated that Superman's red and yellow 'S' symbol and Batman's black and yellow 'bat' symbol were among the most commonly identified images in the world. Neither is actually a hybrid, but central to both characters is a dual identity. Superman, powerful, seemingly immortal and possessed of inner strength, masquerades as meek, mild-mannered Clark Kent. Many of the comic-strip stories, right up to the *New Adventures of Superman* (*Lois and Clark* in the US), examine the humour and pain inherent in that split personality. In the films starring Christopher Reeve, Superman 'confronts himself' many times, not least in *Superman 3*, when he is physically split and ends up fighting a 'thug-like' version of himself. There is also the obvious emotional conflict between his memories of his parents on their home planet, Krypton, and his care and love for humanity and his adoptive human parents, the Kents. Batman's alter ego is Bruce Wayne, and the three recent films, culminating in *Batman Forever*, have been dominated by his inner battle to understand his own true identity.

And Spiderman, Green Lantern, Flash and Wonder Woman, to name but a few, all have 'secret identities'. Somewhere in all their stories arises the inevitable inner conflict this causes, typically when a 'civilian' falls in love with one half but not the other.

The American preoccupation with dual identity is perhaps best illustrated by the fate of the British science-fiction character Dr Who, who had survived on British television since 1963 as a time lord from the planet Gallifrey. In the thirty-three years of broadcasts and novelizations the Doctor was never identified as anything other than a pure-bred member of his race. The series had run in the US, but always on the lower-profile networks. Then, in 1996, American backers gave the programme a new lease of life, but imposed many changes. The Master, the Doctor's arch-enemy, discovers the Doctor's greatest secret. In amazed and awed tones the Master reveals: 'The Doctor's half-human!'

GRAYS

Another image which crystallised as a result of Whitley Strieber's account was the appearance of the alien beings themselves. In the early years of the UFO, as the earlier chapters demonstrate, a great variety of entities was reported -giants, dwarfs, hairy creatures, one-eyed beings and so on – but gradually a 'classic' form, the gray, developed. In later accounts we see the image of the grays not just consolidating but also mutating. Although apparently the same creatures – at least, according to the content of the abduction material offered by witnesses – they somehow became 'more alien'. They grew thinner, the head got larger and more domed; the eyes became bigger and lost the pupils the Hills had reported. Other facial features became almost non-existent.

And this has occurred all around the world. For example, in 1994, leading UFO researcher Cynthia Hind investigated a case at Arial School in Ruwa, near Harare in Zimbabwe. An object had landed or hovered near the school and had been seen by many of the children. Afterwards, Cynthia interviewed many of them, and found a common report of a 'little man dressed in a tight-fitting black suit' who had 'huge eyes like rugby balls'. The children drew what they had seen, and many of the pictures show entities we would describe as 'grays'.[7]

This image of 'grays' remains the predominant description, but recently witnesses have introduced a more 'insect-like' quality in reports. Not long ago we spoke to a young man from Somalia whose father had seen entities he described as being like human-sized 'big ants'. And some of Strieber's accounts suggest similarities to praying mantises.

JOHN MACK

The abduction experience came under new focus with the work of Professor Mack, who worked with over 100 abductees and concluded that their experiences were real and involved alien intervention. Many hold that the support of such an eminent individual is proof that abductions are indeed real, and certainly his backing for the theory attracted worldwide attention and publicity. His book[3] is every bit as impressive as those written by Bud Hopkins, David Jacobs and others – but no more so, and this needs to be appreciated.

Mack gives full credit to Hopkins: 'I wish to acknowledge the special place and support of Budd Hopkins, who introduced me to this work, including demonstrating the use and value of hypnosis in working with abductees,' he was quoted as saying in a magazine.[8] At first it may seem surprising that Mack needed to be introduced, and believed that it was already an area of expertise. But Mack himself admits that it was not. 'Very few therapists who are familiar with or open to the abduction phenomenon are trained in the use of hypno-sis. I had little training in hypnosis as a psychiatric resident and had virtually to teach myself, observing and obtaining support from Budd Hopkins.' Curiosity apart, Mack was drawn to the work because (at the time of his writing) 'There is not yet, to my knowledge, a single article describing the abduction phenomenon in a mainstream psychiatric journal, though I have been trying to correct this situation.'

He seems to have become convinced of the reality of abductions well before he wrote his book. In 1992 he wrote: 'I do not regard abductees as patients in the usual sense. Rather, they are, with some exceptions, normal and healthy persons who have undergone disturbing and mysterious experiences.'[8] *Abduction* was published in 1994, allegedly after Mack had tried to persuade Harvard to bring it out as an academic work.[9] Harvard, it seems, did not appreciate the offer, and in 1995 there were strong indications that Mack was to be heavily criticized. A three-man team investigated his work and claims to see whether or not they were in keeping with the standards of the institution. It seems he also upset a few academics by promoting his book on chat shows such as those hosted by Oprah Winfrey and Larry King.[9]

Whatever Harvard thought, in the end they backed down and Mack was lauded by the UFO community for his courage. Of his conclusions he is honest enough to admit the possibility that 'it is my own mind that has created this coherence, and that I have shaped and interpreted the data in line with a structure that I already have in mind'. He believes he has not done so, however, pointing out that he started out as a sceptic. But in the final analysis, Mack does not provide an 'external audit' of the research. He is a committed convert doing the same work as Hopkins, Jacobs and others, and within much the same structure and belief system.

THE COMING OF AGE

In 1947 UFOs became a phenomenon separate from other paranormal phenomena; in the 1990s they have 'come of age', becoming socially acceptable. They are no longer viewed in the context of events of the day, such as the space programme in the 1950s and 1960s; now they are an independent subject of interest. It is just unfortunate that, rather than coming of age in the era of Walter Kronkite, UFOlogy arrived in the era of the game-show mentality, the decade of cynicism.

In the 1990s everything is entertainment, and the truth does not matter; the West is pervaded by cheapness, superficiality and irrelevance. The media treats news as if it were a commodity designed to increase audiences and readerships. Should aliens ever hover over the White House Lawn, they will probably be cajoled by a TV audience to 'Come on down!' UFOs, then, have not been presented as news, but as cheap tabloid sensationalism.

The degree of 'acceptance' of UFOs has been pointed out by our colleague Mark Pilkington. 'A sure sign of UFOs' cultural significance is their use in advertising; in both the UK and the US they have helped to sell, amongst other things, fridges, cars, beer, soft drinks, banks and jeans. *Spaceman*, the song featured in a Levi's jeans commercial, was number one in the singles charts all over the world and featured a "gray" alien face on the record cover.'[10] There is also an advertising sketch using an MIB to sell lager, and grays have been used in advertising campaigns for cigarettes and other products. Hot

Crop circles became a UFO-related subject almost as soon as they were reported in 1980. Over time the flattened patterns in the crops became increasingly more elaborate until there was little question of an intelligence behind them. But an intelligence from where?

on the heels of the film *Independence Day*, a film based on MIBs, *Men in Black*, is due for release in 1997. And the involvement of UFOs in the background of such programmes as *The X-Files*, which has itself created huge interest in the subject, is obvious.

The reaction to *Independence Day*, released in 1996, showed the depths to which dislike of the government had sunk. Columnist William Langley, reporting from Washington, commented: 'In cinemas all over America audiences are rising to their feet and cheering as an alien spaceship's death ray zaps the White House. Their reaction demonstrates that most Americans would consider rule from outer space a preferable alternative to what they are getting. Government has become such a dirty word that not even politicians are using it. The only dirtier word I can think of is "Washington" which can now barely be uttered on TV before 10 p.m.'

Another American columnist wrote: 'Once a beloved and beautiful symbol of the nation, the White House has come to signify a remote and corrupt government.' Langley went on to sum up what is virtually

one of the central themes of this book:

Not long ago the same pundits were writing off the wave of anti-government sentiment as a passing fad stirred up by a handful of right wing cranks and gun nuts. Anyone that complained that Washington was out of control was deemed to believe in screwball conspiracy theories about the US being softened up for take-over by foreign powers and the forces of Satan. Now the dislike of the establishment is so pervasive that even the government is running scared of the government![11]

CROP CIRCLES

Modern ufology was not just delving deeper into its 'standard' examples of manifestation. This coming of age increased its reach, and it began to encompass new areas.

In the 1980s, patterns of flattened cereal crops in fields attracted attention and quickly became associated with the UFO phenomenon. The beginning of the crop-circle story dates back to 'simple-pattern' sightings starting in 1980 – if there were earlier incidents

Doug Baker and Dave Chorley worked with documentary producers John and Jayne Macnish to prove that they could easily produce the features of crop circles that enthusiasts were claiming as proof of extraterrestrial involvement. They worked at night, under constant observation.

they had not triggered awareness or drawn attention to the subject as a new and significant phenomenon within the UFO enigma. The 1980 report was the Kenneth Arnold of circle lore. At first it was concluded that the pattern had been flattened by air pressure, but the circles slowly proliferated and grew in complexity over the years. Then, in the summer of 1990, the first 'pictograms' appeared, the most elaborate at Cheesefoot Head and Fawley Down, and at Alton Barns and West Kennett Long Barrow, in and around Wiltshire. The formations were composed

not only of circles but bars, rectangles, key shapes and more. The wind alone could no longer be held responsible: there had to be an intelligence behind them.

The UFO connection that had earlier been implied, if not stated openly, was the theory that the circles of flattened crops were the landing sites of flying saucers. George Woods, for example, visited the Warminster area and saw 'in a corn field a large triangular shaped area about 30ft by 50ft of flattened corn, caused he believes by an object landing'.[12] That theory had to be abandoned in the face of the pictograms: no one had ever reported anything flying in the air that could remotely have caused these formations if it had landed. But the 'UFO connection', once made, was not easily surrendered, so now the crop circles were interpreted as messages from the aliens:

depictions of codes such as DNA, drawings to inspire the developing minds of the witnesses, or something akin to the plaque we put on the Voyager spacecraft to alert other civilizations to our existence on Earth.

The crop-circle phenomenon could be seen as potentially two separate phenomena. The possibility that some 'simple' circles were formed naturally was strengthened by the explanation of meteorologist Dr Terence Meaden, who said that the circles could be formed by a miniature vortex. Indeed, there are some witness accounts of circles forming in this way. The other aspect was those formations which could not have been caused in this way; those which required planning and intelligence. To critical observers, it seemed unnecessary to look further than human intelligence to find their creators.

The simplest clues were the strongest: the patterns increased greatly in number whenever the media was watching, which was a curious approach for aliens to have decided on. Before 1987, annual sightings were recorded in single figures. That year there were twenty-six reports, and as media attention focused on the mystery, 1988 produced an estimated fifty patterns, and 1989 around thirty. And in 1990, after the media moved into top gear, numbers rose to an estimated 232. Subsequently, as media interest waned, so did the numbers of circles. Sightings increased again when emerging satellite TV channels, starved of material, themselves tried to resurrect interest. At the end of the summer of 1991 two Southampton men, Doug Baker and Dave Chorley, confessed to the hoaxes. They had carved out the patterns for fun, they said, and to watch the antics of the UFO believers.

Even so, Doug and Dave could hardly have created all the circles that were being reported, not just in England but around the world. And the circles continue all over the world to the present day. Yet what two age-ing pranksters could do, others could do too, and there was no reason to believe that the elaborate pictograms, perhaps inspired by the simple creations of a wind vortex and some wishful thinking, were any-thing other than manmade. However, circles research had now taken on a life of its own. Whole groups of people had sprung up and nailed their colours to the mast; people who were famous for their work on the circles and who were frankly not likely to be famous for much else. There were money-making interests: books, television programmes, and so on. The expected division of interested parties into sceptics versus believers occurred almost immediately, each camp finding characteristics in circles and crops that the 'other side' could not see. Each produced

criteria on how to distinguish between real and hoaxed circles, and yet no one could agree on what such criteria should be.

Claims that the crop was somehow genetically mutated or affected were spuri-ous at best. Many of the so-called 'special attributes' of the circles were almost certainly wishful thinking on the part of the observers. Dr Robin Allen, having con-structed a 'fake' which was later surveyed by believers confirmed that 'mistakes we made were actually ascribed significance… so even when you make errors, it's pre-sumed to be significant'.

It was the worst of the UFO arguments all over again. And it was all depressingly familiar: an intelligence with purpose, increasing in complexity (and therefore meaning), targeting certain areas, under-stood only by certain people who have the ability to see the 'real truth' (and on whom we must depend for advice and guidance), defying basic scientific reason because they are 'special'. It was as if contactee claims were being represented in a new guise, with high priests to bring the message of the 'high intelligence' to the people.

It was investigative journalism in the person of John Macnish, a BBC producer, and his wife which broke the back of the phenomenon and put the ball in the other court. He put Doug Baker and Dave Chorley through tests to confirm their claims. Both at night, photographed and filmed through night-vision equipment, and in daylight, they passed all John's tests, carving out huge predesigned pictograms containing all the features professed by so many to be the signs of a 'genuine' circle.[13]

Macnish produced enough evidence to show that the formations were manmade, and it was now up to the believers to prove otherwise. The believers might remain com-mitted, but no such proof has been forth-coming.

Of course, proving that an effect can be

replicated does not mean that it cannot arise otherwise. But even the believers were not claiming that crop circles formed naturally: their argument was that the elab-orate patterns and crop effects could only be achieved by a higher intelligence. Doug and Dave, taking any instructions from Macnish, showed that there were no fea-tures that they, and therefore others, could not reproduce. And no one has disputed that Doug and Dave are human.

The attempts to defend the status quo are sad to watch. Each year pictures of new patterns are handed around 'proving' that no human could have been responsible for this one, or some new idea is put forward that 'proves' there is a special characteris-tic in a crop that cannot be accounted for in 'normal' terms this time.

When all else failed another standard kit was pulled out of the toolbox. There were suggestions that the government was actively disinforming the public about crop circles to hide a mysterious 'truth'. Rumours abounded at lectures and confer-ences that Baker, Chorley and Macnish were government agents sent out to disin-form people about the government's involvement. Now crop circles had really taken on the characteristics of their UFO counterparts.

ANIMAL MUTILATIONS

A second feature being introduced into the UFO phenomenon was animal mutilations. On 8 September 1967, a colt named Lady ('Snippy' in early reports) was found to be missing from a ranch in Alamosa, Colorado. Her dead and mutilated corpse turned up the following day a quarter of a mile away. The body was intact from the neck down-wards, but the head was completely denu-ded of flesh. It was said that the line where the flesh was removed was so defined that it appeared to have been made surgically.

No blood was found around the animal. A rash of UFO reports in the area at the time led to speculation that the two phenomena were in some way connected.

Many cases of animal mutilations particularly involving cattle, have since been reported. For example, in Denver Colorado in 1987, a witness who had seen strange lights in the sky the previous night saw a farmer dealing with two mutilated dead cows at the same site. And in 1989 there was a case involving five mutilated pregnant cows. There are occasional incidents which more closely connect mutilations to UFOs, such as the 1980 report from a farmer of two 'grays' carrying a cow carcass that was later found mutilated. Timothy Good reports that there have been thousands of cases since that of Lady, affecting various types of animals. It seems that specific parts of the body have been targeted, including sense and reproductive organs.[14]

UFO researchers are keen to point out that, along with abductions, these mutilations started in the 1960s. But for many years there was little acknowledgement of the latter phenomenon, even while abductions were being studied. Mutilations have become prominent in this last decade only due to continued pressure by proponents of the subject. The evidence put forward is often hearsay or speculative at best.

Some researchers have rejected the connection between UFOs and animal mutilations. Kevin Randle, for example, comments: 'I found no evidence that linked the two.'[15] Others, such as Timothy Good, believe that understanding animal mutilations provides valuable research into UFOs.

The proposal for the link between UFOs and the mutilations hinted at in just a few cases where UFOs are seen in the proximity of such carcasses, is that aliens are using the cattle for some sort of experimentation, perhaps to produce a foodstuff they can use during their stay on Earth. Another theory connects the two phenomena to a process by which the aliens aim to create human–alien hybrids, suggesting that perhaps experimentation on the tissue of animals is part of this work. Why apparently secret work – executed in remote locations and often in the dead of night – should be carried out so clumsily is not explained: surely the whole animal could be removed rather than left lying around full of vital clues, or at least they could dispose of the carcasses in the sea instead of on land. Even the alternative proposition, that such mutilations are the product of government biological or other experimentation, would have to take into account that the government might also be tidier with the evidence.

One recurrent counter-claim is that the animals have been used by satanic cultists in weird rituals. This may be true, but in all the years since this phenomenon was first recognized no one has been prosecuted for such a crime. And it would be a rather reckless act for any cultists: farmers in more remote regions coming across someone killing their livestock are likely to shoot first and ask questions later. This lack of prosecutions, or even accusations, supports the notion that at the very least something strange is happening.

An explanation offered for the almost surgical nature of these mutilations is that although large predators eating a dead animal might cause 'ripping' and 'gashing' damage, small predators would nibble into the animal through soft tissues such as the eyes and genitals, and might eat apparently selected areas rather than roaming all over the carcass. It has been suggested that damage by many small teeth could seem as precise as surgical incisions.

A prominent researcher in the field is journalist Linda Moulton Howe. She more than anyone is responsible for connecting the two areas of study in her book *Alien Harvest* and video *Strange Harvest*. Asked what hard evidence there was for such a link she admitted: 'This issue of hard evidence that would connect the animal mutilations to something from beyond our planet or non-human life forms is frustrating for all of us. We seek harder and harder proof but what we have is circumstantial, eyewitness testimony . . . After fourteen years I personally am convinced that there is enough evidence, even if it's circumstantial, that something that's not human is involved with animal mutilations worldwide.' Howe has pointed out that in both abductions and animal mutilations, interest seems to be focused on the same tissues, with an emphasis on the reproductive organs, although the humans come out better since they are 'returned' alive. But she also mentions reports, from Vietnam, for example, of what could be human mutilations resulting in death, and certainly there has been increasing interest in this in recent years. Helmut Lammer of Austria told us he was just beginning examinations of such claims in Europe.

Howe seems to have been targeted for disinformation by AFOSI agents (as we saw in Chapter 4). Whether their remark to her that her documentary on animal mutilations was antagonizing the government was true, or part of a disinformation plan, is unclear. The mystery is, it seems, set to deepen.

TRIANGLES

Saucer shapes have always been erroneously regarded as the classic shape for UFOs; in fact UFOs have been seen in a wide variety of forms over the years, notably egg shapes and cigar shapes. In recent years there has been a huge wave of sightings around the world of triangular-shaped objects.

On 29 November 1989, two Belgian

Artist's impression of the triangular UFOs – 'silent vulcans' – which have been widely reported since 1989. Some appear to be military aircraft under test, but there are cases that seem to defy such explanation: triangles that hover soundlessly and disappear instantaneously.

state police officers driving from Eupen to Eynatten encountered a low-level object travelling above their car. They were almost blinded by three bright lights, and as the object passed over them they observed a fourth, dimmer, light, 'red to yellow', in the middle. The officers described the object as a dark, enormous triangle. They followed it and found it hovering above the Gileppe dam. Several other local reports either corroborate this sighting or describe similar-shaped objects around the same time in roughly the same area. Indeed, the sightings continued for over a month. Reports

were received of various sizes of triangles, and some witnesses described additional features such as domes or cupolas.

On 30 March 1990 there were more eyewitness accounts, radar confirmation and film footage. Reports of triangular shaped UFOs were also received from the air force. At one point the catalogue of such reports from Belgium and the surrounding countries exceeded 700, which suggests that something real was flying over that part of Europe in the early 1990s. Further sightings of triangular UFOs have been made in southern Sweden and various areas of England, and such shapes are now regularly reported from America and around the world.

The most mysterious of the claims include huge football-field sized objects that hover silently, and fly off at astonishing speed, still in silence. Sometimes they

disappear without being seen to move away, which has led to speculation that at least some of the triangles may be something akin to holograms rather than solid objects.

Liverpool researcher Tony Eccles investigated a report of a huge triangle seen over Southport, Merseyside in the early hours of 24 February 1996.[16] He found that the same object, or a similar one, had been reported by other witnesses in the locality within days. The first witness was woken up by a persistent rumbling sound. Above the house were three bright white lights at the corners of a triangular shape with two flashing lights at the centre. The object remained there for some time, possibly as long as twenty minutes. At around the same time a similar object was being seen by John Muir of Ardrishaig, Scotland. He described it as 'a massive black triangular shape followed by four red flashing lights'. The local newspaper speculated on the possibility that it was a top-secret spy plane being followed by fighter jets.[17]

Although it is only recently that triangular UFOs have been sighted in such numbers, the phenomenon itself is not new. The magazine *UFO 1980* published by the Tasmanian UFO Investigation Centre reports the sighting of the 'Tunbridge Triangle'.[18] According to the article, TUFOIC received several reports from around Tasmania of a humming triangle shape. Three witnesses driving on the Midland Highway watched it in the early hours of one morning. One of them, Mrs Pennicott, first saw something low over the pine trees at the northern end of Tunbridge. They stopped the car, turned off the engine and listened to a clear humming noise, which faded after a short while. 'A larger than moon sized dark triangular shape was visible with a steady red light on each side. There was a red light on the centre of the shape. Beneath was a white light whilst at the top was yet another light of an undetermined colour. The object was stationary but after they had stopped the car the lights seemed to dull a bit.' The witnesses drove on, noting that the object had not moved, but when they made their return journey some time later it was gone. Another Tasmanian triangle was reported on 29 May in the Ben Lomond area. The witnesses said that 'as it descended it illuminated a very light cloud cover with a golden orange'.

In January 1983 several people reported a triangular object over Cardiff and Swansea in south Wales. Carole Griffiths said: 'It looked like Concorde taking off, but it was stationary in the sky.'[19] Mrs Rita Bradley claimed: 'I saw two triangular objects close together.'[20]

Among the wave of reports in the 1990s was an incident aboard a civilian aircraft. On 6 January 1995 a Boeing 737, British Airways flight 5061 from Milan, was approaching Manchester Airport when Captain Roger Wills and First Officer Mark Stuart both saw a dark triangular object, illuminated by lights along its side, flash past the aircraft to the right. It was alarmingly close, and they filed a formal air miss report. The Joint Air Miss Working Group, who studied the report for a year, concluded in early 1996: 'There is no doubt that the pilots both saw an object . . . the nature and identity of this object remain unknown.'[21]

It seems most likely that the object was one of the triangles which had been seen flying over Belgium and Europe, and in a wave of sightings over New York State, since the late 1980s. Alien technology? Military hardware under test? Non-physical object? The questions remained unanswered. What was inevitable was that the press would crave a connection between the sighting and aliens. With no obvious source or other basis, the *Daily Mail* filled their report on the incident with references to 'a triangular shaped space-

ship', and gratuitous comments such as 'ET has not gone home', and 'nothing like it this side of *Star Trek*'. They even tried to create the myth of a 'Pennine corridor', describing the location of the incident as 'Britain's equivalent of the Bermuda Triangle'.[21]

From 1992 to the time of writing, a massive wave of UFOs has been reported in Scotland, particularly around the coast, many of which are triangular shapes. A particularly intense focus seems to have arisen around Bonnybridge near Falkirk. This was examined by both leading UFO researcher Malcolm Robinson and local councillor Billy Buchanan.[22] As happens with most waves, the existence of a designated person or two, like Arthur Shuttlewood in Warminster, to whom sightings can be reported, leads to the accumulation of information that would otherwise have been missed. The publicity surrounding the Bonnybridge sightings brought a huge number of witnesses, and Buchanan stated: 'Now that it's out in the open more people are coming forward. Before, they said nothing for fear of being laughed at.[23] At one point 8,000 sightings had been claimed for the area. The wave has been a very intense one, and sightings have of course varied considerably. They include many strange light phenomena, which, Robinson points out, 'seem similar to those "Earth Light Phenomena" that researcher and author Paul Devereux writes about'. Others, particularly the coastal sightings, may be accounted for by military vehicles under test, such as the Aurora, which is rumoured to fly at over 5,000mph and is 'understood to have been flying since the mid-eighties'.[24] However, there are many mysteries yet to be examined.

The question of the shape is intriguing. The upsurge in triangle reports came at a time when the triangular Stealth aircraft is known to have been under test, and many sightings of triangular crafts almost certainly

have to be of those planes. And the history of technology suggests that developments in one country will be mirrored by research in others, so it is no surprise that these shapes are reported elsewhere, too. We have already mentioned the Aurora, and there are almost certainly other top-secret aircraft in development. Sonic booms in the Los Angeles areas have been recorded which indicate a plane flying at speeds of Mach 3 and Mach 4.

Even so, it would seem to stretch credibility to claim that these planes can do everything that is reported of them: silent hovering, astonishing acceleration from a standing start, and so on. Nick Pope, who worked on

One of the Stealth aircraft. Could this be an explanation for at least some of the sightings of triangular UFOs? Stealth has been under development since the 1960s. Are today's UFOs the aircraft we shall see in the skies in 2020?

the Ministry of Defence's UFO desk for three years, stated of this type of 'Silent Vulcan' object: 'It behaves in a way that is beyond the cutting edge of our own technology.'[21]

If a terrestrial technology is not responsible, then either we have a truly alien presence or – possibly and – creativity born of expectation. Once the triangle became an 'accepted' and 'expected' shape, so many more people began to report it. In some

cases, perhaps they are seeing triangular arrangements of lights on objects of other shapes, and assuming the edges. In others, perhaps it is being supposed that unconnected lights seen at night are part of an object that may not be there at all. Earthlight phenomena could account for some of these silent, fast-moving reports if in fact no physical object is involved.

In 1991 another vast wave of sightings was arising in Mexico, which is also ongoing. It started with the eclipse of the sun on 11 July, when thousands of people saw UFOs in the sky. Seventeen camcorders recorded UFOs from several locations, and TV journalist Jaime Maussan put together

video evidence which began a process that led to widespread publication.

Videos of the Mexican sightings have been widely available at UFO conferences and through specialist outlets for some years. It is too early yet to assess the validity of all the reports from Mexico, but what is apparent already is that the country is set to become a microcosm of all that has been both good and bad in the study of UFOs over the past decades. Genuine sightings are inspiring wishful thinking: listening to the dialogue of witnesses watching specks of light in the distance, you can hear them making references to 'seeing the saucers'. 'Lights in the sky' would be a fair description; 'saucers' is overstating the case. So speculation is rife, and exaggerated reports and downright hoaxes are emerging.

AREA 51

Another aspect of the modern decade of UFOs has been the acceleration in beliefs about crash retrievals, and associated paranoia. There is no better illustration of this than the beliefs inspired by Area 51.

Area 51, also known as 'Dreamland', is at Groom Lake in Nevada, USA. In the mid-1950s it was the location for the development of the U2 spy plane which was to figure so prominently in the Cold War when US pilot Gary Powers was shot down over Russia in 1960. The area is particularly suitable for the development and testing of high-speed aircraft: it is isolated, so there are few locals to offend, or who might spy, and the mountains which surround it largely conceal it from prying eyes. Furthermore, it is one of the regions of huge, rock-hard, dry saltbeds so favoured for land-speed record attempts because of its natural firmness and levelness which make for effective, long runways. In more recent years mass communication has made it more difficult for any part of the world, let alone an area within the highly populated USA, to be truly isolated, but Groom Lake is as secluded as is likely to be found.

Nearby is the settlement of Rachel, which, in recent years, has become a centre for UFO buffs from all over the world. It consists of a cluster of trailer homes and a few fixed houses and, most famously, the Little Ale-Inn, the local watering-hole, which changed its name to appeal to the new visitors. The bar is decked out with pictures of flying saucers and mug shots of personalities within the subject. Glen Campbell, a local 'character' living in Rachel, is an investigator and watcher of Area 51. He keeps his feet firmly on the ground and produces a few useful publications setting out his stories of the locality.

Travel along the highway to the junction of the few dirt tracks which form the area's 'communication network' and you will come across the little black mailbox. Actually it is the postbox of a local farmer, but since it is the nearest point to Groom Lake you can easily – or legally – reach, it has become a meeting point for UFO buffs and a good position from which to watch the comings and goings at the base. Stay there all night and you get freezing cold, but you are also pretty well guaranteed to see some very strange lights and objects moving around in the skies. Something of an advanced technology is flying out from and around Area 51. You can see lots of unusual stuff flying in and out of military bases if you take the time to stand and stare. Locals may have been aware of the activity on their doorstep for years and yet are still surprised when their attention is drawn to it by a UFO claimant.

Area 51 is the breeding ground of 'black projects', those funded through taxes but not explained to the public and kept out of the public eye. It is here that Stealth was worked on, and, it is thought, some of the development of the Star Wars defence systems. The officially denied

Many UFO researchers believe that Area 51 in Nevada is the present location of US government work on UFO research. The 'black mailbox' – seen here with researcher Mark Pilkington – is the location for the best views of the aerial tests.

Aurora Mach 6 plane and its cousins are believed to be currently under development in Area 51.

The government welcomes visitors, and particularly the recent influx of UFO buffs, to the area about as enthusiastically as Bill Clinton welcomes the Whitewatergate inquiries. The area is anonymously described as 'RESTRICTED MILITARY INSTALLATION' and signs pointedly warn visitors: 'USE OF DEADLY FORCE AUTHORIZED'. In other words, you could be shot for just entering the area, although we are not aware that anyone has been so far. In some ways even more alarmingly, there is no perimeter fence, just orange posts marking out the restricted areas.

Should you miss the signs, you do not need to ring any doorbells. Semiburied sensors detect incoming vehicles and alert the base personnel, who will come out to greet you. If they are in a good mood they will do so with the local privatized security force, known as the camodudes (camouflaged personnel), who drive out in four-tracks to extend an invitation to you to go away. They will also ask you to make a small donation to Groom Lake of any video or films you might be carrying. If they are feeling slightly more tetchy they send a fully armed black helicopter to fly so low over your head that it hurts your eardrums, whips stones up around your face and blows you off your feet. They make a point of videoing you at close range, and you are not advised to smile or pose as the pilots exhibit very little humour.

Despite the security, more than enough people made it through the defences and took illicit photographs from Freedom Ridge, which offered a very clear view of the base, to prompt the US government in April 1995 to pull an Act out of its pocket (not the one in which it keeps the Freedom of Information Act) and buy up acres of land around the area from the public. This has extended the cordon and made it far more difficult to reach anywhere from which the base can be viewed.

Our colleague Mark Pilkington summed up Area 51 well when he described being there as 'like being in a conspiracy theme park'. But even now, when you do get near the base, you can watch the secrecy in action. When a plane – often black and unmarked – lands, it is immediately covered by mobile hangars which are brought on to the runway. The Cold War has not ended in Area 51: it seems the military are still trying to keep their projects from the prying eyes of Russian satellites and high-flying spy planes. And not without reason, either, but perhaps with a conspicuous lack of success: one colleague claims that you can buy satellite photographs of Area 51 in shops in Moscow!

But it is the belief that this is the location for the reverse engineering of alien technology that is the most relevant to the UFO industry, and such claims have made headlines in the UFO press around the world. It is believed that alien craft captured or found are taken to Area 51, taken apart to find out how they work, and the technology used for military purposes. The main source of rumour that UFOs are in any way connected with Groom Lake is one man, Bob Lazar, who claims to have worked

there on such projects – or, to be more precise, at a nearby complex buried in the mountains known as S4 – for a few weeks during the late 1980s. He claims he saw nine 'alien spacecraft', mostly in good working order, and worked on their propulsion system. Lazar was allegedly sacked for taking UFO buffs to the black mailbox on days when the 'alien technology' was being flown. Lazar has also hinted, albeit pretty vaguely, that he saw an alien on the base.

Lazar is a character with question-marks after his name. He says he is a nuclear physicist and claims to have worked at Los Alamos; he claims he got degrees from both Cal-Tech and MIT, but that the record of his achievements was wiped out by the government as part of a cover-up. But his answers to questions such as 'Who were your professors?' have been pretty unenlightening. Lazar's lifestyle does not inspire faith in his reliability – he was pulled up on a charge of pandering after running a brothel in Vegas – so it is only committed conspiracists who trust his claims.

AT LAST THE SUBJECT GETS AN EXTERNAL AUDIT
———

Common sense would seem to dictate that the more closely the facts relating to something are examined, the most likely it is that the correct analysis will be arrived at. However, there is great validity in the proverb about not being able to see the wood for the trees. We have argued many times that if UFOs truly hold as monumental a secret as proof of extraterrestrial visitation, then the subject ought to attract the attention not just of committed ufologists but of investigative journalists. And yet the only investigative journalists who seem to get involved are those with considerable interest in the subject in the first place.

Where are the Roger Cooks and the Duncan Campbells? They do not need to be experts: after all, they are not experts in smuggling or corporate fraud or in particular political areas. They succeed there because they are experts in investigative journalism. It is in the nature of such journalists to involve themselves in a subject for its own sake when there is something important at stake, and yet presumably they have deemed UFOlogy and the 'great revelations' it promises unworthy of their attention.

It was with pleasure, then, that during a trip to the United States in 1990 we heard many a lively discussion among ufologists about a forthcoming book which would break the mould in that it was being written by just such an investigative journalist. Howard Blum's *Out There* was duly published that year.[25] Blum was no ufologist: he was an award-winning reporter for the *New York Times* and had written several non-fiction books regarded as triumphs of investigative journalism, including *Wanted! The Search for Nazis in America* and *I Pledged Allegiance . . . The True Story of the Walkers: An American Spy Family*. It was during his investigations into the Walker spy case that he first became interested in the subject of UFOs following a comment made to him in passing.

Now we had the perfect model for external audit: a non-committed, non-interested successful investigative journalist brought into the debate not by diehard ufologists but by someone with an ear to the ground in intelligence circles who mentioned the subject in passing. It was a real opportunity for a truly independent piece of investigative journalism.

But what did we actually get? *Out There* is a good book, and Blum can be justly proud of penning an interesting read in a lively and evocative way. Moreover, he brought new information to light, and very useful information it was, too. It is a book that, for the most part, we would probably be happy to put our names to, and we are sure that a good many ufologists around the world would share that view. But therein lies the problem. *Out There* is a ufologist's book: long on rumour but short on proven facts. It could have been written by any ufologist, and indeed similar books have been.

Blum evocatively describes how he came across a government group known as the UFO Working Group, and how their study was linked to other paranormal research such as remote viewing (the ability to visualize beyond the seer's visual range). He goes into some detail about the background of prominent characters in the group and describes a dialogue in which senior government investigators consider the possibility that UFOs are alien space-craft. (This leads him to ask, 'Did the government in the decades immediately following World War II have proof of the existence of extraterrestrial life? Or, ultimately, was it as ignorant as any man in the street?') A considerable chunk of the book is devoted to the US SETI and Soviet CETI programmes, which are, of course, very relevant if UFOs are extraterrestrial space-craft, but not at all so if UFOs have some other explanation. The book therefore strongly confirms its thrust as an examination of UFOs with a view to proving or dis-proving their existence as extraterrestrial. That is fair enough – Blum made that the centrepiece of his investigation and stated so clearly.

He then delves into some UFO cases centred around the town of Elmwood, Wisconsin, apparently selected for the quality of its reports by the UFO Working Group. Whether or not the reports from that town are any better than others from around the world is debatable. Finally, Blum

enters the murky debate over the MJ12 documents and treats the two most polar-ized sides, as represented by Stanton Friedman (who supports the validity of the documents) and Philip Klass (who rejects it), fairly.

Yet frankly, the conclusion of the book is difficult to find. Blum does reach the ver-dict that the government has been covering up its knowledge and investigation of UFOs, but many people have arrived at that using similar documentary proof, in particu-lar Timothy Good, in his bestselling and ground-breaking book *Above Top Secret*.[26] Blum also states in his final chapter: 'I have become a believer. There are other worlds.' But he does so in a paragraph that seems to be more related to the SETI programme than UFO visitation, and in any case it seems that, like other believers, he was won over by conviction, not by certain, hard facts. In the end we found no real conclu-sion on the origin of UFOs merely evidence of Blum's conversion to the existence of extraterrestrial life.

So what went wrong? In one sense, nothing. It is a worthwhile, indeed essential, part of UFO literature. But it is not a com-mentary on it. What seems to have hap-pened is that Blum went the same way as the ufologists. He could prove that the gov-ernment was lying about its involvement in UFO research but could not prove why. Are they covering up their knowledge or their ignorance? He appears none the wiser, and no other ufologist is any the wiser, either (although they all have very strong opinions to the contrary). We can assume that Blum gave it his best, but his best did not do for our 'cosmic Watergate' what Woodward and Bernstein did for the original,[27] or what Andrew Morton did for the rumours sur-rounding the marriage of Prince Charles and Princess Diana.[28]

Yet it seems unfair to suggest that this was due to any failing on Blum's part. The

failure is in the subject matter: the truth that everybody is desperately seeking – that the government is covering up a com-plex and involved knowledge of UFOs, indeed a working relationship with extrater-restrials – is probably not there simply because it isn't the truth. But like most negatives, it cannot be proven. When the government offers denials the response is the classic echo of Mandy Rice-Davies's famous retort: 'Well, they would say that, wouldn't they?'

But we must consider, unpalatable though it will be to most committed ETH supporters, that Blum may well have gone a long way towards proving the negative. If a person with his skills and contacts cannot find the positive, then the negative looks all the stronger. When we compare the UFO cover-up and conspiracy theo-ries with, say, Watergate – a known con-spiracy with a known outcome – we can see how much easier Blum's task would have been if the truth he sought were really 'out there'. Nixon had only to con-tain a small conspiracy within a few people in his own immediate circle, all of whom stood to gain from the secrecy and to lose by its revelation. Yet two reporters broke the chain right the way through to the president himself, producing irrefutable documentary proof and testi-mony along the way. For the government to conceal fifty years of examination of crashed UFOs and an enormous amount of knowledge, were that the case, there would be thousands involved, all with their own personal agenda, some of whom would benefit by revealing their documentation to just such a person as Blum. What we do not have is the smok-ing gun, and we must really go into the future of UFO research much more gen-erally able to accept the possibility that the reason there is no smoking gun is that the trigger was never pulled.

THE MINISTRY OF DEFENCE SPEAKS OUT

The British Ministry of Defence line on UFOs, as related in 1970 by L.W. Akhurst (he of the Moigne Downs case related in Chapter 2) has been fairly consistent:

The attitude of the Ministry of Defence towards reports of unidentified flying objects is quite straightforward. The Department investigates reports of unidentified flying objects because of their possible air defence implications.

Unidentified flying object reports are examined in the Ministry of Defence by experienced staff. They have access to all information available to the Ministry of Defence. They call on the full scientific and professional resources of the Ministry of Defence and may call in expert advice as necessary from other Government and non-Government bodies.[29]

Akhurst went on to add that reports were not released, but would routinely come to light under the thirty-year rule (the UK government regulation whereby certain classified files are released for public consumption after a thirty-year period).

Perhaps what was needed was the inside story. In 1996 we got it. Nick Pope, an employee of the MoD, published *Open Skies, Closed Minds – For the First Time a Government UFO Expert Speaks Out.[30]* For three years Pope had been desk officer at Secretariat (Air Staff) 2A, responsible for dealing with UFO reports from the public and from government and military establishments. As he described to us, the job involved several duties, of which approximately 20 per cent related to UFOs. Pope comments: 'At first, I must admit, my new job was rather disappointing. There were no flying saucers, no aliens, and there was no dark and mysterious government involvement. Try as I might, I couldn't see a Man in Black anywhere.'

The book is a worthwhile contribution to UFO literature, and anyone who seriously wishes to understand UFOs in recent times should read it. That said, despite what might be implied by the credentials of the author, it does little if anything to change perceptions of UFOs. Pope presents himself honestly and in his own right, stating that it is his own book, in other words, that he is not a ministry pawn dispensing propaganda. We believe him, and indeed recall encouraging him to write the book during lunch meetings with him when he was at Secretariat (Air Staff) 2A.

MoD main building in Whitehall, London. The 'UFO public desk' is based here, but many believe that this is only the public face of the British government's UFO involvement and that other more secret locations are undertaking classified work.

What comes across very clearly from his book is that the government has very little more information than ufologists. They might have, as Pope did, access to a few more cases coming directly from their own establishments, but the quality of those cases is no different from those reported to

Nick Pope manned the 'UFO desk' at the Ministry of Defence and became convinced of the reality of extraterrestrial UFOs.

ufologists and the conclusions which can be drawn are no more or less certain. Pope makes it clear that he became convinced that UFOs were extraterrestrial, and we understand from talking to him that this caused more than just raised eyebrows at the MoD, who initially wished to prevent publication of his book. When it became apparent that no top secrets or national-security implications were involved, they relented. But Pope, like Howard Blum, became convinced of the extraterrestrial nature of UFOs in the same way as anybody else: through a combination of interpretation and belief. It was not, at least as far as *Open Skies, Closed Minds* reveals, because the MoD have an extraordinary amount of information that the rest of us lack.

We might argue that perhaps the MoD and other establishments do have much more astonishing information – aliens in the deep-freeze at the MoD's Rudloe Manor, for example – but if they do it appears that Pope was not privy to it. We must remember that

Pope was not a senior-grade employee, and it seems likely that if something very extraordinary happened it would have been discussed at a higher level. He was the first to admit this to us, though he felt he would certainly have got wind of such an incident had it occurred. But we also have the many comments of Lord Hill-Norton, admiral of the fleet and chief of the defence staff from 1971 to 1973, apparently making clear that he knows of no astonishing secrets – indeed, he has demanded that the government should reveal all it knows about UFOs. Major Sir Patrick Wall, the former Conservative MP for Humberside, spent over thirty years in the House of Commons pushing the cause of the UFO phenomenon. As Nick Pope says, 'He pressurized the Ministry of Defence and, as a consultant to NATO at the height of the Cold War, was directly and closely involved in matters of national security.' We have spoken to Major Sir Patrick Wall and it is very clear that he did not have special knowledge of UFOs beyond that available to ufologists and the general public, despite his high profile in security areas. So if the senior defence staff and junior MoD staff do not have the information, and nor do longstanding MPs, then just who does? The probability is that there is no exotic secret. Pope states: 'I have worked for ten years in the civil service and I am convinced that the UK government is in no way involved in a UFO cover-up.'

However, two very active and diligent researchers, Matthew Williams and Chris Fowler, are of the opinion that Nick Pope might not have been privy to all the information on UFOs fed to the government. They came across two specific instances in which material seems at the very least to indicate a delayed route to Nick's office.[31]

Chris Davies [a UFO researcher] from Bristol found out that Bristol Airport had their own air sightings form for UFOs. But they forward it

Chris Fowler is an energetic and enthusiastic researcher who has travelled the world in his study of UFOs.

to Military Air Information Service at London Air Traffic Control Centre. It gets sent there before it gets sent to Nick Pope. Also: John Holman back in 1992 had a UFO sighting in Wiltshire along with a couple of others. John phoned up Rudloe Manor and said 'I have heard that this is the place where I'm supposed to report UFO sightings.' They took a report off him. They were filling out a standard form; he could tell by the questions that he was being asked. John later asked Nick Pope about his UFO sighting and the report but Nick Pope had never received it. He reported it at Rudloe Manor and yet it didn't get forwarded on to Whitehall and Nick's office. So where did it go? That's an indication that someone else was getting them.

The MoD have admitted in writing that Rudloe Manor was once a collection point for UFO reports. And apart from John Holman, several UFO researchers, including Tim Good, Matthew Williams and Chris Fowler, have tested Rudloe's dependability

(Above) Matthew Williams believes that the British government is hiding some of its UFO secrets at Rudloe Manor.

to pass on UFO reports to Pope's department and have found that they do not. There have been rumours that Rudloe is Britain's Area 51, the place where alien craft and bodies are kept. Williams thinks not: if Rudloe is a secret centre for dealing with UFOs, then it is the paperwork rather than the hardware that it houses, he believes.

The mechanism certainly exists to bypass Pope's old desk at the MoD, and so 'significant' information or 'highly classified' events could be weeded out before they get to the present incumbent.

Pope has accepted that there may be other MoD collection points for UFO sighting reports but believes that their reluctance to deal with the public is simply because they don't have the appropriate staff. He says he would have seen all the reports as he was the person paid to interface with the public. But whether you

accept that depends on what you think the government has to hide in the first place.

It is often argued that knowledge of the existence of aliens would create such a profound change in society that a cover-up would be needed to protect vested interests. If that is so, we must also consider the new political, social and moral arguments it would bring. Inevitably there would be those of different persuasions, and if politicians lied, there would be other politicians waiting to expose them, perhaps prepared to sacrifice their own careers, even their lives, for something so important. Self-interest, political point-scoring, or a grand vision – one or

(Below) Rudloe Manor, in Wiltshire, is thought to be a collection/study point for the UK government's interest in UFOs. Its miles of underground tunnels are thought to conceal the government's most classified files on the subject.

other of them would expose such a cover-up. That it has not done so speaks loudly against such a belief.

In the end, Pope's revelations, like Blum's investigation, provided more of the same and no quantum leap. The only progress is that the evidence against cover-up of dark, terrible secrets seems to weaken.

RECONSTRUCTED RUSSIA: 1989

In this last decade, the collapse of the communist regime in the Soviet Union and the fragmentation of that empire resulted in UFO stories almost immediately emerging from that part of the world.

'Scientists have confirmed that an unidentified flying object recently landed in the Russian city of Voronezh. The scientists have also explored the landing site and found traces of aliens who made a short promenade about the park.'[32] Even in 'reconstructed' Russia, Tass is a serious and sober agency. That it should release such a message to the world media is remarkable enough; that it should do so just days after the event, while an investigation was ongoing, was as much as anything a comment on the emerging freedom of Gorbachev's new Russia.

To put this new Russia into perspective we must consider the incredible and rapid pace of change that befell the Soviet Union, and fragmented it, over just a few years at the end of the 1980s. When Nikita Khrushchev was ousted from power by Kosygin and Brezhnev on 16 October 1964, the pattern that was set to continue for decades was the one inherited from Stalin's Russia. When Brezhnev died in 1982, he was replaced by Yuri Andropov who, until recently, had been head of the KGB. On Andropov's death in February 1984, his successor,

Konstantin Chernenko, looked likely to deliver more of the same. Moreover, the machinery in Russia in any case made change a seemingly difficult concept. But Chernenko himself was dead just a year later, and change of sorts was being forced into the system purely by the lack of continuity in leadership.

A relatively young man, Mikhail Sergeyevich Gorbachev, then just fifty-four years old, came to the fore. Over the next six years he entered into arms-limitation treaties with the West; signed the peace accord with Afghanistan which ended the war there that had become known as 'Russia's Vietnam', and indeed offered $600 million in reparations to Afghanistan; reduced Russia's military strength by 10 per cent, and generally revolutionized the relationship between the Soviet Union and the West. He was trusted and befriended by two of the strongest Western leaders of modern times: American president Ronald Reagan and British prime minister Margaret Thatcher. The watchwords of Gorbachev's reign were *glasnost* (openness) and *perestroika* (restructuring). Even while Chinese communists were massacring students in Tiananmen Square, Gorbachev was overseeing the changes that would open the Berlin Wall and unite Germany for the first time since the Second World War, and ultimately he presided over the breaking up of the Soviet Union into independent republics, effectively ending his own job.

It was during this period of *glasnost* and *perestroika* that the landings at Voronezh occurred – hence the reason why they were so openly and honestly presented to the world.

The first reports of the incident in Britain, from the Tass release, indicated among other sketchy details that 'the route along which the aliens walked as described by the onlookers and the one established

scientifically coincided'.[33] This intriguing reference to a 'scientifically established' track of the aliens' 'promenade' was not elaborated on in the report. It would be some time, and there would be some confusion, before what the Russians were up to became clear. The confusion centred on the Russians' use of the word 'biolocation'.[34]

Not understanding what the Russians meant, the Western news services translated the word as 'bilocation'. The implication therefore was that the aliens had been tracked by some sort of 'homing-in' method; that their position had been determined from two separate points which would allow for a 'position fix'. All very scientific-sounding; all very wrong. By 'biolocation' the Russians meant what we call 'dowsing'. Dowsing, a common and well-tested technique within parapsychology, is the location of objects, minerals, water, energy fields and so on through the use of a divining rod, pendulum or other device. Clearly, the landing site was being examined by parapsychological means, presumably similar to the methods John Spencer had seen and participated in during the examination of an abduction site in Sweden a few years earlier.[35] It was a revealing insight into the Russian approach to the paranormal – they have been acknowledged as the world leaders in this research for many years – and how they linked it to the UFO phenomenon.

Other research was applied, but without using the term 'UFO'. *Moscow News* reported that studies were being undertaken by 'enthusiasts in Voronezh who have come together to study abnormal atmospheric phenomena at the Alexander Popov radioelectronics and communications scientific–technical association'.[36]

It appears that the wave had started around April 1989. One report received then was of a UFO bigger than an aircraft, seen over Cherepovets. In June schoolchildren

Russian ufology has suffered much censorship in its history. Yulii Platov (centre – pictured with the authors), following *perestroika*, was able to come to the West to attend UFO conferences like this one in Sheffield in 1995.

THE QUEST FOR THE UFOLOGICAL HOLY GRAIL

As we saw at the beginning of this chapter, Whitley Strieber's accounts of his abduction experience became for many people the proof that this was a real phenomenon. It has been argued that the case revitalized ufology, and it probably did. But it also resulted in a severe downside for the subject.

Researchers, witnesses, and others came to the conclusion – questionable though it seems – that *one case* could solve the whole UFO mystery. The dogged, case-by-case plodding of many researchers was suddenly replaced by some with what can only be described as a quest for the 'holy grail of ufology'. But just what form would such a prize take? The quest has been characterized by a heady mixture of wishful thinking, optimism, and – at the worst extreme -fraud, ego and greed. The challenge of the years ahead will be to get past such simplistic thinking and back to the detailed work that will gradually put the puzzle together.

Accusations against ufologists by ufologists have been flying in recent years, and never before have they been so vitriolic. It is not confined to arguments between sceptics and believers – even among ETH supporters there has been war war instead of the customary jaw jaw. The cases set out below – the quests for the holy grail – have set former colleagues against each other from the opposite banks of seemingly unbridgeable chasms.

GULF BREEZE

The US town of Pensacola and the nearby area of Gulf Breeze has spent the last decade as a major attraction in world ufology. Pensacola is situated in the Florida Panhandle on the state's north-west gulf

reported a UFO over Konantsevo, which apparently landed and 'something resembling a headless person' was seen. It then became invisible. Later there were other similar sightings. The most famous report was made by a milkmaid, Lyubov Medvedev, who saw an alien in the Perm region of the Urals. He was taller than a man, but with short legs and a tiny head. This, it seems, was the origin of the reports of 'giant' entities which were described in the early newspaper coverages. In some of the later entity sightings there were many witnesses: forty adults to one close-encounter case.[37]

There appears to have been something of a division within Russia over the approach to be taken in these investigations. There is a 'traditional' school of science, subscribed to by such as Yulii Platov, whom we met at the Sheffield, England, UFO Conference in 1995, and there are 'non-traditionalists' more open to paranormal experiences and techniques. For example, leading Russian researcher Professor Vladimir Azhazha commented: 'We must consider the psychophysical interaction that may take place between object, the witness, and the noosphere – the plane of human consciousness. If we don't consider such interaction, the sightings make no sense at all.'

A good account of the modern Russian experience, and the wave of sightings in particular, is given in Jacques Vallee's book on his journey to the Soviet Union.[34] It brings the history of Russian UFOlogy up to date and thoughtfully examines the 1989 wave in detail, and could well be one of the most important books on the subject ever written.

coast. It had its share of sightings during the 1973 wave across the gulf states, and indeed the *Pensacola News Journal* of 27 July 1952 reported a sighting of disc-shaped objects over the area at that time. But the case that arose in 1987 was the first which appeared to represent the 'holy grail', for several reasons. It seemed to provide considerable photographic evidence to support close encounters and even abduction claims; it was studied as it took place, with teams of researchers on site throughout (investigator Gary Watson told us he spent every night for two years on skywatch there), and it appears to be a multiple-witness case.

On 11 November local businessman Ed Walters saw a flying saucer and took five Polaroid photographs of it. It was 'right out of a Spielberg movie that had somehow escaped from the film studio', he wrote in his account of the experience.[38] As Walters

Ed Walters is the principle witness of the Gulf Breeze wave of sightings in America, reported since November 1987.

was watching the object he was paralysed and lifted into the air by a blue beam. From that time until 1 May 1988, he saw and photographed many flying saucers. MUFON instigated tests, asking Walters to produce images on sealed multilens '3D' cameras, on video, and on crude stereo cameras (actually two Polaroids on a separating pole to produce a 'stereo' impression of the objects). The sightings were often preceded by a buzzing noise in Walters' head. It was suggested that this came from an implant and arrangements were being made to check this when Walters was apparently abducted on 1 May – he reports over an hour of missing time while alone on a beach

– and the implant removed. His closest moments with the UFOs were over.

Walters took lie-detector tests, and one examiner stated that the witness 'truly believes that the photographs and personal sightings he has described are true and factual to the best of his ability'.

The stakes were high, and if Gulf Breeze was ever to be proven, then some belief systems would be justified and others destroyed. The result was inevitable: American, and eventually world ufology was split, and many former friendships were damaged beyond repair. As Jerome Clarke wrote, 'An emotional dispute ensued, generating far more heat than light.'[39] MUFON backed the

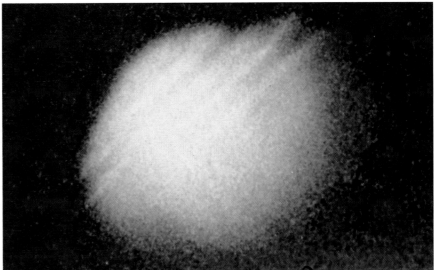

(Left) It is said that even without Ed Walters the Gulf Breeze case would still have validity; sightings and photography have continued to the present day. This photograph was taken by researcher Bland Pugh during recent sightings.

(Above) Art Hufford's 1991 photograph of a UFO over Gulf Breeze. Many reports have included the striation seen on this picture. In the ten years since Walters first photographed his UFOs, over two hundred witnesses have come forward with claims of their own.

case as 'proof positive' of alien intervention; sceptics such as Dr Willy Smith were scathing about it. The local mayor, Ed Gray, commented: 'Never . . . have I ever witnessed so clever and successful a deception of the public as the charade by Ed Walters and his accomplices.' He also said: 'It would be naïve to think we're the only life forms in all these galaxies. They may come. But I can tell you right now, they haven't come to Gulf Breeze.' Carol and Rex Salisbury studied the case and declared: 'Our investigation and analysis lend to the conclusion that several, if not all of the photos, are probable hoaxes.' A reinvestigation was made by Gary Watson, which was more supportive of Walters' claim.

There were resignations from MUFON in protest against the organization's support for the case, and rumours that MUFON was threatening to withdraw the membership and status of members who did not actively support it. In more recent years the MUFON split has created two warring chapters in Florida.[41]

The controversy was further fuelled by a circulation war between local newspapers. The *Florida Sentinel*, which had first published the early photographs, backed Walters; rival publications tried to shoot down his claims. On one occasion what seemed to be a model of the object Walters photographed was found in a loft in his former home, but this was almost certainly a plant to discredit him, possibly inspired by the circulation war.

Over time hundreds of witnesses came forward to claim that they too could see the UFOs, and even today many claim that Walters' role has now become unimpor-

tant; that even without him Gulf Breeze is still a major case. Yet investigation revealed that most of those claims were 'distant-light' sightings and UFOlogy has learned to be cautious. Gulf Breeze is situated near major military installations, in particular the Pensacola Naval Air Station, and a lot of curious traffic moves around there.

Many witnesses inspired to watch the skies would see in a new light objects that they had probably previously ignored: the 'me too' syndrome was well attested to during the Warminster sightings of the 1960s and 1970s in England. One or two of the witnesses have produced photographs and videos strikingly similar to Walters' descriptions, but have failed to come forward under their own names, prompting speculation that Walters himself is using pseudonyms to boost acceptance of his sightings.

But in any case some of the sightings, including, of course, the Ed Walters photographs, cannot be explained by misidentification. The objects seen seem unambiguously to be 'flying saucers'. The following possibilities should be considered.

• Hoax. With enough motive any photographs can be faked.
• Alien intervention. The objects are genuinely extraterrestrial visitations.
• Government devices. If so, then there can be little doubt that they were intended to be interpreted as flying saucers.
• Government experiments designed to fool people into thinking they were seeing what they were not.

The first two possible explanations have been explored by ufologists, but they have not been able to produce a conclusion; the last two are examined in Chapter 6.

Whatever the truth, there can be little doubt that, as ever, people are finding the evidence they want to substantiate their beliefs, and ignoring that which is unsupportive. Gulf Breeze will not be resolved because the waters have been too muddied, mostly by the ufologists themselves.

The case failed for ufologists in the most fundamental way: it failed to be the holy grail. If a massive case including photographic evidence, supported by many photographic experts (if rejected by plenty, too) could not do the trick, then what could?

Another argument doing the rounds was that, despite the many claims of abductions, one feature of them was clear: they were basically single-person events. Abductees were not witnessed undergoing their experiences. It was apparent from discussions at UFO conferences and in many writings of the time, that the hunt was on for a witnessed abduction. Perhaps that would be the holy grail. And on 30 November 1989 we had a witnessed abduction. Not only that, but a figure of world renown was claimed to be a participant.

THE BROOKLYN BRIDGE CASE

Budd Hopkins, the investigator of this case, describes it as 'what seems to be an alien display of an abduction for the benefit of an important political figure who was a witness to this'. Walt Andrus, head of MUFON, confirmed to us that the individual concerned was Javier Perez de Cuellar, then the secretary-general of the UN, who apparently happened to be nearby with two government agents.

Artist's impression of the latest type of UFO abduction claim: a witnessed kidnapping by aliens from a high rise apartment block in the middle of New York. The case includes a claim that Javier Perez de Cuella was also part of the abduction.

Although the case has generated a lengthy book[4] and a storm of controversy it is essentially a very simple one. 'Linda Cortile' was abducted at 3.15am, floating out of a twelfth-storey window in a blue beam of light. A UFO hovered overhead. Three 'grays' floated around her in the air and led her up into the UFO. Hopkins has a report from one woman who claims to have seen the incident from the Brooklyn Bridge and thought a film was being made. She noticed that her car had stopped, and that its lights had gone out.

Over a year after the incident Budd Hopkins received a letter from the two government agents who had been with Perez de Cuellar, Richard and Dan, stating that they had seen the abduction. Later revelations suggest that they, along with Perez de Cuellar, were also abducted as part of a complex alien intervention into our ecological thinking. Still later it was discovered that one of the agents and Cortile had been abducted together many times during their lives, another recurring motif in Hopkins' cases. If the alien abduction wasn't strange enough, Cortile also claimed to have later been kidnapped, and sexually harassed, by the two agents, although she would not file a police report on the matter. Of even further concern is the fact that Dan allegedly spent time in a mental institution.

Hopkins says that this case involves large numbers of people, although it seems that virtually all of the evidence is being channelled to Hopkins through just one source, the abductee herself. He has not met Richard and Dan, and their existence is shadowy, to say the least. They confirmed the incident through Cortile and 'correspond' with Hopkins by post and via recorded audio tapes.

Cortile confirms that the woman on the bridge did contact Hopkins directly,[40] and she therefore becomes an important witness. However, researcher Willy Smith has asked why Hopkins has not presented her as witness to audiences, nor explained why he has not. He has also pointed out that it was curious that a woman who thought a film was being made should report that fact

to a well-known abduction researcher. Smith suggests: 'There is a strong presumption that she really does not exist.'[42]

George Hansen, former MUFON state director Joe Stefula and Rich Butler found 'striking similarities between Cortile's story and a book called *Nighteyes*, by Garfield Reeves-Stevens, first published in April 1989, a few months before Linda Cortile first told her story to Hopkins'.[43] Those common features are as follows.

• Cortile was abducted into a UFO hovering over her high-rise apartment building in New York City; so was Sarah, a character in the book.
• Dan and Richard initially claimed to have been on a stake-out that night and were involved in a UFO abduction during early-morning hours; so were Derek and Merril, the two government agents in the book.
• Linda was later kidnapped and thrown into a car by Richard and Dan; in the book Wendy was similarly kidnapped by Derek and Merril.
• Dan was hospitalized for emotional trauma, as was one of the government agents in the book.
• During the kidnapping Dan took Linda to a safe house on a beach; during the fictional kidnapping Derek took Wendy to a safe house on a beach.
• Budd Hopkins is a prominent UFO abduction researcher living in New York City and an author who has written books on the topic, as is a character called Charles Edward Starr in *Nighteyes*.
• Before her kidnapping, Linda contacted Budd Hopkins about her abduction; Wendy contacted Starr before hers.
• Linda and one of the agents had sometimes been abducted at the same time and communicated with each other during their abduction; in the book Wendy and Derek shared the same experiences.
• Dan, in correspondence, expressed a

romantic interest in Linda; Derek became romantically involved with Wendy.
• Photographs of Linda were taken on the beach and sent to Hopkins; in the book, photographs taken on a beach played a central role.

Claim and counter-claim have bedevilled the case. Many believe that Hopkins has taken too much on trust, and has been desperate to believe in the case whatever facts there may be to the contrary. Certainly relevant key figures have not come forward in their own right in support of the claims. Just as some believe that Ed Walters published some pictures under other names (Jane, Believer Bill, etc.), so many hold that Cortile is generating some of the so-called independent testimony herself. Frankly, without the direct testimony and proven credentials of Richard and Dan, the case largely amounts to one person's unverified account. For one thing, the agents are said to have directly implicated their supposed charge – the important VIP. If they are genuine, this is the most important aspect of the case; if they are not, then the most important aspect is a fraud and the rest therefore probably worthless. If Hopkins is right and the aliens abducted Cortile partly to demonstrate their abilities and concerns to a leading world figure, they must be kicking themselves that they picked the night he had the two most mentally unstable security agents on the planet with him.

Hopkins points out in his book that he is amazed by the precision with which aliens control abductees, leaving them 'normal' most of the time but following their behest to the letter on occasions. Furthermore, the aliens seem to be playing a game of releasing information to abductees, and to him, on precise cue. He states: 'There is an unsettling – and unearthly – precision in all of this.' In which case, why is Perez de Cuellar not doing as they want? Why is he silent on the subject, and why are we not hearing anything from him or his offices which would 'acclimatize' us to the aliens? The most logical answer would be that he is not involved. Claims that he has tacitly confirmed his involvement seem to be wishful thinking at best. The *Independent on Sunday* reports that a meeting was arranged at Chicago Airport between Jay Sapir, a UFO enthusiast, Hopkins and Perez de Cuellar while the VIP was between flights. Even according to Sapir, Perez de Cuellar 'shook his head with a mixture of amusement and amazement'. Hopkins has three letters purporting to be from the VIP, but all are unsigned and of unproven authenticity. And the explanation for the precision of the release of information in this case could be that it was not unearthly at all, but a deliberate release of information to Hopkins by human hoaxers.

A few people believe that Hopkins is faking the case in collusion with the witness, presumably for money, but that we reject. Hopkins is committed to his work, strongly believes in it and would not involve himself, in our view, in dishonesty. But he could have been misled, and there is a possibility that if the bait were seemingly good enough he might have oversold the case to himself, and then to the world.

But while the Brooklyn Bridge case, like Gulf Breeze, will prove one thing to some and another thing to others, it will not be the holy grail. Perhaps the most interesting aspect of the case is its similarity to the book *Nighteyes*. If it is genuine then staging the abduction for the benefit of Perez de Cuellar was not the aliens' only clever coup: they also screened current literature to create an inherent unbelievability in the case. But why? And if the case is a fake, then to so overtly base it on a recently published fiction is an insult to ufology. Has the study of UFOs degenerated to such an extent that hoaxers can afford to treat

researchers with so little respect? Is so little effort needed by hoaxers because of the certain knowledge that ufologists would dig their own graves in their own greedy search for the holy grail?

Consider Cortile's identification of Dan on a video of security operations for visiting dignitaries. She contacted Hopkins; she was '150 per cent sure' it was him. Hopkins points out that if she were not telling the truth it would be a dangerous gamble; that 'no hoaxer would ever run the risk of identifying someone in this way'; that the real identity of the person picked out might be revealed, and then her claims would fall apart. But a clever hoaxer might have worked out that that is not how ufology works, that the ratchet effect – evidence in support is accepted; evidence against is ignored – would come into play. If someone identified 'Dan' as Fred Bloggs and proved conclusively that he was not the person Cortile said he was, would that be the end of the matter? No, it would simply be passed off as a case of mistaken identity. Hoaxers have learned by now that ufologists do most of their work for them. Play a mind game: read Hopkins' account of this story from the point of view that Cortile set out to deceive him and engineered the whole thing to manipulate an honest and trusting man. It is alarming how easily that theory fits.

There are, however, arguments against this. For example, Cortile's nine-year-old son has been involved, and has described a meeting with aliens at which he was given a valuable diving helmet as a present, which he kept hidden from his mother. That she could persuade her son to lie so convincingly about a fiction she had created seems questionable, and potentially reckless. And inventing a scenario to hoodwink her son would be difficult, and would involve many co-conspirators. There are further valid objections to the hoax theory raised by

Hopkins in his book which cannot easily be dismissed. But in the end, the case went the way of Gulf Breeze, and controversy has been the only visible outcome.

THE 'ROSWELL AUTOPSY' FOOTAGE

Whatever the truth of the Cortile case, the next candidate for the holy grail certainly seems to have been based on an assumption that ufologists would do the work of the hoaxers for them, and so far it seems to have been borne out. On 21 September 1993, Philip Mantle told John Spencer that he had been contacted by a man claiming to have film of the Roswell incident. Mantle thought the likelihood pretty remote: 'I don't believe in aliens anyway, as you know,' he said. But he added that he would keep in contact with the man and see what developed.

Apart from a few vague passing references, Mantle rarely mentioned the story again for two years. He has said that he only infrequently contacted the man again[44] and did not meet him until March 1995, when he was preparing the list of speakers for that year's UFO conference. But James Easton[45] says he has seen a 'CV' issued by Mantle which reads: 'In 1993 I was asked to be a consultant to the Merlin Group in London. The managing director of this group is Ray Santilli. Mr Santilli is the man who claims to have obtained the now highly controversial "alien autopsy footage" shown on TV around the world. My consultancy on this project ended in December 1995.' In fact, just three days prior to the September 1993 meeting with John Spencer, Mantle had faxed BUFORA documentary film-maker Bob Digby stating that Santilli's company wanted to make a BUFORA documentary and that 'I am to co-ordinate this project'.[46] Indeed, the degree of Mantle's involvement with

The UFO museum at Roswell, New Mexico, contains a great deal of fascinating material. It now also contains images from a film purporting to be that of a government/military autopsy on retrieved aliens. Few serious researchers have any faith in the claims.

Santilli's company has caused controversy over the last few years.

When the 'Roswell film' emerged, it appeared to show an autopsy being performed on an alien supposedly recovered at Roswell. The most frequently screened section of the film depicts an alleged alien on a mortuary table, one leg badly wounded, being systematically dissected by two people in what look like biological isolation suits, occasionally watched by a third observer. The chest is cut open and the organs removed; the eyes are examined by removing their dark 'covers', and the brain is extracted.

Although Mantle 'didn't believe in aliens', he wrote in the *Independent* on 29 March 1995 the 'Dear Disbeliever' letter containing such statements as: 'The time is fast approaching for me to say, "I told you

so" and for you to eat your words,' and 'A film has arrived from North America which . . . is the closest we have yet come to proving not only that UFOs are plying our skies but also that aliens have landed on earth', and 'The film . . . is the best proof we have yet obtained that an alien spacecraft did crash that summer in 1947.'[47] Mantle claimed he was misquoted but, coincidentally, he has since come around to the positive viewpoint expressed in that newspaper article. His views are due to be expressed in a book he has written on the Roswell story.

The minutiae of the film have been debated ad nauseam. Apart from the unresolvable arguments about the alien itself, there has been debate as to whether or not a curly telephone wire in the autopsy room is an anachronism, whether the clock on the wall was correct for the period, and so on. In the end, if the film is a hoax, any decent hoaxer ought to be able to get such few facts right. It has also been alleged that security markings on the film 'disappeared' after their authenticity was called into question.

The autopsy itself has fuelled debate.

The techniques used are said to be very authentic, and therein lies the problem. Even if the film genuinely shows an alien, the operation is not an autopsy in the true sense – it is not an attempt to determine a cause of death, it is the dissection of an extraterrestrial. Such a rare opportunity would surely merit the use of many cinematic cameras and the colour film available at the time, not to mention stills cameras, so that every aspect would be faithfully recorded. The slow, painstaking, and carefully documented examination, removal and preservation of organs would be required. This was not just a John Doe found dead on the streets of New York. Yet the 'autopsy' is swift, according to the clock in the background; there is only one hand-held film camera in use, which misses a great deal of important action, and the work looks 'routine'.

It goes without saying that special-effects techniques would be able to recreate any features of the films, given the limited amount of analysis that would be possible. Even Santilli acknowledged this: 'Yes, I think any special-effects company worth their salt should be able to recreate anything . . . they should be able to have you and I sitting in the car beside Kennedy in Dealy Plaza – that's their job.'[48] This kind of analysis plays into any hoaxer's hands. It keeps the subject alive and valuable. And it is pointless: verification of the film must depend on the 'big picture', not on a few props.

Part of the 'big picture' is the existence of not one, but several films. In particular, there is a film of what is alleged to be the 'field examination' of the alien bodies. Indeed, this was the first of the Roswell 'autopsy' films released by Ray Santilli for viewing by the BUFORA council. It differs greatly from the much-scrutinized 'wounded-leg alien' autopsy film. The action takes place not in a brightly lit hospital-like room, but in a sort of dark, apparently tent-like enclosure. A figure lies stretched out on a platform bed of some kind, covered for the most part by a sheet with the head, feet and hands showing. Two white-coated doctors spend a great deal of time concentrating on the subject's left hand. They seem to be being watched, perhaps supervised, by a dark-coated figure who could be a military man. The scene is dimly lit by a single lamp. The head of the 'alien' seems to be that of a classical 'gray': bald, domed head with very large, black eyes. It is evidently very slim and flat-bellied – strikingly different from the alien in the autopsy film, which is pot-bellied and has a human-like head.

The implication is that the 'tent' film shows the 'emergency' examination of a recovered alien body. Does this fit with the Roswell story? In fact, it fits with astonishing accuracy. In Friedman and Berliner's book on the Roswell incident, *Crash at Corona*,[49] there is a description of a dimly lit tent set up at the site of the retrieval to contain the bodies.

The tent footage and autopsy footage have come from the same source. Author and crop-circle researcher Colin Andrews states in his newsletter: 'Santilli verified that the photographer does indeed claim that this was an emergency procedure carried out in a barn at the crash site after discovering that one of the two aliens was in fact still alive.' So we have one source, one incident, but two different types of alien.

In the various witness descriptions of aliens at Roswell, one consistent feature is that no witness has reported that the aliens looked different from each other. Surely we are not being asked to believe that two separate races of aliens crashed in the same locality within a short space of time? That is surely one bridge too far, even for the uncritical. But how, then, do we account for Santilli's two different aliens?

The logic of the Roswell recovery dictates

that both pieces of footage cannot be genuine, although one could be. If the tent footage is genuine, then the autopsy footage (and another similar film of an identical alien) is not. But why make a fake film if you believe you already have the real thing? And if the autopsy footage is genuine, where did the tent footage originate, bearing in mind that Santilli released them both? We must consider that the existence of the two films is a good reason to view them both as fakes. But then why make two films? We don't know, but two possibilities have presented themselves.

One is that the tent footage was made to conform with current literature on the subject but was rejected when it was realized that it was boring and would not make enough of a splash: all that happens is that the doctors hold hands with the alien. The autopsy footage might then have been made paying less attention to reports and more to sensation. Experienced UFO researchers are well aware that those who want to will make the film fit their beliefs, despite the facts. If this film was hoaxed, then the hoaxer was someone who understood the psychology of UFO belief.

Steve Gamble, director of research for BUFORA, has suggested a second possibility based on the 'burn-out' of lighting effects on the tent footage. He believes that the original footage might have been shot directly on videotape, and that perhaps the hoaxers then grew nervous and decided they might need to have something on authentic contemporary film. Film stock and cameras from 1947 are available, as determined by researcher Matthew Williams, so perhaps a new film was made, now taking into account a desire for a little more sensationalism.

Why both films were then released is uncertain. Possibly the tent footage was used because, as a truer reflection of the existing literature on Roswell, it was a safer

bet. If that really caused a sensation, then the other footage might not need to be used. More likely, even if the tent film did cause a sensation, the others could be released a year or so later to keep interest alive once the general principle of recovered-autopsy film had been accepted and the second batch of footage would therefore be less critically examined.

Of course a great deal of effort has been put into verifying the authenticity of the film itself. Again, this has been a fiasco. Santilli has claimed that Kodak authenticated at least the date of the film, but there has been controversy even on that point. G.V. Cadogan, the managing director of Kodak's motion-picture and television-imaging division, wrote to us on 31 March 1995: 'I cannot find anybody in our organisation who has any knowledge of such a film and therefore we are unable to make any statement on the authentication of the film concerned.'[50] The only valid tests would have to be made from the actual reel of film containing the images. At the very start of the whole business BUFORA, through John Spencer, offered Santilli non-destructive testing (except for some leader film) under the supervision of John Parsons-Smith, then chairman of Kodak's film division in the UK. The testing team was to include film archivists, special-effects people, computer analysts and an award-winning film company with access to a great deal of analytical equipment. The offer was never taken up.

United States photographic researcher Bob Shell has been interested in UFOs for years. He offered to analyse the film and seems to have done as good a job as possible on the small sample that was sent to him. He believes it is likely to be of around 1947 vintage. The sample showed the autopsy room without the alien, and Santilli has confirmed to us in recorded interview that no cuts of frames featuring the alien were made for examination. But Shell did not actually see the piece of film he analysed being removed from the footage that was being screened, and only a few frames were sent to him. One point our own special-effects advisers made was that a piece of 1947 footage from a 'normal' hospital room or laboratory could have been used as the basis for a 'recreation'. In other words, a hospital room in a genuine 1947 film could have been reconstructed to shoot the alien sequences, and the original 'empty room' film offered for authentication. But even this ignores the fact that 1947 film stock is available for purchase.

In any case, Kodak have confirmed directly to us that considerable quantities of such film (they suggested 16ft) would need to be available for analysis for any study to be conclusive. That quantity of footage simply has not been made available to anyone. So the chase is still on as far as analysis is concerned. Despite offers from authoritative sources, whose confirmation would be of great value, the latest person to be 'approved of' by Santilli was Professor Corrado Malanga in Italy. A leading Italian researcher, Edoardo Russo of CISU, stated that although he believed Malanga was well qualified for the job, 'I would rather object that he is not exactly an independent scientist analysing the evidence, because of his deep involvement in UFOlogy . . . and because of his past and present liaison with Santilli's representative in Italy . . . plus his public, oft-repeated favorable opinions as to the authenticity of the footage.' And that was before undertaking any analysis.

At a BUFORA council meeting Philip Mantle suggested that Santilli and his team were recovering images from a canister supposedly containing footage of 'debris', and another piece of film which allegedly features President Truman. This point was picked up by Kent Jeffrey in an article he wrote:

The most spectacular claim of all was that of the debris-site footage. On January 20, 1995, I spoke to a movie producer, who has a serious interest in the 1947 Roswell event, just hours after he had spoken with Ray Santilli. Santilli had given a detailed description of the debris site. According to Santilli, the terrain was somewhat hilly. The craft was visible, not in one piece, but in a large number of pieces, necessitating the use of a large crane. Also, numerous soldiers in uniform were visible, in some cases clearly enough for their faces to be seen. Santilli described the debris site in detail to others, including Philip Mantle, Colin Andrews, and Reg Presley . . .

Back in January 1995, we were told that the footage included an autopsy scene with President Truman. Truman was described as standing with other individuals behind a glass window, his face so clearly visible that it would be possible to lip-read his words. Author and crop circle researcher Colin Andrews, one of those who has been in direct contact with Ray Santilli, asked Santilli 'what had convinced him that it was authentic'. Santilli responded, 'I had no doubts when I saw President Truman.'

In the event, the debris turned out to be a few struts with hieroglyphics on them which someone was holding towards a camera. There is no location shot. Santilli later explained that many of the canisters were too badly damaged for him to be able to recover an image, though this seems to contradict his earlier statements about the 'field of debris' description.

And Truman did not put in an appearance. The film of the president, Santilli told John Spencer, was also damaged beyond recovery. Santilli claimed only to have known Truman was featured from the canister labels. 'We have . . . about twelve or more canisters that were damaged and on one of them . . . Truman's name is clearly on the canister.'[48]

The most obvious big-picture examination was to identify and interview the cameraman. The duty of authentication falls to the presenter of the film, and is only as good as the story that comes with it. So what of the man who allegedly shot it?

Talking about his acquisition of the films and the camera man, Santilli said: 'He shot hundreds of reels of film . . . he set aside a certain number of reels that he thought had processing problems . . . and then once he finished whatever he had to do with the problem reels he called Washington to hand over the remainder . . . *Washington never bothered picking them up* [our emphasis]. . . That is a very peculiar story, but that's unfortunately the truth.'[48] In fact it is a very fortunate truth, for if that is the case the government can be regarded as having abandoned their copyright, and renewed copyright would be vested in the first person to register it. These 'peculiar' circumstances would seem to make Santilli the legal copyright owner, with full rights of copyright enforcement.

One prominent UFO researcher, Michael Hessemann – who wrote the book promoting the authenticity of the film with Philip Mantle – told a wide audience that he had spoken to the original cameraman. If that is true, it would move verification of the footage a long way forward. However, we pinned him down on this in an interview and he finally admitted, on camera, that what had actually happened was that he had telephoned Santilli, Santilli had telephoned the cameraman, and Santilli had then phoned him back.[51] That is a very different matter, and it relegates the cameraman once again to the shadowy 'maybe, maybe not' world. And yet we heard Hessemann give a lecture to 700 people the following day, and state again that he had spoken to the cameraman. This lapse of memory on his part may unfortunately have created false impressions in the audience.

But just who was the cameraman? Santilli got to hear about the film while he was researching early footage of 1950s musicians such as Elvis Presley. John Powell[52] commented on the Internet: 'Santilli has given the name of the cameraman as "Jack Barnett". In January 1995, he confided the name to Philip Mantle, Reg Presley, and Colin Andrews. On June 22, 1995, Philip Mantle, by prior arrangement with Santilli, received a telephone call from the alleged cameraman, who identified himself as Jack Barnett.' Mantle also confirmed that name to John Spencer in response to a direct question and sent letters to UFO researchers around the world asking for information on 'Jack Barnett', based on the fact that Santilli had informed him that that was the name of the cameraman.

John Powell reveals: 'Reporter Nicolas Maillard located Cleveland, Ohio, disc jockey Bill Randle, the real source of the early Elvis Presley footage . . . the purchase of the Elvis film actually took place in Bill Randle's office on July 4, 1992, . . . Both performances [on the Elvis film] were filmed by a freelance photographer who had been hired by Bill Randle – a photographer named Jack Barnett. We now know the origin of the name "Jack Barnett".'

But Barnett died in 1967. Confronted with this fact on a TV show, Santilli said, 'Well, firstly, I'm very pleased that you have found Bill Randle . . .'

Powell continues his analysis: '(If Santilli was so pleased, why did Bill Randle have to be found in the first place?) At that point, Santilli described a new and changed scenario in which the person from whom he had purchased the Elvis footage was not really the military cameraman after all. He

now claimed that he had met the real cameraman *after* he purchased the rights to the Elvis film from Bill Randle . . . Everyone, including the [TV show] host, Jacques Pradel, seemed incredulous.'

Despite his claims to the contrary, and the letter sent by Mantle to researchers, Santilli responded to questions about 'Barnett' from BUFORA publications director Mike Wootten: 'I have never confirmed the name of the cameraman.'[53]

It was inevitable that the cameraman would have to put in an appearance in the end. If the film was genuine it was understandable that he would want to be associated with it; if it was a fake then this was the next logical step in keeping the controversy alive. At the time of writing we hear from Michael Hessemann that the cameraman plans to make a TV appearance with his face 'distorted'. Anyone claiming to be the cameraman is going to have to prove it: that this individual intends to hide his identity is hardly going to add authenticity to this mounting fiasco.

If the film is a hoax, and if Santilli is not one of the perpetrators but a victim of it, then this cameraman may hold necessary answers to who the hoaxers are.

In conclusion, let us leave aside for a moment the details of the films and stand back to take a broader view. Does anyone seriously think that this film has been treated as a genuine product would have been treated? Why should the source contact Ray Santilli or Philip Mantle; indeed, why contact any committed-interest group with a predictable bias? Why not approach an organization like the Smithsonian? Their stamp of approval would greatly increase the film's value. The reason for not doing so could be a nagging doubt as to the film's authenticity: the Smithsonian's rejection of it would greatly decrease its worth. Therefore we have by implication 'Jack Barnett's' own distrust in the film.

Given the rejection of 'open' avenues and offers of independent authentications, and the back-door or lacklustre way almost everything about this film has been handled by those with most to gain, there is every justification for the doubts expressed by most serious UFO researchers.

As ufology's potential 'holy grail' the 'Roswell' film falls shorter than almost any other recent possibility. It is a serious insult to ufology and those involved in it. On a lighter note: in an episode of the cult science-fiction series *The X-Files*, Agent Mulder informs his colleague, Agent Scully, that the 'alien autopsy' film footage is a fraud. We think it highly appropriate to end this item with the fictional conclusion of fictional characters.

And so the hunt for the holy grail seems set to continue. At the time of writing a few ufologists are desperately trying to pump up a handful of disconnected circumstantial points to turn a genuine low-level light sighting into a UK Roswell-style crash retrieval: the Rendlesham Forest incident has been blown up out of all proportion and it has become 'not the done thing' to criticize the case at all.

Other attempts have been made to 'argue up' Bermuda Triangles in areas of Britain with data that owe more to sensationalism than case quality, and the media are pressurizing ufologists to 'beef up' their stories with little or no regard for truth. This is probably a side-effect of series like *The X-Files*. So the quest for truth is increasingly beginning to look like the quest for film rights or the TV mini-series, and there have been some high-profile programmes masquerading as documentaries but leaning far too far towards sensationalism.

We have no doubt that ufology will change again; and it should improve. It can hardly degenerate any further.

UFOS AND THE PARANORMAL INTERFACE

But if the fifth decade has brought out the worst in ufology, it has also brought some much-needed radical thinking, and the dawn of new approaches.

'A near-death experience mixed with a UFO experience would be the best way to describe it,' Whitley Strieber told us of his impressions of one aspect of his lifetime encounters. He added: 'The near-death experience and the appearance of ghosts and so forth are very intimately involved with the alien encounter.'

In *Breakthrough*,[6] Strieber recounts that he received 139,914 letters following the publication of *Communion*, and that 'people were not reporting the scenario of abduction and manhandling that is so often referred to in the media and UFO publications'. He describes the 'classic' abduction as 'rare', and comments: 'People report interactions at a far higher level of strangeness.' This bears out our argument that it may be UFO investigators who are imposing the imagery on to the subject. Left to themselves, people view the subject more widely.

If the state of research in the 1990s is characterized by one element, it is the belated recognition that UFOs cannot be separated from other paranormal studies. In past decades this connection was either dismissed or denied. Parapsychologists themselves fought shy of involvement with UFOs, although this was probably mainly because of the predominance of the extraterrestrial hypothesis.

The starting point for opening up these possibilities lies, in our view, in recognizing first that there is not one UFO subject, but two separate areas, and secondly that these two areas may not have any real connection at all. The distinction we should make is between *sightings* of objects, or lights in the sky, where there is no sensation of personal involvement, and *experiences*, which are usually closer encounters, often one-on-one encounters with entities, featuring other personal involvement, such as capture and examination aboard a perceived flying saucer.

'Mainstream' UFO research, and particularly the ETH, has demanded that these two phenomena are related and should be lumped together in any overall study. That link has, in our view, been artificially created by UFO researchers dedicated to the ETH, because in order to support that theory the two *need* to be linked. If these objects flying about in our atmosphere are visitors from other worlds, what are they doing? The answer suggested is that they are going to places where they can abduct people. Looking at it from the other side, if these flying saucers really are sitting at the roadside, or hovering outside bedrooms, waiting for a subject into whom they can stick probes, then how did they get there? The 'answer' is in those same little things seen flying around in the atmosphere.

What this does, of course, is create not only a cohesive argument, but one that is largely concerned with a physical reality. Certainly the predominant American view, which dictates a good deal of world ufology, is that flying saucers are as physical as our own space probes. When they do seemingly nonphysical things like moving through rock, or their occupants pass people through walls, it is argued that this is the product of superior technology. In short, these beings and their craft are physical realities with an edge over our own command of physics. This argument seems to be further supported by the evidence of crash retrievals. However, as we have seen, crash retrieval is a largely American phenomenon which grew out of the American political paranoia post-Watergate, and it is arguably a third division of the overall UFO subject, and again one which may not be genuinely connected to the other two.

So what happens if we divorce these three phenomena? Does the whole UFO subject fall apart? Do we discover that we have all been wasting our time over the last fifty years? No. What we discover is that we are faced with rich possibilities for study; possibilities which provide for legitimate links with parapsychology and conventional science.

SIGHTINGS

These are largely of identifiable objects – estimates have suggested that 90 to 95 per cent of reported sightings can be explained satisfactorily. However, a recent study by BUFORA researcher Robert Bull, has at least shown that those IFO (identified flying object) figures are based on very diverse and uncontrolled samples and criteria, the percentage may be significantly lower.[54] Of the UFOs not included within whatever percentage we consider appropriate, a good deal probably (although it is a big 'probably') might have been identified as originating from 'normal' sources if the information could have been located or had been to hand – had light aircraft logged accurate flight plans, and so on. That would leave a small percentage, though still an impressive number, of unidentifiable objects which might possibly represent something as yet unknown to science. The study of these unknown energies and luminosities may be a future path for UFO research, working alongside conventional meteorology and physics.

EXPERIENCES

We might conclude that, stripped of dependence on the ETH, the closer encounters may be a facet of the spectrum we call the paranormal. Something real is happening to people, but a good deal of what they actually believe it to be is dependent on their predisposition, cultural background, beliefs, the normal human misperceptions inherent in any experience and the struggle to classify the unknown. This is by no means to say that all experiences are imaginary or psychological, but it recognizes that such experiences must have an imaginary or psychological component special to each witness.

It is a sobering thought that, if that were not true, UFOlogy really would be a field apart. Such interpretations are a normal part of the way in which we understand our place in the world and in every situation in which we find ourselves. When witnesses defend their experiences against that position, they are not only denying a reality of the way the human brain works, but they are showing that their perception of those experiences comes from conviction and not from evidence.

It is the experiences that offer the prospect of rich pickings for the UFO–paranormal interface. If these experiences are not the result of contact with extraterrestrials, then what are they? There are several areas to be considered.

MARKS ON ABDUCTEES

A strong piece of evidence put forward in support of the physical reality of alien abductions is that many of the abductees have marks on their bodies which correspond with what they believe happened to them on a flying saucer: scoop marks in the skin, which are so strange and so unique that they could only be alien, where the other-worlders took skin and tissue samples; bleeding from the nose or ears, where probes are believed to have been inserted into the head; warts around the genitalia where instruments were clamped

during examination, such as those Barney Hill suffered from. Something like a radiation burn is said to have affected Antonio Villas Boas during his encounter in 1957. Set against this, however, is the evidence of religious stigmata, the phenomenon where the marks associated with Christ's crucifixion spontaneously appear on the

skin of the stigmatic. Stigmata can rightly be regarded as a form of psychosomatic illness – self-created – but the condition deserves a special classification because of the *intensity* of belief needed to produce the effects. Many UFO abductees exhibit, in our experience, the same sort of passion. Not always the passion of

Photographer's reconstruction of a lighted UFO. But many lights are perhaps not part of a solid object; recent research has suggested that a study of 'Earthlights' might answer many UFO questions – and produce a new understandings of the Earth's own energies.

blessing, as is normal in religious stigmata, but an equal and overwhelming passion of belief, fear or fascination, that could create stigmata which match the conviction of the witness. So if they truly, truly, believe they have been probed and sampled, they could manifest marks to match that belief.

GHOST PHENOMENA

The direct involvement of other paranormal areas in UFO cases is indicated by several experiences we have investigated in which ghost or poltergeist phenomena are reported. This was true of the Aveley case, for example (see Chapter 3). And Whitley Strieber had extraordinary ghost sightings linked with the experiences he described in his books. He told us: 'We have had cases at our own home where there were aliens being encountered by people in the living room and in the basement right below them two people were waking up to see the ghost of the woman who had died a few years before.' He never discussed this aspect in his books, though it is something he plans to explore in his next book, *Secret School*. 'Something that I didn't report in *Communion*, because I did not know quite what to make of it, was that an old friend of mine [who Strieber later discovered had died by this time] was with the visitors during the experience.' (Strieber generally refers to the entities as 'visitors' rather than 'aliens', as he believes it important to keep open the question of their origin.) 'I saw him and even talked to him . . . The presence of this individual during my encounter experience I suppressed, not because I thought it was something that I shouldn't say but because I just couldn't understand how to fit it in with what I was writing. I couldn't understand it. I didn't understand well enough. But now that I understand it better I'm fairly sure that his presence there was an artefact of the experience.'

CHANNELLING

There have always been levels of acceptability in UFO lore. In the early days it was acceptable to see UFOs, even to ascribe an extraterrestrial origin to them, but not to see aliens. Later it was all right to see aliens, but not too often: witnesses claiming repeated experiences were regarded as fantasy-prone and unreliable. As we begin to recognize that certain mindsets may be necessary in people to perceive UFO phenomena, as we do with ghost and other paranormal claims, so repeater witnesses are becoming acceptable.

But still on the outside of the field are the channellers, who have never gained any acceptability among 'scientific' researchers because of the nature of their claims. They deliver generally asinine messages from aliens telling us what we already know, or what it appears the channeller himself or herself personally fears or desires. On that level of analysis such claims are of course rejected: they do not seem to offer reliable evidence of the ETH and therefore appear not to fit into 'worthwhile' research.

But when we divorce ourselves from the ETH and attach ourselves to the spectrum of the paranormal, we have comparative studies to assist us. The channellers have close – indeed virtually identical – parallels in religious and spiritual channelling. The same effect is apparent: the channeller receives messages that reinforce their own beliefs and desires. What we seem to be learning from the message, and the manner in which it is given, is that there appear to be several 'layers' or 'compartments' in the mind where information is stored. Channelling is highly likely to be a complex, even brilliant, way in which the conscious mind can access information in subconscious compartments. But because it feels like new knowledge and new ideas it seems to come from without: from beyond the grave, from God, from aliens.

So channelling may be an incredible short cut to learning how to use the brain far more efficiently than we do at present, and one worthy of diligent study.

FURTHER INTO THE RIGHT BRAIN

It is possible that the right hemisphere of the brain houses the special attributes that make us 'superhumans', but that, unfortunately, our move towards rationalism and technology has cut us off from those abilities. The paranormal, in this model, becomes those rare 'blasts' when we perceive with the right brain, and see the world quite differently – and then try to make sense of it with the left brain and all the attendant problems that brings.

In the UFO-experience field we have worked with many abductees who, following their encounters, have undergone life-changing effects such as becoming vegetarian; developing ecological concern or a desire for artistic expression through music, art or sculpting (the latter crudely hinted at in the film *Close Encounters of the Third Kind*); feeling a need for 'new-age' associations with Earth and the universe, and so on. And it is not just desire: the talent also appears, which suggests that a real change is taking place. One gardener, following such an experience, started painting and selling his work for thousands of pounds. Another witness, Bryan, has since become a successful graphic designer.[55] Debbie Jordan told John Spencer in 1990:

I was interested when you and Budd were talking . . . about the creative, the artistic ability. I've experienced that, you know. Budd says he doesn't know whether it comes from within us or may be external. But it's as if, because of the traumatic experience, you develop a heightened sense of awareness of what goes on around you which kind of

breathes in and affects other things. I developed a heightened sense of what goes on inside me in my head and in my heart. And it continues to grow. It's like somebody put a seed there and now it's grown, you know. And I'm not saying they put the seed there, maybe it was already there.

Our colleague Leo Rutherford of the Eagles Wing Centre for Contemporary Shamanism commented on this 'development' from his context. 'If a person has not got much self-awareness and reaches a crisis point, the "demons" – which basically takes in fear, anger, grief, rage, jealousy and more – can appear like an overwhelming threatening external force. And it is, of course, much easier to see one's own demons as external and disown them, and in fact that makes them something very, very powerful.' By that reasoning, as Debbie better came to terms with herself, so her experiences shifted in quality.

On 8 November 1954 thirteen-year-old Philip Molava, of Croydon, Surrey, was in his garden feeding his pet rabbits when a small disc-shaped UFO flew by. Shortly thereafter Philip ended up in bed, paralysed. He became aware of three entities materializing in his room out of a glowing mist, then remembers waking up fit and well. This was the start of many psychic experiences, such as ESP, out-of-body experiences, telepathy and clairvoyance. He commented: 'I wasn't awake until they came.' He was suggesting that a whole aspect of his being was 'switched on' by this encounter, a theme we have heard many, many times when talking to close-encounter witnesses.

Finnish experiencer Dr Rauni-Leena Luukanen-Kilde says of the close-encounter experience: 'Take it as a fantastic opportunity to develop yourself spiritually and understand more about the universe! You will experience exciting things!'[56]

But we do not believe that alien astronauts visit Earth to make people into musicians and artists. We believe that when someone is faced with a potentially frightening alien abduction scenario, faculties not previously realized are switched on. Perhaps it happens as a defence mechanism – the brain draws on its latent abilities in case it needs them. But once the right brain is 'triggered' perhaps it stays active, and the artistic and other expressions are a byproduct of this. Whatever the case, they remain a clue to the mechanisms that might be involved, and again offer potential for study.

SHAMANISM

Leo Rutherford believes that understanding the UFO experience, and gaining benefit from it, might be being hampered by the current approach.

I was at the Association for Transpersonal Psychology Conference in May 1995 talking to one of John Mack's subjects. Listening to his story of abduction, I felt as if I was listening to a shamanic journey. It sounded as if he had gone into an altered state of consciousness, experienced a significant journey out of himself, an out-of-body journey or at least an out-of-mind journey. And it had in it very much the feeling of the lower world and power animals. Power animals are generally known as the way that energies in that world most usually communicate with us. [We had already discussed the idea that the 'alien' could be a 'power animal'.] It doesn't have to be animals, it can be people. After all, it's one's imagination converting the energy of the spirit world into something we can understand. So it sounded to me as if he was telling a visionary journey. But it was translated in the UFO conventional language instead of shamanic language, and it was taken as real in the three-dimensional world.

Rutherford believes that the language of UFOs can be constraining and negative, whereas the language of shamanism (which is based on the concept of a person making a journey to the world of good and evil spirits) allows for more flexibility of interpretation. 'In shamanic journeys one tries not to lead anybody. People do their own journeys and what comes and what happens is theirs. And you don't use your analytical mind whatsoever until *after* you come back, and then you work with the images as to what they actually mean, what they are teaching you. This might suggest that, because the UFO is thought of by its proponents as a scientifically verifiable experience, the analytical mind is being forced into the equation too quickly.'

But a UFO language has existed since 1947, so when people go into altered states they can apply that framework. The fact that they already know the framework tends to lead them on. Prior to this recognition of UFOs, the journeys would have been framed in another way. One of the things that is so important in all this work is to try not to impose one's own structure, because the client is dealing with difficult issues without a framework, and therefore is vulnerable to taking on a framework. And the person's own fears can be manifested through a collectively agreed framework of UFOs and abductors and so on. It is possible that these people are experiencing their own darkness.

Investigators are, consciously or unconsciously, putting a framework on everything and they are feeding a structure of people's experiences to fit into it. And we human beings can be terribly obliging, and quite unconsciously adjust our experiences to fit, because, after all, we don't know what the hell the experiences are. It's very easy to quite unconsciously and well-meaningly fit them into what the investigator is feeding you.

But when witnesses, usually over a period of time, break free of that framework, we find significant changes in them, and in their understanding of their experiences. They often move from a state of fear or anxiety to a state of increased spirituality.

INCREASED SPIRITUALITY

Many UFO researchers, in America in particular, are cautious or even dismissive of claims that abductees became almost 'contactee-like' and increasingly spiritual as a result of their encounters. Despite the investigator's views, it is clear that growing numbers of witnesses are opening up about these aspects of their experience, and it is equally clear that these areas have always been within many people's accounts, although either they have been ignored by investigators, or the witnesses have not previously been forthcoming as they presently are. We have in other books related the account of Elsie Oakensen, whose abduction–examination seemed, to her, to be more spiritual than medical in nature, and who went on to exhibit many psychic abilities, and that of Finnish doctor Rauni-Leena Luukanen-Kilde, who claimed out-of-body abductions.[55]

When we spoke to Debbie Jordan in 1996 she explained her feelings on this. 'The experiences changed from once being a physical experience to being more of a mental, psychological, psychic and spiritual level . . . I have come to find on my own things that were taught in Hinduism and Eastern religions and stuff that I didn't have any knowledge of at all.' Debbie described what she called 'virtual-reality' dreams: very realistic, and exhausting. They acted as a form of education for her. 'It's like going to school. It opens . . . my mind. It's changing everything about me inside, the way I look at life and God and myself and my fellow man and my world and my future.'

Elsie Oakensen is an experiencer who has benefitted from her encounter. She believes her experience to have been basically spiritual.

One case in which this has been very thoroughly examined by a ground-breaking researcher is that of Betty Andreasson, which was investigated by Raymond Fowler. In *Perspectives*[35] in 1988 and *Gifts of the Gods?*[55] in 1994, John Spencer outlined the need for a new mode of 'witness-driven' investigation which puts the witness very much in the driving seat. Whitley Strieber wrote in the foreword to *The Watchers*, the third book documenting the experiences of Betty Andreasson and later her husband, Bob Luca, 'From the beginning Ray has allowed Betty to lead him. Instead of rejecting the stranger aspects of her experience and hypnotising – in effect brainwashing – her into believing that she has been a victim of the typical abduction scenario, he has *listened* to her with an open mind.'[56]

The case started on 25 January 1967, just after Betty's thirtieth birthday. She was in the kitchen of her home, and her parents and seven children were in the living room.

Artist's impression of probably the most thoroughly researched case involving a wider range of the paranormal within UFO literature. The case – explored over four books – started when four entities walked through the walls of Betty Andreasson's house.

Her husband was in hospital following a car accident. An orange-red light was shining into the kitchen from outside, and then the house lights faltered and went out. Betty's father went outside to see where the light was coming from and was astonished to see four non-human figures 'like Halloween freaks . . . they jumped one after the other, just like grasshoppers'. The creatures passed through the door of the house and into the kitchen. They were fairly classical grays, dressed in shiny blue uniforms, gloves and high shoes or boots. Unaware

of UFOs, and coming from a religious background, Betty interpreted the experience as a visitation by angels, and it was eight years before she reported the experience to UFO researchers.

During regression hypnosis it emerged that the entities had 'switched off' Betty's family, telepathically controlled her and taken her outside to their oval-shaped craft. The craft appears to have taken off and docked with a 'mothership', aboard which Betty was subjected to a medical examination. She experienced images of birth, death and recreation. She was then returned to her home.

In later years Betty and her husband divorced and she married Bob Luca who, it turned out, had also had a UFO experience in 1967. Further investigation indicated that both Bob and Betty had undergone a series

of abductions throughout their lives as well as experiencing many paranormal phenomena in their house. These included precognition, telepathy, out-of-body experiences (one of which was a joint out-of-body abduction of both Betty and Bob) and much more. Indeed an entire chapter is dedicated to this interface in Fowler's *The Watchers*. During one of her recalls Betty stated: 'And I am standing there and I am coming out of myself! There is two of me there.' Her description of a 'world of light' which was 'indescribably beautiful' is very similar to the near-death experience (NDE), where people believe they enter another world spiritually.

Betty Andreasson's case must be read in full to be fully appreciated, and the books by Raymond Fowler relate them in all their richness.

The recognition of this connection with other paranormal areas may have been a long time coming, but it is not new. A comparison to the NDE can be seen in the claim of one of the early contactees, Orfeo Angelucci. In *Saucer Diary*, I Norkin comments of Angelucci: 'He had been taken up in a balloon-shaped spacecraft to a great height above the Earth and then given the opportunity to view it from that height . . . It was a beautiful sight, but Orfeo said he wept unashamedly. The realisation came that underneath that surface beauty was a sick humanity suffering from untold misery. He didn't want to come back but was told he had to because it was now his mission to tell the people the truth.' This is very similar to NDEs in which people are confronted with the choice of going on into death or coming back, usually to fulfil a perceived mission, personal or otherwise. For example, in Raymond Moody's book *Life After Life*[57] a fairly typical near-death experiencer explains: 'I wondered whether I should stay there, but as I did I remembered my family, my three children and my husband. Now, this is the part that is hard to get across: When I had this wonderful feeling, there in the presence of that light, I really didn't want to come back. But I take my responsibilities very seriously, and I knew that I had a duty to my family. So I decided to try to come back.'

There is a large body of work building up on the similarity, and possible interconnected nature, of the abduction and NDE, as is examined, for example, in *The Omega Project*, by Kenneth Ring.[58]

Ufology has now been fifty years in the melting pot. It has mutated over that time and come of age, unfortunately, in an era of ego, greed and dishonesty, and at a time when we learn the tricks of the trade and not the trade itself; go for the 'holy grail' and forget the hard piece-by-piecing of the jigsaw puzzle. The climate of the times is such that it is difficult to pick one image that illustrates the state of ufology, but we shall end this chapter with one that would have probably been unthinkable in the early days of ufology.

You can now buy an insurance policy that pays out if you are abducted by aliens. One such policy pays out £100,000 if you are abducted, £200,000 if you are impregnated by the extraterrestrials and £300,000 if they eat you.[59] The policy was created by a special broker, GRIP, and costs £100 per annum. In the first month GRIP received over 1,000 inquiries. Similar policies exist in the United States: in one of them, the claimant must obtain the signature of an abducting alien as proof of the event!

A feature arising more frequently within UFO claims now that recognition has been given to the paranormal aspects of cases: the 'out-of-body' abduction. Many witnesses believe that it is not their physical but their spiritual body which undergoes the experience.

Conclusions

'The more we know, the more fantastic the world becomes.'

Aldous Huxley

This review of UFOs provides us with the opportunity, even the obligation, to set out tentative conclusions to date. In the introducton we pointed out that UFOs have an evolution, unlike other paranormal phenomena such as poltergeists and ghosts, and we believe that this is the result of mis-interpretation of circumstantial evidence to fit predetermined beliefs. We contend that there is merit in examining the reality of UFOs by looking at the stabilities over time. The components arguably remain unchanged – it is only the way they have been fitted into the story that has varied and is artificial.

LITS

We shall start by looking at what many regard as the 'core business' of the subject: the LITS, lights in the sky. Arnold's 'flying saucers' have never been positively identi-fied as anything other than lights. Whether these lights were attached to anything or not is unknown. His belief that he had seen objects was the result of Cold War para-noia, and this set the tone for future exami-nations. Looking back at UFOs in history, they might well have been the same. Pliny, in *De Natura Rerum*, written around 2,000 years ago, refers to 'burning shields', 'flying torches', 'gleaming beams' and so on. Perhaps they had structure; but perhaps not. In the *Historia Francorum*, Gregory of Tours records sightings in the year 584 –

'brilliant rays of light'. Matthew of Paris mentions a sighting in 1239, 'a great star like a torch'. In the *Nurnberg Gazette* is a report from 1561, when an array of 'objects' filled the skies and seemed to 'fight one another', and a similar scene arose in 1566, as depicted in the Basel woodcut. The dominant feature would appear to be the lighted brilliance of these 'objects': in other-words they were LITS.

We could go on throughout the cen-turies to the present day: the majority of well-documented, well-witnessed reports are of lights which either the observers or other interpreters have assumed were attached to something physical. But Devereux's 1982 work on earthlights shows that there are probably natural ener-gies that can become luminous in the atmosphere. Had Cold War and postwar fears not been so prevalent in the early years, then perhaps we would not have spent five decades chasing unlikely aliens.

Let us tentatively conclude, therefore, that one part of the UFO phenomenon has stability: LITS have been reported consis-tently for centuries. They are probably there-fore 'real'. They are widely seen, and in the modern era they register on radar; they inter-act with aircraft, and possibly some charac-teristics of their energy affects the running of engines, accounting for the failure of vehicle engines and vehicle lights. A great many 'nor-mal' lights will be misinterpreted in this cate-

Peter Holding's artworks created since his UFO encounter have expressed his feelings about the experience. He was drawn to open his curtains, and saw in front of him a huge swirling vortex in which he believed he could 'feel' the presence of entities.

gory (lights on planes, astronomical objects, meteors, and so on), and true examples will be rare, but they are important for study. The young Australian pilot Frederick Valentich probably encountered one, and died as a result. As we said when recounting his story, that alone is reason enough for continued study. Earthlights theory suggests that by understanding the nature of some of these lights we may be able to predict earthquakes, so there is valuable knowledge to be gained.

BUFORA has for some years been working on the BOLIDE (Ball of Light Information Data Exchange) Project, star-ted by researcher Hilary Evans, which has been studying sources of luminous ener-gies. Its first report is due in 1997. In a small way this may represent a return to the core business' of UFO research, which many organizations and investigators have ignored in favour of 'sexier' subject areas.

OBJECTS

What, then, of objects in the sky? There are times, particularly during daylight hours, when witnesses report what seem much

Many natural phenomena are often interpreted as UFOs: this is a perfectly natural, lenticular, cloud formation. Typically, other phenomena which can stimulate UFO reports include aurora, astronomical objects and mirages, in addition to man-made causes such as laser-light displays.

more likely to be physical objects. Firstly, many will be the same LITS we have examined above. Nature falls into symmetry, and it would not be surprising if these luminous energies formed globular shapes like bubbles, or flattened lenticular shapes ('saucers') when spinning. In daylight many such shapes might look solid. Into a second category fall those objects which are vaguely or distantly seen, but are clearly physical. Apart from the misidentification of 'normal' planes and other misperceived technology, we should bear in mind that our skies are frequently invaded by secret, mostly military, technology under development. Remember the words of Angus Brooks, who saw a UFO over Moigne Downs: 'If you had seen Stealth years ago you would have thought you were crazy that anything could look like that.' And Stealth has been in development for decades; the technology that will be routinely flying in the 2020s is probably being tested now.

The combination of strange craft clearly seen and lights at night apparently performing impossible manoeuvres, if they are assumed to be physical, easily leads to a belief in extraterrestrial technology. But it may be a false lead.

CONTACTEES

And what of George Adamski and his successors? Do contactees offer proof of extraterrestrials? Are they deluded? Is there stability through history for their claims? There may be a rich field for study here too, if aliens are left out of the equation.

For contactees did not appear for the first time with Adamski in 1952. They have a long history, but their experiences have usually been interpreted through religion or spiritualism rather than through the newly emerging UFO phenomenon. We might consider Joan of Arc: was she not a contactee? She heard a divine message telling her that she should lead the French armies to expel the English from Northern France and set Charles VII on the throne. She succeeded at Orléans and Patay, and Charles was duly crowned. However, she was betrayed and sold to the English, who burned her as a

Illustrator Bryan Ellis has depicted some of the features of his own close-encounter experiences. For some reason, the number three – in this case symbolized by the three aliens – is significant in his experiences.

So are abductees just a different form of contactee? They seem to have arisen only recently. Where is their stable, consistent history? Several factors need to be considered in this context. First, we can find enough similarities in the fairy lore of Celtic and other traditions to suggest that the abduction experience is not new, only newly applied to UFOs. These early stories tell of people abducted into fairy rings and emerging after lengthy periods of 'missing time'; or people meeting non-humans and human–fairy hybrids; even of people finding themselves in magical places that have superficial similarities to flying saucers (such as illumination from no obvious source). Whether this experience is entirely mythical, whether it reflects interaction with a non-human intelligence or whether it is an expression of 'channelling' is open to debate. What is important is that it is not dependent on 'flying saucers'.

Secondly, the abductees were a reaction to the major criticism of the contactees: that the latter did not offer proof or opportunity for study. In a world increasingly slavishly bound to the 'religion' of science, proof is absolute. Now here we have people who can show the marks of their experiences: apparent implants, scars from their medical examinations and so on. The evidence seems impressive until we look at the 700-year-plus history of stigmata and realize that even implants and skin markings may have 'internal' origins. According to St Francis of Assisi's biographer, Thomas of Celano, St Francis not only 'produced' wound markings but 'the nails themselves formed out of his flesh and retaining the blackness of iron.'[1]

Thirdly, the abductees look more like 'victims' than the 'chosen' contactees. Budd Hopkins writes in *Witnessed*, of specific cases he mentions, 'instead of

witch. In short, the message she received was precisely right for the mood of the times. She was convinced of its authenticity, it gave her strength to act, and it engendered belief so strong that others were prepared to follow her. We should not be so cynical as to assume that Adamski felt any differently. He received a message from the aliens (a superior race morally, physically and technologically) which happened to precisely fit the mood of the times (fears of the atomic age). He believed it with a passion that persuaded others to believe it too.

So where did these messages come from? God? Aliens? In fact, almost certainly from within the 'receiver'. A study of channelling, far from being a laughable or derisory subject, might well lead us to understand more about the way our brains work. We spoke to witnesses who had watched one 'automatic writer' (a person channelling in a trance) fill pages with neat script at astonishing speed ('it was like watching Superman in the movies,' they said). It is highly possible that the intuitive use of the brain has been lost and replaced by mechanistic teachings. If people could 'channel' from their subconscious to their conscious mind, perhaps they could access more, and faster, than they can by using conventional memory recall. In times of stress or passion, perhaps these abilities surface. They are so unfamiliar in modern times that it is hardly surprising that even to the 'recipient' they appear to be 'from without'. We might learn from channelling if we put aside prejudices of interpretation, and study the people rather than the messages themselves.

claiming any special wisdom, they admitted to ignorance and confusion.' But we must consider that the abduction experience perhaps also fulfils a need. Abductees partake in the exploration of the experience and its deeper meaning. To be selected by 'aliens' is still very special, and if the selection takes the form of an experience which can seemingly be verified, then it fits well with the requirements of a mechanistic society.

Fourthly, the abduction experience is similar in many ways to the NDE and shamanistic-type experiences, which have a long history. Shamanistic experiences occur in virtually all cultures and possibly go as far back as the dawn of mankind. Perhaps UFO abductions are the same experience interpreted through a modern, constructed storyline. The modern stereotype was established by the encounter of Barney and Betty Hill, and while they certainly seem to have seen a UFO in the sky, the nature of their close encounter is less clear. It could perhaps consist of dreams, or a misunderstood spiritual experience.

So abductions, too, have a long and stable history, though only when viewed without the constraints of the ETH.

CRASH RETRIEVALS

Surely crash retrievals offer the proof that these diverse strands can legitimately be pulled together under the 'flying saucer' and 'alien' banner? After all, the very aliens said to be behind abductions are reportedly found in crashed flying saucers which

Bryan Ellis began having experiences as a young child, seeing 'grays' in his bedroom and encountering UFOs in several locations. They seem to have provided a guidance and stimulation for him. Over time he has developed an artistic flair which he now explores to the full in his career.

might be the LITS and objects seen flying in the skies.

But we would argue that if there is one completely mythical aspect to UFOs, it is crash retrievals. Because the prospect of crashed, retrieved, stored and studied aliens seems to offer so much, it is hardly surprising that so much effort and belief has been poured into this one facet. But in the end all we have are bar rumours, third-hand recollections of the children and friends of the original witnesses, and little substance. The whole subject of crash retrievals is based almost entirely on just one incident – Roswell – and there is little reason to suppose that anything other than terrestrial, military technology was involved in both the crash and the retrieval. That so much should happen in one small location – the most highly classified location in the world at that time – is itself

telling: 'flying saucers' have been reported at plenty of comparable sites, such as rocket bases in Africa and Australia and military installations across Russia. Why no crashes there? Despite attempts by a few researchers to conjure up crash retrievals around the world it is basically a phenomenon exclusive to the United States. And it arose in post-Watergate America at a time when youth was joined by the establishment in distrust of the government, and it reflects the resultant paranoia about government manipulation and dishonesty. The documentary evidence is ambiguous,and what seems to be the strongest documentary evidence – MJ12, for example – has been discovered in circumstances which suggest either fraud or disinformation.

GOVERNMENT INVOLVEMENT

Is the belief that governments are covering up their involvement in UFOs simply paranoia, or does it have substance? Critics of the subject cry 'paranoia', and it would be unfair not to admit that paranoia is certainly high among sectors of UFO believers. When a member of the Russian embassy turned up at one UFO conference some years ago a large group of ufologists backed away, looking like the surviving members of the Moran gang after the St Valentine's Day massacre.

However, the evidence that governments have been deeply involved in the UFO subject is strong. The question becomes: what is their involvement based on? The most popular belief nurtured for the most part by the media and extremists, is that governments – in particular the US government – knows that flying saucers are extraterrestrial but does not want to panic the world's population by admitting it. Variations on this theme are that secrecy is maintained to protect the self-interest of financial and religious institutions, etc., all of which would be threatened by the revelation that aliens are present on Earth, and that the government has entered a pact with the aliens to exchange something of value to both.

All of this flies in the face of historical and other evidence. There have always been committed individuals who get the truth out when there is a truth to be revealed, even if it takes their own death to do so. People may be motivated by reasons of greed, ego or idealism. In the fifty-year history of UFOs those people would have emerged, and despite the bar rumours, they have not done so. Investigations by people like Howard Blum, who should have had the ways, means and motives to uncover the truth, have got no further than the ufologists.

The truth being sought simply is not there: there is a truth, but it is a different one. As for institutions collapsing: for every institution that might be at risk there is a competing one which would have an equal vested interest in revealing all. Financial institutions are opposed by third-world institutions; religions compete at fundamental levels. Yet the status quo remains firm.

And all of this takes no account of the wishes of the alleged aliens themselves. They would need to be involved if there were such a cover-up. Why should they be concerned about protecting political and religious institutions? Does that level of involvement with the fundamentals of humanity equate with the 'explorers' that poked and prodded around in Maurice Masse's lavender field, then paralysed him and sped off when they were 'caught'?

But the identification of UFOs might only be a small, and relatively insignificant, part of government involvement. We suggest that from the beginning, right from the Cold War, postwar paranoid days, factions within governments have wanted to test how vulnerable a population is to rumour, to belief, to disinformation. Remember J. Allen Hynek's statement when he was officially employed by the Air Force on the importance of examining rumour. And the Condon committee's own conclusion that 'UFO reports and beliefs might be of interest to "the social scientist and the communications specialist".'

There is some evidence that interested government factions have watched UFO groups, and given them false information to monitor how vulnerable a specific population would be to such tactics in the hands of the 'other side'. UFOs are the perfect instrument for such experiments. They didn't have to be invented; they arose naturally. Ufologists came with the baggage of certain convictions, and

they were a committed ideological group – all the government had to do was identify the groups and learn how to manipulate them. That is the likeliest interpretation of early CIA involvement, FBI monitoring, and so on. Some of the most dramatic components of the controversy – MJ12, some aspects of Gulf Breeze, Rendlesham Forest and others – may have been staged by government-sponsored factors as disinformation tests.

Consider, for example, Ray Stanford's 'high-level contacts', who told him that a non-terrestrial craft like the one Lonnie Zamora had seen at Socorro had been captured and held at Holloman Air Force Base. Stanford was told: 'They will probably know, eventually, where it came from, but we already know that the thing was not made by terrestrials.' As the statement was made to a known UFO investigator the 'contact' must have realized it would be quoted. But at the same time, without proof, the statement was valueless – another bar rumour, in essence. Even if it was true, it did not give Stanford information of worth. It only seems to make sense as a piece of disinformation. And what about the statement by Albert M. Chop, the former USAF spokesman for Blue Book? 'I've been convinced for a long time that the flying saucers are real and interplanetary. In other words we are being watched by beings from outer space.' And consider the possible disinformation used during the Rendlesham case, as noted in Chapter 5.

All of these lead to the possibility at least that ufologists were, and are, being toyed with. It is unlikely that such a campaign would form part of 'major' government policy, but it is possible that small groups working within government agencies, perhaps on black (secret) budget projects, have used disinformation as part of their work.

FURTHER OFF THE WALL . . .

A possible extension of the disinformation theory should be aired, but it is frankly one for which we have much caution. It has been speculated that the US government might even have gone so far as to try to fool the enemy into believing that they actually *did have* alien technology under study. Researcher Don Ecker believes that the Roswell incident just after the Second World War might have been an attempt to convince the Russians that the US had a captured flying saucer and therefore had access to some incredibly advanced technology. If Ecker's theory is correct, then one reason why the CIA targeted UFO groups for scrutiny (aside from keeping tabs on potential radicals) could have been to suggest, or hint, that the UFO buffs 'might be on to something'. The Soviets could thus be led to wonder why such a level of official interest was being paid to a minority subject.

How far can such thinking be pushed? Could we even consider that something similar might have happened with Gulf Breeze? That case arose just as the Russian 'evil empire' was collapsing, and intelligence reports in the USA would already have indicated that such a change was afoot. So was Gulf Breeze allowed to become a cause célèbre as one small part of a destabilizing campaign launched in the knowledge that the Soviet Union was falling apart, and that a few well-placed hammer blows – such as the news that the 'enemy' was about to make a huge breakthrough with a 'relationship with aliens' – would finish it off? The beauty of this is that, as ever with the UFO phenomenon, they would not have had to invent or control very much. If Ed Walters faked his photographs, they had only to sit back and watch ufologists do their work for them, perhaps dropping a hint in a certain direction here or there.

Far-fetched this may be, but Walters' own book points out that the military moved some very obvious hardware into the area during the time of his sightings, and that there was a 'sudden interest in low-level surveillance shown by the military only a few weeks after my first sighting. Radar equipment such as this had never been seen before in Gulf Breeze.'[2] If some exercise was being undertaken, in view of the furore over the Walters' sighting in all the local press, a cautious military mind might have deemed it wise to move the exercise elsewhere, or delay it, to avoid the attention of UFO buffs. Instead, the military seem almost to have shouted their interest out loud.

Such a campaign would be unlikely to have been effective, to say the least, but if we look at some of the implausible ideas the CIA are known to have proposed in other matters, a plan like this may not be as far-fetched as it sounds. Take the attempts to destabilize Fidel Castro in Cuba, for example. When their bizarre schemes for killing Castro failed to get off the ground, at one time the CIA considered positioning a submarine off Cuba to project a laser sight-and-sound show with the aim of convincing the Cubans that it was signalling the second coming of Christ.[3]

It is also possible that the military are developing 'decoy technology' – perhaps an extension of laser technology using projections designed to confuse, frighten or distract the enemy – and that some UFOs are such images being tested. This might account for the triangles seen over Europe and elsewhere.

These are just some of the possible scenarios which could provide explanations for the major components of the UFO subject. They show that all the aspects of the phenomenon do have a long, consistent history, and therefore probably a basis in reality. They suggest that the recent knitting together of the diverse strands is the falsehood in the subject, and that the evolution of UFOs is its own giveaway. However, none of this explains the fascination for the subject long after the Cold War, even after the collapse of the Soviet empire which for decades coloured the American, and therefore Western, view of UFOs. For that we need to search elsewhere.

MYTHOLOGY

It is in considering UFOs as a modern myth that we find, more than anywhere, the rejection of the phenomenon by science, and more than anything a true, deeper, meaning for the subject. Because even if aliens do not exist, at least not in terms of contact with the Earth, we now live in a world in which their acceptance is widespread.

In Chapter 2 we looked at the sixties; the time when, in the West, values were challenged by youth. The UFOs which might otherwise have died with the Cold War now happened to provide the answer to a new spiritual need, and took on from that need a new lease of life. Churches were emptying, and Western religions were finding it hard to relate to the people. UFOs were not the result of that void, and nor did they cause it, but having come into existence within a largely political framework, they were now to be interpreted within a largely social one.

To understand the role of UFOs here we must examine the question of myths. Author Richard Cavendish, who has studied myths in cultures around the world, has written: 'Myths are the imaginative traditions about the nature, history and destiny of the world, the gods, man and society.'[4] There is not a culture in the present day, or one whose traditions have survived through history, that has not had myths. Myths about its origins, its place in the universe, its destiny. And all cultures have myths which provide for some sort of afterlife, and some sort of contact with a supreme being in some form or other. Myths allow us to express belief, suggest appropriate behaviour and explain social structure. They allow us to understand, often in ways we can visualize and usually through oral tradition, our customs and values.

For example, Adam and Eve, the Garden of Eden (the Hebrew word for 'pleasure') and the serpent probably never existed as a physical reality. But they provide us with a graphic and effective illustration of temptation and of the necessity of adhering to laws or agreements made. Hell as a real locality is largely rejected, even by Christians – in 1996, leading church figures publicly dismissed the idea of a fiery hell, replacing it with a more lonely, isolated place. Nevertheless, Hell gives Christians a strong sense that divorce from, or banishment from, Jesus leads to a world of rejection and desolation. To reject God creates a pain that must be suffered.

If myths die, then they must be replaced by new ones. In the Bible the Book of Genesis describes the creation of the world and the placing of mankind at the highest level among all living things. This served as an unchallenged model for many centuries. Later Charles Darwin's theory of evolution suggested that people evolved naturally and that man was just another animal, but the new theory of 'survival of the fittest' held that man gained ascendancy over other animals through his innate abilities. Therefore mankind continues to reign supreme: the purpose of the original myth is now achieved by the new one. Myths can be shown to reflect those aspects of the world which people hold to be most important or do not understand. Many record the exploits of supernatural beings

and gods. The implication is that the culture in touch with the 'true' gods is the 'highest' culture, the one with the most correct values and the brightest future.

In 1843 John Stuart Mill published *A System of Logic* which was followed in 1858 by Darwin's *Origin of Species*. These works advocated dependence on rationalism, and on the five known senses. They rejected the value of anything that could not be measured. If the West believed that the rational approach was the right one – and it has taken to those principles with vigour – then it has also cut away from under itself a belief in God. God cannot be scientifically proven. His existence depends on faith and intuition, and He does not 'perform on command' under laboratory conditions.

Just as some old myths are replaced, others are resurrected. Hybrid forms of myths combining the old and the new form arise either because times have changed, or because cultures have mingled.

This shift to rationalism and to a dependence solely on what can be validated by science can be held to have been the most important single issue in the creation of UFOs as a phenomenon. In the wake of the destruction of the concept of the supernatural, gods and the traditions that could not be 'scientifically proven', a new myth – UFOs – grew up among a small but expanding group of people across the world because it seemed to offer reconciliation between the old and the new. The gods were back, but now they used technology. They fitted the traditional design of myths, being supernatural entities, near-gods, but they came to us in measurable, predictable, even fallible, flying saucers. And the culture which understands them is the culture with the greatest future, and the most correct set of values.

Myths are allied to rituals in order to explore the edges of human experience.

For example, shamans use among other things deep, rhythmic drum beats, drugs and dance to enter into alternative states of consciousness where they meet and interact with supernatural and god-like figures we would otherwise regard as mythical. UFO contactee experiences occur in this realm at the limits of reality, though usually spontaneously.

Myths allow for a world where taboos can be challenged. In Roman myths, for example, incest, murder, cannibalism, rape, and so on are acceptable. Equally, anything can happen aboard a flying saucer: it is not your responsibility, and if you have to play your role in procreation for the aliens, then this cannot be frowned upon because it takes place in a situation where you are not to blame.

Like art, myths are a way of exploiting thought, of seeing the world as we perceive it or would like it to be. They combine the conscious and the subconscious. The most thought-provoking research into the after-effects of the abduction experience suggests that these aspects of the mind are sometimes triggered by UFO encounters.

And myths not only explain the way the world works, they create it. An individual's responses to the world will be based on his or her belief about it; his understanding of what he believes is true, or ought to be true will colour his way of interpreting what he sees around him. This is particularly true when the data are incomplete or ambiguous. Myths can be built around either 'stories', or realities, and this creates much of the ambiguity. For example, even if it were true that UFOs represent the visitation of aliens to Earth, much of what we think we understand is still mythology. As detailed an understanding as many UFO researchers would like to think they have is simply not possible. We understand less about the animals which share our own world than many UFO researchers think they understand about aliens from others.

UFO myths reflect the fact that people intuitively know that science, rationalism and analysis have failed to reach the soul of mankind; that while they may explain trivial details, and make them seem important, they do not answer even the most basic questions. These new myths, the myths of the new age and its more recent successors, are trying to re-establish the fundamental values we as a society so desperately need. In his ten-volume work *The Republic*, Plato considered whether or not one myth could be constructed which would be believable and meaningful to the whole world. In modern times, perhaps UFOs are a step on the road to the fulfilment of that postulation.

In recent years scientists seem to have fought against the idea that myths are necessary. Science, many argue, can provide all the mental stimulation people require, and can be fascinating and fulfilling. We do not understate the value of what science offers, but we believe that some non-scientific concepts have equal importance for people. History shows us that every culture has created myths. A one hundred per cent score should surely confirm even to the most ardent sceptic that myths must be fulfilling a need that is deeper seated than the transient requirements of politics or society. We in the West have come perilously close to losing our attachment to the values encompassed by myths, and the UFO phenomenon has provided a way back into the mythical, shamanistic world. This does not mean UFOs themselves are mythical – myths do not show up on radar – but they have a significance far beyond their 'reality', and that significance is a real part of the modern world.

AT THE INDIVIDUAL LEVEL

We have studied many abductees whose lives have been transformed for the better as a result of their interpretation of their experiences. Whatever the reality – whether they saw a light in the sky, or were touched by an energy they rightly or wrongly thought intelligent – they have changed. The UFO, whatever it may 'really' be, has become a psychic toy which has encouraged people to think more deeply and therefore to develop. We believe that contact with the unknown stimulates redundant parts of the brain and switches on the intuitive artistic aspects of character, and that, once switched on, they remain at the individual's disposal. As we have seen, many experiencers have developed artistic drive and ability. For many who believed, or were led to believe by researchers, that they have encountered aliens, this process is slow. But eventually they loosen their dependence on this conviction, or relegate it to

Peter Holding is one of many experiencers we have worked with who have discovered and developed talents following their encounters. This picture represents aspects of the religious imagery that often appears in his works – in this case a simple cross.

being only one aspect or explanation, and flourish as they develop 'spiritually'. Whether this is self-generated, or alien- or God-given, becomes largely irrelevant. This is a facet of the subject that should not be lost through prejudicial approaches.

In addition, we have to recognize that having 'come of age', the subject now affects people who have no real interest in it per se. They find it in their newspapers, in their literature ('grays' and abductions now appear in teenage fiction, for example), in advertising. It forms a cultural context, and creates a subliminal level of acceptance, whether they are aware of it or not. We must accommodate this development in our understanding of the modern face of UFOs.

THE ALIEN WITHIN

The theory that extraterrestrials are visiting Earth should not be dismissed out of hand, although we regard it as improbable on the evidence presented even by proponents of the ETH. We are more certain that many people who claim alien encounters are in fact having an 'internal' experience, one more akin to a shamanistic revelation, albeit a spontaneous one. For those people, the imposition on their experience of the ETH by committed researchers is unlikely to be helpful, though we would suggest that total rejection of the 'alien from within' is equally reckless. In shamanistic 'journeys', the experiencer visualizes a 'power animal' which becomes a companion and even a mentor for the exploration. The experiencer can communicate with the animal, which 'knows' the best and worst of his or her inner moods, feelings and frustrations. It is, simply, a way of getting in touch with parts of your own mind that you have difficulty facing up to. Perhaps some 'aliens' are a form of power animals, and the experiencer is creating them in that particular form because they are wrapped up in the mythology, rather than the reality, of the phenomenon. They would be wise not to reject the alien because of the 'bad baggage' that comes with the idea, but should work with the image as a way of accessing their deepest thoughts through their own mythological beliefs. This is a basic self-discovery technique, and of course not a part of the UFO phenomenon itself. It is, however, one way in which this new cultural context in our society can be made to work positively for some.

FUTURE RESEARCH

LITS, objects in the sky, crash-retrieval lore, real and perceived government involvement, mythological contexts affecting cultures and individuals, and a host of affiliated subjects: 'UFOs' have certainly become a complex subject in their fifty-year history. Many 'purist' researchers believe the subject now embraces far more than it should. Perhaps it does, but for the foreseeable future it is all part of the subject, and researchers must deal with the world as it is rather than the one they wish for. We can best approach the next fifty years by not being hidebound by one belief, and travelling along various paths presented by these facets of what we currently label 'ufology'. Each path should lead to fundamental and important discoveries about ourselves and the world around us.

J. Allen Hynek said that the study of UFOs 'could have a profound effect – perhaps even be the springboard to a revolution in man's view of himself and his place in the universe'. In its history to date it has become a more complex subject than he probably imagined when he made that statement. Nonetheless, we feel that those fifty years have proven his prophetic statement correct.

Bryan Ellis' abstract artwork depicting several of the elements he believes is involved in close encounters: the triangle, angelic wings, and the spiritual communion between human and alien as symbolized by the joining of the two faces within the circle.

References

1 1947–57: THE POSTWAR YEARS

1. Bloecher, *Ted: Report on the UFO Wave of 1947 (privately published, 1967).*
2. *East Oregonian*, 26 June 1947.
3. *Life* magazine, 1952.
4. Arnold, Kenneth & Palmer, Ray: *The Coming of the Saucers* (privately published, 1952).
5. Spencer, John & Evans, Hilary (eds): *Phenomenon* (Macdonald & Co, 1988; chapter: 'It seems impossible, but there it is' by Pierre Lagrange).
6. Lusar, Rudolph: *German Secret Weapons of the Second World War* (Philosophic Library, 1959).
7. E.g. *Leicester Mercury*, 21 April 1953.
8. Saunders, David R. & Harkins, R. Roger: *UFOs? Yes!* (Signet, 1968).
9. Hynek, J. Allen: *The UFO Experience* (Abelard–Schuman, 1972).
10. Spencer, John & Anne: *Encyclopaedia of the World's Greatest Unsolved Mysteries* (Headline, 1995).
11. Flammonde, Paris; *UFO Exist!* (Ballantine, 1976).
12. Ruppelt, Edward J: *The Report on Unidentified Flying Objects* (Doubleday, 1956).
13. *New York Times*, 27 July 1952.
14. *True* magazine,1953. Quoted in 'What Radar Tells Us About Flying Saucers' by Donald Keyhoe.
15. Evans, Hilary & Spencer, John (eds); *UFOs 1947–1987* (Fortean Times, 1987).
16. *Sunday Dispatch*, 18 October 1953.
17. Michel, Aimé; *The Truth about Flying Saucers* (Robert Hale, 1957).
18. Steiger, Brad (ed): *Project Blue Book* (Ballantine, 1976).
19. Heard, Gerald: *Riddle of the Flying Saucers* (Carroll and Nicholson, 1950).
20. Associated Press release, Paris, 13 December 1944.
21. Wheatley,Dennis: *Star of Ill-Omen* (Hutchinson, 1952).
22. Spencer, John: *Perspectives* (Macdonald, 1989).
23. Spencer, John: *Gifts of the Gods?* (Virgin, 1994).
24. Leslie, Desmond & Adamski, George: *Flying Saucers Have Landed* (Neville Spearman, 1953).
25. Bethurum, Truman: *Aboard a Flying Saucer* (DeVorss, 1954).
26. Fry, Dr Daniel: *The White Sands Incident* (Horus House, orig. 1954).
27. Angelucci, Orfeo: *Secret of the Saucers* (Amherst Press, 1955).
28. Festinger, Reicher and Schacker: *When Prophecy Fails* (Harper & Row, 1964).
29. *Mail on Sunday*, 3 November 1996.
30. Davis, Isabel & Bloecher, Ted: *Close Encounter at Kelly and Others of 1955* (CUFOS, 1978).
31. Keel, John: *Strange Creatures From Time and Space* (Neville Spearman, 1975).
32. Hynek, J. Allen: *The Hynek UFO Report* (Dell, 1977).
33. *Daily Telegram*, 7 July 1947.
34. Vallee, Jacques: *Passport to Magonia* (Neville Spearman, 1970).
35. Jung, C. G.: *Flying Saucers – Modern Myth of Things Seen in the Sky* (Ark, 1987, orig. 1959).

2 1957–67: THE 'SIXTIES'

1. *Daily Express*, 16 June 1960 (report by Chapman Pincher).
2. *The Sunday Express*, 27 May 1962.
3. Chapman, Robert: *UFO – Flying Saucers Over Britain?* (Granada, 1968).
4. Norman, Rev. E.: 'Flying Saucers over Papua. A Report on Papuan Unidentified Flying Objects' (G. Cruttwell MA Oxon, of the Anglican Mission, Menapi, Papua New Guinea, March 1960).
5. Spencer, John: *Perspectives* (Macdonald, 1989).
6. Fuller, John G.: *The Interrupted Journey* (Dial Press, 1966).
7. *Sunday Mirror*, 25 September 1966.
8. Wolfe, Tom: *The Right Stuff* (Bantam, 1980).
9. Pilkington, Mark: *Screen Memories – An Exploration of the Relationship between Science Fiction Film and the UFO Mythology* (privately published, 1996).
10. Vallee, Jacques: *Passport to Magonia* (Neville Spearman, 1970).
11. Copy of letter from Betty Hill to Donald Keyhoe.
12. Letter from John G. Fuller.
13. Stanford, Ray: *Socorro Saucer* (Blueapple, 1976).
14. Hynek, J. Allen: *The Hynek UFO Report* (Dell, 1977).
15. Friedman, Stanton T. & Berliner, Don: *Crash at Corona* (Paragon, 1992).
16. Quoted in *You* magazine, 15 October 1995.
17. BUFORA files relating to 'Warminster Week'.
18. Rogers, Ken: *The Warminster Triangle* (Coates & Parker, 1994).
19. *Daily Mirror*, 10 September 1965.
20. *Daily Mirror*, 16 September 1965.
21. Shuttlewood, Arthur: *The Warminster Mystery* (Neville Spearman, 1967).
22. Shuttlewood, Arthur: *Warnings From Flying Friends* (Portway, 1968).
23. *West Essex Gazette*, 29 April 1966.
24. Blum, Ralph & Judy: *Beyond Earth* (Corgi, 1974).
25. Evans, Hilary & Spencer, John (eds): *UFOs 1947–1987* (Fortean Tomes, 1987; chapter: 'Exeter, 3 September 1965' by Kim Moller Hansen).
26. Smith, Warren: *UFO Trek* (Sphere, 1977).
27. *Flying Saucer Review*, 14 January and 14 April 1968.
28. *Evening Standard* , 25 October 1967.
29. Chapman, Robert: *UFO – Flying Saucers over Britain?* (Granada, 1968).
30. Angus's own files, lent to the authors.
31. Lorenzen, Jim & Coral: *UFOs over the Americas* (Signet, 1968).

3 1967–77: THE DECADE OF ENDINGS AND CHANGES

1. Saunders, David R. & Harkins, R. Roger: *UFOs? Yes!* (Signet, 1968).
2. *The Times*, 20 January 1966.
3. Lovell, Jim & Kluger, Jeffrey: *Lost Moon* (*Apollo 13*) (Houghton Mifflin, 1994).
4. 'Review of the University of Colorado Report on Unidentified Flying Objects by a Panel of the National Academy of Science', 1969.
5. Copy of original report dated 1 February 1966 sent to the authors by the Ministry of Defence in 1994.
6. Friedman, Stanton T. & Berliner, Don: *Crash at Corona* (Paragon, 1992).
7. Good, Timothy: *Above Top Secret* (Sidgwick & Jackson, 1987).
8. Hobana, Ion & Weverbergh, Julien: *UFOs From Behind the Iron Curtain* (Souvenir Press, 1974).
9. *New York Times*, 10 December 1967.
10. Clancarty, Lord: *The House of Lords UFO Debate* (Open Head Press, 1979).
11. Wilford, John Noble: *We Reach the Moon* (Bantam, 1969).
12. Ryan, Peter: *The Invasion of the Moon* (Penguin, 1969).
13. Von Däniken, Erich: *Chariots of the Gods?* (Souvenir Press, 1969).
14. Story, Ronald: *The Space Gods Revealed* (New English Library, 1976).
15. Von Däniken, Erich: *Gold of the Gods* (Souvenir Press, 1973).
16. Wilson, Colin: *The Giant Book of the Supernatural* (Parragon, 1994).

17. Clarke, Arthur C.: *2001 – A Space Odyssey* (Hutchinson, 1968).

18. Chatelain, Maurice: *Our Ancestors Came From Outer Space* (Dell, 1979).

19. Edwards, Frank: *Flying Saucers Serious Business* (Bantam Books, 1966).

20. Little Rock, *Arkansas Gazette*, 7 September 1973.

21. Clarke, Arthur C.: *2010 – Odyssey Two* (Granada, 1982).

22. Aldrin, Edwin. *Return to Earth* (Random House, 1973).

23. Collins, Michael: *Carrying the Fire* (Farrar, Straus And Giroux, 1974).

24. *UFO* magazine (Sunland, California), Vol. 11, No. 4, July/August 1996.

25. Beckley, Timothy Green: *MJ-12 and the Riddle of Hangar 18* (Inner Light, 1989).

26. Campbell, Steuart: *The UFO Mystery Solved* (Explicit, 1994).

27. Flammonde, Paris: *UFO Exist!* (Ballantine, 1976).

28. Kissinger, Henry A.: *Nuclear Weapons and Foreign Policy* (1957).

29. Hickson, Charles & Mendez, William: *UFO Contact at Pascagoula* (privately published, 1983).

30. Pope, Nick: *Open Skies, Closed Minds* (Simon & Schuster, 1996).

31. Original case investigation by Andy Collins and Barry King.

32. Spencer, John: *Perspectives* (Macdonald, 1989).

33. Keel, John: *Operation Trojan Horse* (Souvenir, 1971).

34. Hopkins, Budd: *Witnessed* (Simon & Schuster, 1996).

35. *Skylook* magazine (the forerunner of The MUFON Journal), April 1976.

4 1977–87: THE DECADE OF CONSPIRACY

1. Pilkington, Mark: *Screen Memories – An Exploration of the Relationship Between Science Fiction Film and the UFO Mythology* (privately published, 1996).

2. Evans, Hilary & Spencer, John (eds): *UFOs 1947–1987* (Fortean Tomes, 1987; chapter: 'The Chase for Proof in a Squirrel's Cage').

3. Friedman, Stanton T. & Berliner, Don *Crash at Corona* (Paragon, 1992).

4. Stringfield, Leonard: *Situation Red – The UFO Siege* (Fawcett Crest, 1977).

5. Evans, Hilary & Spencer, John (eds): *UFOs 1947–1987* (Fortean Tomes, 1987; chapter: 'Saucerful of Secrets').

6. *Flying Saucer Review* Vol. 1, No. 1, spring 1955.

7. Le Poer Trench, Brinsley *The Flying Saucer Story* (Neville Spearman, 1966).

8. Steiger, Brad: *Strangers from the Skies* (Universal-Tandem, 1966).

9. Edwards, Frank: *Flying Saucers Serious Business* (Bantam Books, 1966).

10. Wilkins, Harold T: *Flying Saucers Uncensored* (Arco, 1956).

11. Arnold, Kenneth & Palmer, Ray: *The Coming of the Saucers* (privately published, 1952).

12. *Roswell Daily Record*, 8 July 1947.

13. ABC News radio broadcast, 8 July 1947.

14. *Roswell Daily Record*, 9 July 1947.

15. Scully, Frank: *Behind the Flying Saucers* (Henry Holt, 1950).

16. General Accounting Office report, 28 July 1995.

17. Pope, Nick: *Open Skies, Closed Minds* (Simon & Schuster, 1996).

18. Haines, Richard F: *Project Delta* (LDA Press, 1994).

19. 'The Secret Government – The Origin, Identity and Purpose of MJ-12', 1989.

20. *Groom Lake Desert Rat* magazine.

21. Watkins, Leslie: *Alternative 3* (Sphere, 1978).

22. Blum, Howard: *Out There* (Simon & Schuster, 1990).

23. Moore, William L. & Shandera, Jaime H.: *The MJ-12 Documents: Fair Witness Project* (1990).

24. T. Scott Craine interview: *UFO 18*, Vol. 9, No. 3, 1994.

25. Quotations from a recording of the original radio communication, provided to the authors by Paul Norman of VUFORS.

26. *UFO 1979* Tasmania, No. 26.

27. *UFO 1981* Tasmania, No. 32.

28. Clancarty, Lord: *The House of Lords UFO Debate* (Open Head Press, 1979).

29. BUFORA administration files.

30. *Glasgow Herald*, 10 November 1979.

31. Campbell, Steuart: *The UFO Mystery Solved* (Explicit, 1994).

32. BUFORA Bulletin No. 004, May 1982.

33. *News of the World*, 2 October 1983.

34. Evans, Hilary & Spencer, John (eds); *UFOs 1947–1987* (Fortean Tomes, 1987; chapter: 'Saucerful of Secrets').

35. Evans, Hilary & Spencer, John (eds): *UFOs 1947–1987* (Fortean Tomes, 1987; chapter: 'Hessdalen').

36. Flammonde, Paris: *UFO Exist!* (Ballantine, 1976).

37. Devereux, Paul & McCartney, Paul: *Earthlights* (Thorsons, 1982).
38. Hopkins, Budd: *Missing Time* (Ballantine, 1981).
39. Hopkins, Budd: *Intruders* (Random House, 1987).
40. Jordan, Debbie & Mitchell, Kathy: *Abducted!* (Bantam, 1994).
41. Gatland, Kenneth: *Manned Spacecraft* (Blandford, 1967).
42. Spencer, John: *Gifts of the Gods?* (Virgin, 1994).
43. Randles, Jenny: *Abduction* (Robert Hale, 1988).
44. Smith, Warren: *UFO Trek* (Sphere, 1977).
45. *MUFON UFO Journal*, November 1977.
46. Lawson, Alvin: 'The Aliens Within' in *Unexplained* magazine.
47. Spencer, John: *Perspectives* (Macdonald, 1989).
48. Berlitz, Charles & Moore, William: *The Roswell Incident* (Granada, 1980).
49. Statement from the National Archives, Washington, 22 July 1987.
50. Evans, Hilary: *The Evidence for UFOs* (Aquarian, 1983).
51. Strieber, Whitley: *Communion* (Wilson & Neff, 1987).

5 1987–97: THE DECADE OF AUTONOMY

1. Strieber, Whitley: *Communion* (Wilson & Neff, 1987).
2. Jacobs, David M.: *Secret Life* (Simon & Schuster, 1992).
3. Mack, John E.: *Abduction* (Simon & Schuster, 1994).
4. Hopkins, Budd: *Witnessed* (Simon & Schuster, 1996).
5. Spencer, John & Evans, Hilary (eds): *Phenomenon* (Macdonald & Co., 1988).
6. Strieber, Whitley: *Breakthrough* (HarperCollins, 1995).
7. Correspondence with Cynthia Hind, who was also kind enough to send copies of the childrens' drawings.
8. *International UFO Reporter*, July–August 1992.
9. *Daily Mail*, 6 May 1995.
10. Pilkington, Mark: *Screen Memories – An Exploration of the Relationship between Science Fiction Film and the UFO Mythology* (privately published, 1996).
11. *Sun*, 8 July 1996.
12. *Liverpool Echo*, 23 September 1971.
13. Macnish, John: *Cropcircle Apocalypse* (Circlevision, 1993).
14. Good, Timothy: *Alien Liaison* (Century Arrow, 1991).
15. Randle, Captain Kevin D.: *The UFO Casebook* (Warner, 1989).
16. Correspondence with Tony Eccles.
17. *Argyllshire Advertiser*, 23 February 1996.
18. *UFO 1980*, Tasmania, No. 29.
19. *South Wales Echo*, 21 January 1983.
20. *South Wales Evening Post*, 21 January 1983.
21. *Daily Mail*, 3 February and 5 August 1996.
22. Correspondence with Malcolm Robinson.
23. *Enigmas*, Issue 35, Vol. 4.
24. *Daily Mail*, 15 December 1992.
25. Blum, Howard: *Out There* (Simon & Schuster, 1990).
26. Good, Timothy: *Above Top Secret* (Sidgwick & Jackson, 1987).
27. Bernstein, Carl & Woodward, Bob: *All the President's Men* (Quartet, 1974).
28. Morton, Andrew: *Diana – Her True Story* (Michael O'Mara, 1993).
29. Correspondence From Ministry of Defence to Lionel Beer, dated 8 May 1970.
30. Pope, Nick: *Open Skies, Closed Minds* (Simon & Schuster, 1996).
31. Correspondence and interviews with Matthew Williams and Chris Fowler, who were also good enough to share their years of research and documentation with us.
32. Tass, 8 October, 1989.
33. *Daily Express*, 10 October 1989.
34. Vallee, Jacques: *UFO Chronicles of the Soviet Union* (Ballantine, 1992).
35. Spencer, John: *Perspectives* (Macdonald, 1989).
36. *Moscow News Weekly*, No. 43, 1989.
37. MUFON 1990 International UFO Symposium proceedings.
38. Walters, Ed & Frances: *The Gulf Breeze Sightings* (William Morrow, 1990).
39. *Fate*, November 1990.
40. *Florida MUFON News*, Vol. IV, Issue VI, November–December 1994.

41. Pensacola/Gulf Breeze MUFON Inc. Letter to members, 21 November 1993.

42. *Manhattan Transfer*, a commentary of the Cortile case in the form of a spoof book review by Willy Smith.

43. Monograph circulated by George Hansen, Joe Stefula and Rich Butler.

44. 'The Roswell Film Footage' by Philip Mantle (circulated article).

45. James Easton has circulated interviews and commentary widely through e-mail and the Internet to many ufologists.

46. Copy of correspondence supplied by Bob Digby.

47. *Independent*, 29 March 1995.

48. Filmed interview of Ray Santilli by John Spencer.

49. Friedman, Stanton T. & Berliner, Don: *Crash at Corona* (Paragon, 1992).

50. Correspondence from Kodak.

51. Filmed interview of Michael Hessemann by John Spencer.

52. John Powell has circulated interviews and commentary widely through the Internet to many ufologists.

53. Correspondence between Mike Wootten and Ray Santilli. Copies provided by Mike Wootten.

54. Robert Bull's report for the BUFORA research section.

55. Spencer, John: *Gifts of the Gods?* (Virgin, 1994).

56. Fowler, Raymond: *The Watchers* (Bantam, 1990).

57. Moody, Raymond A.: *Life After Life* (Mockingbird, 1975).

58. Ring, Kenneth: *The Omega Project* (William Morrow, 1992).

59. 'Money Mail', *Daily Mail*, 4 September 1996.

6 CONCLUSIONS

1. Wilson, Ian: *The Bleeding Mind* (G. Weidenfeld & Nicolson, 1988).

2. Walters, Ed & Frances: *The Gulf Breeze Sightings* (William Morrow, 1990).

3. Higham, Charles: *Howard Hughes, the Secret Life* (Putnam Berkeley Group, 1993).

4. Cavendish, Richard (ed.): *Mythology* (Little, Brown & Co., 1992).

In addition, reference has been drawn from private correspondence and interviews, and from historical and biographical works relating to the political, social and cultural historical settings.

Bibliography, Further Reference and Recommended Reading

Angelucci, Orfeo: *Secret of the Saucers* (Amherst Press, 1955).

Arnold, Kenneth & Palmer, Ray: *The Coming of the Saucers* (privately published, 1952).

Beckley, Timothy Green: *MJ-12 and the Riddle of Hangar 18* (Inner Light, 1989).

Beckley, Timothy Green: The *UFO Silencers* (Inner Light, 1990).

Berlitz, Charles & Moore, William: *The Roswell Incident* (Granada, 1980).

Bethurum, Truman: *Aboard a Flying Saucer* (DeVorss, 1954).

Bloecher, Ted: *Report on the UFO Wave of 1947* (privately published, 1967).

Blum, Howard: *Out There* (Simon & Schuster, 1990).

Blum, Ralph & Judy: *Beyond Earth* (Corgi, 1974).

Bowen, Charles (ed.): *Encounter Cases from* Flying Saucer Review (Signet, 1977).

Bowen, Charles (ed.): *The Humanoids* (Neville Spearman, 1969).

Boyce, Chris: *Extraterrestrial Encounter* (David & Charles, 1979).

Campbell, Steuart: *The UFO Mystery Solved* (Explicit, 1994).

Cassirer, Manfred: *Dimensions of Enchantment* (Breese, 1994).

Cassirer, Manfred: *Parapsychology and the UFO* (privately published,1988).

Chapman, Robert: *UFO – Flying Saucers over Britain?* (Granada, 1968).

Chatelain, Maurice: *Our Ancestors Came From Outer Space* (Dell, 1979).

Clancarty, Lord: *The House Of Lords UFO Debate* (Open Head Press, 1979).

Clark, Jerome: *UFO Encounters and Beyond* (Publications Int., 1993).

Davis, Isabel & Bloecher, Ted: *Close Encounter at Kelly and Others of 1955* (CUFOS, 1978).

Devereux, Paul & McCartney, Paul: *Earthlights* (Thorsons, 1982).

Edwards, Frank: *Flying Saucers Serious Business* (Bantam Books, 1966).

Emenegger, Robert: *UFOs Past Present & Future* (Ballantine Books, 1974).

Evans, Dr Christopher: *Cults of Unreason* (Harrap, 1973).

Evans, Hilary & Spencer, John (eds): *UFOs 1947–1987* (Fortean Tomes, 1987).

Evans, Hilary: *The Evidence for UFOs* (Aquarian, 1983).

Evans, Hilary: *Visions. Apparitions. Alien Visitors* (Aquarian, 1984).

Festinger, Reicher and Schacker: *When Prophecy Fails* (Harper & Row, 1964).

Flammonde, Paris *UFO Exist!* (Ballantine, 1976).

Fowler, Raymond: *The Watchers* (Bantam, 1990).

Friedman, Stanton T. & Berliner, Don: *Crash at Corona* (Paragon, 1992).

Fry, Dr Daniel: *The White Sands Incident* (Horus House, orig. 1954).

Fuller, John G.: *The Interrupted Journey* (Dial Press, 1966).

Good, Timothy: *Above Top Secret* (Sidgwick & Jackson, 1987).

Good, Timothy: *Alien Liaison* (Century Arrow, 1991).

Haines, Richard F.: *Advanced Aerial Devices Reported During the Korean War* (LDA Press, 1990).

Haines, Richard F.: *Melbourne Episode* (LDA Press, 1987).

Haines, Richard F.: *Project Delta* (LDA Press, 1994).

Harbinson, W. A.: *Projekt UFO* (Boxtree, 1995).

Heard, Gerald: *Riddle of the Flying Saucers* (Carroll and Nicholson, 1950).

Hickson, Charles & Mendez, William: *UFO Contact at Pascagoula* (privately published, 1983).

Hind, Cynthia: *UFOs – African Encounters* (Gemini, 1982).

Hobana, Ion & Weverbergh, Julien: *UFOs From Behind the Iron Curtain* (Souvenir Press, 1974).

Hopkins, Budd: *Intruders* (Random House, 1987).

Hopkins, Budd: *Missing Time* (Ballantine, 1981).

Hopkins, Budd: *Witnessed* (Simon & Schuster, 1996).

Hynek, J. Allen: *The Hynek UFO Report* (Dell, 1977).

Hynek, J. Allen: *The UFO Experience* (Abelard–Schuman, 1972).

Jacobs, David M.: *Secret Life* (Simon & Schuster,1992).

Jordan, Debbie & Mitchell, Kathy: *Abducted!* (Bantam, 1994).

Jung, C. G.: *Flying Saucers – A Modern Myth of Things Seen in the Sky* (Ark, 1987, orig. 1959).

Keel, John: *Operation Trojan Horse* (Souvenir, 1971).

Keel, John: *Strange Creatures From Time and Space* (Neville Spearman, 1975).

Keel, John: *The Eighth Tower* (E.P. Dutton & Co., 1976).

Keel, John: *The Mothman Prophecies* (E.P. Dutton & Co., 1975).

Keyhoe, Donald E.: *Aliens From Space* (Doubleday, 1973).

Keyhoe, Donald E.: *Flying Saucers From Outer Space* (Wingate and Baker, 1969).

Landsberg, Alan: *In Search of Extraterrestrials* (Corgi, 1977).

Le Poer Trench, Brinsley: *Mysterious Visitors* (Souvenir, 1973).

Le Poer Trench, Brinsley: *Operation Earth* (Neville Spearman, 1969).

Le Poer Trench, Brinsley: *Secrets of the Ages* (Souvenir, 1974).

Le Poer Trench, Brinsley: *Temple of the Stars* (Neville Spearman, 1962).

Le Poer Trench, Brinsley: *The Flying Saucer Story* (Neville Spearman, 1966).

Le Poer Trench, Brinsley: *The Sky People* (Neville Spearman, 1960).

Leslie, Desmond & Adamski, George: *Flying Saucers Have Landed* (Neville Spearman, 1953).

Lorenzen, Coral E.: *Flying Saucers* (Signet, 1966).

Lorenzen, Jim & Coral: *UFOs Over the Americas* (Signet, 1968).

Mack, John E.: *Abduction* (Simon & Schuster, 1994).

Michel, Aimé: *The Truth About Flying Saucers* (Robert Hale, 1957).

Moore, William L. & Shandera, Jaime H.: *The MJ-12 Documents* (Fair Witness Project, 1990).

Pope, Nick: *Open Skies, Closed Minds* (Simon & Schuster, 1996).

Randle, Captain Kevin D.: *The UFO Casebook* (Warner, 1989).

Randles, Jenny: *Abduction* (Robert Hale, 1988).

Ring, Kenneth: *The Omega Project* (William Morrow, 1992).

Rogers, Ken: *The Warminster Triangle* (Coates & Parker, 1994).

Ruppelt, Edward J.: *The Report on Unidentified Flying Objects* (Doubleday, 1956).

Rutherford, Leo: *Principles of Shamanism* (Thorsons, 1997).

Sagan, Carl & Shklovskii, I. S.: *Intelligent Life in the Universe* (Holden–Day, 1966).

Saunders, David R. & Harkins, R. Roger: *UFOs? Yes!* (Signet, 1968).

Scully, Frank: *Behind the Flying Saucers* (Henry Holt, 1950).

Shuttlewood, Arthur: *The Flying Saucerers* (Sphere, 1976).

Shuttlewood, Arthur: *The Warminster Mystery* (Neville Spearman, 1967).

Shuttlewood, Arthur: *Warnings From Flying Friends* (Portway, 1968).

Smith, Warren: *UFO Trek* (Sphere, 1977).

Spencer, John & Evans, Hilary (eds): *Phenomenon* (Macdonald & Co., 1988).

Spencer, John (ed.): *The UFO Encyclopedia* (Headline, 1991).

Spencer, John: *Gifts of the Gods?* (Virgin, 1994).

Spencer, John: *UFOs – The Definitive Casebook* (Hamlyn, 1991).

Spencer, John: *Perspectives* (Macdonald, 1989).

Stanford, Ray: *Socorro Saucer* (Blueapple, 1976).

Steiger, Brad & Whritenour, Joan: *Flying Saucers Are Hostile* (Universal–Tandem, 1967).

Steiger, Brad (ed.): *Project Blue Book* (Ballantine, 1976).

Steiger, Brad: *Strangers From the Skies* (Universal–Tandem, 1966).

Stillings, Dennis (ed.): *Cyber-biological Studies of the Imaginal Component in the UFO Contact Experience* (Archaeus, 1989).

Story, Ronald: *The Space Gods Revealed* (New English Library, 1976).

Strieber, Whitley: *Breakthrough* (HarperCollins, 1995).

Strieber, Whitley: *Communion* (Wilson & Neff, 1987).

Strieber, Whitley: *Transformation* (William Morrow, 1988).

Stringfield, Leonard: *Situation Red* (Fawcett Crest, 1977).

Vallee, Jacques & Janine: *Challenge to Science* (Neville Spearman, 1967).

Vallee, Jacques: *Anatomy of a Phenomenon* (Neville Spearman, 1966).

Vallee, Jacques: *Confrontations* (Ballantine, 1990).

Vallee, Jacques: *Dimensions* (Contemporary, 1988).

Vallee, Jacques: *Passport to Magonia* (Neville Spearman, 1970).

Vallee, Jacques: *Revelations* (Ballantine, 1991).

Vallee, Jacques: *The Invisible College* (E.P. Dutton, 1975).

Vallee, Jacques: *UFO Chronicles of the Soviet Union* (Ballantine, 1992).

Von Däniken, Erich: *Chariots of the Gods?* (Souvenir Press, 1969).

Von Däniken, Erich: *Gold of the Gods* (Souvenir Press, 1973).

Von Däniken, Erich: *In Search of Ancient Gods* (Souvenir Press, 1974).

Von Däniken, Erich: *Return to the Stars* (Souvenir Press, 1970).

Walters, Ed & Frances: *The Gulf Breeze Sightings* (William Morrow, 1990).

Wilkins, Harold T.: *Flying Saucers Uncensored* (Arco, 1956).

Glossary

AFB Air Force Base

APRO Aerial Phenomena Research Organization (US group)

AFOSI Air Force Office of Special Investigations (US government agency)

BUFORA British UFO Research Association (UK group)

CAL-TECH California Institute of Technology

CAUS Citizens Against UFO Secrecy (US pressure group)

CEIIIK *Close Encounters of the Third Kind* (film)

CIA Central Intelligence Agency (US government agency)

COLORADO STUDY A US government-sponsored study of UFOs undertaken by the University of Colorado, headed by Edward Condon

CONDON REPORT The report of the Colorado study

CUFOS The J. Allen Hynek Center for UFO Studies (US group)

ETH Extraterrestrial hypothesis (the theory that UFOs are alien in origin)

FBI Federal Bureau of Investigation (US government agency)

FOIA Freedom of Information Act (the US act here, though some other countries – not the UK – also have such an act)

FSR *Flying Saucer Review* (UK based magazine)

GEPAN *Groupe d'Etudes Phenomenes Aerospatiaux Non-Identifies* French government-supported scientific UFO research group (now known as SEPRA)

GSW Ground Saucer Watch (US group)

LITS Lights in the sky (a type of UFO classification)

MIB Men in Black

MIT Massachusetts Institute of Technology

MJ12 (GROUP) An alleged government-backed force used to retrieve crashed flying saucers

MJ12 (DOCUMENTS) A series of documents which purport to reveal the existence of the MJ12 group

MOD Ministry of Defence (UK government department)

MUFON Mutual UFO Network (US group)

NASA National Aeronautics and Space Administration (US civilian agency)

NDE Near-death experience

NSA National Security Agency (US government agency)

NICAP National Investigation Committee on Aerial Phenomena (US group)

OOBE Out-of-body experience

OPERATION 'RIGHT TO KNOW' US and UK pressure group (re. UFOs and government secrecy)

PROJECT HESSDALEN Scandinavian-based research project

RAF Royal Air Force (UK)

SEPRA *Service d'Expertise des Phenomenes de Reutrees Atmospheriques*

TUOIC Tasmanian UFO Investigation Centre

UFO Unidentified flying object

USAF United States Air Force

VUFORS Victorian UFO Research Society (Australian group)

To Report UFO Experiences

Anyone wishing to report UFO experiences can contact the authors as follows:

BY POST:
The Leys
2c Leyton Road
Harpenden
Herts, AL5 2TL

BY FAX:
+44 (1582) 461979

BY E-MAIL:
jandaspencer @ dial.pipex.com

THE BRITISH UFO RESEARCH ASSOCIATION (BUFORA) can be contacted at:
BM BUFORA
London
WC1N 3XX

Index

Picture Acknowledgements

ANGUS BROOKS 64, 65; ART HUFFORD 155 RIGHT; BLAND PUGH 154–5; BLANDFORD PRESS LTD 126; BRITISH FLYING SAUCER BUREAU 25; BRYAN ELLIS 36, 46, 60, 67, 89, 97, 143, 169, 172 BOTTOM, 174, 179; CAMERA PRESS LTD/DAVID DAPLEY 55; CHRIS FOWLER 154 LEFT; DEBBIE JORDAN-KAUBLE 125; DR G. G. POPE 150 LEFT; FORTEAN PICTURE LIBRARY 103; JOHN AND JAYNE MACNISH 139, 140; JOHN SHAW LBIPP 19, 92, 164–5; KEITH SCAIFE 34–5; LOCKHEED MARTIN 144–5; MARK PILKINGTON 146; MARTIN BOWER (MODEL AND PHOTOGRAPH) 39, 100–1; MARY EVANS PICTURE LIBRARY 10; MARY EVANS PICTURE LIBRARY/MICHAEL BUHLER; 14, 50–1, 106–7, 111, 114–5, 118–9, 135, 156, 168; MATTHEW WILLIAMS 151 BOTTOM; NICK POPE 149; PEREGRINE MENDOZA/FORTEAN PICTURE LIBRARY 159; PETER HOLDING TITLE PAGE, 171, 178; PHILIP MANTLE 58, 78, 128; PPL (PARANORMAL PICTURE LIBRARY) 11, 13, 15, 20–1, 23, 26–7, 29, 31, 32, 41, 42, 43, 45, 48, 49, 56, 59, 63, 68, 70–1, 71 (MAIN PIC), 73, 77, 83, 87, 90, 95, 108, 118 TOP, 121 BOTTOM, 122, 123, 131, 134, 150 RIGHT, 151 TOP, 153, 167, 172–3; PROJECT HESSDALEN 120 TOP, 121; THE RONALD GRANT ARCHIVE 30, 52, 79, 99; SOUVENIR PRESS LTD 47; VUFORS 112.